Leaving is Returning

Leaving is Returning
Robert Kuhn

ISBN: 978-1-948712-51-4

Cover: Samantha Wiley

Weasel Press
Lansing, MI
https://www.weaselpress.com

This is what you shall do: Love the earth and sun and the animals, despise riches, give alms to every one that asks, stand up for the stupid and crazy, devote your income and labor to others, hate tyrants, argue not concerning God, have patience and indulgence toward the people, take off your hat to nothing known or unknown or to any man or number of men, go freely with powerful uneducated persons and with the young and with the mothers of families, read these leaves in the open air every season of the year of your life, re-examine all you have been told at school or church or in any book, dismiss whatever insults your own soul, and your very flesh shall be a great poem and have the richest fluency not only in its words but in the silent lines of its lips and between the lashes of your eyes and in every motion and joint of your body . . . .

—Walt Whitman

Now look at him. He ain't got nothing to do but sit around and write. Take up the minutes in the day and call it work. He ain't made a dollar in years and he calls it work. Just like that old net he's knittin', no end to it and even if there was, there'd just be another net behind that one. Another beginning. That is the beauty, a fresh net in front of you, full of knots to be tied. He can't lift the stones anymore. He can't haul dem pots again. He's gotta try something, even if he ain't no good at all. You gotta walk before you run, and ahora you's caminando.

Song of the Future

Leaving is Returning

Robert Kuhn

The year was two thousand and one. Robert was asleep drunk when everything went down. It was nearly noon and the sun was hot when he finally woke up and turned on the television and saw what was taking place. The date was September Eleventh.

The first thing he did was go wake up his friend Clint. Clint was even drunker than he was and probably would have slept until two or three o'clock if uninterrupted. The two of them rubbed their eyes and moved around the little house nervously as if awaiting an earthquake or some other God ordained natural disaster. They kept asking themselves if this was really happening. Is this the truth. The fighting had already begun.

They were twenty two and living in Galveston, Texas.

Meanwhile in New York, there were flames in the streets. The Twin Towers were in rubbles and people were screaming and running around the streets in a real panic, looking for loved ones who might have been there; praying and hoping they weren't at work that day. It was all a television show for the two hungover college graduates watching the action on the box. They were half shuddering and half wondering what the hell was happening. Robert went through the list of all the people he knew working in New York at their financial jobs, wondering if any of them were around. He almost wanted to know someone there. It was a half secret want that hid behind the shock and sorrow in his voice and mind.

The day was hot. It was a weekday and they had no business being out drinking so late, but that was where they were. They had not taken jobs in the financial world because they did not want to. Robert was damn glad he never took one of those jobs. He was happy waiting tables in Galveston and writing a few articles a week for the Daily News. He wished he would write more, but he just couldn't. He slept too late and drank too much too accomplish anything too serious.

He was happy that he already had his plane ticket to Buenos Aires. He bought the one-way ticket about a week earlier and the morning's events seemed to confirm the path he had not so much chosen but accepted.

After Clint called his mom, the two of them agreed that they needed to go to town and find some greasy food. Things were too shaky inside them. Only a chicken fried steak or cheese enchiladas could settle their nerves now.

They drove Clint's big old beat-up green Chevy Blazer into town to a little Mexican diner that served big cheap lunches. They ordered two iced teas with little lime wedges and tried to catch themselves.

They sat blankly in front of each other and talked about what the hell was happening a little bit. They talked about the night before and about Galveston; about girls and women and tried to believe what they were saying. Everything was foggy underneath the sun hot.

The town moved the way a ghost moves. Everything was absently present, even the parking meters and the waitresses inside the diner. The yellow lines on the road and the oak trees shading the sidewalks near University of Texas' Medical Branch district. Everything was hazy yet clear. Things were sweating, heavy and confused; even the dogs walking their masters on short leashes. It was a good time to leave.

They walked to O'malley's, a little dark Irish bar a few blocks away, and drank two pale ales. That seemed like the right thing. They took their time with everything. Robert had already quit the waiting job and was just trying to hold out a few more days before his plane left. He hoped that the airlines wouldn't try anything crazy like canceling flights. The sooner he left the better. Nothing was here for him now. Everything was here, but he didn't care for any of it. He had a gig playing guitar and singing songs in a Holiday Inn Bar. The bar was too big and usually seemed empty except for the dozen odd people in the back or the where people sat and danced around when they started getting drunk. The gig was fun and paid a hundred dollars a night

It was morning.

The airport was a crazy scene. He didn't understand anything. People were hollering all kinds of things at him. It was full speed. He was confused. He was lucky that he carried on all his possesions, just a backpack, handbag and guitar so it was quick getting out of the airport and into Argentina.

The sun was crisp and bright as he stepped out into the street in front of the large airport parking lot. He needed a taxi. He put on his big gringo sunglasses. He had no idea where he was now. All thoughts of Houston had vanished. He was into reality now. The present was calling. A few days earlier, he anticipated this situation, got on the internet and looked up Buenos Aires. He wrote down the name of a barrio that seemed like a nice place to start off. It was cheap and close to the city center. It said lots of young people lived there. He wrote down the name of a few hostels and hospedajes that were recommended.

"Taxi?" Robert asked to a man sitting on the hood of his taxi.

"Si, . . . " the man said followed by a whole bunch of words that sounded like nothing.

"San Telmo," Robert told the man.

The man knew the place and gave his fare. It seemed reasonable enough, and Robert didn't have any ground to bargain on, so he accepted the price and threw his backpack, handbag and big black guitar case into the back seat and got in.

They got on a big freeway and passed by high buildings and factories, apartments and sprawling warehouses. It is the Capital.

The only thing the driver and Robert talked about was the World Trade Center. It was all over the media all over the world. The driver was happy to have an American in the car with him. They talked about Bin Laden and the terrorists and Bush and everything, and the only thing they really understood each other about was that it was sad. The whole event was sad and an awful pity to lose so much human life. They asked each other why. Why did these people hate the United States so much that they wanted to kill thousands of innocent people? What was the problem? Was there innocence? If they understood the problem then certainly they could find a solution, right? Robert was so naive. He didn't know why people hated the

States so much. The taxi driver probably knew, but Robert couldn't understand too much that he said. His Spanish was much worse than expected, but on the freeway through the city, the two of them began to communicate. Robert didn't know how, but by the time they reached San Telmo and the Hospedaje Mochilero, they understood each other pretty clearly. The man told Robert his Spanish was good, and asked where he'd learned to speak, but Robert was already growing exhausted from trying so hard to speak and understand. His head was hurting and he was relieved when the taxi stopped on the cobblestone street in front of his pension. He paid the driver, carried his stuff inside and asked for a dorm room. They had space for about two dollars a night. Robert checked into his bed. It was only about eight o'clock in the morning, but the innkeeper still allowed him to check in. Robert was happy the room was cool and dark. He picked a bottom bunk that didn't seem to be occupied and put his belongings into a locker that they gave him the key for. He took a shower and laid down for a nap.

When he awoke, the sun was already past its half-way point and he decided to go out for a walk and get to know the place. He was hungry. It didn't seem strange at all that he was completely alone, thousands of miles from home, with no where to go, nothing to do and no direction. Everything was just cool and new. Fresh and crisp.

He heard that Argentina had good steak and good wine, so with that in mind, he set out on the streets of San Telmo. He wanted to find a telephone he could understand and let his family know that everything was fine. He walked round and round the brick streets that seemed like more of a small town than those of a huge city. There were plenty of little cafes, bars, shoe repair zapateros and bakeries. There were surprisingly few cars. The place had a nice feel to it. People walking everywhere. He couldn't find a place to put through his phone call, but it didn't take too long to find a parilla where the sweet smell of red meats grilling over an open fire called him in.

There were old men sitting around tables in a dark low ceilinged brick building, drinking red wine and soda that sprayed from a glass bottle with a trigger on the top. Robert drank a glass with them and ordered some meat that came with a red pepper sauce. The meat was thin, tough and a little over cooked for his taste, but it filled his stomach and he continued on his walk.

He walked into a little grocery store that had all kinds of wine. He didn't know which one to pick out, so he picked one that wasn't the absolute cheapest, but close to it. The bottle cost about seventy-five cents. Robert hadn't tasted it yet, but so far was very pleased with Argentina. He thought he could stay here for a long time.

The sun was soon going down and the sky was changing colors. The hospedaje had a rooftop patio with a few plants, a clothes-line and two tables with chairs. Robert carried up the bottle of wine and a little black journal that his parents gave him the night before he left. He read the inscription his parents left for him. It was simple and endearing. "We know you'll use it," they signed with love. He felt sentimental. He felt like he might just blow off the rooftop in the cool breeze. He felt a dizzy sense of vertigo. He was a long way. What was he doing? He didn't know what he had gotten himself into, but he was in it. There was no turning around now. The September night felt cold.

The wine tasted fine and comfortable. He took his pen and began to write. He wrote something about his girlfriend Nicole that he promised he would return quickly to. "To Nicole, the sweetest thing I have ever tasted and fear that I ever will". It was something cheesy like that he wrote on the first page of the journal but he believed it. He didn't want anything to step in the way of what he felt was love. What is a love that you're running away from? He told himself that he wasn't running away, but this was just something he had to do, to explore the world and bridge the North and the South. He didn't have to be with Nicole, but he didn't want to lose her. If he had to be with her, he would be with her. He promised her that he would soon come home and that this would only reinforce their relationship. Maybe he would be back in a month or two, depending how things were with the road. He said all kinds of shit to her that he really believed. He solemnly gave her his university football ring and told her to hold onto it. He thought everything was so important. He wanted to find a telephone and call her.

He was happy when a funny little Japanese guy came upstairs to smoke a cigarette. Robert offered him a glass of wine that he eagerly accepted. When the bottle finished, the Japanese guy came back with another bottle, and they drank that too. The feeling of fear and vertigo passed away and Robert was ready to sleep. The Japanese guy was ready to go out to the bars and discos for a big night but Robert just wanted to sleep. He retired to the dorm room and slept.

He woke up wanted to explore. The city was huge, and all Robert knew of it was the little bars and cafes of San Telmo. It was beautiful and quaint, tango dancing in the night and Spring in the plazas, but Buenos Aires is huge. Little by little, he started taking longer walks, making bigger circles around the barrio and getting into other urban parts of the city. The river, the football stadium, the sprawling downtown and high-rise women in high heels and men in sleek coats and ties, it was really more of the same.

It was in Buenos Aires that Robert first met James. James was a pretty interesting cat. He was a reincarnation of Robert, just in a little higher class. Robert was a reincarnation of him, just a little bit saltier.

They met in some big urban plaza around midday. The sun was shining, and there was the cool air of Spring keeping everybody happy to be outside. There were all kinds of people hustling around, Argentinian businessmen, attractive waitress GAP representatives, crippled beggars, money changers, little old mamasitas. There was a group of drama students doing some type of demonstration dressed up like bloody tampons and dead people. They were both caught watching the spectacle in a state of dazed bewilderment, when Robert noticed that he had on a sweatshirt sporting the name of his university. It said "Wellesley" or some New England posh university. At the time, Robert knew somebody that went there, so he made a remark about it. Robert had just graduated from Bucknell and all that University stuff still seemed very much a part of him. James looked just like Robert, lost way the hell down in Buenos Aires, just checking out the plazas on a Thursday afternoon.

James said he knew some guy from Bucknell that used to go to prep school with him in Connecticut. Robert knew the guy. He was a twit. He didn't tell James that his friend was a twit, but acknowledged he knew him. That it was enough for them to gain each other's confidence and they became friends.

They spent a few days together bumming around Buenos Aires,

drinking beer and eating dollar pizzas. They were the same age and graduated at the same time. They talked about the business and marketing ideas that filled James' brain. Their brains worked in completely different ways but Robert enjoyed listening to him talk about the way he saw things. Everything was money to James. When he saw a shop window he noticed how the products were arranged on the shelves. He analyzed how the Dollar Pizza place could make a profit. He was a real entrepreneur type. He was obsessed with those things. Robert didn't care about those things in the least. He was just happy to have somebody to talk to.

James already had a job waiting for him when he came back to the states. It was with a big corporation like Proctor and Gamble. He was supposed to be the head of one of their branches. It was a big money thing. He was just coming to the end of a big trip around the world. He'd been through Russia, China, Fiji, Thailand, India, Israel, Europe, Africa, and now was the South America three weeks. He was doing the world in three months. It didn't seem like such an enjoyable thing to Robert, but different strokes for different folks.

James had been drunk with all kinds of people that he'd never see again, screwed all kinds of girls that have disappeared for forever, and bought all kinds of souvenirs. Life was a game. This world was a show. The real world was waiting back in States. Nothing was real here, but he knew it and was having a hell of a time.

The two of them hung out for a few days, and said goodbye without ever thinking too much about it. Robert drifted around Buenos Aires until he figured out how to leave, and in a few days caught a train to the frigid coast town of Mar de Plata. Mar de Plata is a gilded town that was built for rich Buenos Aires people to get away from the city. It is like the Jersey Shore. The wind comes in stiff off the sea and cuts right through your bones if you're not ready. Robert spent his time there walking around, checking out the things. What interested him most were the sea lions that all got together on the rocks down by the fisherman port. Hundreds of them piled up on top of each other, shitting around and slipping in and out of the oily water, bathing in the powerful sun behind a chain linked fence. It was nasty. He took a whole roll of picutres of them, feeling like they were some kind of wild exotic animals from National Geographic. They were more like big rats.

Robert was in his little tidy hotel room, underneath all of the blankets, shivering in all of the clothes he owned, trying to stay warm in the middle of the afternoon, when he heard a gringo voice, trying futilely to communicate with hotel owner in Spanglish. It was James.

Robert got out of his bed and went outside to say hello and wondered what were the two of them doing in this town.

They spent the next couple of days wandering around the streets of Mar de Plata, checking out the rich Argentinean's houses and talking about the good old days of getting drunk at the university and banging girls in beer soaked old houses. They drank big beers in the little sidewalk cafes and tried to make friends with the artesano people. Robert carried him to see the Sea Lions, and after two days, it was time to leave. James was going back to Buenos Aires and flying down to Patagonia towards Tierra del Fuego. Robert was going to take a train out to the highway and hitchhike his way down to Patagonia. Robert didn't plan on going so far South as Tierra del Fuego, but he thought he would go as far down as he could manage with his clothes. There was a mountain town called Bariloche that some Argentineans told him about that sounded nice.

After Patagonia, James was crossing over to Chile, and planned to be in Santiago in about two weeks. That sounded good to Robert so they decided to try to meet up at a place called the Hotel Indiana in Santiago. James had a Lonely Planet book that said it was the cheapest place to stay in town. It was an Israeli hangout.

The two Gringos said goodbye in the night over a few liters of beer and went out in their respective directions. Robert's train carried him South in the night and let him off at a town near the highway in the morning. For several hours Robert waited on the outskirts of town for a car to stop with his thumb out. Bored, he took out his guitar and banged out songs that he made up as the cars roared by and by. It didn't look like a car would ever stop, but one finally did, and he jumped in. It was a father driving his three little girls in the backseat. They were travelling south and would be passing a town called Bahia Blanca where they said Robert could catch a train to Patagonia and Bariloche. The man had his hands full with the three crying, laughing, fighting and playing little girls and was happy to have some help.

The children were fun. Robert took pictures of them and gave him his sunglasses and hat to play with while he smiled and joked with the children. The trip challenged his Spanish, and although it was exhausting for Robert, they somehow communicated.

The car drove and drove through the flat Argentinean Pampas, where the planes rolled a dry brown color of wheat and the white surreal clouds drifted low and endlessly in the hallucinagenic blue sky. The land was infinite and empty except for a few small adobe villages where the car had to take advantage of any gas stations. The driver of the car wouldn't accept anything that Robert tried to give him for gas. He was happy to help the traveler a little further on his way.

The night was cold and windy when Robert got out of the car at the train station of Bahia Blanca. The family waved goodbye and wished him the best as they continued south. The train station was drafty and devoid of life. He doubted a train would really stop here, but an old man soon showed up to sell tickets and confirm that a train was coming. Robert alone waited for the train heading to Bariloche and boarded the train after a few hours of sitting on the floor wrapped up in his Mexican blanket, reading a book about Taoism and health that an Irish fellow in the Buenos Aires hostel gave him. It was an interesting book that was bringing to light several things that Robert had never even considered.

The train reached Bariloche in the morning. It was a long and scenic walk from the train station to the center of town. Robert declined the taxis, suffering the weight of his backpack and guitar.

Bariloche was a mountain town. The air was fresh and glacial. It sat on the edge of a big looking-glass lake that reflected the mountain spires and surrounding glaciers. Cathedral gothic roofs and crosses jutted like out like the sharp snowy peaks above the walled courtyards and plazas on the steep streets. The sky was blue and gray like ice. Robert was sweating by the time he reached the three room low ceilinged hostal above a ski shop. It had a kitchen in the hall and two other rooms that were shared by about eight or ten Argentinean young men who were on vacation as working travelers. They were a good group to be around. They carried Robert around the town, smoked grass and drank wine around the room before going out to the discos in the night. He'd never experienced anything like a night out with the young Argentineans. It was a war when they hit the bars. It was a hunt. It was far different from the calm and carefully slow methods Robert was accustomed to approaching women with in the States. Here it was full speed.

As they smacked the dance floor, the Argentineans started looping around grabbing any girl that wasn't already taken. The girls would fight and squeal trying to get away, but the guachos wouldn't let go. Some of the girls would escape, but they'd flash into a next one like an animal on its prey, holding her tightly and winding their hips with the music, until eventually a girl would give in and start winding along with them. They didn't play around.

Robert tried hopelessly to approach the beautiful Argentinean women and smooth them over with a beer, but before he could blink the girl would be gone. He made zero headway, but kept on drinking, following his friends through the ravaged bar. One by one, the guys disappeared until there were only a few drunks left at the end of the night to go buy a Super-pancho hotdog with and walk home. That was Bariloche.

Robert caught a train across the cordillera for Chile the next day. It was already too cold, and he couldn't take any further South. It was time to start back for the North; towards home.

After a snowy, high mountain border crossing, Chile had a much easier feel to it than the Argentinean Patagonia. He passed through several cold towns in southern Chile, but none grabbed him to stay. Puerto Mont, Punta Arenas, Ovalle, Pucon all led him to the highway that headed North. Route One. The Panamericana.

Robert found a ride with a big rig truck that was going as far as Los Angelas. The driver was a friendly man who bought Robert a lunch of local cheese and some kind of corn thing. He made arrangements for Robert with another trucker that was going to Santiago. They shook hands, parted ways, and the next driver let Robert get in his big old truck.

The driver was a young man, even younger than Robert. He was named Arnoldo. He must have had about seventeen years. The truck was a real dump, but at least the thing moved. Its door wouldn't shut when Robert got in and it didn't have a passenger side seat, only a wooden box. There was no radio and a hole in the floor between Robert's feet. It would never pass any kind of inspection in the States, but it was rolling in Chile. The truck belonged to the boy's father, whom he worked the thing for. The boy showed him a picture of his family that he kept in his wallet, and begged Robert to take a photo of him.

Arnoldo carried Robert by a few tourist stops along the way that he felt Robert should see and take a pictures of; a waterfall and a big gorge that were just off the roadside. He asked Robert to take out the guitar and sing some songs to keep them from falling asleep. Robert played La Bamba, the only Spanish song that he knew, and one from Creedence Clearwater Revival, whom the boy said he liked. They reached Santiago in the night, and the boy said it would be better if Robert spent the night with him and his family outside of the city, and then in the morning, drive him into the city. Santiago was dangerous at night so Robert thanked him for the invitation and was happy to stay with the young man and meet his family.

When they arrived, the big family was waiting and curious about this gringo companion. He proudly introduced Robert to his mother, father, brothers, cousins and who knows who else. They had a big supper with sweet tea and homemade bread, and went to sleep early in the dark earthen floor house.

In the morning, Robert rose at dusk and took a walk around the muddy little village, receiving the same strange looks that he was getting accustomed to. There was a field where people planted corn, a fat pig and some chickens behind their house. By this time, Arnoldo was awake and doing a few things around the yard. He showed Robert around in the daylight and introduced him again to the people that were around. He showed Robert a little garden behind the house that was full of big marijuana plants. People smoke everywhere.

It was about nine o'clock in the morning and the trailer that the truck carried up from the South was already removed from the truck. They ate some breakfast and Arnoldo told him that they could go now if he was ready. Robert threw his backpack and guitar back in the truck and they rumbled towards the city.

The Hotel Indiana was a real funky place. Painted in bright oranges, reds and other swirling colors, the place looked like a tripped out mad house from Alice in Wonderland. The hall had high, ornate ceilings, some swank carpet, a bunch of old couches set in a circle, a few houka bongs that didn't work anymore placed as ornaments and a big chandelier that looked like it was from the thirties hanging down in the middle. There was a courtyard in the center of the ten or twelve rooms with a dry fountain, a few ferns and other plants growing around the place. There were a couple of little turtles walking around. It is hard to say where it got the name Indiana from.

When Robert arrived, James wasn't there yet. He was supposed to be there the following day, so Robert just checked in and watched the scene. There were three communal bathrooms and a communal kitchen that had a fridge and two gas stoves. You had to put your name and room number on anything you put in the fridge because they cleaned it out once a week or so.

Next to the kitchen was a ping-pong table that the Israeli people stayed on. The only language you heard around the place was Hebrew. They were a rowdy group for the most part. Most of them had just gotten out of the military and had a little bit of money to travel around with. They liked to drink and had a reputation for breaking things. Robert didn't mix up with them much. They kept to themselves and seemed pretty serious. Maybe they didn't like Gringos.

James arrived the next day just as Eric Clapton was playing a concert at the football stadium. It seemed like an excellent opportunity until the two of them started playing wine-pong with cheap one-liter cartons of Gato Negro and Carmen vino tinto. They got of some paraguayo, a pressed jacked-up weed, from some white woman that was around there teaching English. It was the first time Robert ever smoked Paraguayo. The night turned around and around making Robert dizzy at the Slowhand concert. He vomited all over the place and had to be escorted by James back to the taxi and to the hostal.

He didn't wake up until the next afternoon with an awful feeling and swore he wouldn't drink again until he had a hit of the Paraguayo roach. He and James took a walk down to the corner store and got another box of Gato Negro. There was a group of four girls who laughed with strong, hot current when the two young men walked in. The girls glowed magnetically. The store quaked and everything was unstable and untranslatable for a second. They blushed and said something about Robert smelling of marijuana. The girls were fast and in a second they bounced out the door and into the darkness of the night street. You couldn't tell which way they went.

Robert and James went back to the hotel, broke the seal on the box of red wine and started feeling better. They aimlessly took to the streets downtown and the Barrio Brasil. James taught Robert an interesting trick with an imaginary stone that he bent down to pick up and scared off a pack of stray aggressive barking dogs. They ducked down some back street in a neighborhood not far from the university. There was loud upbeat music coming through the one of the doors of a courtyard. They slowed their footsteps as they passed and guess who bounces out? The same girls from the corner store. Their eyes were magnets and the two guys slid in. The music played and dancing didn't stop. There were drinks and drugs and all kinds of interesting people at the party. Robert danced with a tall, slim girl named Carmen underneath the fiery stars in the open courtyard. She was a ballerina studying dance at the university. They danced in the streets on the way home passed the government buidings and palacios. They walked up the stairs at two of the girls fifth floor apartment building and ordered a pizza. The pizza was damn good. James paid for it.

They drank some piscola and slipped off to the bedrooms. Pisco is a distilled grape beverage. Mix it with cola and you get piscola. It is cheap and hot. Something happened with James and his girl. It got a little crazy for a minute and James left abruptly. The girl was vexed about something. Robert stayed put.

James didn't speak any Spanish and Robert's was severely limited, so with all the pisco and fire things got confusing. Robert was already in the room with Carmen. The girl who James left came into Carmen's room and eased into the bed. Things got twisted up for a jealous minute, but it all straightened out in the end and Robert woke up with Carmen in the morning. She had amazingly tight and small breasts. He tenderly rubbed her soft hip and thigh. She was the first Latin American woman Robert had ever been with. They talked about Robert moving in with her and all kinds of shit. Robert was in love. Carmen was beautiful. She had to go to class early in the morning, but told Robert to stay there and sleep. Robert stayed until ten thirty or so. It was a cold morning in Santiago, gray and windy, quiet like a Sunday. Robert got dressed, put his wallet into his pocket and realized she had taken all of his money, even took the Jamacian bill that he carried for good luck. Robert walked home with his mind in a mess.

He went back to her apartment in the night. She wasn't home. Only her roommates were. Three other guys and some next girl. They were all students. They all knew Robert somehow and offered him a seat and another Piscola. They told him to wait. They said Carmen would be back later. She didn't come. Robert didn't feel like waiting. He gave the guys something to tell her. He wanted to see her. He walked by her house down constantly for the next couple of months, always looking up to her floor, begging to see her. He was desperate. He went up to her floor another afternoon, but the place was locked. Once he snuck through the gate into the parking lot around the back to see her window and the little ganja plant she had growing on the sill. He wanted to see her and tell her she was a thief. He wanted to kiss her.

Long after James left, he passed by her tortured house everyday on his way to work or the plazas where he sat, read, or practiced mediation and deep breathing. Sometimes we would carry his little black journal and write poems and songs while watching the busy people in the *Plaza de Armas.* Sometimes he carried his guitar and put open his guitar case for change while he sang all his songs behind his father's big sunglasses. He liked hiding people his eyes. It was always interesting.

After a few months in Santiago, he decided to fast. The Taoist book he was reading said that the first step in changing your life is making a seven day fast. Robert was all about change, so he took off work at the language school where he taught English and fasted. It nearly killed him. He went out and got drunk at a Halloween Party the night before it started, but he didn't want to call off the fast because he already cancelled work. He boiled a pot of purple cabbage soup before day and that was the last thing he ate for a week.

He passed through fever, burning stomach and all kinds of feelings, but the fast passed and when he recovered, he left Santiago for the North. He was ready for a change and whether or not the fast had anything to do with it, change came. He unintentionally stopped cutting his hair and his beard and living in cities. He hitchhiked through a bright little fishing village on the hill and rocks named Horcones where he crashed with some fisherman for a few days. He was sleeping on a bluff above the beach, but someone stole his backpack while he was in town buying an onion. They didn't take anything but his two pairs of socks and he found the rest of the rubbage was dashed away in the bush not far from his camp. He carried his guitar with him and sang songs in the *pescadero* with the *borachos, artesanos* and the fishermen. He unknowingly got himself on Santiago tv news. The next day he hitched a ride with a sleepy old truck driver who saw the show told him all about it.

The truck carried him up to La Sirena in north central Chile. It was there he found the Valle de Elqui. He heard the place had brilliant stars and was a nice place to visit from a reliable source, so he thought he'd make the trip off the Panamericana and check it out.

The first town the bus stopped at after Vicuña was Paihuano, up the river and into the valley. A dark skinned Chilean in the bus next to him said it was an Indian word for Big Stars. He got out of the bus. He asked someone in the street if there was a hospedaje near. He had to find somewhere to put down his luggage but before he reached the hospedaje, a funny little fellow with a flute and a drum hanging around his neck approached. The guy spoke a little bit of English and said, "Put your bags down and lets go smoke a joint. C'mon. We can play music."

The little man's name was Raul. He carried Robert by his friend Carmen's house who had two young children playing in the yard. The place had a wonderful garden. Carmen was outside painting a picture on an easel. She was quiet but welcomed them. Raul walked over to a ganja plant growing nearby the house and picked off some leaves to dry in a little clay dish over the fire. They smoked and started playing music that felt magical as rhythms and melodies spontaneously erupted. Carmen and the two younger children danced and sang. It soon got dark and Carmen went and cooked some wheat tortillas and spread a place on the floor where Robert could sleep nearby Raul. Robert didn't quite understand everything that was going on, but all was very comfortable. What was going on with this name Carmen?

They all stayed at Carmen's house for several days until things got a little tight, and they went up in the hills. They walked to a place called La Gua. It was a spring past the old abandoned vineyards, the highest place in the cordillera outside of Paihuano. It was the last place. The place was a desert, but La Gua had *agua* all year round. It was where the water was born. Raul said his grandfather owned the place, but Robert wasn't sure about anything. There was an abandoned mud house and some grapes, pomegranites and apricot trees that needed tending to. There was an old slimy water tank that was full of marrass and wild cane that needed a serious cleaning. There were canals dug and set with rock, but the place was so overgrown, the water couldn't pass. They worked on cleaning the canals and emptying the tank a few times, bringing back the place to life. They carried their rations up there, sugar, rice, flower and beans and they cooked and ate around a fire. There was abundant dry wood. They made apricot *mermalada* and played music under the spinning stars that they studied. They made plans to go to La Sirena and play songs for money and dreamed of the things they could do at the Gua as planted a bunch of seeds.

A few people warned Robert about Raul and the Gua, but Robert didn't pay them too much mind. Robert bought a white, shaggy horse and a saddle with the little money he made teaching English in Santiago. A *llegua*. A "*llegua mancita*," the man said. They named the horse Gringo and rode her all around the desert hills. Robert dreampt of carrying the horse high up into the *cordillera* nearby Argentina, adventuring on the wild trails. A man could get lost up there and never return people told him. There was a trail behind the town Alcohuaz that they say led up there, but the trail cut and crossed a thousand times. The trail passed a lavender farm owned by some Frenchman and from there you keep going up past Cochihuaz and to the wilderness. The saddle was soon stolen and Robert decided to sell the horse to one of Raul's uncles after Gringo bit him in the chest, going for the jugular.

One night, Robert got on a scale at friends house they were crashing at in Paihuano. The house belonged to the municipality who used it to house their social workers. The plump and rosy woman, Claudia, was a supporter of Raul and Robert. She liked to dance and drink wine too. She liked the music and didn't give them any hard time about anything. Not even the food in the kitchen or the gas in the propane tank. She was easy going. Robert got on the scale in her bathroom that night and saw that his weight had dropped to below a hundred and fifty pounds. He lost seventy pounds in the last two years since his football days. He'd lost thirty pounds in Chile. He was shocked. He looked into the mirror at the gaunt bearded face and started to shake. He shook his way out into the street and onto the cold plaza beneath the Rose pepper trees. He crouched down trrembling in the shade of a corner wall. He took a few deep breaths but the cold continued from his inside. He felt like a ghost. He wasn't sure about anything. His orbit was tilting. He vowed to stop smoking Paraguayo and went back to the house when the feeling eased down. Raul told him not to worry and that he was fine. They were going to start eating more *porotos*. More beans.

Robert and Raul would stay and go from *La Gua*, never establishing a permanent residence anywere they went. Sometimes they stayed in the town, sometimes they went to Tres Cruces where Raul had built a mud house nearby his family and sometimes they went to La Quebrada where the beautiful Paz and her sister Loli lived with their father Goyo.

Goyo was a lunatic. He was a pschylogist who had fallen into the trap of his patients and was addicted to drugs. He would spin around his room in the night, hunching up and down, clinching his ears, screaming and listening to high pitch transistor frequencies that howled out of a little radio. He yelled at Robert in words he couldn't verbally understand. He was the most peaceful person that Robert had ever met while he worked in the garden outside in the daytime amongst the apricot trees and peaches; light emanating from his gentle smile but at night he turned into a cracked madman. The first Robert saw of him was from the portrait that Carmen painted on the easel that day. His face was a mask and the blue heavens his eyes. Everything is removed and but something remains.

Goyo was something of a Chilean celebrety. He wrote a book in the seventies or eighties and people came from all over as far as Santiago to talk to him about their problems and what not. He was well known and respected. He believed in marijuana. He prescribed it. He worked one day a week in La Sirena with his daughter Paz who had just graduated from the University of Chile with a masters in psychiatry. They worked on Fridays, and that was enough. They worked together, and along with some other eclectic scholars started a project called "Fractal". Robert loved fractals, which he remembered from his recent, self-similar Mathematics courses. Fractals are everything. Fractals are you and fractals are me, in the heart of everything living thing. They are the star that ran through the heavens tonight. They are the color between the blue of your jeans; the shape of the coastline and the heart of the hurricane that begins at the flap of a butterfly's wings. They are the fingerprint of God.

Goyo and Paz had artists, alchemists, chemists, biologists, nutritionists and poets all working together to put together this project. It was all very abstract and interesting, but it lacked funding. They wanted a mathematics person involved and Robert wanted anything to do with Paz. Her hair was brown and her eyes mirrors. She was the morena with soft clear cheeks and dimples. She was charming. She was enchanting. Her powers of language could make her a witch, the book of changes said. She could read the future. She could strike you dead if she so wanted.

Before they ever met, Paz saw him playing guitar on television when he was in Horcones. She was staying in Horcones with her brother at the same time Robert passed through. She couldn't believe him when he walked into her house with Raul a few months later in the Valle de Elqui looking for Loli. Raul was crazy about Paz's short fat sister Loli.

Robert and Raul were getting by working the harvest in the grapefields and playing music in the touristic town of Pisco de Elqui on weekends. The grape work paid by the box, and the two of them didn't work too very hard. Still they managed to put up a little change during the short season. It wasn't bad. The vineyards were set in high majestic places with fresh views of the valley beneath the shady grape leaves. You ate plenty of grapes. Grapes to the point where Robert got the shittin' for weeks and could only cure it eating coals of burnt Eucalyptus.

San Pedro is the seven sided mescaline cactus patron saint of the desert. Carmen grew the native plant and on New Years Eve, Robert decided he wanted to know about it.

Raul and Robert spent their weekend playing music in the little tourist town of Pisco de Elqui, where anyone with a little extra change in the area came to town to drink eat and enjoy their Sundays. It was full of bars, restaurants, hotels and shops with charms and rustic ornaments. It was here they met the white man and his Chilean wife

Raul and Robert made the rounds of the town with their guitars, drums and other handmade instruments, playing for tips at the all of the spots they were welcomed. At one of the little holes in the wall, they played their three song set, and carried a little wool hat around for any change the patrons wanted to throw in. A white man sitting with his brown skinned woman put a few pesos in and offered the two to sit and have a beer when they were finished. They troubadours gladly accepted the invitation and after the beers ended up driving down through the valley to the river to smoke a joint with the *extranjeros.*

The white man turned out to be a young scientist from Berkley, California where he studied hallucinogenic drugs. The brown skinned woman was the young man's wife. She was a Chilena who lived and worked in California with him. They were passing their Christmas holidays exploring the woman's homeland.

Over the joint, the young people discussed all kinds of drugs and psychological issues. It seemed like everyone had lifetimes more experience than Robert. His limits seemed to be pushed daily. He got a creepy feeling from the couple. The couple drove the two poor musicians home to Paihuano after the smoke and made plans to meet up again on the following evening, New Years Eve.

Carmen prepared the cactus for the ceremony as the sun went down on the old year. Robert prepared a big pot of beef-corn chili that he'd been planning for weeks. It was his way of missing home.

First Carmen peeled the cactus from its mescaline thorns, which she would later dry and mix with her *mate.* She put the fleshy green meat into the blender and gave each of the three young men, Robert, Raul and the doctor, and full shot glass. It was up to the heavens and down the hatch. The drink made you gag. All there was to do then was wait. Wait for the dizzy trembling of the earth beneath your feet. Wait for the roar of the full moon raising above the *cordillera.* Wait for the heat in your face and the naseau in your gut to pass off, and then you realize that this thing is for real and it is far too late to turn back.

You can run but never hide from it, the mad gringo acid scientist told Robert dressed in a tunic like Jesus. "How the hell did I get myself into this?" he asked. The man told him he was just playing music in the wrong bar at the wrong time.

The hole in the chain linked fence they passed through on the trail down to river turned into a spider web. Robert closed his eyes and passed through it. Scarecrows burned in the streets, dressed like their masters. New Year, new life, another chance, they said. Annual apocalypse. Robert ran past the dead in the streets and onto the dark highway that led for down and out of the valley. He was sure he was in hell. He ran in the middle of the road, unafraid of death because he knew he already was. Raul hauled him back onto the side and led him back into town. Robert felt sad for his family. He was sad for what he put them through with his death. He wanted to call them one more time and tell them not to cry. Everything was fine in the world of the dead. It was just like being born, dying. You can't remember any of it, but you know you're there, so it must have happened. He didn't mind being dead, but he wept for his family. They were all just a different dead, one less than him, but that one death would separate them for eternity. Death is life, he thought.

He abandoned the dark highway that led to nowhere, turned around and headed up towards the light of the moon and *La Quebrada del Paihuano*. It was up the mountain break that he wanted to go. It was Paz. It was Goyo. It was the moon and heaven and he had to get moving. He trekked up the moonlit dusty road. A pickup truck stopped and offered Raul and him a ride. It dropped them right at Paz's house at the top of the road. They were waiting for him and Raul she said. There were candles lit and Robert got paranoid. He wanted out. He wanted to run. He felt they were waiting to sacrifice him. Before anyone could tell him otherwise, he was gone running back down the hill. Only Paz' little long eared dog, Rasta, followed.

Their feet carried them quickly through the dark never-ending tunnel of vineyards like purgatory. They stopped to rest on a big rock, and the moon spoke too them. It is too late it said. The moon was the pupil of the night, watching their every move and prayer. Confidence in your life is the only truthful way of looking the moon in the eye. Confidence in your life is the only way through. Did you live the holy life? Were you a part of the world? Did you follow the crowd? You, and only you know what is right. The voice carried throughout the huge universe and Robert knew that excuses were illusions. Don't let death sneak up on you. "Prepare yourself". The voice echoed inside of his soul and radiated through him from the brilliant moon. It was like a huge hole in his gut that took over his whole being and left only his glue souled shoes. This life is one, and if it is wasted, it is all wasted. Did you live for money? Did you live for life? Did you live for love? See your life. Look at your self. You are dead and all is gone. There is no hiding from the moon. There is no way out. The dog was right there the whole time not allowing Robert to sleep. If he slept it would be over. Everything would be over. He would never awake. Rasta was Robert's protector. Raul was Robert's angel.

Dusk found them under the dry wooden cross perched high on the hill overlooking Paihuana, across the creek and up the trail to the Gua. The two of them meditated the sun rising and saw dawn of the morning hours in a clear calmness that appears when the sound stops. He was not dead. He was alive. It was time to go home. It was time to eat a bowl of the corn and ground meat tomato chili that he cooked the day before. It was time to sleep.

The mad gringo acid, vampire scientist from the night before was there with his mad Chilean wife, Carmen and the children, apologizing for scaring him. Robert was still shaken up from the whole experience and didn't know what to make of the night or his life. He needed to rest. The white-guy said the San Pedro didn't do him anything. It didn't even touch him.

It was New Years Eve and demons burned in the streets for our old selves. It was the seven-sided mescaline cactus patron saint of the desert, San Pedro, shaking from inside your bones and visions of all night death under the full moon. Answers to your maker and responsibility for your life were the messages it spoke. It was the spirit world. "Yes, you died because you took too much drugs," Raul confirmed to him in the tiny plaza beneath the flowering rose pepper trees after their escape. Raul stood in the plaza, upright and full of wind like a tragic Indian warrior. Raul ran from the very beginning. Raul could see the man was wicked. Raul could see he was a vampire.

The sleep did him good and in the night, he rode his horse up to *La Quebrada* to see Paz, still a little confused about the reality of everything. He didn't know what he wanted to say to her, but he just wanted to talk. That was the beginning.

He told her about his death and his visions and about the whole night in general. She was a psychiatrist and had studied the nature of the mind, so she had some interesting things to say. She wanted to eat San Pedro and have an experience like that. He never wanted to take drugs again. He felt as if had eaten of the fruit of the tree of the knowledge of good and evil, the one that led to the gates of the tree of life. It felt like he was now fallen, and could never go back. Go back to what? San Pedro showed him the vision for a reason. It was undeniable and unforgettable. He had to use it.

He started reading the Bible plenty and didn't want to go to work anymore at the grape fields. He went up to the Gua and fasted for a couple of days, reading and writing in the little black journal he still had. He broke his fast with Apricots and went back down to the village of Paihuano, where Raul had started practicing with a puppet troup from the municipal government. Robert got in with the group of puppeteers and wrote a puppet show about two friends who leave the city start a life in the hills away from the town. The two friends are making it good in the wilderness until a woman comes up to join in, and before you know it, there is town is full of workers and revelers and a utopian community develops. They make music, dance and eat apricots and there is only one law. "*No traicionar*!" Do not betray.

Someone then starts stealing apricots and selling them. Things go bad until finally the children in the audience have to decide whether or not to forgive the man, or feed him to the *Chupacabra* monster who hungrily awaits a meal. The children always elect to forgive the traitor and apricots go flying for everyone from behind the stage. *DAMASCOS!*

They played guitar and drums with it and performed the show around all the little communites in the municipality. Robert played the hungry *Chupacabra* with his funny accent. The children loved it, and Raul and Robert were awarded several meals and places to stay. They never got any money, but they were never in want.

Raul was a little man with wild bright and wicked eyes. He had tough, dark, high cheekbones and the look of an Indian. He never really had anything. Even the drum that he carried around and beat wasn't his. He had a fiber glass patched up guitar, but it was in the jailhouse for some reason. He didn't worry about anything. He put on whatever clothes were around where he was and didn't pay any mind to who it belonged to. He left his old clothes behind wherever he found new ones. He was a troll that moved fast and slung himself in and out of places with loud laughs. His energy was high one hundred right until the point that he dropped and then it was out. He was a firework. *Chirijue* his family called him. Little bird.

When he ate, he didn't stop. When he smoked, he didn't stop. He killed the roaches and sang with melody. When he was bad, he was evil. When he was good, he'd give you everything. When he was bad he'd give you more. The two were friends and that was it. No matter what Raul used him for or took him for, it was worth it. Robert would never have been carried there without Raul. The fires in the night and the stone man hieroglyphics of antelopes and hunters from *antigua,* where the music played till dawn. The night that he first kissed Paz. The tight rope walkers and acrobat jugglers and clowns. The Sirena Afrosound and the seed filled garden of Peace. The echoes off the walls of the *cordillera*. The orchards of the Gua and who knows what else tells the tale of the missing chagrin and the Frenchman. Lost they are.

They hit it hard one day after fishing music in Pisco de Elqui. Lost in the mountains outside the city where people sleep on the streets and beg rides that are denied in the darkness. The hardest thing is to find a ride in the dark. Its thirty miles to home. Its been a bad day. No money. No sleep. There is neither bed, roof nor food in all of the cold, old, hard road. They were beat. Raul promised that he should have given up the life already. Give up the music. Give up on God. Move to the city. Start a new life with job and tie and blah blah

blah. There are only your feet which you promised you would change a long time ago. And then as if the night had a heart, it sent a pick up truck with eyes out of the darkness. It carried the two beats half the distance home and turned off the highway into the desert.

"You see," he told Raul. "A sign. Ha! God doesn't give up on people. You can't never tell what will take place in the next moment". Robert felt like God was shining on them. He felt like there were universal forces in motion that attached themselves to their chariots. Raul just laughed a wicked laugh and shivered a little bit in the cold. He was wearing a sweater that Robert took off and lent him. Raul was only wearing a t-shirt even though he knew perfectly well how damn cold it got in the night in the desert hills.

Ten miles isn't bad. A house above the road with lights on and voices singing, three women were awaiting a sign that Raul plays on his guitar. "Angels!" they cried out. Angels with the only song they were waiting for. A sweet song about sleep and about dreams, *dulces suenos*. No one else had ever played that song. It held a pleasing, lofty melody that made you tingle a little bit. Raul held a lot of magic. He was full of energy and jumped around like a weird little bird when things were bright.

The band of mystical old women brought the two hungry souls food and courage and the warmth to walk through the rest of the night. A can of tuna, a piece of bread and some juice. Hugs and kisses all around.

Daylight caught them walking into Paihuano. They crashed at Claudia's for a few nights, still trying to get the seven miles down the road to Tres Cruces, where Raul had a mud home, high on the windy hill, steep to the river. The pasture in the valley. The *uva rosada*, the sweetest one of all. The tin roof raisins and sun dried tomatoes. Carmen and the children moved in with them. They had problems in the other house they were staying in. Carmen had a tough life since her husband died.

Her husband and Goyo were partners; associates; contemporaries; colleagues; friends. He was a psychologist too. They were both from well off families in Santiago. The two of them abandoned the city for the rural Elqui Valley. He died in an epileptic fit after taking San Pedro with Goyo. His ghost was still around sometimes, haunting Carmen. Carmen started having an affair with Goyo sometime later, but it was only one mad problem after the other. Carmen and Goyo's wife were friends too. Were. Carmen knew Paz from birth. Her children Antonia and Jose were good friends to Robert. Jose was only five and needed a father figure around. He was extremely intelligent, but an incredible cry-baby. Robert hitched rides into Vicuna, where he could use his old gringo credit card and buy a grocery bag. *Arroz integral, carne de soya* and instant *levadura.* Rice, sugar, oats, beans, flour. Things were looking bright. The grapes were picking for Pisco and Peace was on her way to being revealed. There was powerful heaven in the daylight.

Paz was everything. She was death and life itself. Peace. She was the secret of the moon. She was the coward who ran away from it all. She was a scientist and a naturist by art and the tears she dropped could make even the strongest man change his mind about it all and see the world through a whole different light. They played Adam and Eve and abandoned themselves to the devotion of love.

She smoked all the time, anytime. She had enough in her garden near the corn. They drank wine in the vineyard behind the house.

Loli, Paz' sister, and Raul had broken up. Raul was deeply in love with her. Robert never understood why, but Raul had his reasons. She looked toadish. Raul couldn't take it. His heart was so big that it broke heavy. He was too hot. He wanted to die without her. Raul took a bunch sleeping pills and tried to kill himself. Goyo, the papa and psychologist, prescribed him some other pills to try and make him hold on a little tighter. He threw it all into outerspace.

Then there was Jonus, who changed his name when he realized life was not what he thought it was. He wasn't the same person again after his eyes were open. He couldn't even see the same name again.

He was from the forests of Chiloe, down in the South, but he drifted up here from time to time, floating around and waving everyone hello. Everyone was always happy to see him. He said to breathe plenty. Take plenty of deep breaths, not only some times, when you're meditating or praying, but all the time. He put his hands above his eyes and rolled them back over the top of his head, indicating three hundred and sixty degrees. Vision he tried to explain. It was boiling.

Jonas was a strange little mouse that liked to keep around Goyo even though Goyo got crazy on him just the same way he got crazy on everyone else. Jonas liked to play music too, but he couldn't really play any instruments. He didn't have the rhythm to bang on a drum. When everyone else was lost off in a jam, he'd jump around the room and grab anything that could make noise and throw it in there. A little whistle. The ting of a knife against a metal lampshade. A light switch. A washboard. Anything that could be perceived was added, the funnier the better. Someone would soon step up with some lyrics or chanting or something else. The group was a strange lot.

With cocaine, it's like when you have the thing and everythings fine, but when you don't have it . . . well that's when it grabs you and control is gone.

Goyo hit Paz once. Smacked her good in the face. Left her black and blue and mashed up her silver flute on top of that. She played the girl from ipanema. Bossa Nova Brasilera jazz music. Ba da ba da da bad dah dah. She was good.

Robert was ready to kill her father. He walked right into the house and told him, sir, I love your daughter and I want her to be mine forvever as he screwed her in the feng shui room. Goyo laughed and smiled with them, but Robert still wanted to kill him through his teeth.

They spent all their time together. Paz baked wheat tortillas on the fire burning black iron stove in the kitchen while Goyo and Robert talked about what was happening with the crisis in Argentina and how it was better to live away from the cities.

They made mad love, and she didn't want Robert to wear a condom. She wanted to hold him inside her. She wanted to have his baby.

Robert wasn't quite ready for that. He hauled out and protested about the condom. He was afraid for the first. It soon grew endearing to him and he felt loved. He wanted to stay in her for hours. He heard the words of death and resurrection in his ear. He learned of the cross and wanted to die and be reborn in her. She was holy. Love was God.

He was still reading the Bible a lot in these days. The only three books that he had on him still were the Bible, the Prophet and that white paper back book on Taoism. Those and the little black one that he wrote in. All these too would soon fall. Everything had a pretty religious feel. San Pedro was still playing with him too. He felt that the situation with Paz held the utmost importance. There was nothing else. He abandoned law school; abandoned his abandonement; abandoned even peace.

Robert began to feel his mind slipping away from him with his sanity. A depression was coming over him. They had to leave. They had to leave right away. They could not wait any longer here, for here held danger for them. If Paz did not want him to kill her father, then she must leave with him. She must. That was the only solution. Forget about the university and her debts, Robert could pay that. Forget about the girl down the road you are helping. Forget about your father. They would find something to do and somewhere to go, but go they had to go. She told him they needed to get married. When the time came, they passed by the *Registo Civil* in La Sirena but nothing happened. They went back home to *La Quebrada*, and that was the end. There are no tears that can make a man stay when he is being dragged away by the chain that spins over the teeth of gogs rotating around its axis the sun. The tides rise and fall and nothing remains the same.

There was still one thing hanging over him. There was a doubt that lingered unfinished in his drive. It was his sweet Nicole whom he'd avoided calling for the past several months. He drifted further and further away from her and the past since leaving Santiago. Time, more than miles, drags people away from the past. He felt guilty. He felt she had to be told, and she had to be told the truth. He was a selfish son of a bitch, so he called her. He walked the miles down from *La Quebrada* and Paz's home to the *centro de llamadas* in Paihuano and called sweet Nicole for the first time in months. She couldn't believe he was still in Chile. She thought he was on the road somewhere up towards Mexico by now and couldn't find a phone. She was amazed at his idiocy when he told her what was taking place. She never wanted to speak to him agin. And for what? He ran back home to Paz absent from himself and seeking redemption in her eyes, but he found nothing. Only tears. Her eyes were not the same. He cried and begged her to leave. She cried and begged him stay. He left Paz that night. It was tragic. In a few short hours, he completely did away with everything that ever smelled of romantic love in his life. He destroyed himself. It was brilliant.

He left the Quebrada de Paihuano in a mad rush. Running and stumbling down the dirt, vineyard laden hills through the night, tears running down his confused face. He did not know where to go or what to do. He had to leave. That was the only thing.

He walked all the way through Paihuano and down the long mountainous highway without seeing a soul. His brain rushed. He called out into the night, "Why!" He sobbed. He was punished.

Morning was coming when he finally reached the little mud house house in Tres Cruces where he sometimes slept, and had his bag. He had walked nearly thirty miles since the sun went down yesterday. He gathered his scattered belongings from the house. He threw his three suits of clothes into the backpack, got his guitar, and a piece of Bolivian manta that Carmen had given him, and put everything together near the door. Raul was there. He understood what was happening. Raul was a little bird. *Chirijue*. He realized that this was goodbye for the two friends. Neither had much to say to the other. This is the way it should be with good friends who have shared all kinds of things. The only thing is understanding, support and sincerity. Only positive. They both knew that it was time to go.

While Robert was getting his things together, Raul sat out in the hall by the table and wrapped a joint in a dry corn husk. Some *queca* music played in the background.

For months, Robert had considered leaving, but didn't know how. Now it was the most natural thing in the world. Leaving was the only answer to this heartache. The road awaited as it always does, so Robert shouldered his *mochila*, picked up the guitar, and walked out of the dark cool house into the strong, bright morning sun.

The highway was only a few steps up a small hill from the little house. He walked the dusty path, crossed over to the right hand side and took the bag down off of his shoulder. The little dog, Rasta had been following him all night again. All the way from the Quebrada de Paihuano at Paz's house to here. It was Paz's dog, but it had been sticking with him for sometime. She called him Rasta for the long shaggy ears that he had hanging down. She said that he liked marijuana.

The breeze was blowing strong down the highway where he waited with his thumb outstretched for any passing vehicle. The sun was brilliant that morning. It was cool but bright, like it was closer than anywhere on Earth. A car finally stopped and Robert opened the door to jump in. Rasta fought to get in with him. Robert threw him out, but the dog struggled and got back in before he could shut the door. The driver of the sedan started getting frustrated and told him that he couldn't *llevar el perro.* He eventually got the door shut and the car rolled down the road and out of the Valle de Elqui. He looked back and Rasta was running down the highway after him. The car turned one of the mountain corners, and Robert thought he lost him, but he looked back a minute later, and there was Rasta, still running frantically after the car, so small he could barely be seen. Finally he disappeared from sight, and the car continued on out of the valley and towards the future.

The car carried him for a few hours out of the valley to La Sirena. This was the *Panamericana.* From here could go anywhere. The whole world lay ahead of him. He was still shaking. It was only midday, and he could not believe that he was without Peace. He was dizzy and disoriented. He did not know what to do. He wanted to talk to someone. He found a payphone in a *centro de llamadas* in a shopping mall nearby the bus station, and tried calling his father, but couldn't get through. He got in touch with his brother for a brief conversation that probably left his brother Brian feeling concerned for his safety and sanity. He did not know where to go. He got on the first bus heading North. It was North he wanted. It was the North he was traveling for before he lost himself in the desert mountains and vineyards of love and the Valle de Elqui and North that must continue.

The bus carried him to the desert port town of Arica and then to Antafoghasta. He kept on moving. He did not feel to rest. Through the days and through the nights he kept traveling up and up through the North Central parts of Chile with trucks and buses and any cars he could get a ride with. The first thing that was moving he went with. He did not want to stop. He did not want to wait. When he was moving, the movement occupied his shattered brains. He did not have to think about what lay behind him. When he was moving, he could see what lay ahead of him. When he was stopped, he couldn't.

He finally reached the famous desert town of San Pedro de Atacama. Whether the town was named after the cactus, or the cactus named after the town, he didn't know. He didn't want to touch the cactus ever again, but there was still something mystical about it. It was an oasis in the desert. It was a small collection of mud and straw houses and adobe churches, cantinas and buildings. It was full of artists, travellers, farmers and Indians. He found a place to camp, and decided to stop for a short while. He bought a bottle of wine, and started to drink.

It wasn't long before he met with more travellers from distant parts of Chile. There were people from Santiago and students from Valpariso. Everyone wanted to have fun. He started playing guitar and people started singing. Energies rose with the moon and the wine. They built fires and cooked stews. They danced around the flames. Women twirled fire. Men beat tambors and blew on flutes. Their voices grew loud under the stars and their blood ran hot. They took to the streets and the bars singing, and led by Robert and another Chileno who had a guitar, the band of travellers and revelers raised enough money to buy more wine.

The wine continued flowing for the rest of the week. In the day, they would walk around, cook and waste time in the desert shade, and at night the music would play. Each night more and more people joined the group. More people came to dance, and energies soared. Everyone easily became friends. The women were beautiful. Robert didn't care at all about them. That was the best. As long as he kept singing and drinking, the past disappeared. Peace seemed like another lifetime.

The full moon was the climax. Several people tasted the cactus which Robert solemnly abstained. Everyone smoked, drank and sang, but that night there was a seriousness about it all. A holiness. The travellers took to the deserts under the pale bright moonlight. The sky was clear and cold. They walked through the empty back roads of the town and up into the hills, the Valle de la Luna and beyond. They ended up on a hill full of ancient ruins from the desert dwellers before. The Kechuas or something like that. The corn eaters and harvesters of Amaranto. Amongst their fallen rock walls and shattered pieces of clay pottery the travellers shivered from a cold that grew inside each one of them. It was a coldness that the fire and wine could only intensify. The only warmth that could cure this cold was the warm embrace of someone who cared. Embrace. Embrazar. Brazos. The lonliness is cold. "Words are lonliness".

When the moon reached its peak, high in the southern sky, it began its descent, and the cold began to wear off, leaving only a pallid, clammy sweat. People's fears faded with the holy pale light. The group separated and divided into smaller groups of two and three and each found their own way down the from the hilltop community of Indian ghosts. Some went into the streets alone and some with a partners, but all were alone.

After the full moon, the travelers took to the road again, shook hands, hugged and kissed and made plans to get together again in Santiago or Vina del Mar. They all exchanged phone numbers and email addresses for when their paths would cross again, and then they scattered. Suddenly, they were all gone and only Robert continued North.

Alone again, Robert got back to Antafoghasta and found a train headed North to Bolivia, across the mountains and surrealistic salt flats of Atacama where pink flamencos dance with their reflections on the vast desolate plains that inhabit Northern of Chile.

The train left out from Antafoghasta around 8 o'clock at night, and arrived in Bolivia in the early morning. It was a cold rough ride. The train rocked and shook all night, and the high altitudes the uninsulated old train passed through made sleeping in the ragged bench seats nearly impossible. Morning was a delight to see when the train reached the strange border between Chile and Bolivia.

The train stopped at the ghostly checkpoint and a surly red headed immigration officer came aboard and ordered everyone out of the train. The scene reminded him of Raul and the time when he and an Indian from San Pedro traversed the mountains for a week, smuggling a kilo of cocaine from Bolivia into San Pedro. He said for the week, he lived mostly on cocaine and coca leaves.

Everyone had to get out of the train and present their documents and passports. Robert showed his and thought little about the status that he'd left the country in. In his delerium, he was ignorant that he had been in the country for over seven months, and his tourist visa only allowed for a short stay of ninety days. He was illegal in Chile and way out in the desert at the frontier with Bolivia, there was nowhere to fix it.

The red headed prick took the passport and told him to take the train back to Antafoghasta in the night and fix the papers up at the immigration office there. He would have to pay a fine, explain himself, get the proper papers with the proper stamps, and then take the train back here again next week. What?

This all seemed impossible to Robert. He was in too much of a hurry to even think of turning back now. He could not go back. That was an option he could not imagine. He had to keep moving ahead. He pleaded with the officer if there was anything that they could do, but the red head simply refused and said he had to go back to Antafoghasta. Robert didn't have the money to waste on bullshit like this. Robert didn't have the time to waste on bullshit like this. He was moving North. He had to get to Bolivia. This was no time for Antafoghasta again.

Reluctantly, the red head finally gave Robert back his passport when Robert agreed that he would go back to Chile. He took his passport and got back on the train to get his bag and belongings, when he decided that he was not going back.

The train was stopped at the Chillean side of the border. There was a long, straight two hundred meter stretch of track and road that separated Chile from Bolivia. At the other end of the one hundred meters, lay the Bolivian checkpoint. A few Indian women dressed in big colorful bowl skirts and little round hats crossed the road back and forth. It would be impossible to make a run for it. The immigration officer warned him about this. He told him that if he tried to cross like that, they would jail him. He knew that the train was about to leave off again. He left his bags right there, and ducked down low beneath the window so that the immigration people below couldn't see him. The train started to rock, and made its way for Bolivia. There was no commotion. No officers boarded the train and grabbed him. Everything remained cool. He seemed safe.

The train reached Bolivia and the passengers got out to get their passports stamped. Robert followed along with the rest of the people in the sidecar. Through the cold night and morning the passengers became familiar with each other and formed some kind of bond the way people do when they share a difficult and common experience of suffering. They began to recognize each other's faces and differences in a way that people seldom do in a sterilized society.They had learned each other's names and professions. They learned each other's destinations and origins. They learned each other's stories. There was a fat red headed woman who was going to meet her sick father in La Paz. There was a pair of longhaired artesano puppeteers who were traveling together with their trunk of puppets and props. One was from Chiloe and the other Colombia. Robert asked the guy if the he knew Jonas. They didn't. They were carrying their show to unvisited parts of Bolivia and Brazil, and traveling where the currents carried them. They were angels. They wanted to reach back to Colombia. They told him there were millions of Valles De Elqui's in the world. Finally, there was a man traveling alone and without papers because of some problem he had with his residency in Chile. He was born in Bolivia, but had been living in Chile for the past twelve years. It was now time for him to go home to Sucre. He knew the Valle de Elqui and was in the process of studying a book about a man called the Cristo de Elqui. He had a lot to talk Robert about. The man told Robert to stick close by him. He promised to do all he could to help Robert get through the border. He seemed confident that they wouldn't have any problems.

The passengers were lined into a waiting room with a desk and a few armed guards standing with a stamp and some books with a pen. Routinely, the guards checked each passenger's passport for irregularities and Chilean exit stamps and slammed down the Bolivian entrance. As the line shortened and Robert awaited his turn, his stomach grew anxious and knotted. He did not want to get stuck here in the middle of this desert. Finally, the man who promised to help Robert reached to the front of the line. There was some commotion about his lack of stamps and papers, but without too much of a problem, the guards let the man pass. It seemed easy enough. Now it was Robert's turn. He stepped up to the desk in front of the guards and presented his passport like everyone else. The officer took the passport and began thumbing through the pages, trying to find the page with the departure from Chile. Robert said nothing, but tried to look as serious as possible with his red eyes, shaggy hair and overgrown beard.

"Y hay?" said the officer. *"Donde esta la salida de Chile? Aqui lo mire la entrada, pero me parece que se hace falta la salida".*

Robert said nothing and tried once again to play the dumb gringo tourist.

"Usted tiene que regresar aya a Chile para estancar su passaporte," the man insisted that he return to other side of the border for the exit stamp on his passaport.

He closed the passport and tried to hand it back. Robert did not accept it, and futily tried to explain the situation. He was making no headway. Everyone in the room was staring at him, when the Chilean Bolivian man jumped to his rescue. He began talking to the *chaparo* Bolivian guards for him. He told the guards that Robert was a musician, a troubador. He told them that Robert was an artist and that through the love of a Chilean woman, he was delayed in Chile. He explained to the guards that Robert was a good man and should be admitted into the country of Bolivia. Robert listened to the words they spoke and knew that this approach to migration would never work the in the developed world, but the guards seemed to be softening up a bit. They all looked at each other, and the chief shrugged his shoulders to the next guards. "*Ensena me su guitarra pues*," he ordered Robert to get his guitar.

"*Tocarnos una cancion*," he told Robert to play a song. He took out the guitar and his fingers knew immiediatly which rhythm to begin. It was a cueca by Violeta Para that he learned from Carmen, "*Ya me voy, ya me voy para Bolivia. Sonaron, sonaron los cascabelles*," he hollared over the triplet rhythm his guitar pounded out. The guards all laughed and clapped their hands as he finished the song. Robert blushed and they stamped his passport.

They rushed back into the train, half afraid that someone might call him back in. They all found their seats and laughing in a commotion, the train started rolling again. He blew and the train creaked.

Bolivia. Bolivia is a movie about Butch Cassidy and the Sundance Kid. They took Pancho Villa's cape, and headed for the mountains and the deserts, robbing each bank that they saw and falling in love with the round, skirted little women of the high plains. This time they bussed it as far as they could and then split up, Robert taking the road for the mining towns of Potosi. He played music in the bars at night and took tours of the mines during the day, moved by how hard life hits some people. The mining women, short and stubby, on top of huge, mountainous piles of rocks with a hammer, busting every stone one at a time, checking for silver. The men were hunched over in the dark tunnels all day, blasting dynamite in small holes they bore with a chisel. They thanked the tourists for their gifts of coca leaves and extra sticks of dynamite.

The bus ride to Sucre hugged the edge of a long rocky river. It passed through village after little river village along the way. In one village, there was a group of Bolivians working on the side of the road. Amongst the group of Indians, worked one white woman. The girl was beautiful. Robert tried to stick his face through the window to make some-type of contact with the young blonde, but the bus kept right on rolling into Sucre, a few hours down the road. The girl stuck in Robert's head. He had not seen a gringo girl in so long. She looked soft and pearly. He assumed she must have been in the Peace Corps or something. He didn't care. He just regretted not getting off the bus right then and there and walking straight up to her and something. Something would have had to happen.

He got a cheap little hotel in the cold town of Sucre. In the bar below his hotel room he drank a glass of hot mulled wine. It was perfect. He had another and it was still better. From there the night went on until morning when he had a sick and tired feel to himself. The day was gray and covered with clouds. It was still soon in the morning. He walked around the walled, cobblestone, mediaeval streets and got fed up with his regretting. He went back and got his little things together and carried himself right back to the bus station and back to that little town on the way to Potosi. He was sure he would remember it when he saw it. Maybe the girl was still there. Maybe she lived there with a family and was helping out with some great project. She was sure to be the perfect one.

He stopped the bus when they passed the river again and got out with his backpack and big black guitar case. The bus soared off and left him alone again with community full of little Bolivian people quietly looking at him. What now?

The first thing was getting a place to put down this backpack and guitar. He asked around with at a few of the small roadside, riverside rock and mud homes, but didn't learn anything of a hospedaje. It seemed that he had to walk another forty five minutes to a next town that was supposed to have somewhere to sleep. There was a bus coming, but it wouldn't pass by until evening. He tried asking about the young white girl who was here working the day before, but no one had half a word to say about her. Maybe in the next town.

Robert wasn't about to sit down there and wait for night, so he started walking up the hill to the next town that was supposed to have somewhere to sleep. It was a heavenly autumn day and the sun was bright and cool. The walk was good.

As it turned out, the next town didn't offer any kind of hospedaje services either. Of course no one knew anything about the girl, but someone told him about the government building down the road where the dam workers stayed. They said that he could probably sleep there. It was worth a shot.

There were only two workers at the bunk house when Robert arrived, and one was about to leave. The one who was staying was thrilled about having a Gringo come there and beg for board. The guy was more than happy to let Robert sleep there. He said that there was plenty of room. He even gave Robert a good dish of some corn soup. After the meal and enough exhausting conversation, the big bellied Indian fellow took out a plastic gallon of corn chicha. It was some kind of wine that tasted sweet. Robert didn't quite understand what it was, but it definitely had alcohol in it, and after a few glasses, the guitar was out and they were both singing all of the Spanish songs that Robert knew, plus a little bit of Chuck Berry and Creedence. The Indian played the guitar a little bit, but he was long out of practice and the coordination and mind were slipping into the corn sugar wine.

The dam worker had to go to work in the morning, but left him some bread with cheese and tea to take breakfast with. He told him not to go and that he was more than welcome to stay another night. Robert didn't feel like taking the walk and bus ride back to Sucre again anyway; better to stay and explore the area a little bit. This was Bolivia. There were no tourists anywhere. He met a woman that could speak a little bit of English and was eager to come and talk with Robert. They chatted freely about the States and Chile, and after a short while the woman invited him to come help her break corn. They spent the evening harvesting a small track of young corn that someone had planted and given to her. They chewed on the sweet part of the cane and brought home more than enough corn to eat. They ate corn all kinds of ways, boiled, roasted, raw, with cheese. They had a good feed before he went back in the night to the bunkhouse by the dam. This was an easy night, and they went to bed soon after it got dark. In the morning he left.

Bolivia is a tough place to hitchhike. It is not that the people are mean or unfriendly, it's just that there are so very few cars. When Robert arrived back at the town by the road, the daily bus had already passed. There wasn't another bus until tomorrow. The people said that if he waited, however, he might find a ride.

Robert put down his backpack and the guitar and sat down on a rock not far from the road. He waited and waited and waited, but nothing. He bought a beer and walked down to the wide and shallow river to watch it run. The river was like the Sesquahana in some places, that old ghost of a river that Keruac talked about. He drank the liter and took off his shoes and played on the guitar a little bit, taking in the flow of everything. The were a few women washing down stream from him, and every now and then an Indian man would pass by heading to another town that lay behind the bush on the other side of the creek. A few hours passed and he went back to the road. By this time, there were a few other people waiting for some kind of ride too. Not a car passed. Nothing. It was the kind of road you could have a picnic in the middle of.

Suddenly, towards the evening time at the end of the day, a municipal pick-up truck was passing through that already had couple of riders in the back. They weren't going to Sucre though. They were going to a place called San Miguel, that was a few hours up the road. The driver warned them that it was in the mountains, and was sure to be cold. None of them cared. They wanted to move and that was it. So long as it wasn't here again. Forward. It was La Paz that Robert wanted to reach now. Enough holding up. It was North he wanted. He was ready to get back to Texas along the straightest line. If he could reach back by May, still better. He could reach to his sister's graduation. It would be a good excuse to get home. He called his family in Texas and told them that he meant to do this. This would make her happy. This was important now. Nothing was down here in Bolivia. There was no future in South America right now. The only thing to do was get home. There is still a lot to see on the road. So long as it wasn't in a plane he had to get on, this was a plan. A goal. Sweet Nicole sent him an email advice about a ship out at sea, sailing instead of drifting. This was good advice. It's better to sail. Master destiny. Go where you want to go instead of where the forces want you to go. Death awaits the drifters. Sometimes there is an island or a caye right there. Sometimes it can pass so close by your drifting vessel that you would want to reach out and grab it, but current is a strong thing. The sea is something else. There is no swimming against her when she's running. She goes where she wants with you and begs neither forgiveness nor pardon.

Nicole was right about that. He was sailing back to the North, but don't get too far ahead of yourself, first comes La Paz, the highest capital city in the world. The ride that night was cold and long. He took the dirty blanket off his bag and stuck his head through. One of the Indian riders pulled out a big sheet of plastic, and all the nomads cuddled up beneath it, forgetting all modesty and shame. This was cold.

Mother's had their babies pressed tight against their skin and their young ones held close beneath their wings. Everyone became a family that night before they reached San Miguel on the hill.

It was near midnight when they arrived at the walled town. Robert got a room near the plaza where the truck dropped him. It wasn't far from the bus terminal where Robert went in the morning to check out the schedule of salidas. There was a bus leaving for La Paz at six o'clock in the evening. The night bus. It was scheduled to be in La Paz before day.

Robert passed the day walking around the town and resting in the plaza, reading the Prophet again and writing in his journal. He ate a good plate of food and in the evening he got to the bus on time. The bus rolled cold and calmly through the night and Robert dropped into a deep sleep. He was curled up in his blanket asleep when the chaos erupted. He was awoken to the crash broken glass and screaming. It was just coming on daylight. There was a road block. There were disenfranchised miners throwing rocks and Molotov cocktails at the buses and cars that were coming from all over to get into La Paz. This was the one road coming in from the South, and the miners had taken it, trying to get some rights; trying to get some people to listen to them. Did they really want to hurt innocent people? Probably not, but they had to get some attention, and if your blocking one of the only entrances to the capital city, you are a force that has to be reckoned with. The government has to see their cries and understand their demands if they don't even want to. They want freedom. They want a living wage. They want some working conditions. They demand reform. They want change.

Robert wanted to change his ass right off of this road, but he was already in it. He ducked down on the ground like most of the women and old people did on the bus. Everyone was screaming. Some hollered to go and some to stay. No one knew what to do. Some of the men were brave and opened up the back door of the bus to make a run for it. Robert didn't see where they were running for. There was no town in sight. No village. No next road. They were in the middle of a huge flat plane, a bowl with foothills leading to the mountains far on either side. Maybe there was a town or community hiding in the hills, but Robert didn't see where. Most of the men running were struck down by rocks or chased down by some of the screaming warrior miners. This was serious.

The windows of the bus were still being broken out. Robert covered himself and the woman next to him with the little blanket and didn't look up. There were several cars and trucks and busses stopped and turned off the road. Some were tipped over and burning. Some looked stuck in the mud. They felt the bus start moving. The driver swerved off the road and somehow managed to pass the road block and get us back on the paved highway to La Paz. Everyone was cheering and yelling amongst the scattered broken glass. The miners hurled their rocks after them, but they were flying now.

The dawn wind blew in through the broken windows and the bus got bitterly cold as the road raised into the snowy peaks around La Paz. The front windshield of the bus was completely busted out and the driver and his copilot both bled from their heads and faces. Driving was made difficult, but it was still an hour and a half to La Paz. The road went on in high spirits, passing stonewalls and llama pastures where peasants waited by the side of the road to wave to the windowless bus when it passed by.

When they reached La Paz, everyone congratulated the bus driver for his job well done and went on their own ways. Robert asked around for a hospedaje econmico to stay at and walked for a few good hours trying to find a cheap one. He ended up on the Calle de las Brujas, the witches street, with all kinds of cheap markets and seedy people wandering around. There was nothing pretty about it at all, but there were some carpentry shops that made guitars and charangos, which he learned a little bit about from Raul. Robert walked all around through the markets until he found the strongest looking charango for the cheapest price and bought it. It cost him about twenty dollars. He also bought a jacket that some little Bolivian chaparita woman made from hand with the cloth that he picked out. It was the same kind of cloth as the manta that Carmen gave to him.

That was La Paz, a big market. There were people who sat in little huts and read your fortune in coca leaves, or blessed you with some of their cheap, foul shaman wine. It was their religion. It had some ties with the Catholics, but it was so far gone and mixed up with their Indian traditions, you had to just call it folk medicine. The people really bought it. The market on the high snow peaks of El Alto sold plenty of blessings in their dark huts with burning candles. There was one hut after the other, selling what can't be seen.

Robert bought a little cassette recorder, and sat in his hotel room for the next couple of days recording some of the songs that he had written over the past several months in Chile. He carried the recorder with him into the streets and caught the sounds of the night carried out from the cantinas and closed private parties. After getting all of his songs out of him, he went to a post office and mailed the tape back to his father who would be pleased to hear his son's thoughts and voice, no matter how rough and dry it sounded.

It was in La Paz outside of a blues bar one night that Robert left his ATM bank card in a cash machine on the street. It wasn't until the tropical lowlands passed Coroico that he realized what he'd done.

It was a river town of freight boats that weaved up to the Brazilian border and Puerto Bello. It was hot and muggy, a tributary of the Amazon. There was no getting the card back. He went to a bank and had the card cancelled. He still had nearly two hundred dollars. He had to get thrifty.

He paid the twenty dollar boat pass that would carry him to Brazil. The boat provided three meals a day while they were on the river. The ride was supposed to take three to five days, depending on conditions of the river. The boat was a sprawling system of wooden barges all tied together around one powerful little diesel tug that pushed the freight barges down the calm river at an easy pace. If the breeze picked up at all, then the river would get choppy and too rough for the barges, so the whole system would have to pull over to the edge of the bush and tie on in a calm place until the weather passed. The three to five day journey could easily turn into eight or ten if the weather was bad. It was a huge river. It looked like the Mississippi, brown, muddy, wide and rank.

The first night aboard the boat was spent in port while the sailors loaded her up with freight to carry up the river. There were plenty of bananas, sacks of rice, corn, flour, beans, cement and even a few cars and trucks. Most everything was covered up with big tarps so you couldn't tell what was underneath. Robert found a good enough place above some frieght to hang up the hammock and mosquitero that the captain told him to buy. He went to sleep and woke up before day as the system of barges eased off into the early morning darkness.

By the time day cleared off, they were well on the river. The cook called the passengers four at a time into the small kitchen to get their morning one of fried tortillas with a cup of sweet warm chocolate tea. They finished the breakfast and went back into their hammocks, where they stayed, watching the jungle banks of the river flow slowly past.

There were five other Gringos on the boat, a German pair of young men volunteers, an Agentenian couple, and a solo Frenchman. The Frenchman was a reporter and carried a high tech tape recording machine that he used to make reports for the radio station he worked for. Sometimes they would change up barges and go sit by one another's hammocks, careful not to mash up any of the cargo beneath them. In the evenings, they would smoke joints that Robert wrapped in corn husks and laugh at the stars spinning about their heads. The ride was slow and muggy.

Some days a stiff breeze would blow in, and they'd have to pull the boat onto the bush edge and wait for the river to calm down. Everyone on the boat got to know each other well.

There was nothing to do in the days or nights but lay in the hammock and read, talk, sleep or watch. That was all there was in between the meals. Meals always consisted of the fried tortillas in the morning and a murky river water soup in the afternoon made from a piece of corned beef meet that the cook had hung up near the stove. Sometimes they would get some coffee or hot chocolate in the night with another piece of fried flour or cup of beans. It was plenty of food. If you ever stayed hungry, there were plenty of the small, sweet bananas that were getting ripe on the boat, and the owners were happy to let you eat a few.

The Gringo's were all interesting people. Each had their own stories about their homes and their lives down in South America. The Argentinians were the closest to home, but they might as well have been just as far away as Robert or the Germans. They were all strangers.

Three days passed and five days passed and it looked like due to the weather, they were still going to take a few more days getting up to their destination. It was like Kurtz from Joseph Conrad, inching their way up amongst the pirhanas and the deep jungle. There was nothing to do but stay tranquilo.

One day, they stopped into a little jungle community to get out and check out something with the engine. The locals were all happy to have guests in their community and immediately started up a soccer game while they had an opportunity to play against some new people. There were two teams, the men from the riverboat versus the men from the community. They put Robert as goalkeeper. He said that he could play goalie because he remembered playing when he was a child. Many years had passed since those days on the church grass fields and Robert was terrible. The men from the community played like Pele and Robert had to withdraw himself from the goal and change positions. He would have quit but their team did not have enough people. No one cared how bad he was anyway. It was just good to run around a little bit and stir up the blood.

Before the boat left off, they bought a bottle of rum to continue the journey with. They wouldn't be in Puerto Bello for a few days yet. In the night the gringos sat around taking sips of the clear corn and sugar cane rum. It was strong and went well with the joints that were running out. There was nothing else to do.

One of the nights, an Indian woman in one of the adjacent barges got sick with a fever. She had a young baby daughter and the little girl kept crying and crying form her mama. The captain of the boat said that she had malaria and needed some treatment. He said that she was weak and could die. He went around through the barges asking the gringos if any of them had any medication. Robert was a foolish traveler, and didn't carry things like that in case of emergencies. He always felt that God would be looking over him.

Later on in the evening, the Gringo's were sitting around on the sacks near the bow of the barge, catching the breeze and the last hours of sunlight, discussing the situation. The Germans had some malaria pills. Robert thought that perhaps they didn't understand what the captain was looking for that afternoon and about the girl with the fever, but they understood perfectly well. If malaria was around, they certainly did not want to die from it, and they were sorry for the woman, but they were not giving up their malaria pills. Robert felt puzzled about the situation and thought that the Germans were cowards.

The next day the woman was alive, but still suffereing with the fever. The following day the boat reached its port and the woman lived for all they knew. The travelers felt like they had reached the promise land. The gringos all got off the boat and found a cheap hotel where they all got rooms and a fresh shower before meeting in a bar by the plaza that served big plates of food and cold beer. It was a sweaty town, but it felt like heaven to be on land again, amongst people and space to walk around.

The next day, they all rented moto-scooters for a few dollars and headed out into the bush to explore the countryside. They rented three of them, and Robert got on the back behind the German guy who liked to drive. Robert didn't like to drive at all. He preferred getting high and enjoying the ride. He liked it better to let someone else deal with reality.

Everything was fine. They took the muddy road out of town and into the rainforest, where the road turned into a trail passing by little farms and scattered thatched houses several miles away from the town. They were a few hours into the bush, when the moto that Robert and the Frenchman were on ran out of gas. They assumed all of tanks were full when they left out in the morning. You know what the old drill seargent football coaches say, "assume makes an ass out of you and me".

It looked like a bad situation, but Robert wasn't too worried. He knew that one of the other bikes could go look gas and bring it back to them. The other bikes didn't worry too much either. The Frenchman didn't see it that way though. He whispered to Robert as the other two bikes kept on cruising around and exploring, that he wasn't going to hesitate about killing the two Germans and taking their bike back to town if it came down to that.

Robert thought that he was surely joking and only half laughed at the Frenchman's morbid sense of humor. The Frenchman looked back and Robert and told him he was serious. Robert smiled again, not knowing what to think.

The Germans and the Argentians drove off to go check at some little farm houses for a bit of gas, leaving Robert and the Frenchman alone in the jungle.

"I'm serious," the Frenchman said. "If we don't get some gas, I will kill the two Germans and ride with their bike".

Robert didn't have anything to say. He tried to laugh it off, but couldn't laugh anymore. He started getting dizzy and paranoid like he was high. He was high.

It didn't take long for the Germans to come back to them. They didn't bring gas, but they brought a tube to siphon some out of their bike. Robert hoped the Frenchy didn't try anything crazy. There was really nothing to worry about. They weren't so far in the bush that they couldn't walk somewhere for help, even if the Germans and Argentinians abandoned them.

They got the bike running again and set back on the road for town. They didn't say anything else to one another.

The next day, Robert and the Germans left for Porto Bello in Brazil. The Germans and Robert were traveling together now. They were all trying to reach the North. The Germans wanted to find a ship or something in Guiana and hit back on the either European continent or Africa. Anywhere they could reach home from. They didn't like airplanes either.

They crossed the Rio Negro and into Brazil, but one of the Germans had to go back to get a Yellow Fever vaccination card from the Bolivian side. Robert and the next German, Johan he was named, waited on the Brazilian side. There was a line crossing the border and when Robert and Johan reached the front of the line, Robert suddenly bust out into a dead laugh when he heard the customs agent speak. He knew that Brazil was a Portuguese speaking county, but Robert had never really heard Portuguese so close before. He had to laugh. He had grown accustomed to Spanish and figured Portoguese was somewhat like Spanish. He was wrong.

From the border, they had to hitch a ride through the burned down rainforest cattle pastures to Porto Bello. The seedy port was far from bello. There were whores, rough drunken sailors and vagabonds in the bars and customs houses early in the morning. It was a tough town. There was a boat hauling out in the morning and the captain said that they could put up their hammocks and sleep aboard the boat. They all agreed and bought their tickets.

The Germans sent Robert with some money to find ganja amongst the chaotic scrawl of sin and Robert agreed. He wasn't afraid of anything but the cops, and there were only a few of them creeping around the place.

He hit the closest bar to the wharf. The Portuguese was crazy around him, bouncing around with its birdlike melodies. There were all classes of people in the bars. Most looked dirty. Robert look dirty too, but he still couldn't quite fit in. Robert didn't feel strange about being the only Gringo around. He certainly looked strange, and other people would have felt strange, but Robert was now well accustomed. It didn't take long before he found someone who was ready to bring some ganja. Robert said he wanted to see the thing and the guy ran off while Robert waited in the bar, sipping a beer in the morning hours. Beautiful dark skinned girls walked the bars suggestively, while some mamacitas cooked big pots of soup in the corners and on the sidewalks for the hungry dock workers, hustlers, gangsters and sailors. There was quick movement on the street. There were all kinds of girls. Not the short, chubby Altiplano mamacitas from Bolivia with their big skirts and little hats. These were long legged, body rider Amazonas. Brazileras. So close, but so far from the Andes. Music played from speakers hanging from street lights. Cool groovy jazz that pedestrians glid in the street to. It was like Brazil had a soundtrack.

The guy didn't take long with the ganja, but it was little bit. It looked good, but the thing was very small, only a couple of skinny joints for a high price. He assured Robert it was good, and that he would only have to smoke a little bit. Robert said it was too much money and tried to walk off. The guy was all accelerated and serious. He punched Robert in the back of the head. Robert paid the guy and took the ganja back to the ship where he showed the Germans what he got. They didn't care. They were just happy to have something. It wasn't Robert's money anyway. It is stupid to give people a hard time when you are at their mercy.

In the nighttime, after the Brazilian kitchen served tortillas with hot, sweet coffee, the three travelers went up on the top deck above the bow and admired the stars and fresh breeze aboard their new boat. This was a proper boat, not a bunch of Bolivian homemade barges set to drift. This was a machine that could handle the seas. It had a hull. The Amazon is something else. It is the sea. Its lazy currents could suck down the Earth. It is the blood flowing into the world. It is the heart. It is the lungs. It is the capillaries. It is the mouth and the tongue and the orphis all in one. There are places where you can't see the other side. It was good to ride in a strong fast ship. This ship had a bar and everything. They all bought beers and drank two before their journey, feeling wonderfully safe from the dangerous world outside. In the morning, the ship departed for Manaus, the center of the Amazons. The trip was a three day breeze compared with the last one.

Manuas is the capital of the Amazon, the ruins of a rich rubber trading town. Deep fried pirhanas sold in the streets by the dozen; all classes of different fruits and fried flour goods; bananas by the thousands, skinny iguanas on sticks. It was and oily, greasy, hustle and bustle city. The shiny people moved fast.

Robert didn't have long in the city before a ride he hooked up on the ship was heading North to Venezuela with a load of something from the boat. The boat had to discharge and the truck was to load and leave out after dark. Robert had to be pendient. Everything was delayed with the discharging of the boat and the truck didn't leave until one in the morning. It was a free ride, so Robert didn't mind the wait.

The truck stopped to sleep for and hour before daylight at a stop off the highway. It was a big comfortable truck, easy to sleep in. The driver didn't speak Spanish or English, but after several exhausting hours of brain busting, the two began to communicate. When you're hitchhiking, the sweetest thing is the guilty sleep. The guiltiness makes your eyes even heavier when your only duty is to keep the driver company.

Robert and the Brazillian driver rode that straight thing for two nights and days. They crossed the equator under the full moon and Robert jumped off at the crossroads before big morning on the third day. Brazil is mother of a country.

He dropped Robert at the road to Caracas. There was a man grinding sugarcane and selling fresh juice. It was sweet-sweet, and the cool sun was just coming. It didn't take but a few minutes, and a next truck stopped and offered a ride.

This was no sweet comfy truck. This was a rough jalopy from the past, made of white steel; shaking and rattling down the road at maximum speed. The driver was a rough bearded fellah. Robert didn't ask what he was carrying. This guy was from the bush somewhere. Robert couldn't get a lick of what he was saying. The other driver spoke more slow and clearly, so it was easier to get the meaning. This guy rattled just like the truck. They had to make hand signs and noises to get each other's point, but before long, they were communicating too.

Robert didn't know how far it was to Caracas or where this guy was going to, but they were headed in the same direction. He was from a different region but knew the people and had friends all along the straight road. The two travelers stopped in little wild cane roadside huts along the way that sold heavy shots homemade white rum for ten cents a glass. Cashasa. The land was getting higher, rising out of the Amazon lowlands. The first hut/liquor stand they stopped in, Robert denied the drivers offer to take one. The driver was a little hurt, but motioned for him to suit himself. Robert thought he'd play the good example about drinking and driving. After the second or third little roadside hut, he gave into his better half and accepted a shot of the rum. It was hot. They laughed and got back in the car and rolled on to the North. After the first shot, it all disappeared. At the rate they were stopping for rum at the little huts, they were never going to get where they were going. Neither one of them cared. By this time they were talking freely like they were born speaking the same language. They didn't even need words to understand. They laughed and sighed hysterically. At one point the driver started crying as he swerved back and forth across their side of the two-lane road. Robert was a little bit worried, but just a little. The man still seemed to hold some control of the situation in his hands. The best thing for Robert to do was keep on drinking so long as the guy was buying. There obviously seemed to be no law against it.

Robert didn't remember when he reached Venezuela, but after another night in his hammock sleeping behind a roadside truck-stop, he reached Caracas in the morning with a bus. He was down to about fifty dollars. He checked into a cheap hotel room near the Caribbean port of La Guaira. It was a beach community. He made to the Caribbean. He was just a boat ride away from home. There were black boys beating big tank drums on the beach in the hot sun and meringue in the nights with hips shaking smoothly to the horns and rythms. He bought a small bottle of rum, some bananas, had shower and asked his way around till he found the docks where the big ships come in. He had to find a ship going back to the states, and he had to find it now.

He met a bunch of seaward sailors from Alabama and the Gulf Coast. They were making the trip back with a cargo of containers and carnival rides. Robert imagined sleeping up in the bow, hidden in a bubby baby bumper car. They talked to their captain and told him Robert could cook. The crew all loved a little good home country music, but the captain called the owner and said something about insurance and that was that. It was impossible. The boat was going right to Chorpus Christi. It would have brought him right home, and in time for his sister graduation, a solemn event that he told himself to get to. He thought of just jumping onto the huge barge when no one was looking, but decided it might end up being a long voyage and he could starve.

Chorpus Christi; the body of Christ; back home instead of stuck and broke in this dreaded South America amongst the vultures and hounds.

"There is only one time," he kept telling himself amidst the love song tragedies he filled his little black journal with. There is always the last time. He took his guitar and went for a round about the seaside comedors at lunchtime.

His little cash card was gone, and his money done. The room cost ten dollars for the night. Everything in Venezuela was much more expensive than anywhere else he'd been in the last year. It was a city city. It was metropolitan and urbane. It was built by the Gringo's when they started figuring out how much oil there was. There was a subway, shopping malls, parks with fountains, cars and freeways, sky-scrapers, Burger King sandwiches and Cinabon. There were long legged beautiful women; sophisticated women in snazzy clothes and office wear who looked like maybe they'd do you for a million dollars. They looked like models from magazines. Robert looked like a bum from the streets a South America far away, with his red sweater cheleco and glue bottom shoes, but he made eye contact with them anyway.

He bummed around the streets, trying out the banks but he didn't make any headway. It was a sad situation. He got a room for another night. It was the last night.

He thought about the old friends he had and all the plans they made and how plans don't amount to nothing. How he now sat here alone on the streets of Caracas without money, without help or anywhere to go. He grimaced because he knew it was all of his fault that his plans have all failed.

He thought of his old university friend Jerry Mahl and the little truck. How far away that seemed and how illogical that he was here, but it was not. There was one step etched in the stones of antiguity and pearls of night. It was a part of him. It was real and led him here to where all of the roads have led. Constantinople. A blank page that he cannot jump off of. He must suffer it. He must bear the weight of his past, for now it is taxed.

The payment is the atonement. The pain is enlightening and cleaning.

"God saves us all but once. All but one time".

There was no out of it. He had to swallow his pride and accept himself for the coward and child he was. He wept.

People were telling him to go to the embassy, but that was they last place he wanted to go. He went to the wharf and sang in the seafood market and ate fried shrimp and salads with patacones. The plates were huge. The clients gave money to the begging Gringo musician child. They laughed, sang, clapped and listened. He howled what he knew in Spanish and Chuck Berry and Creedence in English. Anything the people called for or understood. He didn't care. He wanted a hotel room and a bus fare to the airport where maybe his father could send a ticket. He quit. The cooks and managers told him to come back tomorrow and they would give him more food and could open a hat for tips. No problem.

He called home collect. He was in a jam. He was a quitter. A money came through the wire and he forgot all about everything and left the damned airport and made a bus for Colombia.

It was good to get Venezuela behind him. He hit Colombia along the Caribbean border and got out and the National Park, Parque Tyrona. He walked into the bush along the trails and found a campground where he could string his hammock for a few days and cook and eat. He walked the jagged rocks and highland Incan Pre Colombian ruins. Columbus is the mark of death. "It separates us from life".

He found his way to Cartagena and checked into a room on the Calle Media Luna. There were about a dozen cheap hostels on the street along with a pile of hookers and drug dealers. It was the half-moon.

The first room he found was in a dorm at a travelers hostel. It was full of Gringos from all over the world, seeing the sights and doing the things. It offered free coffee. He lasted nearly a week there before he found a cheaper, private local room above a little flowered courtyard with a gazebo.

The room was on the second floor, and opened up to a balcony that ran around all the rooms around the courtyard. Artesanos had their hammocks strung outside while they braided bracelets with seeds and shells. Some worked with silver and some with any kind of trash they could recycle from the streets. They were from all over South America, and one German fellow who was stuck there for some reason. Everyone was stuck there. It was a pleasant place to be stuck. It was for long term people. It was a community.

Drugs were the norm here. No one cared what you did, or where you did it. Colombian press was smoking everywhere.

There was a red room across the courtyard from Robert. It was bright and electric. It was intense fire. They said that a man killed himself in it once a few years ago. Now there was a thin pantomime from Ecuador who rented it. Every evening when the sun eased down into the pre-twilight hours of five o'clock, he stood in front of the open doored room with a hand mirror and transformed into his character. So carefully and precisely he painted the colors onto his white primed face. Everything in Cartagena was fire, roses and sunsets, soft and breezy cutting the heat. Soft were the nights in the Plazas and the banks of old pirate wall, the churchyard cafes of Plaza Santo Domingo where the artists and bums gather around a box of wine or a bottle of rum in the shadows along the perimeters against the high stone walls of the Church of Saint Catherine. Everybody was always there. Marta the artesana and Gill the starving French bum who was trying his hardest to get out of this place, but was so far very unsuccessful. One night Robert carried him out for a bite to eat for some company. Gill was grateful. A few days later Gill gave Robert a necklace made from a nail bent around a piece of broken glass of a building that was bombed that day before. It was the Farc or Paramiltares or some other people that didn't like the highrise financial building. The boom was felt radial kilometers away. That night they warned everyone to stay inside and not around the plazas and public places, but most people didn't pay it any mind at all and came out to catch the life or sell something that they made. They said that thier were other bombs around the city, but no one heard anything else of it.

It was election times. Uribe had his posters up all over town with his "Mano Firme and Corazon Grande". Next door in Venezuela, a coup overthrew the president Chavez, but he double overthrew the coup and took back the seat, lucky to still be alive. The streets of Venezuela were full of talks of revolution. Robert didn't quite understand it at the time. Some people said that Chavez was the pig dictator and others said that the other guy was the corrupt, thiefing swine. The radios played protest music. When he was in La Guaira, army troops rushed into the bar and handsed up the whole place with their guns. They did a quick shake down and carried two young men out into their truck, roughing them up a little bit on the way. Robert didn't know what was taking place, but it was hot.

Colombia and Venezuela were both putting laws into effect prohibiting the people to travel out of the country. They were trapping their people in.

Robert wanted out, but he still didn't want to get a plane. He just wanted to get up to Panama and then he could hit back on the buses and be home within a few days of straight bussing through Costa Rica and the rest of Central America and Mexico. All he cared about was getting home. He'd seen enough.

Cartagena was the end of the road. There were no buses going further on. The Darien Gap stood between North and South America and presented a difficult obstacle to circumvent. There were some boats that made the run across the gap, but they were dangerous things. There were all kinds of stories. You didn't know who or what to believe. Some say it's completely fine and beautiful. Some say its suicide. Two birdwatchers were recently murdered in the uninhabited zone capturing images of rare wildlife nonexistent elsewhere. You had to pay to find out.

There were sailboats that carried you up to Panama, kind of a tourist deal, that cost two hundred dollars at the least. For that money, he could fly up to San Andres and over to Costa Rica and be on the road again, but he still liked the idea of sailing up through the San Blas Islands and onto Colon. He made plans with a captain, but something happened and the boat left without him. The boat was stopped outside the Islas Rosarios just North of Cartagena with a kilo of heroine. It was on the front page of the newspaper. Robert was glad he didn't go with that one.

The time was short before his sister's graduation that he told himself he was going to get back to Texas for. A month passed in Cartagena. He saw a man get stabbed in a broken bottle fight on the Media Luna street outside of his room. The town was full of sex and violence. He made interesting friends and relationships. Rastas and musicians; holed out writers and artisans; whores and drug dealers; fishermen and sailors; all kinds of ragamuffin vagabonds and hustlers. Street children beg for glue money like dogs. The say in Bogota they just shoot them.

He was offered a job at a dive shop in the Islas Rosarios. The resort was Pablo Escobar's Caribbean Vila getaway. When Pablo was assassinated it turned into posh hotel and dive resort. It was the biggest dive outfitter in all of the Caribbean, but no one was there to run it. It sounded like a cool gig, but Robert was traveling.

The time came and he quit again. He bought a plane ticket out of South America and headed for San Andres, the island in the North. The island by itself way out in the middle of the sea. It was neither South nor Central America. From San Andres, the ticket headed to San Jose, Costa Rica and then back to Texas. It was in San Andres, that life changed all over again.

In San Andres, he got a room at the Residencial Restrepo. It was an island place. Islanders. Black men and English speakers. They told him about another island, Provindence, Providence was San Andres's little sister, just smaller and less developed. The sea was pristine and world-class for diving. There was only one road around the island. There was a boat leaving in the night that would make the eighty-mile trip by morning. He could put the ticket off to Costa Rica for a few days and without any harm. Providence seemed like a place to go.

On the boat, there was another Gringo from South Africa, Henry. He'd been working as a dive master for the last three months in San Andres and was traveling to Providence to do two dives before having to leave Colombia by the end of the week. It was his goodbye treat to himself. He was a young guy, with a smooth con-man smile that was good with the women. He had a charm with his smile, and people liked him. He knew people in Providence from his dive shop and had an inside track. While they were waiting by the wharf to board the ship in the darkness he invinted Robert to step out away into the shadows and smoke the last half of a little roach he was saving in a box of matches. Robert readily accepted and got a nice paranoid high as the police snooped around the docks for any kind of contraband movement. There was no problem and the ship set off into the stormy Mid-may seas. The hammocks rocked and rolled from the canvas-draped rooftop above their load of freight. The passengers just had to hold on as the sea splashed in over the deck. By the time morning reached, the passengers were salty and soaked to the bone, looking to get off the boat and find a dry room to change clothes in.

The South African and Robert found a room at a boarding house called Miss Sofias. There was no sign or anything, but everyone knew who Miss Sofia was and that she rented rooms. Miss Sofia was an old white skinned island woman who had a big family and soft and easy ways. She could tell that the young men were hungry after their night on the sea and gave them a heavy dish of Rondon, a rich thick, coconut stew of fish and breadkind; various roots, breadfruit, green plantains, yucca and other potato like things. It looked like a big, rank biscuits and gravy. It was the best thing that Robert felt like he had ever eaten. The South African knew about Rondon and told Robert that it was a traditional dish from the islands that they cook in big pots and share up with the family. It was all right.

Robert and Henry bought a little bag of ganja and smoked a joint before going for a dive with some people that Henry new. Robert got paranoid under water with the narcosis and felt a vertigo feeling that he could not control. He lost his orientation and felt that he would die under the water. The feeling eventually passed and Robert swore he would never smoke and dive again, although the magnetic, electric color of the coral and ambient he floated through were an ecstasy unreachable in any other form. Henry laughed at Robert when he told him his fears. Henry loved to smoke and dive. He loved the colors. He was a master.

The nighttime took them to hammock bars on the beach and ganja gardens behind a pretty Italian girl's house on a green bluff.

There was one road running around the whole conic island. When the moon rose, about a million or billion little crabs crossed the road coming down from the bush and to the sea. They had to cross the road. You couldn't hold up for them to pass. You would be there all night. You had to crush the crabs.

Daylight caught them hungover and trying to get back home to San Andres. The boat left out again that night and carried them back to the island. Instead of going back to his little pension, Henry welcomed Robert to sleep at his apartment until his plane left for Costa Rica. Robert missed his plane the next day and saw Henry off first. Henry was traveling to Cartagena. He was interested in checking out South America before returning to South Africa or London or somewhere for work. He had a contact for a dive job in Cartagena, and had a few months left on his Colombian work visa.

Robert's one month tourist visa expired when he was in Providencia, but he didn't know this yet. Before Henry left, he introduced him to Maria. Aura. Aura Vanegas. Sea Queen, reina del mar. She was the queen of changes. She danced with the breezes and read the rubles. Prophetess landmine. Robert never really understood who she was, but there was something so brief and so rapid, you had to trust it. There was no time for confusion. It was purely spontaneous reaction and luck. It was his last night of the road. It was a furiousity he created out of his madness and schizophrenia. He took her to the room he rented at the Restrepo after Henry left.. He told her he could sing when she asked about his guitar. He said that he sang all over South America in the streets and borders, bars, cafes, comedors and highways, and he sang with his heart for anything. It didn't matter. It was positive and the universe paid him generously. He said that he knew million songs from the air and he shivered because it all was a lie. He couldn't complete a song. He trembled because in his head he knew that his days were all behind him; he was ragged, crushed and beat. His voice disappeared and burned up from the fire of time. He had no voice. His world was a lie. He was a lie. His memory raced, but it could find no songs. She saw through his glass ribcage. She wanted to hug him when she saw how all alone he was with the big guitar on the other side of the bed. He could say nothing. He sat there shaking saying he knew that it was true. He knew that he wasn't lying, but there was no one there now to believe him. He was a lonely soldier unaware of the defeat yet. He was clinging to a rope that already slid out of his hand. Henry laughed when he told him that he was a musician carrying around the guitar. He laughed when he told him that he sang. He never even took the guitar out of its case. Henry knew that he was mad. He whispered it to Aura before he left.

Aura hugged him and told him it was alright. That was all she could say to the poor boy full of disbelief. He quivered as he saw himself where he was. He felt like imploding.

His little black book was full. There were no pages left to expand on the subject he was getting at. No more poems to write. No more sense of urgency. He quit. He drew a little flowing picture on the back cover about the breezes of a woman blowing around the world.

Aura carried him the places she went. She had long straight auburn hair that easily blew in the wind. She took him to the street corner shops where she hung out and introduced him to her friends; places he'd walked by on this sidewalk several times before, but never seen in this way.

She was neither Black nor Spaniard. She was creole. She was and islander. She was Colombian. She was an Indian. She was Aura. She was the mood and the color of the moment; the dried beauganvilla that he saved forever. She was the right now.

They drank two beers, said goodnight and went their respective ways down the lit sidewalk in the salty, wet, warm night air.

The next morning carried him back to the airport to board his flight back to the Estados Unidos. Everything felt a little funny about leaving. He checked in at the ticket counter an hour before the flight left and showed the immigration agents his passport. His Colombian Visa was expired. He wouldn't be making it on that flight right now the Babylon informed him. He had to get his papers fixed up first. This meant paying fines and getting stamps. He argued and protested against the police, but there was no budging. They had him and they weren't going to let him go. He paid the fine and received a bad mark upon his passport. In time the passport got so old, ragged and worn that no one ever saw the stigma. He got everything set up for the plane tomorrow. He wasn't going to miss it again.

He found a phone and called his parents, told them not to bother coming to the airport today, but definitely tomorrow. They'd had this conversation before, but couldn't stop it.

He walked up the long dirt road off the busy sweaty street towards Aura's house. She knew he wasn't leaving just yet. They went to the cave behind her house and sat in the gravel sand with their arms around their knees, talking poetry, philosophy, art and music; the bats and the cats that dreamed to her at night. They listened to each other the way people do and grew fond of one another.

They went to the beach and sat in an abandoned panga, smoked joints and played guitar music with her friends. The songs came out of Robert effortlessly and she looked on him with different eyes while her friends clapped and banged rhythms on the fiberglass. She smiled softly and the evening came upon them. The bright yellow sun shed a bluer note on the beach and crystal sparkling sea.

They went back to Aura's house and sat with her father who drank rum behind his daughter's back. He was a good old easy fellow. He welcomed Robert with the ambivalence and sincerity of transparency and didn't seem to think twice about the Gringo so interested in his daughter. It all seemed very normal.

She took out the I-Ching. The Chinese book of changes and showed Robert how to count the matches sticks that rolled on the ground. She did a reading for Robert and herself. They were the same, Robert thought. She might have heard the fates completely different with her own hidden vision of faces, but to Robert they were the same; wrapped and entwined in each other. The I-Ching is a map of the air, the ether. It is painted in invisible ink. It is a map of the present we cannot see. It shows you the change. It is to be consulted during times of change. It causes change. It illuminates the change. It is a map of the way. It translates the energy of the universe manifested and captured with the position of the sticks at the precise moment in space-time they are dropped. The chaos is coincidental. It comes about naturally in times of need.

Robert didn't understand why this was happening to him. He didn't know why the universe was throwing these urgent feelings inside him. He felt that there had to be a reason. He didn't believe in the randomness of existing. He was a cosmic person now.

The last thing he did was kiss her. She read her own destiny and changes about marriage and Robert swore it concerned him. He swore that their futures were bound to each other in some way, that the very survival of his soul depended on her, the woman he did not even know. He had to leave, that much was clear, but it also became clear that he could not abandon this night if he ever wanted to live to his potentialities, to fullfill his personal legend. Greatness was bound to happen when he returned. Sorrow and failure could be all awaiting if he denies her, the Aura. It was a matter of life and death. She would determine his fate.

He suddenly whispered "I love you," into the night air and walked away from her house, floating on the high promises she created. The walk back to the Restrepo passed in an instant. The airport, the corner shops, the stretch of street along the beach, glid by like he was riding a conveyor belt. His feet flew fast and effortlessly. This chance of a belief in love had him excited. It was finally overriding that depression Peace left him with. Where there is life there is hope. Everything seemed new.

That night he was restless. It did not know how just to conclude this section of his life. He was unsure of his next step, but something would surely take place, and in the morning it did.

He awoke soon and took a fresh shower. He put on a half clean, long sleeved, light green shirt and left his room early with his guitar, backpack, and handbag full of treasurish rubage from the road. We walked out to the road and took a taxi with the little bit of Colombian change he had left. He went directly to Aura's house up the old rocky hill and did the only thing that he could to do. He left his journal with her.

This was the solution that God left for him to choose. It was the only right way. It made complete sense out of the confusion and spinning chaos. He could never leave his journal behind. It was his most prized possession. It was all he had of any importance. The rest could be left in the gutter. A new guitar was not hard to get. His clothes were all ragged and second hand. His books had been left and given away to needy travelers on the road. The journal, however, was irreplaceable. He would turn and walk back up the mountain for it if it. He begged her to care for it and that was all. He stepped out to the road skipping.

No one ever read his journal before. He wasn't shy or hiding the thing, but no one ever cared. He was happy to give it to her because he knew he needed it back. Maybe she would understand him. Maybe it would prepare her for him. Black, beat up journal, divine diary of words and ink, without it, he was gone. It was poetry and inspired prose, images of his awakening. Phone numbers and contact information of all he met on the road. The echoes of his heart and conclusions of his mind. Songs and psalms, unrepeatable and irretraceable. It was all that was left of his memory. It was hope and faith. It was all.

So gone he was one the next flight out to San Jose and right back up to Houston town. He

boarded the plane just in time. As the fast spinning wheels lost contact with the ground and rose into the clouds above the aqua blue reef spotted sea, he began to cry.

It was over, and for a few hours above the Atlantic Ocean, it had not yet begun.

He got off the plane in the crowded Houston airport a blind prophet returning to his hometown. He was the ultimate mad raving schizophrenic with a shaggy beard and colorful gifts tied around his wrists. His eyes gleamed in the reality of the world he never left, this parallel one where no one cared about the stars or fruit trees. Love was an afterthought, a fairy tale misconceived notion of accommodation. There was no *lucha* and no magic. There were neon billboards and parking tickets. The morning was already lifetimes away and it wasn't even middle day. He took a deep breath and sighed because he could finally safely stop. The land never ended though, it just kept rolling on, unsevered; connected to all of the Indian burial grounds and sacred battlefields of the old world, the Pampas of Patagonia and mud flats of Barranquilla, it was in his blood now. It was the Spanish tongue and the evil eye.

One of the first things he did was go buy a notebook. It wasn't no pretty black bound journal with a hard cover, just a cheap high school notebook with plenty of lined pages. Words were in his head that wanted to escape. He cursed his bones and laughed at the fever haunting his sweaty soul. Life continued.

Writings

"These novels will all give way, by and by, to diaries or autobiographies- captivating books, if only a man knew how to choose among what he calls his experiences, and how to record the truth truly."

- Ralph Waldo Emerson

These writings begin in Houston, Texas at a time when Robert just returned from a year of wandering through South America. His traveling concluded on the magical Colombian island of San Andres. He gave up his road dreams, his journal to a girl he thought might hold the answer, and caught a plane to Costa Rica where he flew directly back to Houston. Retreat is an offensive measure in war.

The future looks dark. "I'm not the first one to say it".

We can't see the bright, silver lining, because there is none. There is no better day coming. There is only worserment and destruction; chaos and revolution; storms of all types, plagues, pestilence and famine. There is certain and immanent death awaiting all trapped in our age.

We are sleepless and we cannot sleep. We are hopeless and we cannot hope. We are all free and all in the same boat together, none of us better or more holy than the other; just crumbs of dust blowing off the table that the present has set for the master; swept away by the broom in the mother's hands; left dead in the cold of a no eared branch. I don't know what it means.

You do too.

There is no savior, new president or protest song. There is only the confidence we have in our own lives and the prayers that we make incessantly, leading us to the next fixed step in the course. Of course.

You of course.

There is all that, but there is love as well in the meantime, and that gives us smile. Amen

I gave my last journal away to a woman that I don't even know and found my life in a state of flux and confusion. It is Houston. The real world seems to have me spinning as I turn my head to the computer in search of Hot Jobs. I don't know where I am going, but I need to go, I guess, if nowhere else, in search of the lost journal.

I'm a boy from the suburbs, just like you and different than me. I'm everyone else from your college (who graduated cum laude); from your high school (who graduated cum laude). I am good. Great at mediocrity, but good nonetheless. A lukewarm that makes you spit.

In our minds, all are great. There seem to be two realities in each of us. I guess I can't make facts of your self, seeing as I've never been in your imagination, but I refuse to believe that you believe your inside, your soul, is mediocre and finite. Connecting the two, the internal and the external, became my goal. So I ran. I escaped for the North and South poles, as if in their infinite distances they weren't already as one, and after journeying through all kinds of foreign realities, I've ended up right where I began.

"A man that can sing when he ain't got a thing is a king of the whole wide world." Elvis Presley said that.

I once slept in a blue adobe cottage, on a well-groomed dirt floor with a beautiful *Chilena* named Paz who had multiple orgasms. I loved her very much. Her bed was set with its feet towards the door in accordance with Feng-Shui. Her hands made me comfortable while we slept, and I never wanted to take mine off her. The curtains and lamp had to be put in a precise and strange position to keep the electric line from shorting out and turning the lights off.

We danced to reggae music. We laughed and watered the garden on Saturdays. Saturday was always the water day. The day the dams were let open from the cordillera somewhere high above and precious water rushed through the canals on the side of the streets until everyone's tanks were filled. We ate grapes from the vineyard and apricots from the trees. We played music with our friends. We were inspired by love and magic. We struggled and cried and went mad in the end and just left. What a pity.

Now, I'm here in Houston, as if she were a dream, but I keep telling myself she was not. She was real. Love is real. South America is real. It is there right now. Here it is the dry grind and hot pockets.

The long line to the gates says this: sometimes I just sit here in traffic, and wonder what the hell I'm waiting for. I look over at my other faceless companions with our own private demons and unknown sins. What am I inching towards? Then I realize it's a huge cliff.

You can change your world or go to sleep. You turn around or you weep.

I'm coming back to terms with myself after a short vacation from a long-standing reality. A vacation that was much needed, and is now much need to return from. Life is a vacation. Here's how I go on the road. I just go and I meet people. If they offer me something to eat, I eat it. If they offer me a place to sleep, I sleep. If they don't, I stay at the cheapest place I can find, and eat wherever people go to eat. Sometimes I sleep on the beach or behind a truck stop. I drink at the cheapest place there is to drink. There I sometimes meet other people, and sometimes I just sit and drink, unless someone wants to hear guitar. If there is work to be had, I do it. If not, I don't, and just move on to the next place.

Met a girl named Marylee and right now it's just her and me. She makes me feels alright and I don't care too much about nothing else.

She makes me feel like I can write. She makes me feel like I can sing. She makes me feel like I can feel.

Once I was in Potosi, Bolivia drinking hot and spiced red wine, eating corn with cheese, playing music, screaming and chewing on coca leaves with lime. The miners were unhappy. The government was brutal. All we do here is trifle with the trivial. Make sense out of the nonsensical, make beauty out of the instinctual and call it all love.

I've been unemployed in Houston for the last three weeks, biding my time and waiting to leave. I'm a little worried that I might be wasting my life away as my Mom likes to say, but all in all I'm getting by spending as much time away from home as possible. As far as my dying ambition goes, as long as I don't end up with a corporate job, living in the suburbs, I'm going to be OK. This may lead to a life of seclusion and labor on the pastoral Colombian coast, but so be it. Survive. I spoke with my grandmother today and she was upset about my lack of correspondence. I'll write her a letter and tell her how I feel about stuff. My Marylee habit is growing and it offers little time for writing, work or anything else really. I love it. It seems a strange habit to pick up at such a transient point in my life, but I crave her company.

As I grow closer to leaving again, I notice a five-month rhythmical pattern of disappearance. I feel like these last months at home have been only a stop or a "trip" if you will. It has been an experience but it leaves a sour taste in my stomach. What am I doing so wrong all of the time? I need a mentor.

Here it is the tenth of October and I'm still riding the same wave as last night, I write. I don't have anything to say. Marylee's underwear is in my face on the counter here. There are two roaches on her driver's license. Her cell phone is on top of my Dylan songbook. She is in the bedroom waiting for me. My baby is a hummingbird. Her dragon, Puffarena has a crush on mine. Sometimes she kisses me cold. Sometimes wet.

I'm dreaming of all these empty towers, vacant of all its wardens and cowards. Howling, the dust blows through their halls. I'm dreaming of the day they peacefully fall. They've all had enough and found new ways to spend their time. Democracy and fruit.

November eighth, another day I was "supposed" to leave but postponed for a few more weeks until the Saturday past Thanksgiving. It is a beautiful day here in Memorial Park with the breeze blowing beneath the shade trees.

Houston has been nice lately. I've still been spending time with Marylee who I just dropped off for work before heading to my own job painting with Jimmy at the Coffee Shop/ Electronics Museum. I'm enjoying the time I spend here and there.

It's better to live within your footsteps and bury the names in the pages you'll one day return to read; taking revenge upon tomorrow, for the fallen trees of yesterday. The chimneys of my heart are empty of the swallow's nests you've built then flown away.

May you live as long as you want to and want to as long as you live. May your song always be singing and the gifts you give you get.

Costa Rica

It was a wintery day in Houston just after Thanksgiving when Robert once again boarded a plane for the unknown. His mother and father carried him to the airport to bid him farewell until who knows how long. He was bloated and had a funny haircut that he gave himself a few days earlier. When it came time to board the plane, this time he wept, cause he was hurting his family. The wheels of this departure had been set in motion many lives ago and all Robert could do was keep rolling. In only a few hours, he got off the plane in San Jose, Costa Rica.

Robert knew nothing of Costa Rica. He imagined it had lovely beaches and sea but they were far from the gray and smoggy city. Where they were and how to get there, he had no idea. He left the airport on foot, with his backpack and guitar walked down to a bus stop where he asked people how to get to the beach.

He got on a local bus that left him in the middle of hustling and bustling San Jose, cold and full of trash and vendors. It moved fast. He asked and moved around until he ended up at the Coca Cola bus terminal, waiting for the first bus to take him to the coast. One funny dressed homosexual man from Guatemala told him that he should go to Quepos. He said that there was the beach and a bus was just about to leave for there. Robert bought his ticket and got back on the road. It was a start, and all things must start somewhere.

She reminded me I can break through every mirror in my way! And with that, one day he suddenly just left.

Tell Martha from Cartagena that Elias says hello. The bougainvillea are delicious, as are the sunset and clouds. I've finally slowed down enough to appreciate Costa Rica's beauty and the fact that I am here. I've been so internalized that everything seemed ugly. I could have kept running right through Eden and ended up in hell! Must stop writing and look up through the bus window.

I've just slept walked through two beautiful towns, and I don't know what I'm looking for. San Jose to Quepos to Manuel Antonio to Quepos to Montezuma; where will he take his revenge upon tomorrow?

Quepos, Costa Rica: There's a beautiful *Tiquita* in front of me with her shirt off, showing me her black sports bra. She is number eleven, and is looking in my direction. I am up on a red concrete balcony of the *Hospedaje Familiar Macha.* It costs two thousand *colones* (four to five dollars) and has the best view in town, the soccer field where number eleven was standing with her shirt off showing her black sports bra.

Fireworks are shining across the way, and now I'm gambling on the game. If the blue team wins, I'm getting a beer.

The word on the street is in the *Parque Nacional Corcovado* on the night of November 18th, five Colombians were held in custody, waiting for the Drug Enforcement Agency to arrive and take over. One thousand kilograms of cocaine were seized when the Colombian's skiff hit the beach below Corcovada between the Siera Ranger Station and Carate. Six thousand police officers were called into the huge national park in search of the Colombians who beached their skiff and took to the bush running. A second skiff was stopped by the Coast Guard in the nearby town of Golfito, close to the Panamanian border. It was loaded with *dos toneladas.*

Costa Rica is possibly the most beautiful country I have ever seen. It is too bad it almost completely overrun by us gringos. *Gringolandia.*

I guess that most of the *ticos* don't mind too much. Outside of the cafe where I'm having my *cafecito* at around ten o'clock in the morning, some guy already has started drinking, most likely he never stopped. It beats farming and fishing he probably argues. Despite the Pacific Ocean, which appears to be teeming with the fruits of the sea, there are no fishermen or fresh fish. They say this used to be a fishing village, but either there are new business opportunities or it is all fished out.

Still in Montezuma, having another *cafecito* at the same place I was at yesterday, I sit wavering over an untouched piece of I don't know what that my neighbor here left on his plate. It looks like it could be some kind of tortilla, or maybe cheesecake or something. It gets under my skin to see people waste food when it would go so nicely with this cup of coffee.

I had an interesting evening last night with Claudio, the groundskeeper at my camping. He asked me to walk with him into town and back. "*Muy rapido, cinco minutos,*" he said. I think he needed help to lead him not into temptation. About half way there, he started violently vomiting and dry heaving on the beach. The spell lasted over five minutes and I was reminded of a magical evening spent with Marylee and some rotten not so magic mushrooms. He told me about his alcohol and *coca* disease. The worst part about it is that when he tries to stop, he vomits and can't eat or sleep. Once he lasted eight days without it, and went eight days without food or sleep. He said he goes loco. Now he just tries to take a few swigs of Rum Rico when he needs it, but refraining from getting drunk and out of control, because that when he starts using cocaine, he keeps on it for weeks. He bought some meat to cook and said he'd see about getting some pot today. Ha! When you're hooked you're hooked..

I don't know what the date is. I've asked few people tonight. It has been an interesting evening. I don't know if the "*fuerza publica*" Costa Rican police force is onto us, or I'm just being paranoid, or if I need health insurance, but I'm getting the shakes again. I think it may be the shitloads of ganja we've been smoking tonight. Claudio's Colombian connection came through with several kilos that I helped him break up. I've had a million words that I will never get out; a million letters to a dozen lovers; a handful of lines for my next hit song; a *bolsa* of introductions for my new book and a cure for death if I wasn't out forgetting.

I'm a drug dealer in Costa Rica now, but the thing about a drug dealer is, you got to be quick. You always got to be *"bing bang, bing ting"*. Here and there and move quickly, so when the *policia viene*, you have nothing. "Ting!" I may too lazy for this job. I still like to sleep in. Sometimes it's better just to stay where you're at, instead of always being away from there.

I know that things started going a little strange when Claudio, the loco, is telling his friends that I'm loco. *"Tengo todo pression en mi sangre, en mis dedos, como BOOM BBOOM!"*

Claudio is a mess. He shakes, dry heaves and now his big toe is broken from the bag of cement he dropped on his foot yesterday.

After telling himself *"no hay dolor"*, there's no pain, the doctor did the natural thing and cut the toe open through the nail. He is still bleeding. *"Yo no se que paso, pero el esta loco,"* he says about me and tells people that I'm crazy.

Sometimes I get an unhealthy feeling, but can't point to what is wrong. Nothing on the outside; nothing on the inside maybe.

Someone watching me right now would think I am pretty funny, just sitting here, spinning circles in the sand at my own lost little rhythm, but I found a glass jar washed up on the beach this morning, and I've already put some nice little things in it. Lets see what else I could throw in, la Corazon, a red heart shaped stone I've been holding onto?

All I wanted to do tonight was come home to my hammock under the coconut tree, smoke and write or read something, maybe the Little Prince or some old letters, feel sentimental. Right now I'm waiting outside the bungalow of a well-known drug dealer, where I'm waiting for Claudio to come to the road after making his *negocio*.

Claudio calls the place Saigon. He always wants me to come with him and wait. He talks and talks and when my patience grows anxious to leave, he gives me a subtle nod and wink and pushes his hands down calmingly. Usually I end up waiting a minute longer and then wandering off. I think I'll leave Montezuma tomorrow. Maybe I'll head South to Dominical or North to Ostional and Playa Coyote.

Where I sleep, under a tree in my hammock, there are two Spaniards. They are clean and lightly dressed people with long hair and beards and speak clearly and soothingly. They have a soft, gifted manner about them. They are gypsies. They are mystic angels. They are musicians and one of them carries a drum. He is a gardener. The other one, the thinner one, is a Sushi chef and carries a flute. He has blue, blue eyes and pale skin beneath his brown hair. We make fun music, smoke marijuana and cook food with spaghetti and vegetables. They are nice people.

They came to Montezuma from a place up in the jungle called the *Casa de Piedras*, the house of stones. It is a cave. It is a cave that someone has turned into a house, or a camp up in the mountain rainforest. There are beds. There is a kitchen. It is behind a waterfall. They told me I need to go there. They meant it. They said it as if it was a matter of importance. I don't have anything else too urgent to do. I'll find my way back to San Andres soon enough.

I may have turned *loco* but I try to be nice to everybody. Even Two Horses, the American hippie.

I'm stoned on the beach in Punta Arenas here at ten o'clock at night, waiting for the five o'clock bus to Quepos. By anyone's standards I look like a bum. That's OK, I have the utmost respect for them.

Punta Arenas is a big, polluted town. There are no gringos here tonight. No one likes reality, or big ugly polluted cities. There's a strange Tico Karaoke version of "Tears in Heaven" playing behind me for a bedtime tune.

I hung my hammock in a dark isolated place down the beach but then thought it better to come near the lights of the little Police station. They said they didn't mind if I strung my hammock here for the night, so here I'll rest *tranquillo.* Before day I'll be back on the road in search of the house of stones.

Deep beneath the leaves I find a place where they all turn to dirt, and deep beneath the dirt there lies a man. He told me things they always change, and as he smiled a laurel seed came crashing through the earth, a tree.

My coffee turns my liver black and hidden in my plastic sack, I'm holding for a rainy day a smile. And tucked beneath the waterfall, sleeping in this house of stones, a butterfly below me whispers change and winks.

Down the road I walked, up the trail, for hours passing hours, sweat dripping from my backpack and guitar case, my legs burning from the steep incline. I slipped in the mud, but continued to step up the mountain. I drank from a creek before crossing it. I heard a roaring of water and behind the next curve in the trail, saw it. The dark, steamy jungle gave way to an open clearing of sunshine and there it was. The waterfall, and behind the waterfall a cave, and in the cave, a fire burning.

I approached the fire, and found a note left on a stump of wood. "*Trabajando* on the trails. Will be back," it said.

The note was old and wrinkled and torn in places, smudged with dirt and ash. It looked like it had been used for a long time. I knew not what to think of the note, the fire or the cave, but it was getting dark and I welcomed the warmth of the fire and the comfort of the stone roof.

I pulled out my guitar and sung songs with perfect prophetic nonsense words of disappearing rhymes in my loudest and clearest voice to no one but the trees, wild turkeys, chirping birds, butterflies and sunset that took in my poetry, filtered it, edited it with chlorophyll, and returned it to me with pure energy and oxygen.

I go down to greet the Sun god everyday. I kiss him goodnight when I leave. And just like the trees, I bend to my knees to save the day with a bit of your laughter. Only now is there happy ever after.

If I stay it will be too dark to walk home. If I leave, I'll miss the moment of your eye.

Burning the House of Me seemed an easier task than proved, for a thought is but direction and the stars and trees are always on the move. Yawning beneath me lie my preconsidered generations, dormant as a dream, chained as silhouetted reservations.

So if this house does fall, unveiling a diamond in the coal, a hundred years of solitude could unbind a supersoul. With a father's death and grandpa's lingering sting, a hurricane's inspiration at a butterfly's wings. Fall house oh fall, foundations of lawyers and Pharisees, fingernails scathing my veins, inclined to deny myself me.

I certainly do enjoy this part of my night, finishing dinner, smoking a joint, playing guitar and singing to the ever loving, listening and singing waterfall. I make up songs about everything on my table. Harmonica cases filled with shells and pot, manzanilla with yesterday's dulce, candles are microphones and looking glasses, heart shaped stones, Bibles and Fitzgerald's Swiss Army Knife, everything is looking fine on this side of paradise. Time is the end of all riddles and we are the end of time.

Passing up mirrors but picking up shadows, I've always got a new friend in the cave, tinkering and tattering around in my head whenever I stop to behave. Laura the squirrel is a beautiful girl, but sometimes she might steal your apple. Like turning the radio on, then turning it off, even if the guitar is just ruckus and the words just scribble scrabble. The words are for writing.

Goodmornin' fool, the sun is shining. Have another cup of tea to pass the day. Tell myself to be nice to myself, and call myself an asshole when I say, Shut Up! Turn Off! Don't you listen to what I say? Shut up! Turn off! The radio like to play boy, the radio likes to play, so don't touch the dial while I am at the wheel. Now I must pee.

I have dreams about killing people. Every time I remember my dreams, there is violence. It usually has to do with me or someone close to me. I think that it has been going on for some time now, and I am just now picking up on it. Last night I was at someone's wedding somewhere, and got into a fight with some slick, mafia tied groom. He pulled a gun and tried to shoot me, but I turned the gun on him and he shot himself.

Then there's the one about me being stuck in my dad's office building with a bunch of terrorists. It's like Die Hard.

On the brighter side, I had a wet dream about Marylee the other night. That was cool, but I came quickly.

The sunset was made to imitate her cheeks, which blended to her face like dusk. I have gotten into a habit of thinking about Nicole while appreciating sunsets. Sunrises are nice too, but unfortunately I don't remember ever watching those with her, except through the glass of her wintery windowpane when she was heading off to school.

As I'm on my way to find Aura, or "Ahora", I wonder if I've lost my mind. I have these secret bougainvillea burning a hole at the end of this book, monkeys and *pavos del monte* howling at me in the jungle, and my sunset stick for when it gets dark. I try to work and make trails all day so I can sleep at night.

There is something close making funny noises. I think it might be a *pavo*, wild turkey, but I'm not sure. I can't believe that I used to go hunting those.

I wish I had your address wherever you are Nicole. I'm looking down on a cloud over the Pacific dusk in a hammock in my cave. It is a dream.

So therefore none of you can become my disciple if you do not give up all of your possessions. The Pharisees, who were lovers of money, heard all of this and they ridiculed him. So he said to them, "you are those who justify yourselves in the sight of others".

One of these days I'm going to write you a great letter mi Paz, but until then I just have to wait and contemplate. Since I left you that night a year ago, I've been slowly awaiting the days until my death, but no longer! I lost all faith I once held in God, and am usually quite sure that I no longer believe in love. I've become a pessimist and an agnostic. In my hopelessness, I've discovered a bright light that seems never to dim. It is the light on the other side. It burns heartache and tragedy, for it is hope that brings tragedy. By no longer awaiting or searching, the green leaves shimmer on the trees. The sunlight radiates them and breezes send them through my spine in a euphoric glow. There is a pleasing silence in my ears and fireflies. Deep breaths ignite fireworks behind my eyes. Goodbye. The difficulty comes when

I remember that you still exist, and the only thing holding back my hope is something as shallow and easily overcome as miles.

I have often wondered if I am dead on the inside, *pero nunca mas.* I have since returned to Texas, and fled. While I was once heading North, I am now only heading. Now I live in Costa Rica behind a waterfall. *Hay muchas veces que yo canto en mi Cabeza "Cuando la Paz se fue, la paz se fue," pero en realidad, creo que yo tengo una paz que lo aprendi de ti. Me enseno mucho. Como recordar, parar y escuchar el sonido de las cascadas.*

Marylee arrived. She now accompanies me here in the cave. She is wearing thin on the patience that I work on. She is an interlude from song. She wakes up and comes to life for a brief moment to use the toilet and then its back to bed again until the night. We haven't juked in three or four days. Life in the cave is boring her. Her estrogen roller coaster rides continuously and the Tao escapes my grasp as I rupture and curse and feel the rope of my sanity being forcibly pulled out of my hands. It all shatters like broken glass. She rains a storm upon my shelf, seeking unwrapped attention. "Better end up a fool then to end up alone," says the song.

My friend Jeff,

I was glad to get an email from you this Tuesday morning. I'm wondering how you are and what the hell you're doing. It seems really foreign to me, just as what I'm doing seems foreign to you.

I'm running out of ink in my pen and just wanted to answer your statement that has been a question in my ear for the past few days now. What am I seeking? Nothing and nothingness I thought and I think but in I guess that that is searching for something. I guess that I am searching for truth, and I know that it lies here in the mountains with the trees and waterfalls. I try to listen to the monkeys and macaws, earthquakes and water. That and nothing, and always the path with heart. Adios amigo.

He was sitting on top of a mountain in southern Costa Rica, near a town called Dominical, when he decided that he wanted to write a book about the corruption of the Catholic Church, and its effects on Latin America. There is a ten percent tax on the peasants, and if they don't pay it, they will burn in hell. Ten percent of their corn; ten percent of their beans; ten percent of their goats all belongs to the church. He traced the dollar line from the pews to the pope, checking the percentages and payoffs. Do the people even know they're doing it? Do they even believe it is good? How high do you have to go to find the *infidel*? Either a book about that or a man driven to a southern Costa Rican region on the Osa Peninsula, the best spot in the world to see the rare and secretive Macaw bird in its wild habitat. The birds eventually drive him mad with their endless cawkawing before or after the ending.

Well, just as she came, she left. Marylee couldn't take the cave life, so she took a teaching job in a little beach town named Nosara. Our love is to be continued in a month or so, when I am supposed to go look for her. It is good. I've got to make a trip to Panama to fix my visa anyway, so this is a good time.

The best way to plant a tree, I think, is with the whole fruit. It is a bit of a sacrifice, but in the end how many fruits can you get from a tree? For the first time, here at Pyramis, the little surf camp where I can string a hammock when I come out of the cave, I understand the expression *"no da Papaya"*. Do not give papaya. Don't leave the ripe fruit on the tree. Thou shall not tempt and if tempted, take! As for Marylee, who has taught me so much about living naturally and taking things as they come (*no hacer planes*) and letting them come in time; who taught me so much about love and sex and myself and communicating on higher levels with kisses; who is also a wonderful kisser; you are a butterfly and a hummingbird, and lying here on this concrete floor, dreaming about crazy shit, I've been thinking of you. Today I had a morning of Marylee even though its well passed noon and I'm lying around all day, hungover and stoned.

Traces of Two Horses keep popping up everywhere I turn. A ghetto *pipita* on the floor at Pyramis and his wide mouth roaches; I know he was here.

Like men will, the trees and leaves fight for light, and filled with emptiness, the loser dies.

And we cry, "Is it too late?" Are we too far gone? Too far to turn back? Will the day turn black? Will the night burn? Will we still turn, or are we just too late?

Something has to hurt.

He wanted to kill himself that night watching the sunset. Wondering if he could jump between that crack between the two worlds, he started getting dizzy. Vertigo. There was a sharp pain in his stomach. What is death if you take it instead of letting it take you? Maybe you don't have to go back and finish up your time and the wheels just stop.

It's Wednesday morning in Bocas del Toro, and the *carnaval* has just finished. Even *el Caribe* has the flat, dull, muffled and solitary silence hanging over it. Just as rapidly as it started four days ago, it died out last night at twelve o'clock. It was a sad and interesting feeling, like Cinderella losing her slippers when everyone knew it was over. The music blasting from the *disco-movil* stopped, the drumming and fire spinning ceased, the vendors of *guaro* and fried chicken shut their cash filled cigar boxes and the magic ended. The spirit left and all fled the scene like high school dancers when the lights shot on. The sidewalks are lonely with only drenched debris and traces of smoke and embers. The French Survivor series disclosed the winner and closed the curtains of the house on the corner. I went for one last beer at Mondo Taitu and on the way out passed a troop of *artesanos*. The sight of an enticing fire twirler made me wonder what would have happened if I stuck around for one more. Even in the bars that kept right on rocking through the break and selling their drugs, everyone felt the air leave their lungs and sails; everyone except for the gringos who just kept on smiling.

This is a tribute to Duke, Duke Kahanamaku with his sixteen-foot rosewood surfboard, "The Proclaimed Champion Swimmer of the World"! He had six brothers each of whom surfed, or swam, but none reached the heights of the Duke. From 1911 to 1912, he was the world's fastest swimmer. . .

Entonces, aqui estamos en San Isidro, haunting the same old hotel that Marylee and I stayed in a few weeks ago when I left for Panama and Bocas del Torro, and she for Nosara. I'm back alone this time. With wooden desks and beds and breezes that carry in the *ruida* from the Karaoke across the street, I feel like I could stay here inside for a day or two. I don't have anywhere I'm itching to go, nor do I have anyone or anything to tend to. I don't know what is happening up at the cave. This is what is meant by the "Unbearable Lightness of Being". The freedom and vast openness of the world outside my little room seems enough to make me take a deep breath. It is a vacuum that can suck you in if the moment falls wrong. Walking on an edge, walking the line. I am far away from a friend. The feeling is overwhelming.

I've been around people too much lately. Marylee, Marylee, Marylee, and then Brian, Michael and Frankie have kept me on my toes for awhile now, and since they all left last night, I have returned to you my love, empty handed and empty hearted with a runaway nose and bloodshot eyes. Hello again, it is nice to see you.

I've got bloody eyes that can't keep up with my toes, a pen that writes whatever it knows, summer skies and thoughts of snow.

He dealt his words like blades, how glittering they shown. Every one unbarred a nerve or uncovered bone. The poet in me entices the rest to a life of ceaseless poverty. . . .

Today I turned the fields of a small terrain I picked out to *sembrar*. I chopped and turned about a quarter of the field. It is hard work and my back is sore. The mosquitoes are out tonight in the cave and this asshole Warner took out my mosquito net stakes out and leveled my bed of stones while I was away from the cave. I have been thinking about leaving soon and will surely know when its time. It is just better up here in this monastery.

Old Chepe, the only man who lives higher up the mountain than me, sharpens his machete like I sharpen my guitar, everyday. Does that make me a musician and him a *chopiador*, or me just lazy (yet playful) and him a man?

Under the enhanced fungal stimulated view I found growing on the trail down from Chepe's . . . my pen just can't keep up with my thoughts.

I'm glad that my brother was the person who first observed the smoking plant in front of the bench in the cave. It is true. It really appears to be smoking.

There are two polar views of my life in my head right now. One is the highest, most noble dream of them all, to develop a beautiful piece of land and sustain myself by singing, writing and planting. The other is my biggest fear, a life of ceaseless wandering, never rooting into the ground. The trick is manifesting the right direction without crossing over to the infinitely close polar opposite. They are separated by only a fractal, 1 over n!. It is the difference between zero and one, existence and non. I wonder how is the *caballo*.

So I left my poetic meditative trance to go check on the horse. Barefoot, I crept through the evening jungle behind her so her words would not escape into the waterfall and wind and lost with the drops of oxygen for forever. I dare not disturb her silence or light a torch for a sound would crash through the night like glass, then in my path sat the snake with her hypnotizing spiraling diamond.

A song for the snake who nearly won. Who's triangles and shades with rustling roots and fallen leaves are all one. Who's hypnotic spiraling stare and tempting diamond glare lure a watchful eye into its trap door. Who's manifested appearance echoes off walls in my mind, whispering beware of thou optimism. Who's eyes like diamonds shone the gate at the end of my path and so delicately reflected the moment after my lantern lit; who chose to let me go free a few steps before the leaf like disguise defied my eyes and masqueraded death's door.

A song for the snake for the sake of the man who follows his path as straight as he can; who walked along hopeful and dreamful, with the last lingering drops of sun setting into the night; who's only false shadow deemed venom and fang, just a second too late for the prayer never sang. A song for the second that never passed, frozen meantime defying motion, making a second last.

Stoned on philosophy and poetry I make my way into the snake filled jungle of temptation, literacy and pre-imagined manifestations only to find the white horse that Saint John left behind. He, my Chilean mare Gringo's reincarnation, led me out of the mountains and into the valley of San Salvador, free of harm and malice, only to find the house of Miguel vacant.

My imagination played with notions of contraband and near escapes, but the reality probably bears more resemblance to a short trip to San Isidro.

I once again played the stupid and careless Gringo who lost his horse. Luckily Don Chepe se *recojo* and after a few trips up and down the mountain, reclaimed my beautiful yet pregnant and unmountable *llejua.* It may soon be Pilsen time, accompanied by an overdue phone call home.

At about three thirty P.M. I enjoyed the world's finest shower over looking the San Salvador Valley and the clouds above the Pacific Ocean.

Martin's conclusion was that man was born to suffer from either the anxiety of restlessness or the lethargy of boredom. If one is restless, work, and if uncomfortable, change positions.

There is a green parrot perched on a barren limb, framed by the white, doorless, concrete doorway, and by the clouded sky from behind. Off he flew. Now the limb is truly barren.

Marylee is a flower whose traces are echoing in my hollowed head.

To enjoy Henry Miller, one must first jump into the river.

"America is the incarnation of doom and she will drag us and the whole world down into the bottomless pit".

I open the door, and the daylight is good to see.

There was a seventeen year old boy caught killing horses then raping them down in the valley below the house. "When is the pope going to start letting people fuck?" they ask. The rein of the Catholic Church holds strong in these parts.

The beaches and rivers are my sidewalk cafes and watering hole the moon.

I'm on my way back up to the cave. Tomorrow Saddam is supposed to dump his germ warfare on the soldiers and citizen of the earth. Genocide, what will they think of next?

Is it the wind that makes the waves, or waves that makes the wind? When did this whole thing start up, and wherever will it end. The rope gets longer every day. The ground gets closer to the seeds I dropped.

I finally finished turning over the soil in the *terrenito* I am planting, and then like God's clockwork it came, the rain. Benjamen and Ashley, the Rainbow, people are here at the cave with me.

"The spirits of truth and falsehood struggle within the heart of man; Truth born out of the spring of Light and falsehood from the well of darkness, and according as a man inherits truth, so will he avoid darkness," say the Manual of Discipline of the Dead Sea Scrolls.

Beware of "The world need this now more than ever before" and "the end is coming soon".

I just found my pen in the last place looked. It's a lucky morning. Remnants are rain dripping from stalactite roots and vines, wetting the leaves like a dream. Remnants of night shading the clouds, eyes and bones, yawning in the trees like a dream.

Around here it's Easter for the Spinach and May thirtieth for tomatoes.

"Dear father, send the angel of peace to dwell within me and the angel of life to guide my body."

My candle is a microphone and tongue a fountain, living in a cave in my soul the mountain. Hidden in a bodily disguise, everything is going fine, on this side of paradise.

Her tongue well concealed in a sheath of lips, singing songs revealed in the rhythm if her hips. Ticking time not tocks for a wrist barren of lies. Everything is going fine, on this side of paradise.

Well, things are looking up after a pretty bum morning and late last night. It is strange being here alone again. Its probably strange smoking mushrooms with my pot. I have zero energy. It was so hard to get up last night and this morning. I went and took a shit, then read and came back to sleep, which is where I am now, dreaming of far off magic lands with *duendes* and cavemen, carrots, Marylee and this girl I used to know.

The time I spend in nature with Brother Trees and Mother Earth raises considerations of what we really are. I gave a tree a huge, caressing and trembling hug this morning for five minutes. It embraced me and shared its energy.

I played the didgeridoo to the hibiscus and bananas for close to an hour. We entered a recycling rhythm of fresh filtered oxygen and lifeless stale carbon dioxide.

All this I did sober. I feel the longer I stay here, the more I grow in touch with God, nature. From my medicine to my food, it all grows around here. Perhaps a year from now, when my work here is finished, it will be even more so. Coffee, pot, chicha, onions, carrots, *guanabana*, oranges, bananas, beans, beats, lemon grass, peppers, *palmito*, mangos, mushrooms, water apples and water, water water; it is all straight from the Mother's breast here. I can do this, have a piece of land and live.

The dream has been growing as a tree (of life) since the seed was first dropped in fertile Chilean soil. That was the first time my roots had been removed from the city.

I was thinking this morning, that if I die, I would not mind being reincarnated as a tree. In fact, I wouldn't mind reincarnating into a tree right now.

If a soul is really a soul, and not just some brain matter dream (for the mind is a very strong thing), I feel like it, the soul, is energy. It is life. One thing I have learned from my life in the cave, and in high school physics books, is that life continues. It grows and regrows. It falls and re-dies. It is a leaf. It is dirt. It is roots and it is fruit. It is me, Brother Tree and my music, the mountain.

Anyway, I was going to say, that I feel like a bum this morning, but I've got to admit its getting better all the time with the help of my good friend *Marijuanita.*

You can cry Aye Aye Aye!, but you get what you deserve. Like a honeybee stuck in my honey, or the bank man out of money. So you lost your corporate job, for lack of a better word, forward progress initiated, for the start of a better world. Fallen towers trumpeting defeat, empty halls where battles once fought, pens and pocketbooks killed for clouds covered with soot. Minds covered with television, hearts covered with fear, and lights covered with darkness. Memories like weeds grown over life and all its shades and rich organic soil. Sprouts of meantime and now from pods that shadows have not drowned out. Fasting and air be my blades. *Limpiarse*! Clean yourself.

The sunset kissed me goodnight again this evening. It is worth the pain. Walk and see it. Love is a sunset. The more beautiful it is, the faster it sinks into the sea.

It is definitely April by now, and I'm growing impatient with all the delaying I've been doing with my life and my love. It seems I'm constantly delaying something that's always just ahead of me. That's better than having it all behind me I guess. That is death, the absence of movement, of time.

Time like a river, is not alive. It gives life, but does not posses it. On second thought, perhaps it does have life. It does not contain the carbon element that Western man has stamped as the prerequisite on life, but it does contain energy. Movement predicts energy, and what is life but energy, and energy but life, the soul.

In that sense, a river on the whole would have life, but water alone, as a stagnant glass of water, would have no movement and thus be dead or dying, depending on how long it has been stagnant. Water should be fresh and alive.

Some pretty cool people from Boulder, Colorado showed up yesterday in the cave while I was standing in the kitchen, naked. They brought some pretty pessimizing news.

It seems that all of the "environmentally friendly" alternative energy methods that have been forecasted to save our future from the big global fall it is on a crash course with, are futile. They, Green Mountain, Solar, Wind, Hydro . . . are all what they call negative producers. They burn more energy in oil in their fabrication and distribution process, than they actually generate.

Robert Kuhn of the Cave Pessimist Society in Costa Rica says "*buenos dias*".

Most non-experts agree that the only real solution is self-sufficiency. If you want something done right, you've got to do it yourself.

I recently squeezed a *torsalo* (beef) worm from my swollen left calf. It started as a small irritated mosquito bite and grew into a boilish pea size bump. After two days of intense pain, squeezing, and bush medicine from Don Chepe up the hill, I eventually popped him out alive and squirming on the rocks near the waterfall. It was a huge relief.

People ask me sometimes what I think God meant by the fall. I think it just means watch out for snakes and what you eat.

Here it is, my last night in the cave, sitting here wondering how to make the second last, its gone. There is nothing keeping me here anymore but myself. I see no future here. Warner will come up here and take my place as the guardian. All I can say is that I wish I'd recorded more.

Like the coal in my pipe, rising and dying, glowing and shining and fading into dark and quiet, and resurrected with breath. From the lips lent to me, dream filled smoke finding its way to heaven and to you. May this too be delivered.

So I left the cave and crossed the valley to a friend, Drennan's, organic farm, Pura Suerte. Plant beds, manure tea, mountain beds of stones and fleas, *espalderas cortando maderas*, seedlings heeding to pot and papayas, hummingbirds and *rayas* higher than me, confused at the way things seem, looking for shade in the sweetness of the red hibiscus in the morning and of the arms of the *reina de la noche* at night. She encompasses me and makes me high with her half moon perfume.

Got very sick here for a few days, migraine, fever, chills and sweat, then vomiting, then more of the same. It is Thursday of *Semana* Santa, Easter week, and we're about to finish the Green Mansion, a huge green house Drennan and I have been constructing, and then I'll be off to see Marylee up in Nosara. The buses seem to have been shut down until after Easter, so Gatito and my departure won't be until Monday I guess. Patience.

That's me sitting here alone in the dark Pyramis bar, mango beard, gut pained, facing the ocean, a green ragged book in my hand, Pilsen bottle on the table with a purple *nazarena* cashed pipe. Next-door crickets are chirping sounds of God. Lights are out and I'm in the silent shadows. The contraband moonshine Caicique bottle and hammocks are empty, swaying in the breeze.

Memories like weeds grow over time. Cut them down, free the now and let it take its place in the future. Don't mobilize, but let mobility come with the spinning of the Holy One.

I called Marylee tonight and was reminded how awkward it is talking on phones. She says that she'll meet me in San Jose on Saturday afternoon in that Central Plaza, where it is nice to be outside and watch people if it isn't raining and cold. My only complaint is that I can't see her sooner. She tells me stories about stories about stories. She laughs and I pout. I am ugly as a monster biting his tongue, as ugly as she is beautiful. She wants to read the Tropic of Cancer.

El Caribe

So he split from the Pacific and headed down the road towards destiny and the Caribbean lowlands; a small beach called Playa Chiquita outside of Old Harbor Puerto Viejo, Limon.

Dear Marylee,

You just went outside to smoke a cigarette and come back and now you've left to go brush your teeth. That is thoughtful of you. I've certainly lost my mind or my patience, if the two of them are not synonyms. Someone said that there are no synonyms.

You are back and underneath the mosquito net. You did not look up at me on your dart back to refuge. I don't know if you want to talk or not.

I have returned and you are a sleeping beauty and the rain is still tapping of the roof. Lying here next to you, I feel it is better that I have not spread my seed. Better I eat the seeds of sterility and abandon the goal of my manhood; give up my soul for the good of mankind in the gracious name of overpopulation. Maybe this will get me into heaven. Marriage, the Pope, prophylactics and the deadly game of knots and devils and masturbation, rubbing their wings with perverted fantasies, I am now numb to it all.

I was twenty-four when I met my first vampire.

Marylee says she's going to leave tomorrow. Again. She smells of beer and cigarettes. I do not want her to leave. Downstairs two lovers are quarrelling. Their baby is crying, and Ronaldo is drunk. He is so drunk that he seems retarded. He is a Panamanian Bri-Bri Indian. He is a worker and an *artesano*. I think that Marylee is also drunk.

Marylee's friend Rhonda makes herself ugly because she is what she hates. I have shattered my dreams like mirrors. All that you once believed is now unbelievable. Unobligated to anything, but destined for something. The only failure is death. The only triumph, living, and drawing another breath from the spring. Hopeless for hopes, hope in the hopelessness. Thoughtless for words, words in thoughtlessness, the pen in my mouth is put to the floor.

I am in Puerto Viejo. I am living in the Casa de *Silvio*. I have infiltrated the Caribbean Italian mafia.

Mario just came by. He said he's coming back tonight. He smells Italian, smooth like.

Elena is Italian, blonde and pimple faced, Kiara is from the North of Italy, the same town as Silvio. Marcos is Italian, Juancito and Tony the pot guy.

We've been bootlegging Noni and *chicha de yuca* and selling it out the back of the *feria*,. We work construction downtown, contracting out ranches and free labor. We are the teamsters.

The skies feathered with dusk tremor at the sound of her name. Marylee! Marylee, what have you done with my soul? What have you done with my heart? They've flittered to flat-lines, where ones turn to zeros and leaves turn to dirt.

Gone with the day and the night and all I've been promised of Sundays.

The *Caribe* is moving well. I've slipped into a home on the beach of Playa Chiquita with Marylee. I am making Noni and *chicha* and constructing bamboo ránchos. I plan on becoming a fisherman. A fisher of men, cannibal, vampire, breaking up families and burning bridges, cursing lives ever after, blessing hospitals and fleets and getting high on taking away people's souls, so they too can be like me and understand that it is best to live.

There are two movies being filmed around here that I would like to check out. One is called *Caribe*, and the other the *Petrolera.*

Last night I bought a bottle of Ron Viejo and picked a *limon* and tried to get drunk, but lost interest before I passed out.

Marylee is tired of being ignored. I am tired of ignoring her.

In the night's sun feathered skies, poetry lies waiting, somewhere between red and blue, words only steal from her silence.

Last night Marylee and I sat on the rug blanket *pancho* on the wooden rubbery floor and listened to the Panamanian *Caribe* Indians downstairs play my guitar after their fish fry. They played happy and loud enough. Ronaldo works with me on the rancho when there is work. When there is not, he and his wife, a name that I cannot remember, fish and make *artesania.* He carves parrots and animals in wood and makes bracelets and necklaces of seeds he finds in the rainforests. She weaves baskets and hanging shelves and other detailed pieces from some type of vine that grows in the *selva.* They eat well. I am an unskilled laborer. Moving things and washing bamboo and handing people higher up the wall tools for making their building higher. I am an assistant. A beautiful girl with pink capri flowing pants and a camera in her hand walks in between my hammock and the ocean. She smiles. I am taking her picture right now. She just doubled back and passed behind my hammock. Her ass is full and should have dimples as it smiles at me. She glances over her shoulder and looks at my eyes before she disappears into the bush.

Gatito left me. So did my pocket knife. So did Marylee. I have given all outlets other than this pen to the martyred name of freedom. Freedom to get lost. Redistribution of wealth. The spoon I was carving has to be delayed. It is a shame because there was someone who was ready to buy it when I finished.

Marylee is inside the *mosquitero.* I am out. She just went to the outhouse for a cold shower. She is grabbing my arms to pull me inside, and I reply with "In a minute". I cannot muster up the sexual energy to sex Marylee again. It has become a job that I must tackle every morning or face the consequences of her innards wrenching bitchy bellyaching.

She's on her last cigarette. The smoke of it is burning sweet in my nostrils and eyes. "We're running out of money" she says.

I say it's a relief. Hunger breeds genius the way cigarettes breed death.

This morning I stuck my tongue down Marylee's throat, trying to suck a drop of feeling from her tonsils. A drop of dew from her dying flower. I was trying to infect her mouth with the nauseating odor of my Noni breath. I knash my teeth into her breast and nipples and try to draw a sip of milk or love as if it was blood. She doesn't even respond. It hurts her much deeper than nervous skin pain.
She is confused and thinks I make love like a Tasmanian devil.

The harder I squeeze her nipple, the drier my mouth and soul become. It is ugly.

The aki outside of this yellow termite eaten windowsill are red and nearly ready to split, but green *todavia.*

Marylee has a heavy head. She's come complete circle.

"Oh Robert" she whines from inside the mosquito net. She rubs my arm and asks what I'm writing. She rips the pen out of my hand and complains that she's not whining. She asks why I'm doing this. We're leaving here tomorrow. I'm carrying her to Limon. From there she's going back to the States. She has had enough.

Marylee is gone. I hope she's not pregnant.

I spent yesterday running around Limon looking for a *negro* called Lindo. He is the man to talk to around the docks about the boat the Dona Olga, which heads for San Andres every fifteen days or so. I needed to talk to the Captain, but the boat never showed. I walked from gate to gate, asking from guard to guard for any information I could drip or bribe from their tight tongues. Some people do not like Gringos here.

In the afternoon, I ran into Ronaldo and Alexis in the plaza and got drunk in a dusty *cantina China.* We missed the last bus back to Puerto Viejo and ended up staying the night with some bartender/hooker who thought I was cute and ended up feeling sorry for us. She lives in the barrio Cieneguitas. The swamps. The houses are all on stilts and sidewalks little rotten wooden bridges on posts. She left us in the house when she left for work and we ended up spending the rest of our money on beers and looking for *muchachas* in town. I feel sick.

Last night I dreamt myself from afar. I saw my hut and my friends from the sky with their relation to everything else in the large world, and all I can recall is that I was pleased and scared. I then recall the magnificent blooming of a lotus flower, unfolding its infinite colors, petal by petal and turning its insides out, one leaf at a time.

We live poorly here at the Casa de la Playa. We live poor, but well.

We collect our rainwater and make our firewater. We spear our fish and pick our Noni, the real fruit of the sea.

The poets have all left the marketplace the way man crawled out of the sea. The corn has all turned to wine again and the wine has turned to ink. Ashes to ashes, dust to dust. God bless America. Amen.

Ronaldo just stumbled home with a flag wrapped around his head and his shirt torn off. "*Ya vengo! Ya vengo*," he cries as he passes below the balcony.

He bangs on the door for his wife to let him in. She apparently does not want o unlock it.

He has a big goofy grin on his face. His bareback horse whinnies in the background. It sounds drunk too.

Ronaldo wanted to borrow the flute I made from a piece of bamboo. The flute has a full, beautifully deep sound and carries light melodies when played well. It is like a well-bodied and aged bottle of red wine.

I taught Ronaldo to play the flute the other day. In exchange he invited me a drink of his Noni before bedtime.

The Noni drink was smooth and strong. It was easy to drink, but only a small taste was enough. We had the drink from a little one-ounce glass of clay, poured from a ceramic jug.

They are artisans and Indians. Everything they made was art. The only making that is not art is money. That is the anti-art. It is piss sour vinegar.

The termites are busy eating away at the support beams of this rotting chicken shack, Casa del Arte, Casa de la Playa.

The inhabitants of the Casa are interesting and a little stoned. They rarely participate actively in the exchange of commerce.

I wonder if this humming in the wall to my left is the hissing of termites, or the rattle of a snake.

Someone else bought the vegetables for the *feria* today as I spent the morning chasing Sylvio's horses. The house is quietly sleeping, except for me, who is just as well, staring out the window and muttering nonsense and small talk at the page in front of me, who is attentively listen. I can tell by the delayed reflection of my thoughts in its white eyes.

I need to sweep the floor of cigarette ash and bat guano. They are both good for the soil. I just planted spinach, lettuce and marijuana, all of the necessary greens. Tomorrow is the full moon. There will be a large fire and strong drum circle. Ashes to ashes, dust to dust, they said at the church where we went every Sunday to remind us of death.

The coals are still burning from last night's bon-fire. The sun is *bajando*. The rhythms are still with the symphony that's starting to ching and chime in my ears.

It is Monday. The moon is still full, but feels to be waning. A sloth has climbed its way to the roof of our meager house and after realizing that is nothing here at all to eat, he has found his way back down. Nothing can just sit there like a sloth, just sit there and gaze contently and deliberately.

Things here at the Casa have taken a turn for the crazy. Sylvio split for Italy and left Maria in charge. Maria finally flipped and ordered everyone out of the house. Felipe with his drum, Hazel and the *gordita* from Cartago, Christian and Adriano, the skinny jugglers and the painters who sit in the room all day and smoke pot, everyone out. I don't know where I fit into the whole scene. Everyone seems to pay me some kind of respect and ask my permission about things. It must because Silvio left me with the big room. I have something people want.

The *locura* continues at the Casa de la Playa. I awoke this morning to find a crying, helplessly dejected girl in her dirty bra and panties lying in the yard. She looked like she'd been awake all night vomiting and heaving, and now in the dusk come to a calm daze in which she no longer had the energy nor sustenance to continue in any dramatics other than simply laying there. She looked give up.

She was pale and disheveled.

I asked Adriano what was the matter with her, and he replied that she is just crazy.

Yesterday she spent all afternoon resting her head on the foot of Christian and Adriano's bed staring at a bottle of water. Hanz moved away the bottle of water once, and she flipped out until he moved it back.

She is the same girl who showed up at the spontaneous organic music jam hurricane at Sylvio's the other night, covered from head to toe in mud. She wasn't wearing any clothes then either. Perhaps she doesn't wear clothes. That is interesting.

Harrington told me that she was on mushrooms for certain, the way that she was shaking and refusing to talk to anyone.

I thought she was taking a mud bath.

Ronaldo told me that he thought Harrington raped her. He said that Harrington would do that just to screw with her.

Harrington smashed in all high on crack last night to eat the lentils he bought. I was just happy that he bought a little bit of food for once.

Hanz was the one that told me about Harrington. He is good and bad, and he just doesn't care. He is a crazy man. "He don't give a fuck about money, he can live with it or he can live without it. He is a drug man. He may fuck up every once in awhile, but as long as he doesn't hurt anybody, he figures he's alright."

I don't know if he raped that girl or not. I told Christian that he just had to get rid of her, and he did.

Now she's gone, and I'm out on the veranda that is just about ready to cave in. I hope I am not here when it does. I am thinking of going up in the bush to the *finca* when I have an opportunity to leave and quit this game.

Brian, the prophet of Judah and Rastafari from California, told me that he foresaw the situation progressing to a struggle for power for the king of kings who have no castle.

I told Brian and his good for nothing girlfriend Maria Angel, that they could not stay here any longer. Brian did not seem to understand. I do not think that he can hear from inside of the little world where he resides. Nor can he cook or contribute anything of any use to any greater cause than himself. I however, have my room that I am generously contributing to Felipe and the *tica gordita* for one of his raki sessions.

The *gordita* and her friend Hazel will be leaving today.

Hazel invited herself to my bed a few nights ago, so I politely agreed. What a saint I am. After nothing became of it, I shut my door the next night. After a few more nights, she finally left.

There is no privacy here. All that I write is forced and strained. All that I think is forgotten, and even that is of no worth.

It is all worthless, like a treasure chest I keep locked around my neck; a treasure chest of ideas and schemes and poetry that would all lead to fame and fortune if I wasn't so scrambled up to unlock it.

Instead I'll just continue with first lines to other stories that seem interesting at the moment, but loose their inspiration and enthusiasm with my patience. But how is a man supposed to write in this nuthouse? How can one think in the midst of chaos? I'm going for a coffee and make myself appear useful at something. The only time I can feel useful is when I am away from here, but the thunder is prophesizing rain and beckoning a day of the *Casa*. . . .

Today I went with Harrington to the *monte* for bananas and sugar cane. Oh, the things I do to waste my precious time: making the bed, brushing my teeth, flushing the toilet, flossing, looking for my pen, losing my lighter, listening to the birds, dropping my roach, having a coffee, pacing back and forth across the room forgetting what is behind me, checking on my plants and writing poems.

The woodpeckers are banging their heads against the coconut trees looking for an ounce of sap. That is how I feel writing. This is the story of the snake.

Harrington cut off the main trail into a banana field where he saw some ripening bunches of bananas. We were probably thieving.

I followed him into the bush to carry out what he was going to cut, crossing over fallen trees stumps and thick boot stealing mud.

I left the smaller *racimo* I was carrying where a tree had fallen, deciding to pick it up on the way out. I entered further and he handed me a heavy bunch with a few yellow half varmint eaten skins already at the bottom. They'd already started to ripen. Better we eat them than the animals right? We were happy because we knew we'd have bananas tomorrow instead of the monkeys, rats and raccoons picking away at them.

I shouldered the bunch and turned towards the exit, watching for snakes and stepping over wet fallen trees.

Harrington was telling me the other day about how little snakes are more poisonous than the big old ones because their venom is fresh. They haven't begun yet to diminish the store of venom they are born with. They are virgins.

I picked up the bunch I'd left on the ground and continued out of the bush, when I heard Harrington shouting something at me. His words were stuck.

Then I understood to drop the bananas, and I threw down the bunch I'd just picked up.

"No, the other one!" he yelled in broken Creole English.

I threw the bananas down, and out crawled a skinny *terciopela*, the most poisonous snake in the jungle. As it slithered away from the fallen fruit, Harrington pulled his machete and chopped off its head. I took a deep breath.

Harrington thanked God, and I thanked him too. Tomorrow I'll go back for the snake's carcass and make a cross from its hide.

Last night I walked up on Leonardo and Alexis and the family sitting below the deck in the *cocina*, eating dinner around the candles. I walked in with the flashlight around my head.

"*Me asusto Roberto*," Alexis said that I scared him.

He said that he thought that I was the *Gordo Malo*.

The *Gordo Malo* is a notorious criminal from Playa Chiquita that had been put away in prison for the past several years. Word has it that he just broke out and is back in town.

His wanted poster was posted on the pole outside the gate to the house, but was ripped off.

The owner of the place next door, the Playa Chiquita lodge, somehow had him sent to jail for theft, and now it seems that he's come back for the vengeance he's sworn. I know a few of the *Espanolas* that work there and they say he's shitting a brick.

The past several weeks have been littered with sightings of him and his gang that travels armed and dangerously through Puerto Viejo's suburbs and jungles, robbing and burning down houses.

Four gang members/*guerilleros* were recently involved with the attempted robbery of a gringo Vietnam veteran who's living down here on his social security and war pension. He was involved in the break up.

The gringo burst out of his house when he heard them on his property. He fired two shots into the darkness, one from each hand's revolver, and each shot connected.

One gang member was shot directly though the cheek and got away with two of his teammates. Another was shot in the knee and could not go anywhere quickly enough.

The gringo came down to the wounded *Tico*, stuck the gun into his mouth and said if he ever comes back there again, he will die.

It was the *Gordo Malo's* guys that supposedly broke into my unlocked house and stole a backpack and some money from a few friends staying in the front room.

Hanz, my roommate, met him once. Someone brought the Gordo to his house in search of a place to sleep one night. Hanz let him in, and the Gordo Malo started asking if he had a gun or a knife or anything. Hanz said no, that all he had was his little switchblade, and the Gordo took it to sleep with it under his pillow.

When Hanz awoke in the morning, he and the switchblade were gone.

Hanz said the Gordo was shot once, but it did not kill him. "He does not give a fuck," Hanz says.

He is not a Christian. He makes anyone that has anything scared. The rest tear his wanted posters off the poles.

I was dead. Then I was alive, and now again I'm dead, speaking to you directly from the Casa de la Playa.

The need for Peace is growing in me like a fire, like a moon, pulling my insides out and waning the distance between us.

I get stoned and pace back and forth across the room, looking for nonexistent things I've misplaced. My footsteps on the rotting wooden floor must sound like the dance of a madman to the Indians below.

"If you see a boogeyman when you are walking alone in the forest, run at him, and he'll run off afraid." But what if his mother told him the same thing? That is called a collision, and at that point, there is a break.

Harrington told me the other day, that he knows people who have killed their mothers for crack. You have to be strong with to battle with that drug. You have to make yourself work.

"I've lived with money and without it, and man I tell ya, there ain't no difference," he says.

He is a madman that likes to go fly and be close to God.

The bats are whizzing around my room. Everything lately tells me to attack my fears. I don't know what all I'm afraid of. I can't begin to make a list. The things I'm scared of are the things I possess. I am scared of death. I am dead.

I am scared of losing my past, my family and my self, but all that is already lost.

I am scared of loosing my money, but my pockets are already empty.

I must clean my wounds. When staff infection appears to be under control, the bacteria begin to take over the digestible skin.

I fear of breaking a shattered heart. I laugh because I am laughable.

Today I took the horses and rode them. I sailed them. Rapidly dodging trees in stride, powerfully, sinking the mud and dragging through it.

Letting the candles burn down, I no longer worry about writing down the songs in my head. I would like to play them, but the Indigenous *Teribenos* downstairs are occupying the guitar, howling out songs and getting drunk. I'll soon go join them.

For weeks now I have been trying to make myself sit down and write a story, or an article or something other than this dribble that seems to pour out of my hands. Something of worth, something other than vanity and I's from the narcissistic hero spinning out small talk from his central perspective point.

My balls itch.

The hairy part where my dick connects to my body and soul itches incessantly. If its not one thing, its something else. The itching turns to guilt ridden burning.

Walt Whitman turns to Henry Miller.

The Indians downstairs think I'm writing a book and this makes them laugh.

It makes me feel good, that they think I'm working, while really I just sit on my lazy ass all day counting sheep and scratching my balls.

We both hack away at a block of wood for our art. His ends up looking like something, a parrot, a pair of *quetzales* atop each other, or a lizard. Mine evolves into piles and piles of scattered scrawl. I turn a beautiful block of wood into sawdust. It is chaos, a hurricane, a nothingness leaving any possible reader with only a broken mirror and an unfinished story, a plate without food. Just the sight of it is beautifully insane.

Leonardo does not speak a word of English. These letters thrown together could be numbers for all he sees. To him however, it appears to be a book. "In time," I tell him.

I tell myself that I will write something of worth and coherence rather than this slowly flowing drool leaking from my pen, and small talk about the weather.

No hay palabras en el mundo para explicar la verdad, ni realidad para traerle en el profundo. Que viento magia punto, que lluvia tan calmante, que penas tan ondos quedan en mi rostro. Adios al el amor, pero no se da tanto distancia.

When you pass me the wine, touch my hand and I'll know it's you behind those eyes.

Today I went down and stole breadfruit from the Pacheco plantation, the Costa Rican ex-president. I climbed his trees and shook his branches.

Marylee has returned to my life and pen to my hand. I am naked. She is an evolving mirror. We are slowly fusing, I to her and she to me. *Federacion.* My hair, my odor, my clothes; her clothes, her eyes, her stream.

The sun is at midday. I have been scavenging the beach looking for fruit and fun. I am naked with you. We have lost all hope for survival.

Yesterday was a day of mirrors. Mirrors in the morning, mirrors at noon, in the rearview on the bus, mirrors reminding me of you. Today is a day of dreams. Dreams of the future and dreams of the *llano*, dreams when I should be watching the path and guarding the kitchen?

Just when I think the infection in my leg has gone away, I find the red glow of sores against my pale legs illuminate like little *casas de la luna*.

I am in the Casa de la Montana at the *Finca de los Pallasos*, the farm of the clowns, awaiting the arrival of a sweat lodge at the *Casa Comunal.* The nylon string, pink and blue striped hammock is rocking. My name is Roberto and I am in the jungle.

San Pedro will be there, an old prickly saint from Chile whom I once hoped I'd never meet again. It is a Temezcal and said to be cleaning, purifying. I may be ready for a haircut.

We are the last *Guerilleros*, whose souls have been cleansed with fire and water and hands cured with mud. Our feet persist with their path. We are the last *Guerilleros*, fighting the last battle there is to lose, determined to live, and take as many lives with us that will leave.

We are *Guerilleros* of peace, marching to the sound of the stars, planting seeds of rebellion and free thought wherever we tread. Escaped from the cells of Babylon, over the mighty walls of fear, pledging defeat with return, and victory with rotten multinational towers of greed.

Our trenches are the mountains and rifles our songs, beat with drums of anti-commerce and sung with roaring voices. Our colors are worn in the brightness of our eyes, so we'll know another *Guerillero* when they show you your reflection.

After the *Temezcal*, hours of fiery steam and sweat, chanting, crying and holding tightly to consciousness I crawled out of the sweaty hut into the cool muddy night air, exhausted and weak. We limped down to the cold spring and washed the sweat, mud and tears from our bodies. In the cold water, I wept. The tears ran from my body like they were waiting for the door to be opened. Tears neither sad nor joyous released and flowed strongly. It was something that the hours of sweating fire brought from the depths of my being. The tears washed the soul and left me relieved and light.

Having lost faith in everything and not knowing what to believe, I turned to the one God I knew I could trust, nature, and she says that everything must go!

Marylee has a way of her; a way of loosing pens and taking hope; taking hope and music from the air and playing it through little headphones while pouting. She looses pens. She takes pens and looses them. She has lost mind. If she does not take the pen, she takes the thoughts away from behind them and leaves them without air. It is a miracle that this dribble has been allowed out.

Last night she fucked me. She fucked me because she thought that it would make her feel better. She thought that it would make her stop being a bitch. "It will make your life a whole lot easier," she promised, and I agreed.

I put the condom on again and suffered under Pontius Pilot the weight of the plastered body bag. I traded my dick for a plastic dildo and let her ride up and down on it.

It was a ride, and after thirty minutes she stopped having fun and agreed to stop and go to sleep. I laid the whole time, stiff legged and straight on my back, with hands on my side, trying to be as accommodating as possible.

She once grabbed my hand and the open burn on my ring finger. I jerked in pain. It was a sign of life.

"What is going on?" she asked.

"You just grabbed my finger," I replied as calmly as possible.

"Do you want me to stop?" she asked.

"Do whatever you want," I answered sincerely.

That short phrase, "Do whatever you want," has become a cliché in our relationship. She has a difficult time grasping the concept of freedom. We both do.

I ate mushrooms the other day. I was walking up to the *finca*. The *finca de los pallasos*. That is where you can stay for free. Anyone can stay there. That is freedom.

Norberto the painted rasta from Austria lives there. He is a clown. He is an artist.

Moraine lives there. She is from Ireland. She is a lushy vagabond.

Jueves, the Guatemalan folk singer and yogi, lives there. Inti and Milena, the Colombian showmen, and their Chilean sidekicks, Juan Carlos (Catato) and Tatiana from Santiago, stay there also. They are preparing for a grand *spectaculo*.

I am sometimes found there. I vomited there all last night.

I threw up once and my hearing returned in stereo. Twice and came back my vision.

From there I finished the little food that remained in my stomach after my fast and moved on to the thick green stomach bile and other acids that are stored somewhere far off inside. After that, the convulsions of my stomach became more regular and the intervals of peace shorter and shorter. By this time it was dark. I was on the ground in the rain in my underwear. I was shivering. I made Norberto come over with the light because I felt I was throwing up blood. When he showed the light in the water by our feet, it was pink, and he agreed.

He said my face was pale and beneath my eyes and lips was black. We were both a little worried that I might die. He said I showed the signs of toxic mushrooms.

I began to ponder my own death earlier on in my trip while watching the leaf cutter ants marching in a line over my vomit. They move in a straight line as quickly as possible. If something is in their way, they go over it or mold around it. I thought I might die, and ran at that thought. The closer I got to it, the more comfortable I became with it. If I were to die, I was happy to be dying free and on drugs, however stupid that may sound.

I did not die that night, at least any more than I already was. I had visions of lemons. I needed lemonade.

I did not sleep, and when the rain stopped and morning came, I took a nasty shit and went to Sylvio's for his lemon tree. I am still drinking lemonade.

I have been hanging out with Harrington a lot lately. He is more fun than Marylee and cooks like a hungry mad man. He is a hungry mad man.

Harrington is a middle aged Nicaraguan refugee living with us at the Casa de la Playa. He has kind of taken over some of the Indian's spots that haven't been around lately. He stays gone for days then comes running in to eat anything in the kitchen, then crashes into sleep for awhile. When he's up again, he's out. He's alright.

He's been sticking around the house lately, maybe trying to stay out of town and off of crack a little, but who knows.

He told me, "Unless mushrooms got a bit o blue, leave 'm alone". I think I'm gonna leave them alone anyway.

It rained this afternoon. It is raining. I smell pot. It is good to smell pot, but better to smoke it.

A rat came into my room last night and ate all of my pot. I was reasonably disappointed, as I was looking forward to smoking away the rain, but, "If wishes were fishes, we'd be eating sushi." Marylee said that.

Wish and it will be answered, for my wishes just delivered my new friend and roommate downstairs, Ismael. He's always in time.

Marylee is bored and I must tend to her.

She takes her guitar to the ocean, to sing her a song out of control, to ears that always listen, to eyes that do nothing but roll. Paula, you don't know it, but I'm writing a song for you. You're not crazy, just out of control.

You asked me what I'm writing and if I wanted to smoke. From down below my balcony, I said of course and awoke.

She takes her juggling pins to the ocean, so no one will smile if they fall, and no one is worthy to watch, and no one has answered her call.

Her accent seems like Argentina. Her art seems of Ecuador and Peru. Her bag is from *Parque Tyrona.* You don't know it, but I'm writing of you.

I awake every morning with songs in my head, but always fail to write them down. I should take my guitar to the sea and come back with blank pages of nothing.

I have been waiting for a good time to play music with Paula. She sings beautiful songs that I would love to learn. This may be a good opportunity, as I hear her playing in the other room. She did not go to the sea today. I am going to stop writing and go into her room. Right now!

I am coming to learn that solidarity is motion. A time alone is a time of transition. When I become stagnant, I become society. I gather rust. Motion is cleaning. Motion is living. Living is free.

Hurricanes run through the month of September. In October it rain again. August will trick you into believing you know what God is forecasting. The only thing sure is nothing, which will certainly continue. All the rest is c, the unknown constant. No matter how precise we believe to become, chaos is always present. Theory exists at every moment. It could be next to nothing or nearly infinite, big, small or all the same. The margin of error could be a pin drop. It could be point zero, zero one. It could be a billion. It could be a trillion. A mountain, *un monton*, an earthquake or an atom bomb. It could go from zero to lightning in a moment. The moment could be a generation. A birth, a death and a heartache in the flap of a butterflies wings. A hurricane.

Lifetimes are easily broken at the snap of a fingernail. Heartaches are easily stolen when your head is straight. All of this rain is making my nose turn to glue. The pale of my skin grows with the black under your eyes. Eyes, eye, I can see myself in you.

Marylee is reading Henry Miller now and is a little worried about the moral animal in some of us. She says she would not like to be close to anyone like that. I finally screwed her and surrendered my warped sense of right and wrong and good and bad.

I conquered my mind, or let my mind conquer me when Marylee put her hand to my cock this morning. I wanted to rip off her panties and shove myself into her. I did not want to make love with the Tao. I wanted to bury my seed into her barren uterine garden. When she climbed off me, there was blood mixed with semen around the base of my cock. She split from under the mosquito net and shuffled for a roll of toilet paper. I laid there and let my mind wander through words I had already forgotten to write, and into a brief sleep-like state until Marylee crashed back through the mosquito net.

When we finished, she lay on top of me and began to cry. I was not surprised. I was not interested.

"It's not bad," she said smiling. "I just cry sometimes."

I am finally beginning to understand myself. I understand why I am not having sex with Marylee. It is the only way that she will ever leave. It is what she needs. Without it she will shrivel away and wilt. She will find a new host. Why I want her to leave me, I don't understand. Perhaps it is her attachment to Houston. Perhaps she is only my reflection that I am trying to shed. I have not told her that I intend to leave her for Limon.

Marylee tells me that I keep forgetting that she is my friend and not my enemy. She is right.

Today is another morning I awoke into and went to the sea for fish, and returned to the house empty-handed. I am a vegetarian anyway. I will remain so until I become an efficient fish killer. Success is preparation.

It is another morning that I returned to the kitchen and found another serving of last night's bread and warm coffee. I reminded myself to give up bread and coffee again. I am a sinner and a glutton, feeding on death and filling my body with his warm touch.

It is another morning that I awoke to Marylee's hand on my cock, pulling me inside to give her a juke, so she can continue living in my bed. Now she can survive another week. I cut her off, but she tricked me again. She knows what to do to get laid. She knows how to take what she wants. She is learning to become creative.

She can control me with this, for I am weak. It is my Achilles tendon, under which I collapse like a shot deer. It took her no more than thirty seconds for her to raise me into iron, and from there, I am a puppet to her delicate string. She shifts and I roll. When she is ready, she climbs on and works the key into its hole, unlocking our orgasms. Then she leaves and I fall back to sleep.

I am pleased to find that my lack of sexual appetite for Marylee does not signify homosexuality. I am drawn to the imaginations of sexing others.

I am surrounded by beautiful women here, several of which I picture laying on the table and slicing into them, stabbing their uterine sheath. It is only Marylee who I dread.

It is not for her lack of beauty, for I have no idea what she looks like anymore. I do not know if she is fat or skinny, or pleasing to the eye or ugly. I have no point of reference. I am lost. It all looks the same to me, like slowly drifting down a wall of coral deep in the ocean, disoriented with narcosis. I no longer see the top of light above nor the bottom below. I have no depth gauge or anything concrete to judge my actions or perceptions. There is no terra firma, only the flows and infinite drifting of la mar. Her face has become a pure reflection of my own emotion.

She is ugly when she makes herself ugly. When she makes me crazy with frustration and dead with apathy, so too she becomes.

When we make love, she becomes passion. When she bitches she becomes a whore. Her face is constantly changing. This is a disadvantage she has over other girls.

Other girls are still fact. I have not yet infected them with my reflection. They are landmarks and still independent. Their faces are not yet dictated by my mood. Marylee's face is yesterday's reflection. Tomorrow she will be suffering for what I said today.

Downstairs I can hear Leonardo chipping away at his block of *Nispero*. *Nispero* is some hard ass wood. He will sit with it all day until it becomes soft and turns into a parrot, *a loro*, which will fly away. Someday I will fly off and leave my head. These pages will fly away and sing songs for others to hear in the morning. The words to those songs flow freely, melodically and intangible as the parrots, in rhythm with the silence laid over the cricket's backdrop of hum.

They swirl together in crescendos in keys of *Dios*, in harmony with the bass line that the ocean drops, the choreography of the coconuts swaying and the lead fiddle of the mariposas. All is jazz that is alive. Even Marylee is jazz. She is the slow line of the cello that sometimes swings and sometimes screeches.

Sitting in my chair on the porch I get the urge to say something profound and Earth shattering. Something strong enough to bring *campesinos* and bankers and lawyers and military men to their feet and drop their arms and cell phones and pick up shovels and hoes in revolutionary acts of resistance; a word strong enough to turn sons from fathers and babes from the tit, to turn for the seven seas of freedom.

Towers will fall, stock markets collapse and no one will feel a thing except for the for the gentle breeze and gust of wind started at the butterfly's wings of the word I was about to chip away; a parrot so precise that readers would drop their clothes and head off into the jungle. The word was ready for the writing, when I headed for my chisel and found lost air . . .

El tiempo es la musica y color. Time is music in color.

Harrington is downstairs frying a breadfruit that I stole from some rich gringo's yard down the way. One was rotting on the tree, so I took two. I baked one in the oven last night with some bread, but there was too much food so we left it for today. I am going to eat it before I go off chopping *monte* with Ismael. I promised to help him in the spirit of communism, but now in the spirit of capitalism, I feel like sitting on my drug-infested ass and letting him pay his own rent.

Marylee can't go back home anymore now that she's braless. It's like a drug. Her mother always knew that she would be braless. A vampire, undead and unwilling to return to the confined and imprisoned life of the bra, she is free.

The sea beyond the reef is flat. It is reflecting waves of light like the desert. It is hard to tell where the sound of the crashing waves is coming from.

The long outboard canoe fishermen are making their morning

eastward run towards the sun, parallel with the beach, steadily crossing from left to right in front of my reference screen. Hummingbirds are hovering over the hibiscus stamens and the dry avocado tree. The sea seems calm from my balcony, but below she is *fuerte*.

I went out this morning with my mask and spear, but the waves inside the rocks and the channel where the fish hang out in the deep were too great for fishing. I took one desperate shot for flesh, but missed and soon returned to the shore out of air. I wonder how healthy my lungs are.

I feel like I should give up the fire all together and return to the simplicity of darkness at night and light during the day; foods fresh and alive, fruits and *verduras* instead of rice and beans; air cool and clean instead of fiery and sticky brown smoke. My nostrils would be dry and clean instead of thick and runny. My head smart and clear instead of all funny. Here instead of there, bald instead of hair, when instead of where, books instead of cares, flames instead of flares, saying no to the *petroler*-a. On second thought, I think I'll finish this bowl I started before all this contemplation and exploration.

Last night before we went to sleep, Marylee woke me up with a stern and dream shattering stare and told me that if there was anything, and she meant anything, I wanted to talk to her about, I could. "I knew that didn't I?" I asked and it slapped me in the face and rattled in my eardrums.

And she'll be saying, "Please come quick and capture from this boredom. Show me something I can touch and I'll pray for your sanity". But there's nothing around the corner to capture your pleasant freedom except a broomstick and a hoe and a pair of boots that could soon be walking. And that's alright Ma . . . if you believe in Jesus.

My mustache man on the wall has spirals inside his nose and wears infinity across his eyes. He is :cosign:, cos repeating, waving up and down, and time is music and color. He is hungry and has already eaten the flower people who each have their own eyes and own hungry mouths. They will eat a river and drink a mountain, because we all should eat our drink and drink our food. They too are of the same heart, in the center of everything, living on the wall. The vines of blackness eventually overtake everything. They grow into my beard that eventually fades into the ground. Blues had been added to the blacks for color. Blues have been slid into the reds. Color is time minus music. At the core, it is a butterfly flapping its silvery wings.

Reading Emerson this morning, I am struck by his view that everything in nature is beautiful. My mind goes to the sunrise of the Caribbean waves this morning and the beach and bla bla bla . . . and to the rotting *popylomoyo* leprosy spots that Norberto has growing on his back. The flesh eating disease is trying to take over his body. That is its natural bacterial desire.

I think of the burn of fire ants, the smell of the decomposing rat carcass somewhere upstairs, the millions of compounded toilet hole worms in the shit chalet and I wonder what beauty is. I do not believe that it is a quality possessed by all nature. Nature is perfect, but not beautiful.

Harrington is calling for coffee downstairs.

I have been having an interesting time with my breathing.

Reading and writing are completely different things. To write is to let the mind wander; to let it swill around the pools and pockets its streams has carved through deep rock; to let it pass over perjuries and weak skinny thoughts, playing with the divine.

Reading is a work out. It must be disciplined and running one word to the next in an orderly fashion; from left to right, following the rules of the game, as they are printed on the page.

To write is to release, to let the hand and pen flow freely as the tide through holes in the coral bommies or the wind through the drying and dying, pointed, hanging coconut leaves that are ready to fall to the ground and decompose into rich, organic, living dirt. The coconut leaf is dead, but the cellular energy inside it is immortal. It lives as long as it can, starting from the top and growing from the inside until new, live leaves sprout, pushing the old down, demanding fresh sunlight.

I am reluctant to pay the electric bill. I live better without lights yet I do not turn them off. Last night the electricity cut out, but

Harrington and I fixed it. I loved the darkness. I loved the light of the candles, letting me sleep soon in the evening and arise soon in the morning. It was comforting to know that my day was over. Now the electricity is back and so is the modern man, frying his bloodshot, insomniac eyes.

I cannot resist the string from the bulb. It is too easy to pull and support the electric company. They run things in Costa Rica. They are a big ass monopoly. They run the *Petrolera*, supporting the war of terror, the war on drugs, the war of wars, killing little mutilated kids and women across the world. From the bald headed leukemia girl whose chain linked fence backs up to the vinyl chloride factory in Pasadena, Texas, or the Iraqi kindergartener who's school was blasted with some bio-chemical death agent, the energy industry is behind the killing. It is death, death death.

The monkeys are howling in the trees. They throw shit on people that get too close. I like that.

Filling the world with one light bulb at a time, filling the night with little phony, oil powered suns; it is the capitalist destruction of God. We light the darkness and darken the light for rich hogs that think the fatter they get, the happier they will become. They do not know that it is possible to live without artificial light. They do not know that it possible to live without refrigeration. They do not understand the magic of an apple and the beauty of a fernMarylee's father threatens to leave her out of the next family vacation if she is not living a productive lifestyle. What must she produce? He is an oil tycoon who struck it rich beyond belief, but still short of the insatiable and indiscernible mark of comfort and security. His appetite for destruction is unappeasable. His wings for death are spread and he complains of Marylee's production.

He produces barrels and barrels of oil and thinks it is for the best. He drives SUV's through downtown Houston. He is a saint, killing for the good of the country thinking his money is utile.

He cannot spend it. He cannot buy anything of value except a plane ticket for a family vacation. He is the richest slave I know, but poorer than the *Panamenos* working the fields for the *bananeros*. He is poorer than even me, sleeping under a roof full of holes, on a floor full of termites, with a belly full of beans and bananas. I have the horizon from the heavy wooden chair on my balcony. I have his daughter.

Harrington says that if he wrote a book, they'd lock him up. That's 'cause he's a free man.

The only feeling of easiness comes through creation. All other time is postponement, procrastination, frustration and masturbation. Waiting is a madman pacing back and forth across the room like there was a pen or a thought forgotten on the other side; running down the stairs to wash the dishes, running back up to turn off the light; telling myself that today is the day I'm going to paint my masterpiece.

The only relief from the void of non-creativity is sleep. Whether it is making a hammock, or making a bathroom, making *chicha*, or making a book or a song, we must make.

Give me weed, give me wine and give me solitude, and I will make something. I will alchemize these raw materials into gold or excrement, and if I do not, I will erupt. I will implode. The pressure built up around the void inside the chambers of my heart increases exponentially until the space, which was once the size of a dime, will grow inwardly to the magnitude of a black hole. Spinning and reeling, disoriented dizzy, the physical walls of my heart will not stand up to this intense pressure. The pressure must be released. Make. Get something out. Forget about your own thoughts. They'll just chain you up in indecision. Release what is raging through your veins with some expression.

Release, or learn to be content with nothing and the silence of the sea and sway of the coconut trees. Let the air fill your belly and your head, until it lulls the swilling and spinning cry for creation to rest.

Let the birds chirp through you and understand the signals they hint. There is a world beyond to which they are connected. You too are connected. You are a part of it, but you miss the signs because you are detached. At each moment there exists an entire, infinite, wordless story, constantly unfolding between my balcony and the horizon.

The world is silently singing and breathlessly breathing and constantly, infinitely instant. It is reactions based on reactions based on instinct. It is perfect and only breaks down upon distracted thought. It is the only rupture of the rhythm, and even he enters in time without skipping a beat.

A dry weather pillim is sitting atop the headless coconut tree. They call him a pillim because that is the song that he makes. They call him dry weather because some people call him a spin bird. He's got style and sings when he takes to the sky, "Pillim, pillim, pillim." He ain't sayin' nothin', just singin'.

Harrington's uncle was born in the jungle, the bush. The English army came and got his grandfather and made him do the obligatory service to the lord, service with guns, while his granny had the baby alone in hiding. That was wartime.

The Pillims have a secret talk song. Two more appear from the Guava below. The three of them have them a family. He flies out a little dance just for show.

A woodpecker flies up and joins them. He goes into a hollowed out hole in the headless coconut tree. A *carpentero*, he's got himself a young one that he keeps in the hole.

The Dry Weather Pillim is flying, stay away from my territory. A tide bird is calling for the changes. It sounds like the roll of a wave.

The bird of the summer in September, he'll sit there all of the day. At night he may go into his hole, but today he'll just circle and stay.

A man has some animals, a horse, goat and some cows. The fence is broken and off they go free, breaking through other people's fences and onto other people's properties, eating up all the green grass and raising all hell because they're free. They're wild. Soon out came the police and put the animals into jail. Now they're doing three months time in the animal jail with the criminals. The man has to come buy them back out. Buy another car for the police.

When my plants are happy, I am happy. When they are sad, I am sad. When they are dying, I nearly die from the frustration breathing and filling up my airtight veins. The pressure could be released with only a scream so loud it would take out the tops of buildings. It would blow the bottom out of my belly and the head off of my cork.

Live! Live! I want to yell! The more I want to yell, the more they wilt. I drown them in water and kill them with love.

Never underestimate the power of a roach.

I dove into the ocean. I slept inside the sea. When I woke up, I had lost my bed, and found sea horses at my feet. They breathed a bubble from the inside and filled my lungs with words and air. I sat up straight and stretched my legs and floated up the coral reef. I met a turtle on the fly, told me I should come on by and have a look at outer space and said, "You'd better look for food before your hungry".

Today I followed Harrington around looking for coconuts. I picked some. He husked some and left some. I asked him if one that he left was bad. He said no and he cleaned it. I asked him if another one of them was bad. He said, "Ya, da ones bad. Leave him alone," and I threw him in the *monte*.

"How do you know which one's bad?" I asked him.

"Cause da ones got hair like I got on me head," he grinned a crooked, speckled tooth grin.

I looked at the black and grey wiry, curly salty hair on his head, and he was right. The sun dried, frayed coconut husk looked exactly like his hair.

I understand that everything I thought and all of the imaginary words I threw onto the page and all of the speeches and oracles I delivered to Marylee whenever I'd finally open up were not mine. They were not based upon things I was uncovering beneath my skin or some universal wisdom springing from some supersoul. They were neither my moods nor my observations, but merely seeds grown to flowers planted and watered with the words I have read.

If you can leave someone, do it quick. Do it now, cause before you know it, it will be too late. It's like a drug. It's like a wine. You can always say tomorrow, but freedom's passed you by because you wait. I've got the corkscrews in my heart again.

She crawls inside the bed and takes her place on the pillow, then cries about me sleeping far away. She kisses my lips and I know she wants my mouth, but all we got is nothing to say.

Hey little buddy with your finger on the trigger, take a deep breath and spit out your mind. Every time I read back over my writing and notice the pages and pages of scribble scrabble, I promise myself to shut up, but it just keeps going without point or rhyme or reason or direction. Perhaps it is as I like to dream, that it is as the wavy tacking of a sailing vessel at sea, zigzagging in a seemingly incoherent current, but over and enlarged grid circumspection, it is ever drawing closer to some conclusion. The conclusion will conclude only the unfolding of a new beginning.

The winds of traveling filled my nose and lungs this morning and got me high for a few moments. It faded just as low when I realized that today would probably be just another day I will not leave nor do the things I promise myself to do. I am going east.

Today I woke up, cut my hair, walked to the beach, raised my hands above my head, took a deep breath and passed out face down into the sand. I blackened my eye and concussed my brains, shaved my beard, drank rum and cooked bean soup.

Today has been a day of losing. I am losing everything. I am losing my mind the way I lose matches. I lost my hair, my beard, and the pen in my hand. Time looking for something is time lost. Time, time, time; what is it, and why do I care about losing it? It's nothing and it's not mine to lose. The years could turn into Septembers and Septembers could turn into Junes and no one understands why I won't turn on my lights, but I do. Time lost is time spent thinking about money. "Who took my money? Who took my money?" Sometimes it is better to know only one thing, and that thing is nothing.

I just walked downstairs with Harrington and he went into the back room. He told me to come downstairs and take a look and what the guy gave him.

I don't know what I thought I was going to see. I don't know what I thought he was doing. I knew we were talking about crack. I went into the back, and saw a man with different eyes filled with yellow blood.

He was hunched over the compost bucket with a match and an old Pilsen beer can I threw out last night. He had the possessed look of a leprechaun rewarded with a treat from the devil.

Today I saw Jesus hunched over and broken, swollen eyes and puffy cheeks dragged down by his droopy lamb-chop frown. He spent all day at the cantina alone at table where he poured concrete all week. Spent all his money just to be miserable and pissed off. I can do that without working all week.

Harrington just left. He didn't say much. I should not have walked back into the room to watch a man filling his lungs with evil. Why do I see it as evil? Why do I feel it is wrong to smoke crack? Why do I feel it is wrong to die? Nothing makes a thing better or worse. When I was in Chile that was what I was afraid of.

I feared that to become the best I could be, the further I had to fall into darkness. I understood the yin and yang culture and this whole Heaven and Hell thing that God talked about, and I was afraid that to become a real writer, an artist, I had to sell my soul, predetermining that existence of a soul. What is the loss of a soul, but death?

I am not listening to the television anymore. I am looking at the sea and the ants. I am looking with my ears and with my eyes now, and what I see her say is live!

Live free, but live! Smoking crack is dying. If one could harness its powers for good, however, you could stay awake for days filling books and books with scribble scrabble, never once having to stop for food, water or even rest.

What is it to write anyways? What is it to publish? It is something of life, and what is this life, but life only. It is the toss of a coin. If you tell me to play something pretty, I will stop. If you ask me to say something nice, I will shut up.

September.

It is morning on the balcony. It is beautiful and sunny, but was just pouring rain a bit earlier. It will rain some more and be sunny some more too. That is the weather for today, morning in September.

Today I am going to Limon to see about a boat out of this crazy house. If the boat is there and willing, I will leave. I am going to bring my guitar, a small saddlebag of clothes and a book in case.

I have grown so sick and disgusted with my self that I can no longer even kiss Marylee. I lay in bed with her and the thought of it makes my mouth water from underneath my tongue. It makes my skin crawl. She doesn't understand. She says it is all in my head. I told her I know that.

I find her very pretty and sweet, but I do not want to have sex with her. I feel it will only continue to drag on our miserable existence together.

I know what she wants, but I cannot give it to her. She wants me. She wants to consume me and burn me in her fiery womb. She wants me to want her, she says to me crying. This makes me feel so awful that I break down and try to kiss her. She does not want a kiss on the cheek or on the forehead. She wants our tongues swimming, sliding, conversing and screwing inside her mouth. My tongue has nothing left to say to her.

She is beautiful. She says she loves me and I do not reply. "I am incapable of love," I want to respond to her. It has been sucked out of me along with all other emotions on the way up and down to zero. She is too much of the me that I want to lose.

She is too much Houston and too much Texas. She is my mother, my father and my sister up in the oil tower. She is the computer, the bank account and the reminder to call home.

My father tells me that it seems like I have a severe hatred with myself or my past that I am trying to burn. I say that I have seen the light and have changed direction. It is time to leave Costa Rica.

I am going to go sell young coconuts and Noni over at the *feria*.

She says she loves me. It is a love that was introduced to her baby eyes in the form of a father that slept with her mother every night. They were Baptists and good parents until they could stand themselves no longer and divorced. They introduced her to love, and with love they introduced her to violence, love's ever present polar opposite. When Alpha was created so was its Omega.

Society throws to us morality and introduces evil. In a world where no good and bad exist in Nature, we create a bad by instilling goodness. "We live equally out of our bodies and out of our minds."

Society takes us out of our minds and turns us into killers. We are taxpayers, elders and assassins. "We are effectively destroying ourselves by violence masquerading as love."

This is a note to myself reminding me that Marylee is a mother bitch. A reminder so that when she leaves, I will not be sad and miserable. I will remember.

"She rises in the morn and enjoys laying with me in bed. It is one part of the day or time with me that is always special and important to her. I know this so I do my time, take my shit and escape to begin my morning without Marylee," she writes in my little notebook.

It has been a long time since I have been lonely. It has been a long time since I have been alone.

I crush Marylee daily. I have no regard for her feelings. I cannot help it. I've become numb to her daily flares and temper tantrums, and know to accomplish any kind of well being I must sacrifice the two of us.

She is crying right now. She rises in the morning and enjoys laying in bed with me. Her enjoyment soon metamorphasizes itself into loathing and resentment when she finds that I need to get up and take a shit and do things away from the bed. She will yell and scream and swing again, just like every other day, whether I stay or leave.

If I stay in bed, it will not be enough. She will cry now because I don't want to fuck her. I can only apologize for myself so long. I become numb to even my own apologies because they no longer mean anything except . . .

Today would be a good day to travel. If there is a good word to describe me, it is inconsiderate.

They say that a writer is judged by the quality of his suffering and the resonance of his silence.

I will take one more hit from my pipe and listen to what it tells me to do. I can already hear the words walk on.

Alas, there is nothing more to say.

They divided my things among themselves, and for my clothing they cast lots.

"When the ocean comes to you as a lover, marry at once, quickly. Don't postpone it. Existence has no better gift. No amount of searching will find this. A perfect falcon has landed on your shoulder and become yours." And there is nothing to look forward to, nothing. There is nothing but the waves on the horizon. That is Rumi.

Turn off the light killing me! Quit buying plastics.

"*Buenos dias* Harrington".

"Buenos dias".

"Como estas".

"Mas o menos".

Every morning he greets the day equally balanced between good and bad, and then Harrington puts on his rubber boots, grabs his machete and a flour sack, and walks off for the beach.

"I'm gonna see what I can find," he says as he skips away in search of coconuts or whatever else the beach and the ocean have to offer.

In Puerto Viejo, coconuts sell for about twenty cents a cleaned and husked coconut. On a good day, Harrington can back fifty or sixty cocos, and that turns into dollars at any of the many restaurants in town. The restaurants need the beach, because that is the "roots if the kitchen," Harrington says.

"I call this roots food. It is black man's food. It calls for de coconut".

When I was about six years old or so, my sister had a friend named Catania Ryan. She was a beautiful little blonde girl with fragal front teeth, and my sister invited her to spend the night.

I don't remember the circumstances provoking or antecedent to the situation, but I have a somewhat vivid image of chasing Catania around my sister's bed with my dick in my hand. I was firmly punished afterwards and made an embarrassed fool of. I certainly learned my lesson. This was the education of young Bobby Kuhn. The death of the animal and the birth of a conscience whispering a father's voice in my ear. The image sickens me.

Leonardo thinks that I'm crazy, talking about *comida cruda*, writing for pages and pages about absolutely nothing. "*Ya tiene un libro*," he tells me.

I tell him that if it was anything other than listless, unintelligible babble, then yes, I would have a book, but not this is only bound fire starters or toilet paper. If this book were a block of wood, I would turn it into sawdust and space.

I told Marylee tonight that I could not kiss her because it felt like incest.

She told me that I'm crazy and started to cry.

She follows me out of bed and asks me what I'm doing here on the balcony.

I say "Nothing".

She comes out and my words to write are shattered like confidence. Into a dreamlike state of radiance and rapture for plans for the future alone or with Peace I wander. The moon will be full tomorrow. The light bulb is dimming. I am going to give myself a sponge bath because my balls feel hot and sticky.

I am racing to kill myself I frightfully discover. I grew so sick of my life and my past that I want to cut it all off and burn all binds I have tied to it. I let my self go free into the sea of infinity. I am naked.

Lost at sea, one can find love. "Is it true? Does it exist?" I ask myself and imagine reminders and answers from the arid valleys of Chile; from a time in my life that I was not lying.

Chile seems so far from Texas. I am much closer now. If I grow closer, can I still grow farther from home? Is distance relevant? Does space exist or is there only here and there?

The growth is a derivative, a rate of change. At each instant along this axis of time, I possess a growth that is either positive or negative. I am either growing closer to home or closer to away. This increasing or decreasing is based solely upon desire. Do you want to go further or do you want to go back?

Going back always takes on the feeling of homesickness or despair. It is a sad emotion, a negative connotation. The positive energy comes with the manifestation of the increasing rate of desire to go forward into the sea.

Destroy your life. Kill your past. Unwrap the light.

Give life to your body and death to your life. Do not call home. Do not use a computer. Let go for awhile. Travel East to San Andres or North to Cuba. Go South to Chile. Save some money. Buy a farm.

Bugs are everywhere, crawling through my clothes; flying through my hair; slipping into my mouth and in my underwear. Cockroaches, *bichos* and beetles, flees and flies and ants and tweedles, sipping on this morning's coffee, swimming in the bowl of beans; itching, scratching, stinging and singing, some don't do a thing that I see, so most I don't mind.

I am beginning to understand myself, my problems and my reflections. I hate Marylee just as much as I hate myself. I clench my fists in angst with the piercing pain of the hatred, and all of it, all of it is me. I am with her. Location, location, location.

I have not left her. I have not left my self. I only hate it. I still own a car. My parents are still on the phone. My sister is on the way. My past is Marylee and I have her with me still. If I could rip out my sideburns I would.

Why write when language cannot touch what there is to be said? A true language is lacking for the undecipherable flashes and symbols representing the poetry of the soul. The words of my dreams disappear. The words of my dreams in a truer tongue unspoken but precisely understood vanish into the morning air. It feels like the world's draping robes of mystery have just come clean.

In vain, I will try to express my philosophy; what worries me or gets me high; what keeps me down or keeps me distracted. I have gotten through good and bad and entered the eerily silent realm of nothing only to again ask myself if this is good.

I have killed my ambition and my pride only to wonder where

my ambition went and is that good? The truth of this mediocrity and futileness to produce anything mind-blowing depresses me. It creates an un-unity that I constantly struggle to bridge. The words flow out of my pen unhindered only to reveal to me that my poetry is unpoetic. It leaves me in want to unveil this supersoul that I barely believe lives somewhere deep beneath my belly button.

This soul, this magnificent feeling of eternity and mystery and higher being must reside somewhere inside me. Where is the slack between that and the mediocrity of my footsteps? Where is the bridge between what I know and what I write? All seems cliché.

Where is the bridge of creation? Where is the bridge between hope and doubt, between truth and faith? Does it exist? Does anyone know more than I? It certainly seems that some are quite confident that they know the road to heaven. The Hindus know it. The Christians know it. Even the atheists know it, but as far as I know, the dead can still not write.

So where does this leave us and with what, road maps drawn by good imaginations, Upanishads of fiction or the divinely inspired? I'll tell you when I get there.

The streets are filled with faces, each seeming simpler than mine. Believers or infidels, we all end up in the same place.

The Taoist believe that through dedicated meditations one can learn to release the soul from the body at the point of death and soar into a higher realm of light and energy and space without time, or time without space, or something. They say that those who reach this enlightened state leave behind a set of pearl-like indestructible stones from their abdomen. They find them perfectly preserved in the ashes of some masters. These pearls are a product of the energy they've stored.

Christians believe that if you are dedicated to saying your prayers at night, your soul will go to heaven. Are the two beliefs so different?

I am painting a candle and in a fit of terror. I will attempt to describe the warmth that I want to capture. I want it to warm the room like a log fire, the heat blue and then black at its deep center. It is so hot and so black that it is itself removed from the warmth of the flame. It is so black and so dark that it gives light. From its emanating center, its black hole, the light fades into the rest of the night . . .

The light is a natural light, natural but tamed by man, burning a small controlled spot. Let the natural man be a wild fire, not the point of a small candle. Our nature is to burn, so burn! Consume everything that touches your frontier boundary, your skin. The soul is a fire.

They say Nietzsche died in a hospital, completely insane. They say it reflected in his writing. Who is the judge of that? They say it may have been the syphilis. What is deemed in insane is often only misunderstood.

The world is centered around my own perception. There exists only two places, here and there, and what is not here is untouchable. Take care of the here. Be responsible for making the here a perfect world and it will spread. Perception will grow. Here will grow until its light shines over the world. I am responsible for my own dream, but there are no bounds to how vast the dream can grow. The inner world is outer space.

I feed my instincts, but the compassion and respect I hold for your instincts creates humanity. The care I place for my own health protects you. I don't buy processed shit sold by anyone I don't know because I don't need it. I do not support the corporate monsters, for my own selfish purposes, my own health and my own pocketbook, but the compassion I hold for myself thus spreads onto your plate. If everyone held the same compassion and responsibility for themselves, the world's problems would resolve themselves. The holes in everyone's ozone would eventually fill like the holes in people's smog filled lungs. The Earth will cure itself if given the opportunity. The *Pertrolera* would stop rolling and leave peace in place of its rusted tracks.

Wal-Mart's sweatshops, Exxon's missile factories, the United Fruit Company's miles and miles of *bananero* would all crumble under the weight of freedom. Freedom is not buying.

In Spanish, there are two words for free, *gratis* and *libre*. There is an inherent connection between these two words that we condense into our one word, free, which encompasses both the monetary and the spiritual, personal or spatial quality of freedom, but the two are both poetically entwined. You cannot have one without the other. I have to leave this paper and go to work, the only thing jeopardizing my freedom.

"A victorious language is nothing but a frequent sign of successful conquest."

I ask myself, "Why do I write?" There is nothing more to say, and even these words I write, these metaphors connecting themselves to concepts they represent, attaching themselves to nerve stimuli that its sounds immediately generate in your head, are not my own. I read them in books you've never read, and heard them from people you've never met. So why print them down on paper? It is for the vain hope that someone may eventually uncover truth, a coin whose face has been worn away leaving only the metal. This is the truth.

Who remembers what they were just thinking anyway?

See Jah at even the smallest.

The beauty of art is in precision. In freedom, there are no decisions. A potter can be as close and precise as the size of his pick; a painter the tip of his brush; a poet the girth of his vocabulary and the ear for his own voice. A mathematician can come as close as you can count. A collector of beads; a collector of breads; a collector of songs and a collector of heads, everyone is collecting their treasure. The rarer and more specific the item of collection, the better. The rose and her pollen, the day and her dawn. The collection of money is boring and impious. It is an unnatural and fixed quantity. It is a natural number. There are no natural numbers in nature. Nature is much too precise for that. She uses e and pi, and other imaginary symbols for her numbers.

After sitting here in silence for long enough, listening to the Panamanians downstairs frying rice in the kitchen and playing *tipica* songs on my guitar, I begin to sing. Sylvio is back in town after three months in Italy and he's kicking Harrington out of the house. I think he wants me to stay and work for him again, but I can't handle his shit.

He's schizophrenic and obsessively compulsive. He is as outwardly insane as I am tucked away inside. He is a child with temper tantrums, who is too spoiled to do his own work. He is however keeping a roof over my head.

Today I did not leave the house. It was deemed a day of rest for my feet and legs. They are bruised and beaten from my past three days of incessant barefoot walking to and from the farm and Puerto Viejo. My feet still have not recovered from the walk through the mountain jungles of Teribe with my Indian friends. I was barefoot there too. I got drunk and fell asleep on the bus. I woke up in a hurry and hopped out into the border town of Sixaola in the rain at night, leaving my black rubber boots in the bus. All of the excitement was too much for my feeble brain to handle.

We crossed the border illegally so as to escape the ten-dollar entrance and departure fees the government taxes us every time we cross the border. I don't support their laziness, or respect their international imaginary boundary lines placed by some rich descendants of the conquistadors, a wealthy Spanish landowner and loyal subject to the king.

Ronaldo says "los Indios no saben de fronteras". The Indians don't know of borders.

Politicians cause starvation with their borders, keeping people stuck in famine stricken lands rather than roaming with the buffalo and the rains. We don't respect them, so we crossed the Costa Rican side of the Rio Sixaola incognito, but we were stopped by a police officer upon entrance to Panama. He told us to go back to Costa Rica and get our passports stamped. I told him that the office was closed and that we'd have to wait until morning, but our friends were leaving now. At first he seemed unsympathetic, but eventually let Marylee and I go with our Indian friends to San San Drui. He warned us not to continue to Changinola because there would be *guardias* there. He didn't want us to get him into trouble.

From San San Drui, we walked higher into the mountain, further from Babylon towards Teribe, the center of the mountain Indian's communities and farms. We walked hours of rainforest to watch the women's softball game. We drank *chicha* and visited farms and houses of Leonardo and Ronaldo's families, playing with children and understanding the men. The women were silent. They carried and fed us everywhere until our bellies were full with the food they grew. It was an important weekend.

We are a group here in Playa Chiquita at the house of Sylvio. We play with tons of ganja all day and it's hard for me to tell what the hell is going on.

Harrington is in his underwear, cooking up the coconut, waiting for his clothes on the line. I'm watching shadows and the lights in between them, breaking up fights. An alien, illuminated by a mushroom from another planet, once inhabited Hanz. We are all along with the jellyfish, floating along in the chaos of the sea, a non-repeating mathematical equation.

Something organic has the ability to process information and to act accordingly. Trees are animals, people, that move very slowly, and very *grande*. My head is filled with inactivity, and conscious reminders of the heart.

"*Que pasa con mi vida*?" we sang all day at the communal house at the farm of clowns. What happened with my life? Thoughts escaped like words to our songs, passing with the river of fresh spring water.

"I'm a rebel!" Harrington sings as he saws off a point on a spear. He sees his black bandana in the back of the house, on my guitar. He says Alberto stole it.

"*De quien es*?" I ask Alberto in the back while Harrington put on his clothes.

"*Es mio,*" he said. Now we have I problem, I think.

"I'm a rebel . . . soul rebel".

"I left the Bluff (Bluefields) on a boat. A paddle, like that. The first guys I see, military guys I see, when I's leaving, is a group of four. Behind them was a group of twenty or so. That was the *Mano* Negro. 'Oh shit' I says, because the *Mano Negro* him de baddest man of all the *tenientes* dem. Bad fellas dem Sandinistas," Harrington told me.

"I was coming down to check them out, them Contras, to see what them deh' fighting for. That's why I was leaving the country. That's why I's still here now, cause I want to attack Ortega. I want to fight and take back my country where I can live like a free man."

"You can't do that here?" I ask.

He looks me real good in the eye and says, "You tink dis country free?"

"A country is free when dem men out in the town everyday with arms?" he asks. "A free country is when the police carry around a stick and some handcuffs. This country's got arms boy. They got M-16's to carry around. What they need M-16's for here?"

"Hey, before Ortega, when deh was Somosa, you can walk down de street widout no man ask you for papers; askin' you where you goin' and what is you business".

Two gunshots ring off in Playa Chiquita's *tranquilo* forefront. I am at the Casa de Tao. The world forces have drawn me here, dirty, idle fingernails and all, to escape the *locura* at Sylvio's.

I ask Harrington how to get to Bluefields. He said you gotta cross a lot of rivers.

"You gotta cross the Colorado, El San Juan- man there are alot of rivers that sometimes get high with plenty current. Man at some rivers them not be nobody there".

"But are there any roads?" I ask.

"Playa!" he laughs. "*La playa alla* man". It is only beach there.

"You can go in boat up the river to Rama. *De alla se puede andar por todo el pais. De alla se va en Caretera.*" The highway starts in Rama. From there its only boats.

"I tell you man, every county you travel to, dems have different life. Every country have the life different. Me no traveled too much, but that much I know. I think from Nicaragua to Çosta Rica is enough to show that everywhere different".

From what I've read, I would like to go to Big Sur. First I'm headed to Bluefields though.

"Immoral, in the case of the virgin who looses her way, is not to be able to bear a displeasure despite the thought of the power that makes the rules. Being moral means being highly accessible to fear. Fear is the power by which the community is preserved. What is contemptible in the girl is the weakness of her fear". This is what Nietzsche has to say. I say nothing, but I think I agree.

Harrington knew cocaine for the first time in 1988, in San Jose.

That was when he was a Contra. He was on call in case of immediate need for support from the South, but was not actually fighting, or on any official duty. It was really just shelter, food and a little bit of spending money. They seemed to do a lot of drinking.

This particular time, he and a friend were sharing a bottle of Flor de Cana, the rum of Nicaragua. The friend offered some to Harrington. They did six lines and Harrington said, "Hey man, that stuff change my mind. It make it hot".

Right now, Harrington is asleep in my bed because his back cannot take the hard wood floor anymore, much less the wild cane communal bed with its irregularly jutting out chutes. Cana brava they call it.

It is good to finally have some rain. All of our throats were dry, and Harrington needs some sleep. If he is not sleeping, he is going crazy, waiting to smoke crack. His sleep is full of nightmares, but it is still better to sleep.

Marylee is still.

He says that he is going to stop smoking crack. He is going to start drinking rum again he says.

"I gonna just get my bottle, take my seat and open it, and if you want to sit and have a drink . . . " and he slices his hands in the air. "Then the dream takes over".

It is not his style to take a drink on the road. Him rather drink in a he home or in one place. That is his style.

"Let us remove the conscience of sin from the world and let us soon send home the concept of punishment after it. May these banished monsters live somewhere else henceforth," says Nietzsche.

I hear the Indians downstairs reading the cruel propaganda stories about the Word of God distributed by the Evangelical Conquistadors of San Jose, speaking of the huge guilt that we carry with us for our sins that we cannot avoid. I tell them that it is a *mentira*! They roll their eyes and goes back to the fried eggs and white rice.

The children sing hymns about how they want to die, "*Quiero morir, quiero morir*".

They are afraid of sin, but not death. They welcome death with their diets of rice and pork.

"But where is your inner worth when you no longer know what

it means to breath freely? When you no longer have the slightest control of your selves? When you frequently become sick of yourselves as a stale drink. When you listen to the newspapers and leer at your rich neighbor. When you no longer have any faith in philosophy, which wears rags, and in the candor of those who have no wants? When the voluntary idyllic life of poverty without occupation or marriage, which might suit the more spiritual among you, has become a laughingstock to you?

No, against all this, I would sooner emigrate and in a savage fresh region seek to become master of the world and above all, master of my self; keep changing location as long as a single sign of slavery still begons me".

"An insight has come to me: companions I need: living ones, not dead companions and corpses, who follow me because they want to follow themselves, wherever I want".

"'We have invented happiness', say the last men, and they blink". Nietzsche said those things.

She kisses me a story. She loves me up a tale, pulling on the lever, searching for the grail. Knocking at the gates, sliding through the yard, putting up a fight, but giving in before she's tired. Luring me in, filling my nose with want, make me believe I have won. Feign me in truth of your coming, bite and bring me back to your eyes. Squeeze the muscles hard between your thighs, send a lightning bolt from your trigger, and invite me to the room where I cannot return. Take my life from me in the name of pleasure. In her name I am resurrected.

Her fingers reminded me of last night's spaghetti, which reminds me last night I did not eat. Tonight I ate till I vomited all of the stew on my plate.

Harrington's got seventeen kids with seventeen women. He had eighteen, but one of them died. I wonder what happened to the woman that gave him two.

It upsets me, the mess my life has become. Standing on the road, going one-way or the other, but nowhere at all. To a bed where I cannot sleep; to a woman I cannot kiss; to a page I cannot fill; and a decision I cannot make.

I am sick, and here on the side of the road, in the middle of a night full of rum, the only direction I can go is down. All I have the energy for is lying down and dying.

With those thoughts, I knew I had to continue my life and my journey. I set out for San Andres so long ago I can hardly remember to even remind myself that I need to go there. It has become a dream. I must wake up and move.

I am living here in a state of deja vu. Even the word seems to have been written on the page before. The bottle of alcohol on the table, the black of the bus window, it all reminds me of some parallel time or familiar future that occasionally crosses into the meantime.

If everything is what they say it is, and half of your life is but a dream, and the other half of light is dark, and between every moment there's another moment, just like the red between blue in a green, or the valleys between each mountain and the distance between a touch, dreams exist uncovered during consciousness. They are sewn in between the seams of waking hours, and crossed between the shadows of ego.

There is a moment in the morning when the rain stops and silence starts. For just an instant, a brief pause, smooth, not abrupt. Then the music fades back in. It is like a V. From there the day is broken, and put back together again.

It is no use complaining, for it is you who have chosen this location that you sit. Perhaps you did not choose it, but you settled for it. Otherwise, you would have kept on moving. It is you who sits in the company of fools and morons, thieves and liars. I have settled for this community of beggars and leeches, for it is me who has yet to walk away in favor of solitude. All that I want, all I must do is take it. Whatever you see, it is yours if you are brave.

Show me a man who is not a fool, and I'll show you one who has never loved nor cared to.

We are now in the house of the dying dogs. We are watching them die. It is a miserable condition.

I just saw the nectar glistening on the tip of the beak of a hummingbird. My eyes seemed to zoom in on the still frame moving one hundred beats per second.

We are watching them die and killing them.

One of the young ones has some kind of scabies and is covered in raw bald patches. The mange.

The radio still softly interrupts consciousness from down below with the Indians. The rain cleaned me today. There are no voices in my head to record, only Indians.

They are peaceful Indians. They have been baptized, Christianized, sterilized and finalized, but they are still beautifully calm and peaceful people. They have warm eyes and sincere smiles.

Leonardo comes home from work and must wonder what the hell I'm doing. He makes me feel guilty. He makes me feel lazy, like a father coming home in the evening.

I can see my father walking in through the back door and into the kitchen where we are all eating spaghetti with meat sauce, drinking a big glass of milk, watching television (maybe a show like Alf or something). He walks in with his tie already off and top button unbuttoned so he can breathe, his heels clicking against the orangish red rectangular tile floor, and he goes to his chair where he throws his coat. He grabs a beer and sits down, pissed off at something my mother's done wrong. Some careless mistake probably induced by her frontal lobotomy and altered character. . .

Hanz's dog Asia is dying. We don't know of what, but it seems to be starting to suffer. It has begun to keep away from the house and others. She goes alone and sits in the *monte* when Hanz is not around.

Alberto just arrived and nearly shattered my connection with the words, but I overpowered him and his sucking thumb and annoying cough. He comes up the stairs making sure to make as much noise as possible, and just stands there, feeble brained and egg shaped. He has a stupid cross-eyed look to him. He is a burden to have around. He is a worthless mouth that always expects to be fed. He comes into my room to ask for a rolling paper. I have to come in from the balcony and write in my room when he is around. No one likes a thief. I don't like to have to be on the look out for my things, but so one must be with a thief; either that, or kill them.

I have considered killing Alberto, but he is like the son of Sylvio. A thief is worse than a dog. Perhaps after I kill Asia, I will kill Alberto. They say that after the first one, it becomes much easier to kill dogs.

The yellow haired dog that Ronaldo brought has grown so skinny that it is beginning to look like a rat. I gave it some coconut last night, but it did not want to eat. It just looked at me with big dumb eyes that seemed to ask for something else. You can see its bony ribs that funnel rapidly down to his asshole. I am sick of writing and all of my creations.

When I finally awoke to the truth of the consummating lifestyle I was being milked into, I vomited and was shaken so violently that I wandered directly in the opposite direction. Instead of wanting to be updated with the newest model and the next highest price range for a vehicle, I went immediately to unemployment and rags with paint stains and holes in the soles of my bare feet.

I stretch my eyeballs for a bit, roll them around in my head and return focus to the page with new clarity.

I see a multitude of stars in the black sky of my head, each shining and twinkling there own personal color of red, blue, green, cranberry, violet, orange, yellow, pale white and indigo with two or three blotches of energy roaming around.

Like painting your face on a mirror or letting your lips wander in song, let your art go. Release it. Throw it like a fastball and hit it like a homerun, without thought or hesitation. At the full moon party, I jumped through the fire. Its sparks splashed up into the darkness and all of the drums simultaneously stopped as if God gave us all the cue to cut. There was a loud cheer and the rhythms began again.

I smoke a joint and the drums from the ocean beat. The guitars begin to bang in my head. My pen begins to write and my ambition goes.

The drums have now stopped, leaving only the sea and the Indians. Leonardo is leaving the house. He does not want to work for Sylvio. I went and got a beer with him at the cantina. It was an unsympathetic goodbye.

Ronaldo must think that I am a lunatic. I rant and rave like a mad preacher of some ancient religion of truth and the anti-Christ. I tell him that the missionaries that invaded his village are spreading lies.

They have been tamed. Their tiger is in a canasta. They have been civilized, Christianized, socialized and prioritized, putting heaven as their end all and be all.

Marylee loves the instant that I first enter her. The moment, that all is feeling, all is new. It is her favorite part. One might say that if her favorite part is the beginning, then she could never be disappointed. This is false.

"Uh oh," she says. Something has just happened that is irreversible. The only things that are irreversible are broken. Everything is broken. First and foremost is seconds. Secant is Marylee's glasses case. Next will be her glasses. That is the beginning.

I believe in the God of the circle; the God of the fern and the God of the vein; the God of the broccoli and the cauliflower; the God of the split; the God of self-similarity that explodes with the splitting of the atom. Gods have always meant nothing but violence. The God at the tip of the butterfly's wings, moving around at the heart of all things, teaching itself to rhyme, portraying herself in her rhythms.

I am living in another world. I cannot say that it is an alternate world, because there is no choice in the matter. I am rotting.

There is an infection eating away the face of my right ankle. I have been battling it now for two weeks and have little to say for its current status of improvement. I am unsure of its present derivative, its rate of change. Everyday I tell myself that it seems to be getting better, but in the real world, it grows uglier everyday. It is a puss-covered crater the size of a dime. The puss may not be only a cover. It seems to be attached to the meat.

I have not eaten in four days. I have passed the time with lemon water and garlic.

My head aches. There is a sore on my hand that may be on its way to the staff. It began as some type of prickle or spider bite. I feel that my defenses were preoccupied fighting the infection on my hand and the staff sneakily snuck in through an unassuming scratch on my ankle.

My head is spinning. My eyes see in different shades. I have visions of bright colored stars giving from themselves as a fountain, an empty void from which springs a trumpet of color. It is the flesh re-growing I tell myself. Words come from my mouth that I have no control over. I don't know where they come from or who is saying them, but their sounds and meanings astound me. It is sick.

My outbursts at Marylee are completely uncalled for, these negative jolts at her character. I cannot control it. She curses me for not wanting to screw. I call her friends bitches. I call her a bitch. I call her a whore. I scream and crawl up in a ball under the covers because the tightening knot inside my soul pulls me in.

I see things that do not exist. Small translucent spirals float their way up from the sea towards heaven. I watch it go all the way up like a balloon.

I have been fasting for a week. I have been gone for a year. I have been alive and awakened for two. Marylee says I have been an extremist for...? I have been here too long.

I have been stretching when I wake up for the past two years, and have been slowly developing a peaceful form of martial arts based on circles. It is stretching and breathing and moving the body in the most perfect form that nature has given us. It all begins and ends in the belly with a breath and then rises to above my head then stretches outward and down, filling up the body as the rising of the sun.

It is mathematics and physics, yoga, tae kwon do and kung fu disciplines and poetry.

I inhale, inspire and turn my ears to stethoscopes and listen through the air in my auditory and respiratory canals. I can hear the beating of my heart in my lungs and wind. It is in rhythm with the rain.

In the everlasting, resonating moments of silence, the veil of perception is dropped from the face of reality and behold, a blanket of dawn. The day is broken. As my arms descend and fall from my head, warm currents of energy run through the veins of my chest, and I know that it is good.

Maybe leaving is better in the afternoon, when the rain doesn't fall so hard, but maybe its better in the morning when nothing has time to change. In the morning it's better to sleep and wait till tomorrow spreads its wings, but today Ernesto, the communist Taoist Sandinista, found somebody to rent our room, so out the door we went.

I told Marylee that I will not eat again until I see her. She is leaving for good on Sunday for Houston town.

We have fled the lowland Caribbean swamps of Puerto Viejo and returned again to the cool mountain valley town of San Isidro de General. It is nice to be back in San Isidro. We are hoping that the change to a higher, dryer climate will improve our chances of healing this leperic flesh eating disease called *popylomoyo* that we thought was an infection and both now have. Whether it will or not, I don't know, but the strong mountain sun and crisp air feel damn good. It feels like Colorado. It feels like spring or fall. It feels like change.

We are lodged up in the same old hotel Amaneli where we stayed in before, only in a different room. We are in one with a television. Marylee said that she was willing to pay the difference.

I have to pee desperately, but know that it will interrupt the stream of my writing, so I squeeze my dick and tell myself to focus. I have been drinking quarts and quarts of water. That is the key to this disease. That is the key to this world. Water and piss. As I promised, I have now lost all words.

I enter the day with a joint, like jumping into the river behind the hotel. It is dirty and polluted looking. It has trash and garbage and broken glass scattered along its banks. Rotting coconut shells and mangos, broken locks, cinderblocks, syringes, snakeskin and absolutely nothing of any use except for the space, the view of the river and the coconut tree, who gives me a hug sometimes in the morning.

When I return to the room, Marylee is always sleeping. That is why the morning is good to greet. She carries gifts with her named solitude, peace and freshness. She brings her niece Freedom with her and she and her auntie promise unconditionally of return and forgiveness with the sun. The dead are asleep and the alive are alive with her and her breath.

In the morning I will not feel guilty about ignoring the present and reading or writing, because this is my time, when Marylee is sleeping. When the baker's doors are locked. When Clemente's shirt is still on and Agnell is yet to come home to change clothes from the gringo's she screws house in the projects.

Marylee just rolled. Her face is beautifully shaped when she is looking at me. When she looks away, she is as ugly as her mother, who is still pretty.

It would be wrong of me to disturb her. She likes to smoke soon and go back to sleep for another hour; to have pretty dreams of being ground back to consciousness.

I nearly screwed her in the ass last night when I was sleeping. I woke up dreaming with my dick rock hard, trying to find its way through her pretty pink panties. It was a bone with a nose of its own, feeling its was to daylight.

I awoke in a somewhat frenzied and disoriented state, confused about the time and location and afraid and apathetic of getting a condom and having sex. Instead, I rolled over and went back to sleep. What the hell?

Marylee was rightfully pissed off. She could not go back to sleep. She was wet, and not just a switch that could be turned on and off as I was. She had to smoke a cigarette, my punishment and her own sadistic retribution.

I make myself a little sad at myself when I do that. It doesn't make sense to me. I'm embarrassed of myself and am no doubt causing problems for Marylee.

Her skin delicately coats her soul.

To enjoy Henry Miller, one must first jump into the river.

"America is the incarnation of doom and she will drag us and the whole world down into the bottomless pit".

I open the door, and the daylight is good to see.

Marylee and I were sitting in the bed, back to the wall and heads in the rafters. The lizard with no tail crawls across the corner of the ceiling. Thunder sounds and Marylee asks God, "Is it gonna rain?" The tin roof answers affirmatively.

She wonders how my walk went this afternoon. Where I went. What hills did I climb, side trails I took into the monte; what I saw; the view of the valley, the people and fruit trees that crossed my path. Mud and brick wood burning ovens and *chicharon* frying pots of lard filling the pork scented air. . .

"I had such a nice walk today," I respond to Marylee's thoughts which she swears are bouncing off the mahogany and *manglare* striped hard wood ceiling.

"It's this damn room!" she bursts out. "I was just thinking about that again. I'm getting claustrophobic again. I need to smoke a cigarette". Marylee relates the buzz found with fresh air, positive ions and unsealed skies with nicotine.

I light a roach when she leaves the room. The first match had already been spent. Hard times when you're saving all your used matches. Scrap wood.

Miles Davis trumpets from the Rancho Tico. Jazz. That's the good thing about jazz. You can write to it. You can make love to it and drive with it. The words don't slow you down or lock you up. It lets you roll with it and sing your own songs in your brain, but shocking you back down into the trumpet with a sharp pop, piercing your song.

This is not a short story anymore. It's not even a long story anymore. It's just a song. A jazz song that might get smooth and sticky at times, but always promises to roll, even when the playing stops. The power goes off and speakers may blow, but the song still rolls, up until the next number hits. It's like a nine tenths repeating into one. So am I. And so is the dawn, rising in the morning sky. So is the five o'clock bus to Nicoya. So am I. One, two three goes the snare from the bar. Triplets that Marylee taught me. The cornerstone of all rhythm. One, two three, three to one, no one here likes to have no fun.

Triplet.

Triplet.

Triplet. Three syllable words. Two syllable endings. Menstrual cycles roll along with the moon and me, coming and going at just the right time. The moon is almost full, but already foreboding her quick return to nothingness.

"If anyone ever dared to translate all that is in his heart, to put down what is really his experience, what is truly his truth, I think the world would go to smash, that it would be blown to smithereens and no god, no accident, no will could ever again assemble the pieces, the atoms, the indestructible elements that have gone to make up the world". Henry Miller said this.

If it could be translated, it would be in a tongue of numbers and symbols, a complex maze of shining hieroglyphics flashing through the purple darkness, so that only a child could decipher it. Seeing as I have and will fall far short of raising any kind of real hell and really smashing shit up, I will print the partial truth that I experience in some type of readable form.

I am not a writer. I am a nothing who has held many occupations with many different names. I was a carpenter before I was a musician and a puppeteer. I was a grape harvester and a gardener. A student and a drunk. A painter and a clerk. An English teacher and a legal intern making fake ID's on the copy machines. The jazz is still rolling and I resume reading.

I always have to say I love you twice to Marylee. The first time doesn't quite sound right. It is a little off key or a bit out of tune. I need to say it again. The second time always sounds more natural. The way she waits to hear it, to believe it. I love you. The second time sounds sincere, nicer, organic, lighter, warmer, loving. I like the way it sounds the second time. I like believing myself and giving into myself instead of fighting it. This is all very humorous to me, as I know leaving will happen promptly. I am obviously just digging and scratching for a little bit of pain or suffering to hold on to. To pretend I'm lonely. To pretend I still feel and have feelings, even if it is remorse. Remorse is good to sleep with. A tear is an orgasm. Dry is death and the absence of running water.

One more love song from my pen and guitar to woo myself into feeling.

I just look down at the pages and pages of scrawl and scribble scrabble I have leaked onto the pages of Marylee's notebook and giggle inside at the lunatic I have become. The one o'clock bus will not leave us here in San Isidro together.

Then Marylee left. It was a day that was coming for some time. She had left before. I had left before. I left her for Costa Rica, and she left me for the States, but we knew that those were just for a time. This is the future. She was going home, and so was I. Our homes were different. My home is the uncertain. The uncertain was certainly not for her anymore.

We walked across the street to the bus stop. The bus for San Jose left at 7:30 AM, and would reach the capital before midday. Her plane was leaving in the afternoon, and she would be back in Houston before night. She would go out to dinner with her father and her mother who would be thanking God that she finally rid herself of me. She would be back in plenty of time for Christmas.

I was worried about the hole she had her leg. It was our common bind. It was holding us together in our misery. We loved each other, despite of our hatefulness and jealous rages. We both made too many mistakes to be forgiven. We had both thrown too deep a cut of slicing dagger words. We were awful. We were beautiful. We knew that this life was impossible, but neither one of us held it against each other. We were smiling. We were crying.

Before she left we had the most wonderful sex ever. I never even finished.

Before she got on the bus we hugged. She gave me a few thousand *colones* that she still had and wouldn't be able to spend before she got on the plane. She said that she was contributing them to my cause, whatever that was. She hoped that I never had to come back. She wanted me to come back and get a job, but she dreamed that I never would. She hoped that I could continue this dream of youth for forever, never giving an inch to the real world that her parents so often preached of. She wanted me to follow her, but she loved me for staying.

The infinite was here. It lay ahead in the lonely stretches of dark roads and abandoned plazas throughout Latin America. It lay in bus rides and free rides going to wherever the hell they were going. It was a fruitless dream, but a dream nonetheless, in which survival and is the only goal and sheer instinct the only tool.

She hoped that her open sore would close before her parents Christmas party. I hoped that it would too. Her father would carry her to the best doctors that specialized in tropical diseases, and they would take care of it. The bacteria eating away at us would probably die when it reached a frozen climate anyway. I knew she would be fine, but worried anyway.

I put her bags on the bus for her, and she stuck her head out the window. It was a real goodbye. All bets and promises were off. All negativity was forgotten. It was tragically romantic how much we loved pain, how much we begged to be released then mourned for our granted wishes. Life is funny like that. People get used to people. That's how love is I guess. With time we grow used to anything.

The bus pulled out of the dark, carbon stained warehouse station and onto the morning highway. I walked out and watched it speed up the road towards the cordillera mountains separating San Isidro from San Jose. I could not see Marylee anymore. I wondered if she was looking back watching me. I held up my hand and the lonely fresh breeze blew through my knotted hair. I took a deep breath and looked around. I turned a circle on the sidewalk. There are so many directions; so many degrees and half degrees. Fruit stands selling mangos, cantaloupe, oranges and watermelons; little *pulperias* and juice stands; *cafetins* with black or strong *cafe con leche*, *gallo pinto*, fried plantains, scrambled eggs with onion, garlic and diced tomatoes; *discoteca* keepers mopping out last night's stale spilt beer underneath shiny Imperial signs; tortilla makers; *carnicerias*; coffee factories running the product of the valley; the list goes on and on and on. I bought a young coconut and went back to the hotel room to sit on the veranda and breathe.

I haven't come down or brushed my teeth since Marylee left, but now I'm going out to the plaza. As I promised, I still haven't eaten a bit of food, but don't know if I'll last until I see her again. Maybe I'll look a bite of food on the street.

The streets are full of people walking around doing their own little things. There's a McDonalds selling Big Macs to these poor people.

I saw a few kids getting trouble with the cops for stealing something. It feels blue to be so free again. I wander up and down the streets with nothing to guide me. No food seems appetizing. I can't imagine eating any of it. I'm going to head back into the valley tomorrow. I have nothing to do here. I'm going to go back to San Salvador. Maybe I'll head back up to the cave for a few days. Maybe I'll go up to Pura Suerte and see Drennan. I want to be alone in nature. Eat fresh live things. Write awhile. Get my head clean. Get my hole filled. Prepare myself for the next part of this journey.

The rain is beginning to fall.

The morning is inspiring here in San Salvador. The clouds nestle in small mountain pocket of green then hover their way across the valley like majestic boats through these ancient rivers of sky. It is good to have sky beneath you, especially in the morning.

I came down from Pura Suerte yesterday and found John's old little house here abandoned. I decided to crash for a few days until the bus leaves out of here on Monday. I'm reminded of all the time I used to spend here with Michael and Barbara and little Frankie Lee. I wonder what happened to them. Someone told me they moved to San Jose or Alejuela or something. Maybe Michael started up his dentist practice he was always talking about. The people here all remember me. No one is going to give me a hard time about crashing here for a little while. They all ask me if I've seen Michael or Barbara or el *bebe*, but I have to tell them no. I guess the bush life was a little too much for them. We had some fun times here though, picking beans and smoking joints, going in the woods in search of bat guano. Most of the time I'd just pass a few days resting before going back up to the cave. It is good to have friends.

The only thing that they had to cook with here was a microwave. They cooked everything in it. Spaghetti, fried eggs, they even boiled beans in the microwave. I often wondered how long one could live like that, with straight nuked food. To me it killed out all of the life and goodness, but well, they seemed to be doing alright.

I don't know what I do with all the letters I write. I somehow always let them get away from me. They just seem to slip out of the books and into the forgotten lost world of no return.

I have come back from the Caribbean to the Pacific and will soon begin to circle my way back North again to Nicaragua when Monday's bus out of here comes. I have been waiting around in a comfortable, *tranquilo* atmosphere with cooler, dryer, *mas fresco* air until this *popylomoyo* (a strange flesh eating paramecium that eats holes into our skin) disappears. I got it from a white mosquito bite about a month ago and have focused my life on filling in that hole since then. Today is a grand day! It is a day of celebration, but only in moderation. It is the day that the wound has finally closed. I have become whole.

You can imagine the types of things I have been saying I will not do until this open sore closes. I have been denying myself every vice and indulgence that you can think of.

I began with a five day fast that started when I realized that this mosquito bite on my ankle was growing at an incontrollable rate. I quit everything but lemon water and garlic, which I used because my lymph nodes were all swollen and I needed some type of anti-biotic.

After that, I started eating all live foods, fruits and vegetables and no carbohydrates except for the occasional bite of a ripe banana. No alcohol, no coffee, no sugar, no oil, no grease, blah, blah blah. Anyway I woke up this morning and looked at it and knew that it was finally closed. This does not however mean that it will not open again. It is not yet completely filled, but it is no longer open and bleeding/pussing. It is a relief, but it will leave me with a good scar.

Popylomoyo, they say is a form of leprosy. Most people that get it down here go straight to the doctor and get shot up with dangerous heavy metal injections of mercury and other toxins. I went a more natural and safe route, trying just about everything and sticking with a few things that helped me through some of the more critical stages along the way. Even battery acid I tried dripping into the sore to kill the flesh-eating microbes.

The stronger of the topical antibiotics I used to kill it was the milk of a vine called "bulls balls", which I applied after scrubbing the twice-daily buildup of yellowy pussy stickiness, with a lemon peel. I then turned the peel around and squirt the citric acid spray into the wound.

When that all dried somewhat, it was important to cover the

wound with something to keep it clean. I sometimes used a gauze and sometimes *arcilla*, a volcanic clay that dries and sucks the moisture out of the hole. I have used the clay throughout the entire process, and have found it to be helpful.

I finally finished the sore off with what may be the simplest, most effective of all cures, rubbing my own three day fermented urine, which contains the exact anti-bodies the body needs for healing. Piss.

It all came down to two things in the end, piss and water. Drinking extreme amounts of water to clean the blood and drinking and applying my piss. This is what God has given every one of us to heal ourselves.

The rain has paused, but commenced anew before I had the chance to go out for candles. Give me darkness instead of your light. I have changed my morals over good and evil. No more fire to burn away the truth of darkness.

Outside of the farmers market in San Isidro, I found a wild tomato vine in the parking lot, growing stronger and bigger tomatoes than the ones inside. Nearby I found the cilantro in the earth that I was trying to buy in the market. The trees are full of *limon.*

Should I feel guilty because they want me to? Do you think I should feel the urge to go home, back to the concrete jungle, with the iron trees and rivers of traffic full of beasts of preys who drive their cars over lands of the free, leaving their scars with the things that they buy and food that they shove into their fat asses? "The West Wasn't Won on Salads," I saw on a bumper sticker on a huge pick truck in Houston. That is true.

Last night I fell prey to more dreams of violence as I was stabbed with a corkscrew about my right breast. My friends and family denied me help again and again as I walked and walked and walked in search of assistance. Finally my vision began to tunnel, blood began to salivate in my mouth and I knew that I was dead.

A monarch butterfly is stretching its wings on a *negro madero* leaf.

This is a book of poetry. A book of poems. It will predict the future and recall the past, and all with the same word. That word is

She opens her mouth when she wants to. She closes her eyes when she is finished. She shakes the rocks with the voice. Violeta Para.

The waves run through my soul in the morning, as the sun penetrates my eye. I enter the day with a poem.

Everything is a joke. Everything. If something is not a joke, then something is wrong.

I walked into San Isidro barefoot and ragged this morning reeking of urine on my breath and on my feet.

My new pants are getting dirty. My old shirt is already torn. I must find a needle and fix it. My new shoes are getting worn. My hole is filling with new; flesh creating flesh; nature is the ultimate artist. It looks like this.

This is a book of poetry because it lacks the discipline and coherence of thought to create any type of literature other than the short fragments of words that barely enter my head before permanently expiring. It is representative of my work ethic and relationship experience. . . .

In one hour, the bus leaves for San Jose. Hopefully I'll catch a night bus for Nicaragua.

Little Corn Island

The bus left out at 3:30. It reached the border of Nicaragua outside of a town called Rivas at about 9:00 at night. It was dark, and all of the frontier services had all gone to sleep except for a few neon lights accepting money and giving out stamps. Robert got off the bus, stamped out of Costa Rica and walked down a narrow road lined with policia and immigration officers. He was nervous. He was carrying a half a pound of Costa Rican marijuana from the Talamanca Indians who planted in the mountains near Puerto Viejo. He hoped there were no dogs.

He reached the Nicaraguan side of the border and was relieved to find no hard time. Everything went cool as he paid a small fee and received a ninety-day tourist visa to enter the country. The only problem was that it was by now long past dark, and there were no busses running into the country. He caught a taxi to Rivas which lay about twenty miles up the road.

He reached Rivas and walked around looking for a hotel. The first two little hospedajes he found were full. He found one that had space. It was all lit up. Drunken truck drivers, Spanish whores, old women outside frying chicken and green plantains, it seemed like a nice place. It cost about five dollars a night. Robert was out of his head. He decided to save the five dollars for something that might be more important up the road, and go find somewhere to sleep on the road. It's hard to say where he would find money again in these types of places.

Not far away, there was a bus parked on the street that was leaving out for Managua at 3:30 in the morning. It was already nearly midnight, so he begged the driver if he could board the bus early and get a little sleep before the bus left out.

He got on the dark, empty school bus and found a seat towards the back and put up his bags. He slid his guitar into the bag rack above his head and laid his backpack on the bench seat next to him. He loaded a small ceramic pipe that his half German artisan friend Hanz had given him, smoked a bowl, and sunk down into his seat. Nicaragua was a different place. Nicaragua was for real. He felt snug and safe to be inside the bus, hidden from the rumbling, hustling world outside. It wasn't long before he dropped asleep.

It was just daylight, when Robert was awoken by a tap on his shoulder. He felt another shake of his shoulders and looked up half dazed and half still asleep. "Sus papeles," greeted a big bearded police officer. He thought he might be dreaming. "Sus papeles," the man repeated, holding an AK-47 rifle around his chest.

A large thud hit in Roberts belly bottom as he realized this was reality. He was surprised to see the once empty bus was now packed with people, all looking on him to see what was going to happen.

Robert calmly pulled out his passport and showed the officer. The man checked it good and held onto to it.

"Y la mochila?" the man asked, pointing to his backpack with the gun.

Robert felt the thud in his stomach tighten into a knot. He knew this could be a big problem, but in his sleepiness, he just rolled the bag onto his lap, tried to remain cool, praying the man didn't find the ganja. He hoped that it was well hidden.

The officer put his gun to his side and started digging through the bag. He lifted his shirts and towel on the top and poked around through the contents at the bottom. After a few heavy moments, the man looked up at Robert and said OK, handed him back his passport and got off the bus. "Thank God" Robert thought to himself as the knot in his stomach loosened and he leaned back into his chair. It was a beautiful morning.

Outside the window he saw the pink blue glow of some rice mills and some kind of factory just opening up in the dawn. He was about to reach Managua.

The bus made its way into the busy city of Managua before seven o'clock. The terminal was a fast moving market, where the old ladies in their little aprons were sitting around their fruit and vegetable set ups, talking amongst themselves. Robert saw all of the fruits and natural things in abundance that he could only rarely find deep in the bush in Costa Rica. He bought up a pile of sweet fruits and nuts for what turned out to be a little bit of money. Nicaragua was cheap.

He asked around about how to catch a bus going to Bluefields. He had to take a taxi to a different market where a different set of busses left from, and he had to hurry up. Everything here was hurry up.

He got the taxi that flew round and round through busy streets an side corners, till it slammed to a stop in the middle of another market, this one even bigger and more hustling than the one before. As the taxi pulled to a stop, it was swarmed by circle of small fast moving Spaniard people, all creating a large sense of confusion. Robert gave the driver a money and ran to the trunk to protect his bags. As he stepped out of the car, the driver sped off with his change. Robert chased after him, trying to get back his little money, but it was useless. He was glad to still have his bags and his wallet.

He bought some corn tortillas and a few bananas and got on the bus that was going across the country to the town of Rama, from where it seemed that he would be able to find a boat to Bluefields.

The bus left out in the sweaty part of the morning, slowly making its way through the hot crowded city streets.

The bus ride was interminable. After it left the city, it bumped through the rolling, dry hills, hitting every pothole that filled the rocky road, dust filling the open windows. The old school bus bench bruised his butt, which seemed extra bony after so many days of fasting and traveling.

Along the road, women in aprons sold warm cheese and cream with cabbage salad wrapped in corn tortillas. "Quesillos, quesillos!" they hollered after the slow moving bus.

The bus stopped in every dusty small village on the way picking up and letting out passengers. Little girls made their way through the aisle of the bus selling little plastic bags of cold natural juices and peeled oranges, deep fried pork skins, chicharon, and roasted corn.

The bus cooled down as the afternoon approached and the bus cruised through the cordillera separating the Atlantic and the Pacific, and slowly down into the Caribbean lowlands and river valley. At about four o'clock, the bus reached Rama. Robert shouldered his backpack and guitar and headed onto the streets, looking for the wharf and a boat that headed to Bluefields.

There was a large flat barge loading up with all types of cargo waiting there, scheduled to depart for Bluefields in an hour or so. Robert purchased his ticket, and found a place to tie up his hammock behind a truck and one of the ships pilings. A few Spaniards approached him when they saw he had a guitar and begged him to play a few songs. He took out the guitar and sang the only Spanish songs he knew and passed the guitar around to a few of the other men who cried out some ranchero songs in their saddest voices. It is easy to make friends when you travel with a guitar.

The boat set out on the calm oily river just as the sun was setting. The jungle along the banks was alive. Birds and monkeys howled in the approaching night. Robert swayed gently in his hammock and was pleased to be on the boat and off of the bus. The evening and its breeze were invigorating. As night set in, the crowd of inquisitive Nicaraguan folk singers left him alone in search of their own hammocks and a nap before the barge reached Bluefields. Robert took a few deep breaths and fell asleep to loud hum of the diesel engines.

Bluefields came in the middle of the night with its bright lights shining over the bay and the swamp. Upon arrival, the people filed out of the boat and disappeared into the city night. There were a few crackheads and drunkards still hustling about on the streets, but other than that, the street was deserted. One rockman who looked just like his old friend Harrington approached him wide eyed and strung out, offering to carry him anywhere he wanted to go. They had the same nose and same big forehead. Robert assumed that they must have been brothers or some kind of family. He wanted to ask the man if he knew Harrington, but he decided it better just to try and loose the man as quickly as possible.

There was a dirty narrow road that led down to the wharf lined with some seedy little bars and hospedajes for the sailors and fishermen. Robert carried his bag nervously up the street and asked around at some of the hotels for the best price for a room for the night. He ended up in a dark, damp alleyway at a little two-story house with a light on. There was no sign or name on the hotel, but there was a man sitting in the doorway who said they rented rooms. It didn't seem like they came any cheaper than this, so Robert asked to see the room.

The walls were made of thin ply board, and the room was large enough to hold his bag and his guitar and the small bed with a fan. The door had a padlock. It would be good enough until the morning.

The morning came, and Bluefields was a different town. It was sunny and alive with all classes and colors of people walking the streets and market doing their own things. There were gleaming white churches with red rooftops, and dirty little wooden shanties built over swamps. Black people, white people, Indians and Spaniards all mixed up like a pot of rice and beans.

Robert went into the market and ate a plate of fried fish with corn tortillas. The market was hot and steamy with about ten different women frying fish and shrimps over their coal burning furnaces. There were another ten women baking corn tortillas over red clay pans. There were bananas top of bananas, red, green, yellow and black. There were pineapples and coconuts by the sack. There was plenty of movement.

After a satisfying and cheap breakfast, Robert started getting to the business of finding a way out of Bluefields and to San Andres. He asked the women who sold him the food, and she told him to go down to the wharf. Maybe someone down there would know something.

Down at the wharf was the same. No one seemed to know anything about the Colombian Island of San Andres. One thing that seemed certain was that no boat went there from Bluefields. Perhaps someone could tell him something at the Bluff, the port of Bluefields.

After a few hours of walking the streets of Bluefields, Robert paid the three dollars and fifty cents for the hotel and carried his bags back down to the wharf, where he caught a small outboard motorboat to the Bluff.

The story at the Bluff wasn't much better, but a few people told him that maybe he could get there from Corn Island. There was a boat, the Captain D, heading to Corn Island that afternoon. It was the only way to go. Robert took a seat in a long line in the sun, and waited to board the famous boat, the Captain D.

The Captain D was an old US Navy boat that somehow changed hands in the last ten years to a man named Norman Downs. The Downs family is one of the most powerful families on the Caribbean coast of Nicaragua. They have a major hand in the lobster and fishing industries, along with anything else that is moving on the coast. They run things.

The line for the Captain D ran from the gates of the wharf and down the street around the pulperia and up a small hill past the past the spot where the police and Navy keep an eye on things. Little children played with wooden balls on strings, banging the balls together in cluttered rhythms. The wooden balls surrounded him. Their scattered rhythms entered his ears from all directions. The knocking was deafening as the sun was burning the tops of his cheaply sandaled feet and the back of his neck.

There were a few sunken ships in the Bluff harbor that were there from the war time or the hurricane Johanna, which destroyed the Bluefields are in the early nineties. "Quesillos!" were selling. The cargero from Corn Island was already an hour late and showed no signs of accepting passengers anytime soon. He soon got bored waiting and walked around in search of an isolated alone place where he could take a haul from his little pipe. He wandered further up the little hill until he reached the peak. At the peak was an old abandoned military fort over looking the bay. It was half falling down and growing over with bush. It looked like an ancient ruin from ages past. It smelled like people went up there and shit when they didn't have a toilet. No one was around, so he smoked a bowl, admired the view for a moment and made his way back down to line. Robert found some shade and a little bit of breeze to cool down the situation. Words began racing through his head and he pulled out his journal, recorded a few thoughts and drew a picture of the Bluff harbor from his elevated perspective. It wasn't long till the Captain D began accepting passengers and pulled out into the open Sargasso Sea.

"One must love an evening at sea, to be in the belly of the beast. A part of its breathing, pulsating rhythms, when you know that things are alright for right now. Swaying with it up the stairs, waiting and letting her let you go," he wrote.

The freight and passenger ship docked into Corn Island at about ten o'clock at night. Robert shouldered his gear and headed out on to the wharf and the road. He stood there for a moment, studying the street with the movement of the people. The street was dark except for the lights of a few fisherman bars blasting reggae and calypso music. Robert had no idea where he was going.

He started walking up the street along the shoreline. He was awake and content to be walking a little to get the sea out of his legs. A hustling crackhead rock-man soon approached him and started pestering him for anything he wanted. At first Robert tried to ignore him until he mentioned that his mother had a room that she would rent out for much cheaper than anywhere else on the island. The few hotels that Robert already saw were about three times the price of a comparable hotel on the mainland. It seemed like a good deal so Robert agreed to walk with the funny-eyed, twist-up faced rock-man to his mother's house.

To his surprise, the fat old mother kept a clean little house near the beach and had a fine little room with a lock on it where he could sleep in for the night. The rest of her children seemed to be normal enough. He put his bag up in the room and told the old lady that he wanted to go sit down on the beach for a little while. She said it was no problem and gave Robert a key to the house.

At the beach, Robert found a little fishing skiff to sit in, and wrapped a joint and took a few deep breaths enjoying the fresh sea breeze and the myriad of stars hanging over the Caribbean. The rock-man who showed him his home soon arrived with a bottle of rum offering him a drink. Why not he thought and took a small taste of the clean white Nicaraguan rum, Rum Plata. It tasted sweet in the night air. He gave the boy a handful of ganja for his help, which he wrapped up with a small piece of crack, breaking it up and spreading it over the joint the way Europeans smoke hash. Robert took another sip of the rum and felt it start to move his head. The boy kept drinking and smoking, and soon things began to get uncomfortably hot and Robert just wanted to be alone. He tried and tried to get rid of the boy, but it was useless. He finally had to excuse himself and leave. He walked down the beach a bit but then just decided to go back to the house and get some rest. The rock man found Robert again before he reached the house, this time begging for some money. Robert awkwardly told him no and bluntly left him alone again. He got back inside the house, locked the door and took a drink of water and went to sleep comfortably in the bed behind a light mosquito net and thin ply board walls.

The next morning was sunny and crisp. Robert awoke soon and made his way down to the sea. It is amazing how much things change from the night to the morning. In the daylight the island looked far different than how he had imagined it when he went to sleep. A few late leaving fishing boats were making there way through the tides and into the sea looking for fish and lobster.

Robert took a walk down the beach to stretch out his mind and tired body. After a few days of traveling like this, his back and his legs felt tight. He was a long way from Costa Rica. He made his way up the beach towards the point of the island, passing several small board houses along the way. The sand was thick and white. The sea was a strong color blue. The breeze came in off the sea and filled his lungs with power. He found a comfortable spot away from the scattered house and took a deep breath. He took another and raised his hands above his head. He leaned his body to the right and to the left and rolled his eyes around the low morning Eastern sun. He leaned backwards, arching his back towards the sand behind him and came back up. The day crashed through the silence of the waves and was properly bro-

ken open anew.

He performed a few more stretches, touching his toes a few kinds of ways, rolling his hips around and twisting his back around until he felt the blood sufficiently warm through his veins. He walked back down the beach again. A black man passed him by and told him that was doing a good thing, starting the day off like that. He said that he liked to see those exercises.

Robert took his time walking back to the house, exploring this side of the island a bit. He found a young man hauling some young coconuts off of tree. Robert begged the man one. He was happy to share. He drank it and it felt like he was living.

He reached back to the house and found the fat mamma with her apron on and head tied. She had just finished gratering coconuts and was beginning to knead out the flour and coconut milk for baking bread. "Johnny Cakes" the woman said when Robert asked her what she was making. It looked nice. He unlocked his little room door and went inside to tidy up his belongings and see what business needed to be tended to. The first order was to see about getting some money.

The sixty dollars that he took out of a pulse machine in Managua was just about done. There must be a bank or something on this island where he could get some money he assumed. It would make his life much easier. He gathered up his documents and went out the door. He told the woman that he was going to go look some fish that they could cook up for lunch. The fat woman smiled and said that would be fine.

He walked out the back door this time and took a look around the yard. Behind the dusty front street, was a beautiful lush backyard with all kinds of greenness growing. There was a huge breadfruit tree with plenty small breadfruits scattered across the yard underneath. He asked the woman if they were good, but she said no. There was a strong storm that blew through and blasted the young fruits off the tree before time. They would never ripe, only rot.

In the shade of the tree's lofty limbs was an old tombstone of some old relative from generations ago. These were original island people. They've been there from the time before graveyards were in style; when you just buried your people in the backyard like a dog or pet bird. Everything was very normal here.

It was about nine-thirty in the morning when Robert finally got out on the road and started trying to figure out what happening around this island.

He soon found the bank, and after waiting in a long hot line, the teller told him that it was impossible for him to withdraw any kind of money. Credit cards were non-existent. He asked the young woman if there were any other banks on the island, but she said no. She didn't offer any suggestions about how he could get money.

He walked out of the bank into the burning sun and began sweating profusely. He was at a loss for anything to do. He began to feel a little bit worried. He did not know how he would make life here without any money. He saw the people working on the roads and by the wharf, unloading heavy things and carrying them on their back. He did not know how he would be able to compete with these people for work. This was Nicaragua. These people were serious. He would have to stay here for a year before he could save enough money to pay for a pass to San Andres. What would he eat, he wondered.

He saw a ripe papaya on a tree off the side of the road. He remembered the expression that the girl in San Andres told him, "No Da Papaya". Don't give temptation. He thought about his promise to her to return, and thought about how long ago that it was. Could this be the end of it? Should he turn back for Managua and the western world or keep going Eastward into the Caribbean? He had less than twenty dollars in his wallet, and decided that he had better forget about the fish that he was going to bring back for lunch. He walked of the road and grabbed the skinny Papaya tree and started to shake its leafy head. It took only a few shakes, and the ripe papaya fell. He caught it like a big orange softball. He walked off into the bush a little bit and found a big rock in the shade of an almond tree and burst open the Papaya. It was sweet and tasted delicious. He stopped fretting for a minute. He had to find a way off of this island.

After the Papaya, he walked down to the wharf and started asking around about which boats were going to San Andres. Everyone looked at him like he was crazy. No one had ever heard of any boats going to San Andres. The only boat leaving today seemed to be a panga that was getting ready to leave for Little Corn Island. In two days, there was a boat going to Puerto Cabeza. He asked where Puerto Cabeza was and the people told him that it was in the North. The people that worked at the wharf showed him a map of the Atlantic Coast of Nicaragua, and Puerto Cabeza was in the opposite direction of San Andres, and besides, that wasn't leaving for another two days. He wanted off the island now. Little Corn Island looked a little bit closer to San Andres, and that boat was leaving in a few hours. It was Little Corn Island he was heading for. La Islita.

He hurried back to the house and got his things together. He asked the lady how he could take a bath. She showed him the bathroom out back nearby the well. It was four sticks with a sheet of black plastic wrapped around it to hide the bather. Inside the plastic box was a bucket with a little bowl for a dipper. She said she already had her son fill the water for him. He took off his clothes and threw some cool water over his sweaty sticky skin. He felt new again.

He gave the lady five dollars for the room and she accepted it with a smile. He threw his heavy backpack over his shoulders and grabbed his guitar and started for the door.

"Wait a minute," the woman said. "Take these. These are for the journey." Robert took the three Johnny Cakes in a pink plastic bag and gave his most sincere thank you. He touched the woman on her shoulder and hurried out the door.

It was a twenty-minute walk down to the wharf from the woman's house. By the time he arrived he was soaked with sweat again. The panga was already loading up with passengers. The panga was a large, open skiff with two, two hundred horsepower engines behind it. It looked like a powerful thing. When he entered the gates, he saw a woman sitting with a large canasta full of cabbages. They were big, round and white. They looked nice, so he bought one. There was another man with a sack full of raisins. It looked like he had brought them from the Pacific side. He bought a small bag, and moved quickly down to the landing where the panga was loading.

"One hundred cordovas," the captain of the skiff demanded. Robert paid the five-dollar toll and took his seat to the bow of the skiff. In a few minutes, the skiff was off on the open sea, leaving Big Corn Island behind them. In front, about eight miles to the North was Little Corn Island, the only thing on the horizon. The breeze was fresh and exhilarating. He sat up straight and took a deep breath, smiling to himself. The salty sea splashed in his face. He held on to the edge of the skiff. Movement is life. Thank God.

I have come, it seems, to the end of the road; the place where all boats stop and none continue, and even if they did, I wouldn't have the money to get on one. I've spent the money I was saving to get on an exiting boat, but that too has already left me. I have burned the bridges. There are no banks, no work and no traveler's checks. All food has finally fallen. Lucky for me, I stuffed myself with fish yesterday and the day before. I told the tourist people I'd clean their fish for them if they'd let me eat with them. Afterwards I even cooked up a coconut cake dessert with the evaporated molasses I was carrying with me. The meal was terrific. The food was so good that the people talked me into grabbing my guitar and singing them songs that I belted out until well past midnight as they kept providing more and more rum. They gave me all the left over fish the next day. It was going to spoil anyway. That will give me strength for some time.

If it ever stops raining, I will begin walking with my eyes open for anything edible. There may be some bananas between here and the village that I would not be above stealing. I have been eating coconuts for my other meals and am getting sick of the way they make me feel. I need a change for a few days. The damn cats here got into my bag last night and ate my last piece of Johnny Cake that I was saving for today's lunch. "*Lo quien guarda la comida guarda la pena*". He that saves food saves pain.

I found someone who may need help a few hundred meters up the beach. He runs a little bed and breakfast and is constructing. He told me to come by when it's sunny, but the fierce cold wind seems to be circling the island. My only hope for some money lies in the few ounces of ganja that I carried from Talamanca. I'm hoping to sell it when I get outside. If there is no one to buy, I may be in trouble. Spending the last of my money is like going into debt because it leaves no way out of here except for with the *narco-traficantes* who sometimes run between here and San Andres. How do I get hooked up with them?

We are only eighty miles from San Andres where all my problems will be solved, but here I am, stuck in the rain on Little Corn Island, thinking, waiting and fasting.

I have thoughts of cooking up one of the cats if things don't go well. They might make a nice Ron Don with some coconut milk. I need to sell this ganja. I am tired of traveling with it. I guess it doesn't matter if I'm leaving on a cocaine boat, but still. "It is better to have pot and no money than money and no pot," Ernesto said. I need to go look for food.

I have found food. Perhaps it is better that I have not sold my pot. I am not hungry right now for any of the shit they are selling. I may not be traveling again so soon anyway.

It is a cold and rainy Christmas morning here on Little Corn Island. I should call it Treasure Island because that is what it seems people do here. They walk the beach, making *vueltas*, keeping their eyes peeled for any of the white gold that might wash up on the beach from one of the many sunken pirate ships that make the run from San Andres, Colombia to here. It is on one of these "*pangas*" that I need to hitch a ride with. If not, it means going all the way back to San Jose via Managua, via Rama, via Bluefields, via Corn Island. That's a trip I don't feel like running back. There are too many bumps on the road and I've already come too far. My ass is still sore from the last ride. It gave me hemorrhoids. I am much too close now to turn back. I have found ways of surviving here for now, so long as I don't weird out my employers Ramon and his wife Marian anymore. I asked them if they knew anyone that needed to buy any ganja around here, and things got really strange and uncomfortable. They still have not warmed back up.

Ramon is a strange sort of mad scientist. He reminds me of Goyo,

Paz's crazy father. He used to be some type of biologist, dealing with the social behavior of monkeys and animals. Now he's in the tourist business. He goes off a little crazy sometimes, a dreamlike state where his eyes roll off towards the horizon and his voice changes key to a surreal, peaceful whimsical tone like he's saying something mysterious or poisonous. He talks like that when he speaks of the island.

"What is it about this *Islita*? There is something here, something special that has stopped me here," he says in his floaty voice.

"Ahh *hombre*. It has no special flora or fauna, only the typical cocos, boa, toucans, Noni and fish, but something has drawn me here".

"It is the end of the road," I tell him. "Ends of the road are always interesting places."

"Yes, but there's something more" he says. "There are faces here. Faces hidden behind faces. You may never see the true *cara* of the *Islita*. There needs to be a documentary done here". He then told me how he used to work for National Geographic, making documentaries about monkeys and things. Ramon may be a big liar. That's alright. He's pretty interesting. The name of his place is *Ensuenos*. That means dreaming the kind of dream that you can control and direct. There is no word for it in English that I'm aware of. It is kind of Spanish feeling, like magical realism. The English are too grounded in reality.

Little Corn Island is really an *islita* and nothing more. It takes only a few hours to walk around and there are less than a thousand people. You could count the little houses, but there is a lot of shit going down.

There is no law here. That is why it is best to stay out of trouble. If you screw around here, you can get yourself *matared*, killed. I am going to take my knife in my guitar sack and go into town this afternoon. It being Christmas, people will be out in the bars and restaurants. Maybe I can hustle a few dollars as a *mariachi* with a couple of Christmas carols. I wish I had a band of carolers behind me instead of just me.

My wounds are now like red roses, full of joy.

Get as high as you want to, it's Christmas. It's never too late to fall off the deep end. It's never too late to let go. The one place you always know will be there is the road.

Sometimes I don't feel like doing anything, writing or playing guitar or going to sleep. Sometimes I don't even feel like sitting here, in the dark, in the deep.

There is beauty in the darkness. There is color in her seems. There is light and there are visions when I don't know if my eyes are open or closed.

I don't even want to watch anymore.

When people lose all ego, they begin to sing. They begin to dance and create because they're not so caught up in their self.

They begin to write. Their words take meaning out of the chaotic wheel of subconscious light playing through a strange flute. The words become poetry and the poetry grows into literature.

I think that my stomach is getting sick of coconut but I must say that I love it. I'm hard put to say what I would buy if I had some money. I would buy more light. With a hundred *cordovas*, I would buy ninety-nine candles, and one box of matches.

I might as well sit here and smoke until my fire is gone.

I guess that I was wrong. Today seems to be Christmas, and it has been full of joy hungover my head like mistletoe. I am growing rich.

I awoke this morning a little high from last night's rum to my crackhead friend asking to buy some ganja to smoke his rock with. He gave me ten cordovans, the equivalent of seventy-five cents. I am happy for tomorrow I will go to the village and buy more light, my favorite drug. Instead of ninety-nine candles, I will buy nine, and the box of matches. As I look around this dark, dirty wet room, I have a feeling that I may have been robbed. Oh well. I have found bananas. A full fallen bunch of *cuadrado* bananas. I have as much food as any man could want.

Dear Me,

I guess that the funniest part of this whole thing is that all ambition has fallen from me except the distant dream of creating something beautiful and expressing that emotion brought about only through proximity to God. To paint something beautiful. But what can be created through words? They are nothing to look at. Can they describe something beautiful? Look deeply into your eyes they would say. Look outside they would say. See what God and man have planted. The farmer is the only true artist. God is the artist. The farmer is the prophet, letting the seeds of life be planted, allowing the dormant magic of life its necessary spark.

You must clean your lantern so that the light can shine through freely and brightly. Let your brown eyes be blue.

You've really gotten yourself into a jam again. Here you are, Monday morning, high on rum coffee and ganja, starting trouble with the folks around town, trying to sell off a little pot to make this load a little lighter. Playing Sherlock Holmes, trying to track down Diko the thief who broke into your room two days ago and stole your money, papers and credit cards, on Little Corn Island.

Living on breadfruit, bananas, papaya, pot, sour oranges, coconuts, rum and handouts. I was at dead zero two days ago, and I've now found two jobs, one at the dive shop and one as a painter/ police officer. The former pays nothing but free fish lunches and the latter has already advanced me twenty dollars, a *gallo pinto con pollo* and enough rum *plata* to keep me up till now.

As for Diko, the purse thief, I caught him sneaking out from behind my bathroom with the haircut and face of a monkey. I should keep my handless machete up here in the loft with me. It was his word against mine until I ran into his auntie at the wooden shop in town and caught him in a lie about his whereabouts upon the morning of the crime. He said he was at home sleeping off a *goma*, hangover. His auntie said he was still out drunk in the morning.

So I'm out a credit card, a whole past of phone numbers of so called friends and a few dollars. I could take what I've got now and run back to Bluefields or I could stay, work and wait for a ship to come and carry me to San Andres. I could get myself killed in the process. My plate is completely full and empty. My feet are torn, tired, shoeless and dirty. I accidentally smoked crack last night. I pray that I never do it again.

It is about time to get off of this expensive little island. I think that my waiting time is about up. There is a cargo ship that arrives every Saturday, or sometimes Friday or Sunday, and heads back to Bluefields via Big Corn Island. I've heard that if you come to town on Friday, you can ride it to Bluefields. I've got twenty dollars. That's enough to get me home, or to the safety and security of a cash machine. I could buy a little time in Bluefields until I feel well enough to go back to San Jose and fly to San Andres. I am crazy. I am in bed right now, praying for rain because my lower back is in real pain. I am afraid that it may be my kidneys. I got busted stealing some ripe bananas from a tree in the bush behind a Gringo's hostal, Derrick's Place. I saw the ripe bunch on the tree two days ago, and filled my pockets with a few of the ripe ones falling off. I said if that if the bunch was still there yesterday, I was going with the whole thing before the animals ate it. "*No me da papaya*," I say to Derrick who calls me a thief. Next time, perhaps I'll beg the fruit before I steal it. Perhaps I'll just take it again. I only hope that my back will hold up through the week.

I don't want no learnin', dignity, or respectablity.
I want this music and this dawn
And the warmth of your cheek against mine.

What hurts you sadly blesses you.

Well, I am out of food, except for a few green bananas, a yucca and a couple of bitter-sweet oranges. I guess that I'm just not hungry enough yet. I'm almost out of light again. I have plenty of rum and plenty to smoke, but those too will be out again soon. No matter how it can seem, all soon will return again to the dark night and new moon. Now however, the moon is full. The air is light and so am I, enough to be writing in the dark instead of cooking.

There was a police boat inside the reef today. It was watching out for some drug boats headed out to Puerto Cabeza. "They'll never catch any of them unless their drunk and stupid, and not paying attention," said Joe the raker man.

Joe has one eye rolling around the other side of his head, but the other will catch you right square in the eye. "Not unless them Colombian boys been sittin' in the bar, they not gonna catch no one. Dem' Babylon," he says.

Dem' Babylon were however smart enough to know that a load was going up to Puerto Cabeza. Catching it is another thing. The young men running the boats are boys from the islands. They are seamen. They were born on the reefs and rocks around Little Island and San Andres. They know the tides and where and when they can pass to slide through the waters undetected. This is their life. The police may have been chasing them around for a few years, but it is just a job for them. It is a life for the island men. Babylon, what the people here call the police, Navy, Coast Guard, or any other government agency, will always lose.

This is one of the gas stops for the pangas. They go from San Andres, to Little Corn Island to Puerto Cabeza, stopping only to refuel or pick up a load. This is apparently where the loaded panga was headed that ran up on the beach near the swamp here at Little Corn before Christmas. It was a huge skiff with three, two hundred horsepower engines, one for each ton of cocaine it was holding in the hull. Some Babylon coast guard was chasing the skiff when the captain made the decision to run ashore and abandon the load. This happened a few weeks ago. The news spread over the whole island like fire. "Cokes on the beach! Cokes on the beach!" people were yelling through the community as they raced to see what they could find.

People hurled themselves into the beached panga and carried away as much cocaine as they could back before the fast approaching Babylon arrived. Men grabbed the kilos by the sack and ran back into town or into the swamps and bush where they could bury or hide their load. Women frantically tried to with run sacks that were too heavy for their backs. Some collapsed or had their load stolen by other islanders caught up in the rush. By the time the police came the skiff was empty, completely discharged. The island was rich. It was a white Christmas and the party is still hot in the bars and ranches. I arrived about three days to late.

Today is another day dedicated to not being able to do anything. I will stop trying.

I almost killed the cat today but he bit into the fleshy part of my palm and got away. He got me pretty good. There is blood on the page I am writing on. That is the second animal that has bit me this week.

The first was Bing, the neighbor's, dog, which bit me as I was going to steal the ripe bananas falling from the tree, begging to be taken and enjoyed. I was to take the bite as an omen. I would still be enjoying those bananas had Derrick not caught me backing out the racimo. I gave them back.

I threw the cat out of my second story loft, because he ate the cheese I bought with five *cordovas* of credit this morning while out scavaging for food after a long night of drinking rum and smoking crack that I mistook for a joint that someone passed me. He was a fisherman that was to get me work this morning unloading cement from a cargo ship. I slept in town in the hammock of a Honduran rock-man named Matagalpa. They call him that because he was a bus driver in Matagalpa until he crashed the bus killing sixteen passengers. Now he's a terrible alcoholic, spending anything he makes fishing on the ocean or backing heavy loads on rum and crack. The families of the deceased were tracking him down to kill him, so he ran to this far corner of Nicaragua where no one would find him. I woke up with the chickens this morning and went to wake up my fisherman friend, but he was asleep for the rain. The cement has to wait for dry weather.

The rain left me out ravaging around drunk with dirty pants rolled up, barefoot, shaking orange papayas from people's trees. Hunger makes a man do strange things. There was one that I knew I shouldn't take despite the fact that it was going to rot or be eaten by birds like the two others around it. I was too tempted though by its size and lightly delicious sweet and juicy color. I crossed over the fence and pierced it with a stick just as I heard a neighbor tell me no. I left the papaya on the tree and ran off down muddy sidewalk. I must learn to listen more to my instincts. They are always right.

Yohan, a German staying nearby, went to town to buy fish. I need some flesh I think. I have not eaten any meat in three weeks or so, since Christmas.

It is Sunday. I have been locked in with depression all day. It will be better to sleep and awake tomorrow. I hope that I never smoke rock again. It is a *busqueta inutil*.

My kidneys show some signs of improvement sometimes, but now my back hurts too bad to sit up. I am in pretty rough shape.

Can I change my mood by what I write? Can I create my own destiny and reality? Am I my own God? I am happy. I can do everything well today. I feel great.

Worship yourself. Praise yourself in the morning with devotion to your body. Cleanliness is next to Godliness. Wash your feet with kisses.

Adventure. A man is stuck on an island. The only problem is, he doesn't know yet that it is deserted. He gives it a shot because he's got no way to get off anyway. Just drug boats loaded with guns heading back to San Andres. Night boats. *Escondido*. Rather than come back empty handed, they sell off the product of Colombia, cocaine, and buy up what Nicaragua has plenty of, guns; AK-47's and other weapons of war that the Colombians can use in their revolution.

I'm hard put to say whether one lives better without money; without the extra bullshit spices and meats that *lleva la muerte*; without the rum and artificial lights. With the bananas and breadfruits, oranges and papayas, coconuts and shooting stars. Without the medicines, soaps, sandals and cigarettes.

So for some reason or another, the man wants out. He thinks that there might exist love out there, something waiting in San Andres. He doesn't believe it's deserted.

Dirty and bearded, blind and barefoot, he breaks through his reflection, his fear and he takes off his mask. All that has been promised to him by a return to San Andres is fulfilled.

"Where's the ocean?" he asks.

"You're in it," someone replies. He is surrounded.

He remembers that patience is a virtue, but retreat is still a very effective method of war. He is only one step away from freedom. Can he take it or are we back to step ten?

Tonight I was walking home from Benito, my San Andres connection's, house again across the baseball/*futbol* field, where you can almost see the whole sky, all except the part that the earth underneath you is blocking out, and I wondered what the hell is all of this for? I could see a myriad of burning suns in the heavens. There are heavens and huge things going on up there. What is their purpose? What exists but has no purpose? What has no function? Is it all just there to give us dreams of grander things than ourselves? Is it there to make us imagine a sense of order, a sense of chaotic reasoning?

A coconut just dropped with a powerful thud. I am living in the middle of a bomb field. Each year in the world, falling coconuts kill more people than sharks. I ate so much coconut today for lunch that I didn't eat dinner. My stomach still feels sick. They say that you can live on coconuts, but I'm not sure if I believe it.

My ride to San Andres is coming. It is here. The boat came in a few days ago and the captain of the panga agreed to take me back with him. I don't know if I would want to be here in Little Corn Island in a couple of years. There is tons of crack. Benito is the community's biggest rock seller and it seems like the whole island passes by there. Everyone seems to smoke. It is only the beginning of a desolate problem. I can see it in a few of the people's eyes already. They don't even know that it's bad for them yet.

I spend most of my evenings at the crack dealer's house. There are guns and crack and a little pot. I could have made three times as much money selling off the rest of my Talamancan ganja here, but some asshole named Cho snatched my sack out of my hand the other night at Benito's. He was all fast and accelerated on crack, telling me to sell him it to him for a hundred *cordovas*. I told him no and he snatched my plastic bag, slipped me fifty *cordovas* and ran off into the night. I should have sold it.

Benito says he'll help me get to San Andres, and I believe him. We just have to wait for the police boat to leave the island. "Maybe tomorrow," he says.

The police all have big scary machine guns. It pisses me off that someone tells them that they can use them on people who aren't even looking for trouble. They just want to steal all the drugs and they think they're aloud to.

I took my last injection for malaria today, which reminds me, I must take my pills. I need to leave this place. I'm sick of working everyday. I do not like to work my body too hard everyday. It hurts me. I need to become a writer and sleep and dream.

I woke up again this morning about an hour before the sun and told myself to go back to sleep, but I couldn't. I told myself to get some citric juice. It is bitter and burns my lips. Today is another day I tell myself I'm leaving. I suddenly feel sick. My strength is leaving me. It was an awful idea to smoke.

The Caribbean Sea is as flat as a lake this morning. There is no wind. There are sand flies instead. The air feels too still. It is sickening.

I think of so many people, but see no one. I think of you Marylee and of you Nicole. I think of you Jerry, that you are the type of person who can do anything you want.

I think of the letters I should send you all that only get lost in the hesitation of thought. All I do is sit and listen.

I've lost the will to read. I've lost the will to write and play music. All I can do now is listen, to the waves; to the whooing of the birds; the crowing of the chickadoes; the swooshing of the waves, filling my head. That is all there is.

The only thing that really is, when you cut away all the extra crap that gets added on top, all there is, is the great silence. Stripped of everything else, it is a great loud silence. I must rest. I have been going too much.

It is Sunday, and I'm still here. Another week on Little Island it seems like. I have plenty of time to tell this little story.

So anyway, I left San Andres almost two years ago, leaving only the promise to come back for my priceless, precious journal full of addresses, phone numbers, poems and other unimportant piles of horseshit that in my delicate and deluded head I've been telling myself will make me a great writer someday. I don't know where the hell I got the idea that I was going to become a writer, but here I am sitting on some old wooden lobster traps on the Nicaraguan Caribbean coast telling a story, so I guess I am. Good is a subjective word. I have at least four more days to be stuck here, so I'm going to explain everything the best and briefest way that I can. How I got here, and how I plan to get off.

Little Corn Island is the *puerta* to the North for the South American cocaine producers. It is the back door. Shit from as far south as Bolivia sneaks its way up the rivers and muddy roads of the Amazon till it meets up with the rest of the Colombian crop and has to make a jump across the Darien Gap to Central America. This is easier said than done. I have nearly done it, but without the coke. From the mainland of Colombia, much of the drugs go to San Andres.

San Andres used to be a Nicaraguan island. She was one of the twin sisters with Corn Island. The two islands are only eighty miles apart. It is no where near Colombia, but for some strange reason, the forces and governments running the world and its God given boundaries, the island changed possession. Now it seems to be an easy stopover point for the tons and tons of cocaine making its way up to the United States via Mexico. From San Andres, some of the cokeheads to Puerto Limon in Costa Rica, some heads to Panama, but plenty heads through Nicaragua. This is the Atlantic route. Some drug lords go with the Pacific route, and pass the drugs up the Pacific coast of Panama and Costa Rica and so on, but I really don't know much about this. I have seen that tons and tons pass through Little Corn Island on its way up to Mexico.

I fell in love in San Andres. Well, that's not exactly true. I became curiously interested in the notion that love may exist. This curiosity was reawakened in me in San Andres; that there may be some benevolence of the soul in our bellies, moving our pens and our feet. That same soul might meet its mirror image in God granted love. I was led to believe that maybe, just maybe there is a chance for something more, something important, in this mundane world of silence; that there may be a right and a wrong. That there might be a destiny that we must all actively seek out and follow or else be doomed to a hell on Earth in a life of mediocrity and suburbia. It is the belief in a saint, and the belief of a call to heed. So somehow this girl made me believe in all this mumbo jumbo bullshit. She made me speculative that there may be a chance of it. Even a chance of it is worth everything. What else is there in life? Who are you if you neglect this possibility of the divine? What has a poor boy to lose but his soul, and to abandon and deny a feeling is to lose it.

I smoke a bowl out the back window at Smoothie's house to aid my siesta hours, and the voice begins in my head. You are listening to it.

It says that people here are treating me like a king. I am poor and dirty and they keep me drunk and full of meat. They are putting money into my hands and giving me things. They say it is out of friendship. I hardly know the people.

They invite me out and buy me beers at the bar. Some people cannot stand to indulge in sin alone. I must make them feel guilty.

I started off the morning looking all over the yard for the shitter, till finally I had to run off into the bush. I moved out of Ramone's "Ensuenos" place, and moved into a more comfortable and convenient room in town at an old black man named Smoothie's house. He told me I can crash here until my ship comes for San Andres. It is infinitely better than my situation around the dark and windy other side of the island. It was wearing me down having to run back and forth every night checking on skiffs headed out of here and every day slaving for Ramon for the wet little shack he let me sleep in.

After shitting, I went down to the wharf and waited to go out on a lobster boat, but was denied another trip to sea. Everyone already has their sailors. The sea is not ready to take me yet. I guess that I haven't spent enough time with her. Perhaps I need to get to know her better first.

I wonder what ever happened to my sense of humor. I wonder if I have one at all.

Benito is a king around the *islita*. The people look at him like he is some kind of savior or a leader. Everyone is grateful to talk to him. He is a crack dealer.

I saw him today carrying the biggest fish I've seen anyone carrying around this lobster town. It was a grouper he told me before inviting me to come eat some of it a little later. I thanked him again for everything and smiled and went on my way down the sidewalk to call my parents on the telephone from the *centro de llamadas* and tell them that I'm not dead yet. It's more like them telling me I'm not dead.

Well, Big Joe Smoothie just came home drunk as piss looking for a fight with Jose the crackhead neighbor. "Yo soy un boxeador! Yo soy un boxeador!" he keeps chanting. He is a boxer. Smoothie Joe is about eighty years old and tough as a piece of dry leather. His white eyes squint so it barely looks like he can see out of them. I hope he doesn't hit the boy. Things might get bad.

Smoothie kept screaming at him about some money he took last night to go buy rum and never came home with. Jose stayed out all night and went out for lobster before day. He came home around ten this morning with the *viejo's* flashlight, a hundred *cordobas* and a shitload of lobster. It looked so damn good. He said we'd eat it later. Joe doesn't understand any of this, but he's drunk and letting out a bunch of shit that he's been waiting to get out since last night when Jose left and didn't bring back the rum. I would tell him, but I don't want to get in the way of a hurricane like this, especially when he's keeping a roof over my head right now and food in my belly. I cooked us up a pile of food this morning, but I'll let him figure that out when he comes down and gets hungry. I hope it doesn't spoil first. He won't even care.

He's eighty years old, but still as hard a black rock. "*Yo soy un hombre*!" he's roaring outside like a lion. He swings his fists in the air like Joe Frazier. His fists look like bricks. He likes to swing his fists around and yell in Spanish when he gets drunk.

He's been at it since last night when we were all sitting around drinking rum on the veranda. Everyone knew it was going to get ugly when he started off the morning with a beer at Tom's. The wheels started rolling. He came back home with another open pint of rum plata. The wheels are coming off now. I wish I was drunk as piss and completely out of control and no one would do a damn thing. That must be a comforting feeling.

I saw him on the little walk I took this morning playing with a group of children, laughing in the middle of them in the shade of a big breadfruit tree on the beach.

I've finally gotten my wish and have all kinds of food brought home from the shop, like everyone tells me I need. I feel awful. My stomach feels like it has a big hole burning through it. I tried to shit this morning, but was so constipated, it was like going through labor.

It felt like trying to push a huge watermelon through a slowly stretching bleeding raisin on the verge of tearing. These drastic changes of lifestyle are taking its toll on my innards. I haven't eaten papaya or coconut for three days. I am dying for a piece of breadfruit. I'm still okay without the bitter oranges, but I miss the bananas. I no longer have any fear of going hungry.

Joe is a hit with the ladies. He walks with a hunch but moves like he's going somewhere. I walk with a straight back and my nose in the clouds like I don't have a clue about my next step. Joe keeps a scowl on his face and barely grouches out a word when he's sober and half of the time when he's drunk. The other half of the time, he's all lit up with smiles, tears and firecrackers.

He's been to San Andres. He's trying to help me get there. What the hell is going to happen when I get there, I have no idea. Something. Should I go to customs? The American consulate? Cartagena? Something will happen.

I like listening to the radio at Joe's. It's nicer than the blaring reggae, *romantico* and dance party mixes playing over all the new lit up CD players around town. It is *volero, vallenato* and *salsa cubana*. It has swing in its *vallenato* hips and *suave* in the *alma* of the piano. It sounds good until the Christian voice comes on and Joe starts getting religious and preacher like. That must be where his son, Olin, gets it from. He's a preacher, carpenter and drug dealer. The other son is in jail for running drugs up in Veracruz, Mexico. His daughter died across the way in San Andres during childbirth. He always talks about his son the preacher. Joe would love to go to church. It would bring peace into his soul he believes. He can't go though. He is a fornicator, living a life of sin after taking another woman after the death of his wife Esther.

He took another woman to get laid like a man, but he really believes it will send his soul to hell to burn in coconut husk fires for eternity. The only thing that's going to send him to hell now is the bottle of rum he can't put down. As for his wife Esther, the real reason he can't go into to church now is because he came running into church piss drunk with a machete looking for her, screaming and cursing her name like the real devil. Shortly afterwards, they say he chopped her Achilles tendon with the same machete, leaving her crippled for the rest of her life.

Right now, his speech is getting slurred as he's yelling at the trail in front of his house. That's why he drinks he says. He's going to hell anyway and this is easing the way. Maybe he's right. Its sure not making heaven on Earth last any longer. He tells me "There's rum you know". I accept and take a sip.

I let the sea into my soul in the morning.

Today there is no wind and the sea is like a lake of salt. The ripples of waves seem to have to hurl themselves onto the beach. They curl up into themselves and wait until the forces that be finally break them smoothly onto the sliding sand. They just ride it in.

There is supposed to be a boat to San Andres today. Benito is sleeping and Kim is finding a phone. I am as the waves, waiting patiently. I have sold my soul to the sea.

Smoothie tells me that two hills can never meet, but two men can. He calls me Jimmy, but I don't correct him. Nor do I say anything when he tells me that gringos don't know nothin' about their history. About when we bombed Yokomate to finish World War Two. About how Moses led his people into Egypt, the littlest country in the East that will one day control the whole world. God's chosen folk. About how we bought Hawaii from the Russians. "It says so right here in the bible. I'm talkin' bout the joke on Lazarus boy!" His eyes light up as he turns his head and spits tobacco juice from the cigarette he's been chewing on. I need to send him some chew when I get back to the states for letting me sleep in the room of one of his dead kids.

Robert slept at Smoothie's place for about a week longer, just trying to pass the time as smoothly as possible, without molesting anyone too much. He found a few little odd jobs around town, helping people carry cargo up from the boat, or picking up rocks from around the beach for the foundation for someone's new house. He tried to buy a little rice and sugar when he could, but mostly he spent his time dodging the pass to San Andres. Several days passed in which he was supposed to leave, but always there was some problem and the boat would never come, or would leave without him or wouldn't go at all. On his last night there, Benito told Robert to be ready, because the panga was going in the night. It was certain, so Robert had to be ready. He packed his bags and said goodbye to Smoothie. It was becoming clear that Smoothie was about ready for him to leave as well. He gave him a cup of black, sweet coffee and a little bit of rice and beans and wished Robert off.

It wasn't certain what time the boat was going to reach. They only new that it would be at night, so at about nine o'clock, he carried his back pack and guitar down to the beach in front and found a beached panga to sit in. There was no one around. He wrapped a joint and looked up at the stars and waited for any sign of movement. There was nothing, only the silence of the night. The village behind him was dark and sleeping and Robert had no idea what to expect. He waited and waited for some sign to come out of the dark sea, but there was nothing. Eventually he fell asleep in the bow of the old panga, but every minute he awoke, thinking that he might have heard something. He walked up the beach a few times but still nothing. He came back to the panga to rest off again, saying he would just sleep there until morning, but across the dark sea, he could hear a breeze blowing in from the Northeast. It was a squall, and he was about to get wet. He threw his be-

longings into the small hull of the panga and tried to squeeze in as best as he could, but it was of little use. The rain began to blow in with the cold wind, and little by little, he was getting soaked. There was nothing to do but wait. The squall soon passed off, but from by the way the weather appeared, there would soon be another one. He grabbed his bag and guitar, and hit back on the sidewalk for Smoothie's. By this time, it was well passed midnight and it didn't look like the Panga was coming anyway. He reached Smoothie's, but it was dark and he was sleeping. He called Smoothie's name outside of his window, but not loud enough to wake anyone up. Things looked bad. What was this low-some life that Robert had led himself into? He remembered an abandoned shed across the way behind a mango tree and a few green coconut trees. He felt sure that he could get in there and rest off from the rain until daylight. No one would molest him there. He hurried over to the shed, pried open one of the windows, and was pleasantly surprised to find an old wooded bed where he could crash. The squall came again, but this time he was safe and warm. He felt happy, like the Gods were smiling upon him. He spread his blanket over the bed and slept sweetly until the sun rose up above the horizon.

In the morning he saw Smoothie. It was clear that he heard his calls the other night, but that didn't matter. They talked and had another cup of coffee and a piece of bread and sat on the veranda like before, listening to the radio silently. After the radio session, Robert hit for the ghetto, where Benito stayed, to see what was the latest. He said that the panga never came in the night before, but was certainly coming tonight. There were two other people there who came from Pearl Lagoon on the mainland, also traveling to San Andres. It was a man and a woman. The man's name was Marlon and the woman was Sonja. It was tonight's panga that they came to meet. Benito told him that he could trust them and not to worry. Marlon would help get him on the panga. He told him just to be ready and to come back at about seven o'clock in the night. "No problem," he said.

San Andres

I made it.

The panga pulled in down the beach aways from where Marlon and I were waiting. It came near the Hotel Delfines. I was already starting to get drunk on the rum some "friend" kept shoving down my throat. Then I found out it was spiked with cocaine or crack. I spit out what I could and felt the numbness of my lips and throat and went to grab my backpack, which was taken from the beached panga where we were awaiting the pick up. I start running around crazy trying to find my bag. The Colombian skiff was already on the shore. The bartender has it I find out, and he's got my bag emptied out on the floor. He doesn't believe it's me in the ID picture. I look at it. I don't believe either.

It's too dark to write. Turn on the light and disconnect from the train you were in.

Stuck in a moment of indecision, whether or not to step outside. Stuck in a moment with the mirror, staring at a maniac.

I finally get the bag back from the bartender, away from Tom the fag, and hurry down the beach hoping to catch the panga before it leaves. I'm feeling the cocaine and thinking it might not be such a bad thing on a trip like this.

By the time I reach the boat, it is just getting ready to launch. I neither hesitate nor ask questions. I ran into the water and jumped up into the skiff.

It was a big panga with a huge hull and two two hundred horsepower engines. It had some muscle.

As soon as I was in, it was a cluster fuck. I could smell Colombian joints being passed around over the thick air of gasoline. I was a little worried for our safety.

The captain was yelling and messing around with one of the engines that kept cutting off. They were trying to siphon gas out of one of the tanks on deck and into the engine, but they were too rushed and couldn't succeed. Everyone was flipping out. They didn't even notice that I was there. They need light to see, but every time someone turned on a flashlight, another yelled about the police.

The captain was a big black guy that reminded me of a Rasta Ton Loc. He had a big belly, and a big bass crass voice. He kept shouting for rum, weed, whiskey or beer. "Rum! Weed!" he would holler, and one of the mates would pass it to him.

By the time that we got out of the *Islita's* harbor, things cooled down a little bit and they realized that they had no idea who I was. "What the fuck? Who the fuck is this?" they yelled.

"*Cual panga*?" someone finally calmed down and asked me.

"*Para San Andres*," I replied.

"How the fuck does he know where we're going?" one of the crew asked themselves.

Then someone vouches for me, that they saw me standing on the beach when Marlon was doing the negotiating.

"Two hundred and fifty dollars," they told me. If not, they said they would drop me back off on the rocks.

We were in such a hurry to get out of there I knew that was a lie. I was a little worried that they might just shoot me and throw me overboard though.

"*No tengo*," I told them. I told them all I had was about forty dollars, which was still an exaggeration. I knew that I had less than thirty dollars in Nicaraguan and Colombian bills together after the few beers I had at the bar and the forty *cordovas* I got swindled out of by two crackheads. It costs twenty *cordovas* a piece.

It didn't matter anymore. I gave them all I had and knew they wouldn't count it until the morning anyway. They took it, but were not happy.

We sped off over the dark, cold sea, crashing over the top of every wave in our way. It didn't matter what was in our way. We were flying blindly.

I got the last space in the boat. I was ass down in the bow, with no foot room on a plastic gas tank lodged in between two big plastic gas drums that held sixty gallons apiece. There was gasoline everywhere. My pants were soaked with it. My dick and balls started to burn from it. I knew this was going to be a long hard ride. I already had to pee. I knew I could hold it for a little bit, but the discomfort was rising.

The boat cracked down after every wave, and each wave cracked me down onto the plastic handle of the gas tank that I knew would soon either smash my tailbone or shoot up my ass. It was uncomfortable to say the least, a condition that would soon rise to pain and anguish and later to joy and recovery.

By the time we saw the helicopter and the first police boat, the captain of the panga was so drunk that he was slurring his speech and it was difficult for anyone to understand what he was saying. At first, the boats were little more than red lights in the distance. The plane could have been a star.

"Hey, you watch for da plane," he said. "Keep eye on dat boat. Where de boat gone?" he stammered.

"Gimme de gun. Get de guns!" he slurred.

One of the crew jumped past me into the hull, pulled out a black canvas bag and handed it back behind me. I didn't look back to see what type of guns they were.

"Keep watchin' da plane! Whe de plane? Whe de plane?"

We were getting much closer to the boats now. I feel certain that if they were looking, they could have seen us. We took it nice and slow, trying to sneak away without them hearing or seeing the white of our wake in the black sea. I was just waiting for a big spotlight to shine right on us. We were so close we could see the lights on in their ship.

There was no light at all on in our panga. They put away the GPS when we got close like this. They weren't even smoking.

I was wondering what else there was down in the hull and if I would be expected to shoot if things started to get hot. By this point, I'd already pissed in my pants once and feeling it warm and pleasant, decided to let the pressure go again.

A few days ago on the *Islita*, I got some work going on a panga to pick up a load of rocks. On the way to the other side of the island where the rocks were, we had orders to dump out all of the *patron*'s garbage into the sea. It was a disgusting thing to do, but we didn't ask questions, and just did it. I feel that I could have just as easily shot back at the police if it came down to it. I cannot believe that I was rationalizing these things.

After sneaking around the last police boat at an angle so they could not cut us off if we were seen, the captain hit the mother-fucking gas, and we felt the power that his twin engines could thrust. He turned it up to eleven. It was like we reached a point where he no longer cared if they heard us or saw us, because he was sure they weren't going to catch us. He just hit it and didn't give a ras about the Babylon.

The boat crashed and toppled over the waves. The boat felt as drunk as the captain, jumping back and forth and cracking up and down. The boat felt unstable. It felt out of control.

I had already pissed in my pants several times and no longer worried at all about the pain in my bladder. The new pain was from the smashing of the boat and the gas tanks in my ribs, forearms and ass.

It was so dark you couldn't see the waves coming. I had to constantly brace myself by flexing my leg and arm muscles in hope supporting my weight a bit.

I tucked my left arm in against my side in effort to block my ribs at the cost of my forearms. I knew that a broken arm would be better than a broken rib.

All I could do was count the hours and spit out the salt water that splashed into my face, burning my eyes. The trip was only supposed to take three or four hours, so we should nearly have been there by now. The only concession was the faster we raced away from the police, the quicker we would arrive. We were flying.

Just as the boats seemed to be safely out of site, problems began. One of the engines shut down and we stopped.

Nobody knew what to do. All I could do was thank God for the little bit of rest. I did not know how much more cracking I could take before I passed out. I was happy for a minute, and then I realized that we could be in serious problems, floating around out here on the sea without any chance of outrunning the Babylon if they showed up, we would be screwed.

The captain and crew kept getting the engine running for a moment, only to have it die a few seconds later. We were getting nowhere.

The sun began to rise, and the booze and ganja were beginning to wear off the captain. Everyone was tired. They were hungover. We were supposed to be there already.

There was a lot of arguing about whether or not to try and fix it, or just limp back into San Andres on one engine. But what if there was a problem and we had to move, the captain said. On one engine we would move too slow, and wouldn't reach back till noon anyway. This was too slow.

We were all getting hungry. There was no food. We were getting thirsty, but there was no water. The sun rose higher and hotter, and before long, we were sitting ducks in broad daylight.

Marlon seemed to know about engines and was telling them it was the power pack. Finally they listened to him and got the engine running again. I was relieved but pained again by our newly acquired speed. I was the only one without a seat and on top of that, located up in the bow. The bruising began again.

It was the hardest, most enduring test I had ever undergone, but eventually we spotted land and the hills of San Andres ahead on the horizon. No one knew how to go about making an arrival like this in broad daylight, but there was nothing to do but just go for it. We got a little bit closer, and they ordered me and Marlon to get down.

I crouched up in a ball underneath a chair in the stern, ducked my hooded head and didn't look up. They said the coast guard would be watching, and a gringo would look suspicious. I took their word for it and prayed that this ride would be over soon.

When the panga pulled into Rocky Caye, San Andres, everything got crazy. I was hunched down in the back corner of the boat, underneath some Colombians, in a pool of gasoline and saltwater.

"*Levantase*! Get up! Hurry man! Run!" The captain and crew started yelling at me. I moved.

Surprised to finally see land, I jumped right out of the panga and cut my feet on the coral rocks below. "*Rapida! Rapida!*" they hollered as one of the crew threw by guitar and my bag into a docked fishing skiff.

"*Y las chanelas*?" I yelled to the man to throw my sandals, but it was no use.

Marlon and Sonja were already on land when I saw them, but they told me to run fast. There was no time to talk, only to move.

I didn't look back. I realized that I must have looked like a lunatic, soaking wet, barefoot in a big blue sweatshirt and long grey pants, but there was nothing I could do about any of that now. I waved down the first cab that drove by and rolled in.

We dropped off the other two passengers and I told the driver to drive to a cash machine. The first one we found wouldn't accept my card. There was a problem with the next one too. I started to get nervous again. I kept looking around behind us to see if there were any police following us. Everything seemed cool. After checking a few more cash machines, I finally found a bank to give me some money. I took a huge sigh of relief and told the driver to just wait a minute. I walked into a little cafe next door, used the bathroom, changed my clothes and ordered a big glass of *nispero* juice. It felt good to be back in Colombia.

The first order of business, now that I had a little money, dry clothes and a little something in my dehydrated stomach, was to get some sandals on my feet. I told the taxi driver to find a little *zapateria*, but before we turned off the street, there was a little stand on the corner with all kinds of cheap plastic sandals. I bought an inexpensive denim pair that nearly fit, and got back in the cab. I couldn't tell the driver the name of the place I was headed to, but if he got to the airport, I could find it. I didn't remember what the name of the hotel-like place that I stayed in the last time I was in San Andres, but I remembered that it was within walking distance of the airport.

As we reached closer to the airport, things began looking familiar. I still kept looking behind us, but nothing followed. Everything was cool.

I told the driver to go around the long curve, to take a left when we hit the beach, to take another left when we reached the corner at the *pescadero*, and then in front of us on the left hand side, there it was again, the same as it was before, the Residencial Restrepo.

"*Aqui, aqui senor*," I told the driver. I told him to wait while I went and checked everything out. They had rooms, and it cost about four dollars a night. That was fine for right now. Just get me inside where I can shut the door and lay down. I paid off the taxi driver, gave him a little tip for his helpfulness and had the tall, balding, brown skinned workman show me the room. It was the same room as before, up the stairs and the last room on the left. It was perfect.

The room had a double bed and little glass window with bars on the outside. There was a bathroom with a shower and toilet, and a small desk with a mirror above it.

I set down my backpack, took of my clothes, took a long cool shower and examined my battered body. I smoked a small piece of a mashed up joint that I picked up in the panga when I was squatted down underneath the captain coming into San Andres. Something for the brains.

After the joint and a minute in front of the mirror, I made my way down the stairs to check out the situation in this little pension I had just checked into. There was a little *kiosko* outside of the front gates that seemed like the neighborhood gathering place. They sold beer, juice, *gaseosas*, chips, candy, toilet paper and some other little things that people like to buy. It offered a few white plastic chairs where eight or nine people could sit around and listen to music and talk about whatever was happening. I grabbed an open seat and ordered a Colombian tree tomato juice. I remembered the loud-mouthed lady who ran the thing. Her name was Estella. She was in the pension when I was here before. She had a funny quality to her. She reminded me of medusa in some kind of way, with her long hair extensions that she sat and let the young girls tie in. She had a mysterious way that made her look like she understood the black arts of witchcraft. Maybe she didn't know anything, but she had something that set her apart from the rest of the other people in this world that you see one time and don't remember at all.

Estella put the tree tomatoes and sugar into the blender and served me the "*liquado*" cold. I drank my juice and tried not to look too high. It was sweet. I didn't feel hungry. I walked back into the shady pension from the sunny street, and retired to my room again. I slept for the rest of the day.

The pension was well planted up. All kinds of trees grew around the yard. Noni, coconuts, mangos and avocados were all around, keeping the place with a cool ambient. There were basil, vervine, wandering Jew and oregano plants growing scattered about, not to mention the other flowers and bush that I didn't know. It wouldn't be a bad place to relax for a few days until I found somewhere else.

I am getting a warm tingling feeling throughout chest, chin, fingers and shins. I don't know if it's the water or the wine. I don't know if I should seek help or give it.

Upon my arrival, all I cared to do was sleep, drink good water and smoke a tiny bit of ganja, sleep, sleep, sleep and drink juice of *tomate del arbol,* the Colombian tree tomato.

I saw two *militares* here at the *residencial*, when I went to refill my water bottle, and I wondered what they were doing.

I fell to a fever yesterday. In the morning I had diarrhea. I thought I was shitting blood, but that must have been from the beats I ate with breakfast. Today has been a *dia vegetariana.* Not even a little butter.

My ribs, shins, hips and forearms are black and blue from the trip, but feeling better. My upper left hamstring and lower back are still sore. It could be my kidneys, or just a muscle problem. They could both use some rest.

Today my shit is better. My bruises are starting to heal. Getting here was a crazy and rough adventure. Racing and chasing with cops and choppers with guns that are ready to shoot beneath the moonless night. It is no joke when you're dealing with the mafia.

It amazes me how one can have so little to do that he turns to art. Or drinking. Then eventually working.

I want to paint and rest my body when I finally move in someplace. Perhaps I see a doctor about this pain in the back of my leg. Maybe a week without booze, coffee or work will help. Painting sounds like a pleasant way to pass the time.

If I wrote down half of the poems that dream through my head, I would be a prophet instead of this two bit vagabond bum living in the cheapest room to rent underneath the airport until his money runs out or health recovers enough to travel again.

So for the meantime now, what should I paint? A portrait of my guitar, battered and shattered; crooked and bent, out of time and out of key and out of the bag to breathe. There's a crack in the neck about to blow up. The strings are a mixture classic and steel strings, just trying to keep together a full set. The first string is a second string and the fourth sting is a third. Some kind of way.

I'd like to write and explain what is happening to me write now, but I think I'd rather just lie down again. I have a feeling that I've got some kidney problems.

If my hamstring, fevers and nausea don't stop by Monday, I'm going to the hospital. I hope I last till Monday.

I'm in San Andres. In a cheap hotel/hospital room where I've been hiding out for the past five days, I am hoping to heal my self.

I haven't been getting out much lately. I made it outside for a little while today to sit in the driveway and watch things pass by on the street. Mostly I sit in this room locked down, reading *War and Peace,* touching the guitar and breathing deeply.

Stella gave me three quarters of the money I lent her back. I'm in no hurry.

I wonder if I have AIDS. I was scared to even write that.

I tell myself not to worry and just listen to the silence. That's all there is anyway, just a big silence that is as loud or quiet as we can take it. We're all just a part of it.

I have cut my diet down to lemon water and ganja, but only one or two hauls a day.

A fast has a mental and physical side to it, if there is a distinction between the two. All of a sudden, you have nothing to fill your day with. The worry of food has completely vanished, or completely filled your life, never appeasing itself. There is no worry of looking for food, preparation or buying of food. That part of life that is so much a part of us leaves. In its place, we are left with a great opening. There is nothing to look forward to but rest and meditation. No treats, no pleasures. Only lemon water. Lemon is the only flare of taste or preparation. Lemon joy.

Two bananas and a bag of bread I bought yesterday just caught my attention. I wonder if they will spoil by the time I feel well enough to eat.

So here I am, beginning to smell this hotel room, the same one I was in a few years ago, just waiting to recover enough of my health to move on again. Either move on, or find out why the hell the waving forces of God have swirled me back to this same room. It was certainly not for love or answers. To find the answer would take generations, eternities. It is futile to try to find some kind of beginning. If there is one, we must all share it. If there is one, we're all the same.

It would seem logical to say that existence implies beginning. That if one is, then one once began. That if one is, then they once were not. It is not so. Where does a sperm come from? God? It is not so.

Aura has gone to Bogotá with her *marido*.

And they all say "Why did you want to get back to San Andres so bad?" And all I can say is "For a woman."

I think of all the perfectly good women I've left, just to get here alone and estranged, and I must ask, "Who you gonna run from now?"

Sitting around all day with absolutely nothing to do, a little bit of marijuana goes a long way.

Someone just reminded me what happens to Americans in Colombia who start getting involved with drugs and the guerilla. Kids whose parents want them to come home. They get kidnapped and ransomed.

Ahh! "Good," I say. I'll tell my parents it is for a good cause; that they can use it as a tax write of for charity.

Or they get killed for fucking around. Or they get busted by the police.

In my new Rasta man friend Octavius', Tattoo's, room, he was showing me how he could smuggle one hundred and fifty grams of cocaine inside an aluminum perfume canister. The side of it said "TESTER. If you are offered this product, someone has stolen it". It was written in English and Italian. He can't read. I didn't like that.

It's not like that in the *Islita* though. In the *Islita*, everything is cool.

Jesus took a hooker, Mary Magdalene, and called her his Alma. He never had to pay for her. She just liked being around him, that's all, like normal girls do. Even if she was addicted to cocaine and whoring herself out in the bars on the side, she never did any of that when Jesus was around. And he loved her, and she him.

A pound of pot here in San Andres sells for about seventy dollars. Just across the way in Little Island right now, it sells for three hundred dollars. From there, the price goes up the further North and inland you go.

In Cartagena, a pound only costs about twenty dollars. That's before the long and treacherous boat ride across the Wide Sargasso Sea to San Andres.

They run it along with the cocaine in big ass pangas with huge hulls and three two hundred horsepower engines, one for each of the three tons of cocaine they carry.

A kilo of cocaine in the *Islita* is going for three thousand eight hundred dollars. I don't know what one costs here, probably about two thousand dollars or less.

I know a kid in the *Islita*, a neighbor boy of mine from when I lived back in the bush. He lived a little bit further back in the bush. He found a bunch of coke washed up on the beach in front of my house one morning.

He tried to sell it so they could start a better life for themselves off of other people's farms. He must have found about twenty kilos. He tried to sell the stuff, but was robbed during the deal at gunpoint. They came to his house with AK-47's and took the stuff.

Wicho, the boy, told me that they still had some more buried back in the bush. He told me he would sell it to me for two thousand five hundred dollars. All I would have to do is take it to a guy on the other side of the island who buys for thirty-eight, and I make thirteen hundred bucks a kilo. If he has five kilos, that a pile of money for everyone. I start a better life for myself, and buy a farm and Wicho's enormous family gets off the farm.

If I make the right connection, which could be given to me by Estrella's husband, I could make this trip to San Andres worth my time. I only have to wait now for the right boat out of here and back to the *Istlia*, carry six pounds of marijuana, leaving me with one thousand dollars and the connection. For some reason, I don't feel right about taking it by Benito's place. I'll bring him a pound as a present for helping me out.

I am starting to feel little bit stronger. There is a little spring in my step. I am starting to have less difficulties eating. Perhaps I will even sleep tonight.

Morning has come and I feel the strength to accomplish anything, even write.

I have another full day ahead of me with nothing at all to accomplish. I tell myself I'm going to go to the post office or go use the telephone to call Maria's father and see if he had any luck recovering my journal that Maria might have left behind. It's probably a long shot anyway. These things can surely wait and so can I.

I feel like I may be waiting here in San Andres for a little while longer. It is good for me. It is good for the moon and the light for traveling. "I believe in the moon," Drennan told me once.

A week more of recovering and hotel living will be alright. I've got a deal worked out with Estella that she gives me my food everyday for the interest on the money I lent her. It's a rice and beans lunch, but it is good for me.

It is good that I lent her the money. She says she's going to help me get off this island. Whatever happens with the little money I have left now, the money is already down to leave when my time is up.

Sometimes I feel like San Andres is a prison and my room a cell. Perhaps it is because I'm out of pot. I've made friends with some guys on the lower rows who have been here for a while in the cheapest place to stay.

That's what prisons end up being, the absolute cheapest place to stay. Where people go when they have no more money and turn to a life of crime on the streets. The big boys have all the right people paid off already.

To get around San Andres, you just have to be cool and not draw any attention to yourself. It is difficult to do sometimes being a gringo hanging out with locks headed Rasta men.

Maria Vanegas, Aura, was not here when our hero, the author, arrived in San Andres.

After a few days of sleeping, resting and gathering strength, I finally made it back to her house on a long walk through the hot midday sun.

"*A la orden*?" someone asked as I was snooping around her neighbor's yards looking for her house.

I walked over and looked the neighbor in the eye and ask if the man knew where a *muchacha* named Aura lived. The neighbor did not understand.

I then remembered the name Maria Vanegas as the image of an old hotmail inbox computer screen flashed across my third eye.

He knew her and smiled and directed me around the corner towards her door.

I walked up the stone steps to say "*Halo*?" where two skinny sickly looking dogs stood barking feebly in the yard.

I said hello again, but no one seemed to be home.

I turned around to leave and saw a man walking up the stairs whose appearance resembled the dogs a little bit. It was her father Roberto.

"*Te conoces*?" he asked with a comforting smile. I remembered how much I had sincerely liked her father the last time we had met.

Aura had a magical relation with her father. Every other girl I had ever been with has had a father that I couldn't stand being around for one reason or another. Roberto felt warmly comfortable.

I wanted to ask him if he wanted to go out for a beer and a smoke, but I decided to wait. He said that he remembered me from the other year.

Maria's gone to Bogotá he tells me, with her new husband Greg. Everything is just as I imagine, always.

I ask him if he knows anything about the little black book that I left with her and he says, "*Ah, el diario*".

"Yes" I said, feeling uplifted that he remembered the book.

"*No se que hizo con eso*," he said. He didn't know if she took it to Bogotá or left it here.

I was relieved not to hear "or she threw it out," as one of the possible locations.

He said he'd have to ask his wife about it and then gave me his phone number, and told me to call.

I walked down the hill with a strange and indescribable feeling in my head. It made me want to chuckle.

I continued my long walk afterwards and laughed about how many perfectly good women I'd left to come her alone, miles and miles and miles and miles away from anyone I knew, in the middle of this huge sea of lulling waves and *brisas*.

The *volero* music has stopped playing on Estella's radio down below. I have a wonderful balcony to observe the breezes and voices above the courtyard here at the Residencial Restrepo.

Turn on the fan. Blow out the light. Turn on the light. Turn off the night.

Everything in life repeats in some way. Maybe if these things can be resolved, they will stop repeating. Maybe that is why they keep coming up again and again, demanding that they be resolved, that a new solution to some conflict is needed.

Sunday morning. Went to church in the ocean. My eyes are still red from the swimming. My breeze is blowing. The words aren't flowing. Put up the pen and take a walk to the seaside. Sit at the *pescadero*. Take a nap. *Almorzar*. Get out de trap of this island. Drink some water.

Octavio's been downstairs since yesterday morning, shaking off the last several days of hard living with rum and cocaine and without food or water. Food and water, especially water, are the two things that drugs take away from you. If water is life, death works by stealing her. That is how drugs sneak into people's lives and suck it away.

Octavio's been shivering with a fever and vomiting up his innards. He is jittery and fidgety and talking one hundred miles per hour. He is desperate.

He threw some stones at my window last night and told me to come quick. He needed a hundred pesos. I came down and found Jennifer with him. He looked sick. He looked like an emaciated rodent about to die.

His bony legs shook beneath the sheets and he muttered for Advil. He needed Advil.

Jennifer asked me to go next door to the shop for some *fruitilla*, powdered fruit mix to help the water go down like a spoonful of sugar. I told him that I had something better than Advil that I brought from Nicaragua when I remembered my pain and fever pills.

"Uh, Nicaragua," he muttered in a raspy grunt which reminded me of Koto, my old Polish linebacker coach who smoked two packs a day.

I went by the store and brought the pills and *fruitilla*. He threw everything back up right away. His body heaved and convulsed trying to purge itself its surplus of toxins. I mixed some more water with *fruitila*.

Estella is like the mother of this big messed up family here at the Residencial Restrepo. She cooks a big lunch everyday of rice and beans and always gives me and Jorge, the drunk *viejo*, the leftovers at suppertime after we help her close down at night.

There's too much sugar in rum. I feel that I am addicted to sugar. If I do not get it in my beer or coffee, I find it in the sweets on the street. If I'm not getting it there, it's from the fruits on the trees. The bananas and the coconut or the rice. Sugar, salt and cocaine. White powders. Stay away from white powder, legal or illegal, it doesn't matter.

I wonder what kind of role the church has in this drug trade import/export business.

I think that today I'll go for a walk and draw a picture of this big warehouse looking building near the airport. It has a big sign on the outside saying something like "Jesus Christ International" or "Church of God Shipping Co." It must be the Romans from Rome, Italy. There are piles of Italians here. "*Italiano*?" people ask me all the time. All these mafia people must come from the Vatican. What would they make their money on with no drugs and no religion? They've got a huge hand in Latin America. America's got the oil. Italy's got the mafia.

I'm getting a little shaky. I need a water break.

I met a guy out on Johnny Caye the other day named Popeyo. He was huge. He looked like an All-Pro Middle Linebacker. He's got a boat and charters people around the Cayes or wherever they need to go. He's careful about who he gives his card to. He told me a story about the big mafia boss man around San Andres, the richest guy on the island. He is getting old, and about to die, and when he does, all his business, all his shit, his name is going to be handed down to his son, who happens to be a crackhead. He is a bad crackhead. He's always taking things and fucking them up, getting into trouble, selling his stuff for crack.

His father always gave him everything that he wanted. Anything he could ever need, he bought it for him. Cars that he crashed, girls that he fucked, houses he trashed, everything. Finally, his father, who's got nightclubs and businesses all over Colombia, decides to bring a girl up to the island from Bogotá. A beautiful girl. The most beautiful hooker from all of his clubs, all for him, just to settle him down some. He can fuck her, suck her, take her out or take her home or get rid of her, whatever he wants to do with her, just to keep him out of trouble. Well things go well with her. They fall in love and smoke plenty of crack, and it turns out, she's more trouble than he is. Together, they start getting wilder than ever.

Now the old man is about to die and everything is starting to be run by the son. "That is what everyone around here calls good luck," says Popeyo.

Stuck in the room again, afraid of the door, dreaming of prophets and life outside. A deep breath worth breathing. Holy water worth drinking. Salt of the Earth and of the damned. The *Virgen* del Carmen, locking the door, the entrance and the exit are one in the same.

The islanders are talking about revolution. They are speaking in Creole, so no one else understands, taking their part away from the Colombians and giving it back to the colored man.

"It's the *Panas*," says Castillo Bryan. "The *Panas* been trying to kill us off for years. Killing us off with their *Fogata* matches and their poisons, so they can buy our land. All of it."

"Deh's just too many of a dem teefs. Dem teefen' de ho island. Dis Black Man island. We's English. English learned . . . "

It is strange things that will catch your eye sometimes.

A twenty pesos piece that's now out of circulation due to inflation, so someone has tossed it to the street. A papaya across the yard. The third hole on a cane flute on the bed. Perception is limited. Perception is infinite, but what the brain chooses to recognize at any given moment is limited. L I M . . .

I need to negotiate with Stella's mother, the owner of the *residencial*, about the price of my room.

I have been hiding away under the excuse of lethargy and hospital time. My back and leg pain is nearly completely healed, but not completely. I still get a tinge of remembrance. I think that a drink would kill me. Why is that what I want most?

I have finally come to the conclusion that there is nothing of my past left here in San Andres.

After two and a half weeks of being here and waiting on word from Aura's father, our hero received word that his journal of love letters and poems and names and phone numbers and descriptions of the places he had been and women he'd conquered throughout Australia and South America; with sketches and outburst from the God within him; with his first attempts at art without ever knowing what art is; with sappy thoughts and songs about love and forgotten lyrics about his insides; was officially gone.

How could it all be lost? How could his poetry and his past, his dreams be shattered? Where was it resting?

When her father talked with Maria, she said it was supposed to be there. She had not taken it with her to Bogotá, with her *marido* Greg. Who was this *marido* Greg? It just sounded funny and awkward, the two words together, a word so romantic and Latin, "*marido*", and the blunt gringo word Greg.

I don't give a damn about that. It was a lesson about love and expecting people to wait on you. Nothing waits in this world, therefore there are no excuses. There is complete justice without any morals. You love who you are with, like it or not. I live alone. I am alone. Am I a narcissist? If I loved myself, then why would I not care for myself, or is that the nature of love? To kill? To flee. To run. To Colombia, where one can be sure.

Nearly two years passed since he promised to return to retrieve his heart. He said "I love you" into the night wind as he walked away from her house that night. He might have heard the wind reply, but he was probably stoned or drunk, or both. He promised to return. She promised to remove his mask.

I try not to make a habit of having too many cokehead friends because sooner or later, they all end up hitting you up for money. I say that, but the last three friends I have had have been helpless addicts. Smoothie Joe wasn't. He was too old to get hooked. Jose certainly was. Harrington, who got me up to Bluefields, which in turn got me here in the shape I'm in for better or worse, afraid to pick up my pen and write of the story I've been telling myself in my sleep. The wind feels to have been knocked out of me.

I have not yet landed on my feet from the blow after blow the wind continues to give me. If it is the heaviness of the kidneys in my back, or the realization that I will never get back to my past, my words or my thoughts, they are lost and annihilated. Their beautiful matching will never again be so perfectly put together or remembered with the exception of small fragments of songs remembered.

My memory has been destroyed and now too is my collection. My heart has been thrown away into the rubble bubble of yesterday's garbage. Someone looked at it and decided that it was not even worth the space that it occupied and then threw it in the gutter.

Colombia is full of whores. Nothing but whores. The true nature of sexuality and relationships is revealed.

Oh Sweet Nicole Sampson, the sweetest thing I have ever tasted and fear that I ever will, where have you gone?

Oh how many trees our hero has killed with poetic spaces and indentions and time skipping masturbation that have no business existing in the first place. . .

Tonight I got sick and fucking tired of being poor, of being alone, of being sick, of eating rice and beans three times a day (although I must say that beans have never failed to make me happy). So tonight I mixed my pot with some fine German tobacco, picked up my guitar, which has not called to me in some time, and began to sing sad old country loved songs about cowboys and mothers and suns going down. "So what you gonna do when your sun goes down?"

I'm going to rest, sleep and hope that in the morning I awake alive and with energy. If not I will sleep till noon.

I've paid off this room until Tuesday. Forty pounds of ganja came into the airport today, so maybe the guys will want to get rid of a chunk quick and sell me a six pounds for three hundred and fifty dollars. Maybe eight pounds for four hundred. I would settle for six pounds for four hundred. That would leave me with two hundred dollars for the boat back to Little Island, and keep me within my budget.

The Residencial Restrepo becomes very intense three or four times a day, whenever a plane takes off right about our head. A huge roar runs through your heart and ears, filling the world with a vibration that rattles the walls, windows and doors, and for a moment, everything stops. In this hurricane of noise, a silence overtakes everything while all is drowned out by the jet engine. It's intense but after years of being here, the people do not even notice it. They just go right on though moving their lips and talking like nothing is happening. It is like the church bells that chime unnoticed in the streets of a small snowy town in Pennsylvania every quarter an hour to keep the workers on time. It is the dripping of water or ticking of clocks or addiction that sneaks into your heart unnoticed and unfelt. It is the pain I felt when I lost love so long ago, as it faded slowly into the night. It never disappears, one just gets used to living with it. It is how time heals all wounds. They never really heal, we just become accustomed. I have dedicated this night to Norberto the clown who taught me how to be free.

So that's what I'm going to do. I'm going to walk on off of this island with as much pot as I can carry, and if anyone tries to fuck with me, I will stab them in their throat quickly and silently. I will not worry about eating anymore. I am tired of that, but full nonetheless. I am tired of complaining of nothing and being a miser. I hope this deal goes down cool and my health continues to improve as the moon continues to wane. I hope I get out of here again.

The glands beneath my chin are swelling. I look bloated in the neck. I should consider waiting a few days before heading west to Nicaragua, where the next hospital is Managua. It seems strange to me that Houston is only a two to three hour flight. So is Nicaragua.

Willard, the eye twitching drunk fisherman, dances for beer because his heart is filled with joy. He is simple, a simpleton. He is the most intelligent person around here. He was. He used to be the Secretary of Agriculture and an excellent musician before he sold his clarinet for drugs. Now he just drinks rum and fishes. He is renowned as one of the best fishermen on the island when he is sober. He does not fish when he has money. When he has money, he drinks rum. When the money is done, he goes fishing again.

I feel to vomit. I must step away from the mirror and this so called literature.

I am *pegado* in San Andres. Passing my days at the *pescadero* in the beached boats beneath the shade of coconut trees, I wait, watching the old fishermen drink Dorian's Gin and slam dominos. Enjoying the breezes, checking out the fishermen when they come in, weighing their catch of bonitos, baracudas, snapper and mackeral. The fishing seems good. Everyday they come in with their hundred pounds or more. I am jealous of their life. They are strong warriors of the sea. They are hard. They eat well and drink better. I am sustaining myself on rice and beans and pasta and *bienestarina* (well fare flour). I am turning into a watery bread-ball, but haven't the money for fruits and vegetables anymore.

Another helicopter just took off to patrol the island and keep any *lanchas contrabandos* at home again, so here again, I will patiently wait until the good opportunity comes to leave. When you hurry up your dead.

Rubia, the fat *peroncha* across the hall admitted to my Sherlock Holmes imitation, that it was she who stole my one hundred and seventy dollars. Her mother is paying me back the full amount on Monday. I cursed her with the threat of a heart attack and when the Colombian police that I paid off threatened to take the fingerprints, she caved in and turned to begging forgiveness, friendship and a payment plan. I said just give me the money.

I don't know if I look good, bad or crazy. I wish that I had Marylee here to tell me I look like shit. Give me a reality check. The glands in my neck are still swollen. All of this money and drugs give me stress. I am reaching new and interesting levels of meditation at the *Pescadero*.

Sitting here on the balcony, watching the rain come in off the sea again, it is another night I will not be leaving. I can hear Rubia sniffling to her mother down the hall as if I should pity her careless, stupid thievery. This last month in San Andres of waiting endlessly has sucked the money from my pockets and the blood from my veins.

Yesterday, I came back to my room from the balcony, to find the door open. I knew right away that something was wrong. I immediately see my purse laying open on the table. I knew that I had been robbed. At first, I panicked. Then I settled down and knew right away who it was: the fat bitch, Rubia, who lives across the hall.

Immediately, I put on my shoes and walked into town, searching for her at all the shops where she could change a hundred dollars. I didn't have any luck. When I came home, I saw Estella and her husband Pacheco. They were sure that it was Rubia too. They told me not to worry. They would get that money back. It was the money that I needed to pay for the boat that they were getting the contact for. Worse they wanted that money back. Pacheco had some friends that were policemen, and he would beg them to do a favor. He said he'd get them over right away.

In a few hours the police came by, and they were past cool. They went right up to Rubia and told her that they knew it was her. They told her that they had her fingerprints all over the purse and the doorknob, and if she didn't pay back the money right way, they were going to carry her to jail. It was all a lie, just trying to break her down.

That was all that Rubia needed to hear. She started balling. She called her mother to come bail her out, because she'd already spent all the money. She said she'd have the money in a few days, but she just needed a little time. No problem.

I am becoming a master at sitting and waiting. I am gaining weight on my pure carbohydrate diet. I am turning into the Buddha. This quitting of smoking ganja has been fairly unsuccessful. It would be easier if there were anything else to occupy my time than waiting. Tomorrow I should get my money back from Rubia's mother to pay for the boat, and we should be off before midnight. The President Uribe has left the island, and the skies and waters should be once again clear of Babylon.

I know that I'm going to die in my sleep one of these nights. I'll just go to sleep and never return. Who's to say that it hasn't already happened?

I always have these dramatic dreams that I don't recall. I don't even know if they are dreams. All I know is that I wake up, gasping for air, my heart fighting to beat. It's as if I didn't remember to wake up, I wouldn't remember to breathe or beat my heart. Its as if my heart had already stopped and I need to wake up to start it back up in time. I know that one time I will not wake up in time. Tatu know's it too.

"Sure, plenty of people do it," Octavio said. "Just go to sleep and don't wake up".

It is interesting that he said that tonight. It is the one thing I have kept on promising myself to write, but have been too afraid to. Ha! Put it into words and it becomes prophecy.

But can I change it? Just like that, say, "I will live". Create my own destiny with the thoughts in my head. Can it be done? We shall see tomorrow, if the morrow doth come.

Wasting the days of my youth away, sitting on my ass, minding the little shop for Estella.

Take time for what its worth and spend it.

All I really wanted this morning was some beans and a piece of bread. Some bush tea would have been nice, but I have no stove. Harrington always claimed that something warm first thing in the morning was the best, something to take the slime off your stomach. I drink my urine first thing. Then I hit a shot of Noni. Then I look some beans. So what would I do with more money? Be more idle? Impossible. Eat more veggies? Eat more fish. I haven't been drinking, or smoking very much. All I want, is a small piece of land. Perhaps I'd buy some presents for my friends and family at Christmas.

How I got myself to where I am so naturally, I will never understand. The steps I am taking are unconscious. I cannot stop what I am flowing into. The people I associate with. The drug dealers and cokeheads I so casually walk up to and discuss the price of pounds of ganja.

No one can believe it when they see a gringo buying a joint in Vietnam. That's what they call the neighborhood where the drug dealers live. It really favors Vietnam. You have to be careful that you don't get your ass blown up. I catch plenty of looks walking in there. I often forget that I am a gringo. That is probably how I manage to play it so normal. In the back of my head, I wonder if they're all thinking they're going to rob me, but it's really all cool. It's good that Octavio introduced me. They would have never talked to me otherwise. Everyone either thinks that a gringo is DEA or has money. People that know me are sure that I don't have money. I tell myself that I have money, but my life shows me otherwise.

Tomorrow, all of that will change. Stella tells me she's going to help me with the boat ride. She's putting me on a boat with some *Peruanos* and an *Africano* who her husband is helping get across. We are slaves. Someone is paying them to smuggle dirt-poor people across to Nicaragua and then up the coast to Puerto Cabeza and then hopefully up to the States. It is the same route that the drugs make. The *Peruanos* and Africans will probably be carrying a load for someone in exchange for their pass. It reminds me of the Triangle Trade Route that we used to learn about in the history books with the rum, sugar and slaves in the Imperial days. It is the same shit.

She says she's going to call her Italian friend about some ganja that may come in tomorrow. There's no pot in Nicaragua right now. What a hero I am. Risking life, limb and freedom to bring hope and color to the lives of poor people at the hour of sunset. Another night boat across the sea. There is no moon. They say it's a smooth ride back to Nicaragua. The tough part is getting here.

Octavio's nephew, Edwin, who I knew, died in his sleep suddenly on Thursday night.

Love writes words better than the mind, and better than the soul. Love writes words without fear and sings songs without hesitation. It is the only thing worth singing about. It is a shame that I am no longer worthy of its grace of presence or praise or sunshine or shadows. This whole day has seemed like a dreamlike deja vu. San Andres is the only place on the road I have ever returned to.

I have been here over a month now, and am going back tomorrow again. I'm worried about going to jail, but it's too late to turn back. In this game, you don't know whom to trust. Everyone tells you you can't trust someone else. Everyone wants you to believe in them. These things must be felt out.

I believe that God is law. Not the law of right and wrong and church and state, but the laws of motion, dictating every predetermined step. It governs the rising and falling of the tide and the waxing and waning of the moon. The magnetic forces that push and pull particles along their predetermined paths. Movement is life, and laws govern that movement. I have seen it proven over and over again in mathematics with God's invisible tools of numbers; his fingerprints that he has left on everything existing.

Where did it begin, the steps that I took to get me here? To be named Gringo in this cheap hotel with dirty sheets and dirty bathroom. Sitting in the morning, sunrays break through the bars of my Eastern window, preparing me for a journey back to Nicaragua, on which I may or may not return. I left Costa Rica, Cartagena, Chile, Argentina step by step with nowhere left to go but right in front of myself. The only choice I have is whether or not to carry with me some *contrabando* when I go, and that decision was made years ago, before I even needed the money. It is natural. It is no choice at all, only the next step, leading me to jail or to freedom, if such a thing truly exists. The freedom to accept the fate willed to me by God, blowing the leaves on the mango trees and consuming the time that has already passed and producing the future that lies in this next word in return.

As far as love goes, we must only wait for its credence to come back around on the turntable.

There is a strange and mysterious lanky looking gringo old man that stays in a little apartment downstairs. No one knows anything about him, except that he's been here for a long time. He always wears big dark sunglasses, and can only be spotted moving quickly from a taxicab to his room, carrying a bag of groceries. He doesn't say anything, but moves like he's on rails. I've seen him several times, but never said anything to him. I don't think he's ever seen me. He doesn't seem to notice anything on his direct walk into his apartment, except the step right in front of him. Something connected us the other day, and I ended up smoking a joint with him in his apartment, and learned that he was a student of some mad poet, that I can't remember the name of, but have read some of his works. The guy wrote "Bird of Paradise", R.D. Lang or something. We exchanged some books and thoughts about meditation. Anyway, he gave me a few of his letters that he sits stoned in his apartment and throws out of his mad typewriter. This one is called "True Sanity". It makes sense to me.

"True Sanity is arranging yourself so the Divine in you can come out. So God can come to His world through you and everyone else. God wants to come into this Earth through us. So true sanity would be getting yourself so that you could let the Divinity come out through you. It will be in your individual way, as you were put here to do something no one else could do.

True sanity would be serving something bigger than yourself. True sanity is taking a direction in which you know you will be happy. That leads to what you need. The things a human being in your situation, here and now, needs, the way that leads to your being able to satisfy those needs, taking that direction would lead to your fulfillment of those needs, which would be very happy making. To be really happy in reality and with reality is truly sane.

True sanity is using your brain to make conscious what is unconscious about you, so that someday you can know all about what kind of creature you really are, and will be a fully self-aware being here on earth, quite rare relatively speaking.

True sanity is identifying with your individualized spark of God that you are, and telling your body what it should do. True sanity is using the gifts and everything you have to evolve into the next step of evolution, to spiritual man, or, spiritual human being. For this, you have to give up fantasy and use only the imagination.

These things are important: good health; courage; strong sympathies; a warm heart; strong and earnest desire to connect with your Higher Part; and an exalted moral nature. Those qualities are necessary to reach the top level of self aware-man, and from there, someday, one goes into that next state, Cosmic Consciousness, or the heaven within. The blessed state. Bliss. You are universally aware then, and have begun a new journey one far beyond this Time and Space earthly thing you are now.

True sanity is arranging your life so you can love God, the Creator, the Imaginator, here and now."

I woke up today to pray and talk to myself again, and the one thing I've learned for certain is never do or not do something just because you say that you're about to leave. You never know when the wind is about to pick up, or when it is just about to die down.

"*Prend soin de toi!*"

Full moon, storm, March sixteenth. Five days away from Jorge's birthday and I don't think he'll make it. A huge growth on his neck behind his jaw seems to be getting the better of him. Tomorrow he keeps saying he'll take the pills, but tomorrow always begins with a new bottle of gin. I don't have the heart to tell him or anyone else that his magic pills won't do him any good anyway. They're only Ibuprofen, and will not cure a tumor grown from gin and cigarettes. It would take more than a day of soberness and two painkillers to make the growth disappear. So I do what I can to help. Last night I gave him an old, green, long sleeve shirt given to me many years ago by a beautiful girl I used to know. I sewed it up a few weeks ago, so at least it looks respectable. It was raining, and he was complaining of the cold. I knew all he had was the Florida Gators t-shirt that he wears everyday. He says he has a blanket in the abandoned house he sleeps in, but it's doubtful he has anything.

Where he sleeps who knows?

I gave a dime to the blind man who lives at the *pescadero* two days ago. He's still got it. He knows that sometimes it rains. He lent me a scale that I needed to measure off the pounds of *contrabando* I'm leaving with.

"*Seco y mundao*" everyone teases at Jorge. He takes another pull of his Gin just to prove them wrong. "*Hay que hechar gasolina en el caro!*" he says.

Carlos, the night watchman, taunts him, saying he won't live to see the end of the month with a smile. Jorge does a little dance and says, "*Usted primero,*" you first, but inside he knows that Carlos is right. His birthday is three days away.

He had a twin brother that died some twenty odd years ago. He cries for him everyday on his birthday. Everyone gives him little chores to do, washing their *moto* or taking out the trash, to find some excuse to give him a dollar here or there he can spend on rum. They know that if he doesn't have any money he'd probably start to steal. I don't believe that he's spent a dollar on anything except gin in a long time. Dorian's Gin. With Jorge I share my supper every night.

This poem is being written one word at a time. One word per day:

Pearl; Wind; Thousand Fires; Blown fruit from trees; Full Moon; *Busqueta Inutil*; Malaria Dreams.

The beautiful thing about life is that you always win something by taking another deep breath or writing another word.

To dream is to run through the river.

Enough poetry, there is a DAS officer outside of my window right now. At least I believe he is DAS. He is wearing blue. He is some kind of Babylon. Today would be a good day for them to come by if they've been listening to the telephone that Stella just told me was bugged. That's how most of the inexperienced get caught she says. I feel like the guy is off duty. Nonetheless, he's sitting outside my window and in uniform. I think I'll go check out front. I am feeling a bit nervous and wonder what to do with all of the ganja in my room. The plan again is to leave tomorrow. The only thing that could stand in the way is a storm that may be out.

Foolish men die young.

The mind is colorful as the dark.

The eye that you see is not an eye because you see it. It is an eye because it sees you.

Look in the mirror and see what you're controlling. Reflect in your eyes and see who's controlling you.

The day finally came for Robert to leave San Andres again. Everything was hurry up and move. The day was the same as all the other days that he was supposed to leave, so it took him by surprise.

Stella sent her messenger friend Herbie to his room to tell him to gather his things and move. It was about ten o'clock in the morning. Robert had just smoked a joint and returned back from his little walk down to the pescadero where he sat in a beached up panga breathing in the shade of the coconut trees, watching the sea and the ramblings of the drunken fishermen slamming dominoes.

"Where de ras you been?" Herbie exclaimed. "We me waitin fi you from marnin. Le go! Le go! Is time fi move padna. De boat's awaitin fi we reach. Is going now. Movin fa Nicaragua!"

Herbie was a dough-faced looking breadball of a black man. He had about fifty years, a skinny little mustache and a big mole on his left cheek. He was a pretty worthless guy. He never worked. He spent most of his time sitting around the shop, begging little things and cigarettes, waiting for Pacheco or Stella to pass him a little handout. He was some kind of family to them. Robert didn't like him pressuring him like this. He didn't like to be hurried up, worse when he had just smoked a joint. It seemed like a dream having a collision with a pick up truck. He needed just a minute to get his shit together. He told Herbie to leave him alone for a minute and that he would meet him out front by the shop. He told him to get a taxi ready.

So much time had passed from the time when he was supposed to leave, his bags had been packed and unpacked, repacked again and lived out of, that it was just the same as he had never packed. By this time in his travels, he was very adept and practiced at packing his familiar backpack. It would take but a minute to pack again. Robert had the packing down to an art and could fly through the action without thought or hesitation.

He threw his things into the tight bag, zipped up his guitar in the case with a small, rusty, dull, orange handled machete he had found one morning in the bush behind the residencial. Finally, he secured his writing book with the five sealed black plastic ganja pounds in an old canvas military handbag that he found washed up on the beach in Costa Rica. He took one last look around the room and checked under the bed for anything he might have forgotten. He struck a match and finished the piece of joint he had started before his walk to the pescadero and he walked out of his little room in the Residencial Restrepo, leaving the door open behind him, the key on the desk.

Stella and Herbie were out front with the taxi, rushing up everything and giving him direction about where to go meet the panga and who the guy was and this and that and all kind of things. Robert understood everything already and let them go on with their pressure. He needed no explanation. They finally concluded that Herbie would go with him in the taxi to make sure. Robert felt this was unnecessary, but didn't really care too much. He gave Stella a big hug, and thanked her for all the help that she had given him. She wished him well on his trip and told him not to forget them. Robert knew he wouldn't and flowed into the taxi. "A la muele de la gasolinera," he told the driver, and the taxi took off with a cool sunny breeze blowing through the open window.

Robert didn't really want Herbie going with him. He could see Herbie was a ball of nerves, making things more complicated than they need to be. Robert already knew where the salida was and the name of the panga. He knew that Herbie was just going because he would expect a few dollars for the favor he was doing. Whatever. Robert wasn't in the mood to fight things. Everything seemed cool as the taxi rolled through the hot town of San Andres. It rolled down the beachfront and then through the busy streets of the downtown and then turned back towards the ocean and the wharf where the panga was waiting. The sun shown brightly and a cool breeze blew in off of the sea. The air smelled rank of the sea. Pelicans and sea gulls flew from the posts of old wharfs. He stopped at the central corner where all the busses stopped and old black men sold yucca, mamay, bittersweet oranges and anything they could find on their small island farms. Nobody said a word in the taxi. They continued on in silence past the government buildings and high rise hotels, making their way along with the traffic, and then BANG! Right in front of the crowded police station, the taxi suddenly blew a tire and swerved through two lanes of traffic to the shoulder of the road. All coolness and music vanished from the air and things turned crazy.

Robert quickly searched for the money for the taxi and passed it to the driver. He didn't waste anytime. The last thing he felt like dealing with now was a bunch of Colombian police asking for his passport and why he didn't have any Colombian stamps, not to mention the five pounds of ganja in his bag. This was a strange joke from God. He grabbed his bags and jumped out of the car, not even looking towards the hundreds of police officers who were no doubt watching the taxi with the popped tire that rolled up on the curb in front of their station. Herbie grabbed the guitar and followed Robert across the street to the wharf where the panga was waiting. Robert weaved in and out of people and through the gates to the wharf where no one asked him any questions. He never once looked back over his shoulder towards the taxi. He saw the panga, put down his heavy backpack, went back onto the land and ducked behind a small coconut tree where he hid the camouflaged ganja bag in a little patch of bush. He sat down for a minute and caught up with himself. Everything seemed to be cool. He looked back towards the road, but could no longer see the taxi with the popped tire. He didn't see any police. He could see Herbie standing there with the guitar talking to the captain of the boat. Robert left the bag and went to over to the two men. The captain introduced himself to Robert, and the two of them shook hands. They put his bag and guitar into the panga, and said they were just waiting on another guy to reach. The captain said that it was best to leave off in the daytime. It would look like they were going fishing. "No problem," Robert said.

Herbie begged Robert to give him something for the job. Robert didn't have anything left to give him except for a few pesos that couldn't buy much more than his taxi fare back home, but what could he do. It was really all that he had. He told him that he left all his money with Stella. Herbie was vexed but left just the same. What could he do?

The captain told Robert just to wait easy for a few minutes until he called him. "No problem," said Robert again, and went and sat down back beneath the little coconut tree, trying blend in. He was nervous, with a little knot in his belly. He wanted to get in the skiff and hit it but he just had to wait.

Two police officers showed up and were walking around the wharf slowly with their big automatic rifles, making the rounds. They weren't doing anything, just walking around. They took no notice of Robert and just continued making vueltas.

About twenty minutes later, the next man showed up and the captain and three men got into the panga. The police officers were still around somewhere, but Robert couldn't see them. This was it. He grabbed his canvas handbag and put on his red Colombian University hat and walked down to the skiff where the captain told him to get in. The skiff started up its two hundred engine and lifted up into the sea. The five of them bounced off towards the bright sun in the western sky with Nicaragua in the distance somewhere ahead of them.

"Take off your hat," the captain told Robert. "If they're watching us, they could see that red hat from far". Robert understood and took off the cap. He took a look around and the small island getting smaller behind them. He took a deep breath and held on to his seat in the stern of the panga. "Thank God," he whispered to himself.

La Islita

The skiff hit Little Island just after dark. The ride was so smooth and fast that the captain stopped the skiff and turned off the engine to drift for a while as the sun went down. They were ahead of time and didn't want to reach the island before dark. The sun sank into the western sea. A few miles ahead of them, well out of sight, lay Nicaragua with her savage freedom. The captain's mate took out a box of fried chicken that they all shared with bottle of red fanta. They waited for the sun to sink safely down, hauled the engine back on again and started their course West again. The lights from the backside of Little Corn soon appeared on the horizon.

The panga maintained a good distance from the land as it rounded the southern point of the island and crept up silently to the front. They kept a slow enough speed to keep the wake from showing white against the black sea. You never know what could be waiting for you in Little Corn's front harbor, the Babylon with loaded automatic rifles or piratas from the island waiting to hijack your mercancia. They had to be careful.

The panga pulled into a small bite at the top of the island where a high bank came down to meet the sea. A skinny rope ladder hung down the face of the cliff where the skiff pulled up to the beach. The travelers hurried out of the skiff so that it could turn back out of the harbor quickly.

Robert backed his pack and shouldered his guitar over the canvas handbag with the ganja that had not left his side all trip. Following the two Colombians who were making the trip with him, he jumped out of the skiff into the knee-deep surf and walked up onto the beach to where the rope ladder hung down from the night. The Colombians were both carrying bags and mercancia. He never asked what it was that they carried but he assumed it was cocaine. They climbed up the ladder onto the bank of Little Island.

The island was quiet. There was no one else around. Everything was good. Everything seemed to be sleeping.

The skiff already turned back for San Andres. The two Colombians disappeared into the night and Robert stood on the sidewalk with all his bags like a statue waiting for a sign. Everything was silent and alone again. It was time to look a room and get safe. Things were still hot.

The closest lodging was Miss Bridget's Place right down the sidewalk. It was a safe place where Colombians always went. She was a mafia woman and catered to any kind of drugs movement. Stella told him to contact her when he arrived. She told him that she would buy the ganja. If she didn't want it, maybe her brother Tom would. Anyway, she would have a secure room to sleep in for a night or two.

Robert walked down the sidewalk along the sea and in a few minutes got checked into a room by Bridget. Bridget was sleeping, so he'd have to wait until the morning to check her about the mercancia. He looked around the room and thought about a good place to secure the ganja. The only thing in the room was a little board bed and a nightstand in the corner. He threw the ganja as far underneath the bed it could reach and opened up his backpack to take out his towel and have a shower to wash the salt spray of his face.

He opened the room door and walked outside towards the dirty little bathroom. He turned the corner and hit face to face with a group of five military men from the Fuerza Naval, each carrying big ass guns. He stuttered in his steps and panicked for a second. He turned around and went back for his room, but the naval was already running towards him. They rightfully thought he looked suspicious. By the time he shut the door to his room, the Babylon was knocking at the door, demanding him to open up. His stomach was in a knot, but he knew he had to just remain cool and act stupid. It was time to play the role of the gringo.

"De donde viene? Ensename las papeles," the Babylon ordered and said all kind of things in Spanish. Robert fumbled pretended to not understand, speaking words of English along with bits of fragmented Spanish. "Tu passaporte."

"Passaporte?" Robert responded. "Ya, ya, OK, esper, wait," he fumbled around as he took out his passport.

The Babylon was already in the room, digging up his bags and searching through the guitar case. He prayed they didn't look under the bed as they lifted up the little foam mattress.

They didn't see anything. Robert tried to be as cool as possible, but acting reasonably frightened the way a gringo tourist would. He knew that his papers were still valid in Nicaragua. He had about a week before his tourist visa expired.

"OK," the Babylon officer said. "Disculpe para la problema," he apologized as he handed back Robert's passport. They all backed out of the room and left him alone again. Things were again quiet, but his stomach was still unable to release itself fully from the knot it tied itself in. He let out a sigh of relief and made sure the Babylon was really gone. He crawled under the bed and grabbed the bag with the ganja. He opened one of the taped up pounds and took out a handful of pressed ganja and put it in a little plastic bag for himself.

He wrapped up a joint in a dried leaf and went down to the rocks on the beach in front of the Lobster Company, with the joint and a box of Colombian matches. He thanked God to be back in Nicaragua. He laughed.

The stars hungover my head like mistletoe. The clouds are tickling at the quartered out moon. Laughing at myself under the free Nicaraguan sky.

Arrived again to Little Island *limpio*. Cleaned out of money. I'd better get rid of my *mercancia* before it gets rid of me.

Saw Myrta this morning and gave her a hand moving her big old wooden bed down from Smoothie's place. She had some problems there and had to go home. When I reached by her mother, Miss Cherry's, house, she offered me a room to stay in. I guess they had the extra room, and could use a little help. It's plenty better than paying for the room at Bridget's Place. Things are looking fine.

Saw Joe this morning talking bout last night. He showed me the wound on his head. Jose and him had a little fight. Drinking Rum Plata, six bottles or so he says. Jose's hooked on crack and snorting now too. Says he just went crazy and attacked him with a stick. Said he had it out for him long time. He seen the *ojos* Joe had for his wife. Said he don't remember nothin', don't remember nothin'. Me and Joe, we gone to the clinic, got him cleaned and closed up good. Got me some pills and other injections.

I need a spear.

What is that sound you hear way out there in the dark? A mixture of the waves, wind, generators, crickets, dogs and echoes and who knows what else. Murderers and thieves and dealers and me. You never know whom you can trust or what exactly your instincts are saying. My life has become so crazy I don't know where to begin. I'll just open up the window and check on my last two pounds of ganja I've got hidden up in the coconut tree. There's too much color around here right now with Yellow Man, Jose and me and Babylon right around every corner.

Yellow Man thieved me a pound last week and has been going crazy all around town ever since. Calling Babylon after me, telling people he's going to fuck me up, putting his hand on Myrta . . . I need to kill him. I was going to just let it die, but he is leaving me with no other choice. I think about it all the time. How to do it, what to use? Tonight I walked with my machete in my shorts. I think I will use a syringe filled with air. I should have known not to deal up with any rock-men, but nearly everyone is a rock-man.

I promised Miss Cherry I wouldn't go out tonight, but I need to see Benito. I have to move this last two pounds. The price is three hundred. Big money. I have completely lost my mind, for once and for all, because those are the rules.

A little bit of Guinea Hair wine; a clove of garlic and a baby lime in my pocket; a little bit of confidence, and I know that no one can do me no harm.

Sometimes I can just sit for hours, or is it days, in the yard, watching the clouds blowing; the roosters crowing; the hibiscus in blooms; shadows waving at my feet; hands writing and never once give thought to the distant land I once called home. Never think twice of the love I left behind. Three times for rubbish and four times for swine. I never think how strange I have become.

I saw Marlon this morning when I was hauling sand on my back and he reminded me that I need to better my situation. He was sailing home to Haulover after struggling with tomorrow in San Andres. It's been nearly a month since I left him in Colombia and he just made it back.

The days of my life are passing by like years in the Caribbean breeze, but that is good, for one day they will stop and death will arrive like a thief in the night. A *ladron*. And like a *ladron*, I am waiting an opportunity to kill Yellow Man. I have made no plans, only psycho-simulations. Today I passed him while making a *chamba* and I licked my lips. I fantasize about smashing in his face with a club and beating out his life through his bucked teeth. I am getting sick.

Can one kill and be a prophet of life? The only thing holy is life itself. Another breathe, another chance at salvation from death. Good and bad judged in measures of health. Morality by longevity. Yellow Man has done wrong. He is shortening his life with every mistake he makes.

I owe Granny a breadfruit.

Hello whoever you are, reading my message from the bottle. I've been shut up for months with the excuse of no paper, but today, I overcame my fear and marched valiantly across the sidewalk and bought a *cuaderno* for a buck.

I'm here in Little Corn Island again, passing time alive until my ganja sells, an ordeal much more slow and complicated than I ever could have imagined. This was a mistake that I hope never to make again.

Yesterday, I rolled up a half a pound into twenty *cordova* joints to sell at Benito's. Then I got sick to my stomach and curled up in bed all day and night with a fever, freezing from the inside and rattling my teeth. Indigestion.

Today I've been eating mangos. Sugar Mangos. It is the only mango for the true mango connoisseur. It is the only mango people will actually buy on Little Island.

And instead of going out, I smoke a pipe of the strong shit John gave me, and I change my mind and sit down and open the window and watch the sun go down in the safety of my room. Storms a comin'.

The wind blows, drafts change and the window blows shut. I am stoned and paranoid and have every right to be with two pounds of ganja buried away in my room. Every move I make is color.

Open windows. Take a deep breath. Stretch your hands above your head. Drink some water. "It will all be alright," the stranger says to himself.

He's been alone now for so long, he doesn't know what an honest familiar face would say. He doesn't even know what honesty is or any of this mirage. Sane or insane, living or dying. All I know is I can feel the music in my bones, like a pain in my head.

Today the weather is Gray. Dorian Gray. Neither up nor down, skies black nor blue, ugly nor pretty nor purple. I pass the day at Benito's, playing with loops of string and selling (or not selling) ganja. Making the chicken boonky. I fear that I will be chained to this bush for a long time. All I want to do is run free to the North. To travel clean and light and move on to a new life, or rather return to the path I have never really left. Why can't I just drop it? Why not just leave it behind? Why am I always one step behind on my destination? I want to kill my destination and free myself to my present location; cut the hauling string of time, the winch of calendars that *Cristo* has hooked into my chest.

The freight boat is coming in today if the weather permits. Bishop and Granny Menah are heading back to Bluefields with her if she comes. Bishop is a little black boy whose parents are dead. He's been staying here in the house too. We go to the bush, go fishin and things like such. This morning, we gone look coconut and found some big ones boy. He climbed a tree and hauled some down and I husked them. Little Alvarito bagged them up. I got a little vexed at Bishop because he wanted to take all the coconuts back to Bluefields. They cost five cordovas apiece there. They cost one cordova for one here, but they are really free. Every mornin', I goin' take to the beach with my sack and machet' and fill it. We gonna make oil.

Stoned and killing time again, hiding from the rain like excuses. I don't like to force things that don't fit, so my time here has become slower. This life is boring me; too much ganja selling too slowly. If I sell it all however, I will be relatively rich for a short while. I must use my imagination. I go for vagabond walks during the day, eating mangos and mangos and mangos. Life is a mango buffet. I get my bellyful.

Kim had an old AK-47 at Benito's this morning. Oran, who owes me a hundred and fifty cordobas for a machete job I did for him, brought the gun from Big Corn. Someone must have brought it from the main land. I gave them some sand paper I'd been holding onto for a while to help them get the gun cleaned up. They're going to sell the gun in San Andres, where it will be shipped to the Colombian mainland for the *Guerilla*. The whole way, the gun will probably be traded for cocaine. There are plenty of guns in Nicaragua that the people held on to after the Contra war. Some people now choose to sell them. Some are holding onto them in case war comes back with the Babylon.

They shot some poor boy here last week. It was Pablo's *tio*. He was a silver toothed fellow whom I raked the churchyard with, making *chamba*. He was here trying to make a little money, working jobs that no one else wanted, and some asshole hothead, uneducated, untrained policeman shot him trying to be a hero. There is no excuse for this type of behavior.

Sometimes, like now, in the morning, when there is just too much shit to do, it's best to just take a seat and look out the window and pick up the pen and do nothing for a licky while, ignore the constant reminders of the work I should be doing. The cry of the laborers. The joy on their faces. The women washing and starting fires. The children playing in the tambrand tree. *Tamarindo*. Machetes chopping posts. Boys building chicken shacks. The sun is rising. The wheels are turning at their constantly accelerating fixed speed. I am a body at rest.

I am waiting for Benito to wake up to drop of the half pound for the day. After learning the ins and outs of this tricky Nicaraguan ganja business, my best option now seems to drop the bush with him in the morning and pick it up from him in the night, with the money of the day's sales in the bag. At this rate I'll be stuck here in Nicaragua for a long but pleasant time. I rolled two hundred joints that are selling at about ten per day. It is too slow. I need to get rid of this shit. It is not at all like Stella and Pacheco said it would be, a one shot wholesale thing.

I need to get out of this house. It is a beautiful morning. The world is working. I should go out walking and find something, but right now I'd rather just sit and write down this tale.

My clothes are dirty. Go buy soap. Go look mango. Go look coconut. Go look work. I just pace back and forth across the room, and think about my health.

If you could just see this crazy life. All these crazy women in this house, with all their babies and man problems and complaints and crying and spinning and chatting about me and you and you know who. The rain has passed. The sun is out. The lazy white man is hiding inside again.

Drank some rum last night and woke up feeling fine, but am lacking a little something now. I let the sand boat I was working for go and tell myself I'll work tomorrow. It is difficult to make myself break my back when I've got a little money in my pocket. It is slave work. Military work, backing sacks full of wet sand. Now I play the roll of the pusher, and I hate myself. I am ready to change rolls again. Change jobs. Change locations. Change my name and change my clothes and keep with me only the music. Jose told me people are talking about me. On an island this small, people love to talk. Someone saw me hauling a bucket of water by Benito and said I was doing a *chamba* to get a joint or a stone. People are stupid. Myrta tells me that I shouldn't hang out there. "Draws color," she says. I tell her I know, but that sometimes, people just have to do things. Myrta is beautiful. She tells you how it is and she loves Jose.

She truly loves him. Beneath the rock man and bad boy, despite her mother and the rest of the island and the rum and the money, she loves him. She loves him and she loves his baby, Esperanza, more than the houses he's got them thrown out of, the beatings he has given her, the crimes he's committed and the men he's hiding from. She loves him when he comes home from sea with fish and some of the money he made.

The rain is pouring now. When it stops, I will leave.

It has stopped.

Myrta fries beans everyday and makes tortillas with coconut

milk. She cooks the food I like to eat and she makes it with love.

Babylon is off the island right now. Ever since they shot that boy that I cleaned the churchyard with before *Semana Santa*, they haven't been allowed back. "In the mafia world here, that pretty much means we can do whatever we want," says Benito grinning.

Gunshots boom in the background. Kim is cleaning up the AK. Granny is snoring in the bedroom. I'm in the backroom alone. Rain is coming and going. I've got to run up to Benito's and grab the grass.

Dorian Gray was an orphan, dropped off by his father here on Little Island, and Benito never saw the man again. He had eight years, and was adopted by Mister Steadman in the back. He raised Benito, fishing in the sea and planting in the bush.

Dorian took his first wife when he was fourteen. He took her out in the bush and cut sticks and wild cane and made a house for the two of them. Man and wife. From there he never stopped. He's gone from one woman to the next, making houses for each one of them and leaving again to find a next one.

"I've made five houses now. Just left the last one in Bluefields with my wife there. Never got a divorce or nothin'. Just left. She had two kids with me, and a third with someone else. I don't know who. So I left, and have had nothing more to do with her," he says shrugging his shoulders and laughing.

To me it looks like it won't be long until he runs out on this one here too. She likes to give hard time. An Indian woman already. Sometimes I come up there in the morning and find the TV mashed up outside, or a wall in the kitchen torn down, and I know things got hot the night before.

Smoothie says that he's going to kill Jose. I guess that he went to Winnie, the *Alcalde* here, and annulled the charges he had pressed on Jose. He told Winnie not to worry about it, and Winnie said OK.

"If you kill somebody, that's you and you".

Winnie is a very laissez faire kind of sheriff.

Jose is smoking crack again and borrowing up money, hanging out in the shadows at night. Myrta's been rubbing her nose alot and talking to you all over the place. Rock-people.

Rock-man skinny, dirty, hungry and crafty for a buck. Saw one selling Sugar Mangos he stole from some tree today, ten cordovas a dozen. Sugar Mango. The knowledge of the Sugar Mango's sweetness makes all the other mangos taste ordinary and boring. Some are sweet, but they ain't no Sugar Mango. Honey. *Miel.* Make you wanna call yo mamma. Smoothie got Sugar Mango growing back up ina his yard. Tomorrow I'll go pay him a visit. Talk a little. Black magic voodoo shit.

Morning. If I found a woman here, I would stay and marry and build a house. That would solve my visa problems but give me some others no doubt. Maybe I'll try out Pearl Lagoon. They say the rain is coming. The wind is blowing. Miss Cherry is rowing with everyone outside. Yelling at Alvarito for all day walking around and round. Walking bout. That seems like the worst thing one can do. That is why she is always sick and weighs about two hundred and fifty pounds. She never leaves the yard. I don't believe she has left in several years. "I don't go outside for nothin'. Pa-Paw Me? Go outside?! Not for nothin' Pa-Paw," she chuckles.

She's lived here a long time and seen alot of shit, and knows what is good from bad. She knows how people talk on an island this small. She's right. People are calling me a rock-man.

They see me walking around, doing *chambas*, carrying heavy shit around on my back, dirty clothes and "in need of a good scrub," as Miss Cherry says.

Sitting around at Benito's, hanging out with friends like Jose, I guess I can't blame them. Everyone I know uses stone. It's a plague upon the people. It is lack of education.

I'm going to get some bread and coffee and go sit at Smoothie's.

It is never too late for history to start repeating itself, my battle with infection reminds me. I've developed two painful boils on my right shoulder.

Jose is "fucked up." He is outside shoveling or banging on something. He claims to be "working" on his new house. There is a loud racket outside like something metal has fallen. I do not open the door because I care not to witness nor play a part of this nonsense.

He gets a little bit of money then goes on these sprees that last as long as the money does. The favors from the neighbors are all gonna be out soon. History always repeats itself, demanding to be dealt with and changed. It's never too late to change . . . except with the *piedra* it seems.

Get a little bit of melody. Get yourself a soul.

One of Pacheco's boys from San Andres called me out on "Main Street" (the sidewalk) this morning. "Gringo!" he says waving his hand for me to come over.

"You know Pacheco?" he asks me.

I just looked into his eyes and said nothing. Everyone here knows Pacheco. The police, the drug dealers, the old Bluefields people. Everyone here and there in San Andres. Me not knowing which group this man belonged to, had to wait for more information before responding.

It turns out that he just arrived from San Andres last night and brought with him twenty pounds of good *calidad* compressed Colombian ganja. He's trying to get rid of them quick for one hundred and seventy dollars a pound. That's cheap. It will slow down my sales. It will slow down my life. I set out this morning to go for a walk. Jose stopped me with a joint and I ended up changing directions and picking and boiling beans.

I stopped eating mangos. Mangos are the devil disguised as a woman. They lay in abundance beneath the trees like Easter eggs in beautiful pastels of yellow, red, orange and pink. Full like cheeks.

My favorite pastime has been walking around the island to find a good mango tree and sitting and eating as many as I can. I taste each one for sweetness and dash away the ordinaries like a lukewarm soul. I take one in my hand and take for the next tree. My head wanders to Marylee. I have eaten too many mangos. I am only a beginner mango eater. There has been too much mango sweetness in my blood in too quick a time. It cannot handle the twenty to thirty mangos I put away most days. It is emitting the excess of toxins my body has through the skin in the form of painful boils. It could be cleansing. It could be too much sugar. It could be AIDS. It is too much for me.

It is the boils.

The heat of the midday afternoon sun is too much. It makes me want a mango out of the boils bowl I keep full in the corner of the room.

Yendi just walked by the window with a plastic sack of Sugar Mangos. Not being one to fight temptation, I politely asked if she said "Sugar Mango?"

If I could fall in love here I would follow. I would build a home, begin a life and make something. I have not found a place better than this. The soul, the sea, the soil and the money, but there is no love. It would be just as good to sell my ganja and get out of here. Clean my dirty fingernails.

Little Island is wild. It is an adventure. It is untamed and untrained, raw and free. It is more of a tribe than a Babylon town. No police officers, only some enforcers of Island law.

Lord, I just can't stop thinking that things are going bad. Nausea, trembling, fear, consciousness that you're too far-gone to do anything about it right now.

My new family is a trip. Miss Cherry, Jisena, Alvarito, Keisha, Dookie, Yenni, Yendi, Big Belly Rambo and little Erika out in the yard playing with anything the tide brings in.

The candle I was laying by burnt out. I fell asleep and dreamed of a friend I'd just left behind. I awoke to find the candle relit. Resurrected from the dead. Creation. Art.

Light from darkness and water from wine. Inspired, I get up and grab my pen and use it, but once again it has burnt out and left me with darkness to dream of a candle I once had lit. Divinely Inspired Poetry.

I tape up the broken orange handle on my worn out San Andres machete sword as I prepare for the days battle of going to the bush to look coco, cassava and other roots and breadkinds. The tape is useful. It was Brother John's. I gave him a half a pound of ganja to sell. He still owes me close to a hundred bucks, but I call it cool just not to start problems. I took his tape and his flippers and I know that I have something on him.

Yesterday I did not battle. It was a loss to the constant task of fighting infections. I must now wrap up the pussing hole in my knuckle. "It looks like a bullet," someone told me. The hole however is filling with strength and newness.

Went up to Benito's old house last night to see what he had to say. His eyes were rolling around drunk in his head when I arrived. He seems to have done a bit of remodeling in response to some problems with his wife Selea. He smashed down the whole front wall and took out the two walls that once housed the kitchen and the *sala*. He threw her out with all her shit and busted down the house she used to live in.

We sat around and drank a bottle of white rum de Plata and talked about the lion, the bear, the serpent and the twelve tribes of Judah and shit like that. The rest of the day was a dream. Floating around, looking for food, playing music and screaming out songs with Katato and Tatiana, who just arrived from Costa Rica. If I could not laugh at the situation my life has gradually become, I would crack at the core. How far away I have drifted from Houston and Lewisburg and the corporate capitalist lifestyle I was grown into. It makes me sad to feel that my parents at home are probably crying, but it is the pain they must grow through. It makes me sad to feel that my sister spent her five vacation days to visit me and I haven't communicated with her since then. I sleep with a knife on the table.

My mustache is starting to sweat. I'm a month overdue in Nicaragua with no hope of leaving soon.

Jose has been charged since yesterday. Crack has taken Central America like a plague. Crack and AIDS. He sold Myrta's radio after I refused to help him out with twenty cordovas. After all the times I have helped him out, he has never once paid me back. Since my plans of going to the bush have changed, perhaps I'll go pick beans and make myself a useful member of the family.

"Do you want I slap you? Hush up your mouth," Jisena hollers at Alvarito whose eyes are always peeping into the holes in my walls, checking on me to make sure I'm not smoking grass. He's gonna tell his momma.

I have been in Nicaragua now for nearly six months and I recently realized that I have no chance of fixing my papers. I am facing serious fines that I would rather not pay to some Nicaraguan beaurocrats installed by Oliver North's boys and backed by CIA cocaine money and guns.

The other day in Bluefields, four police officers were killed in the streets. Stabbed and cut throated by what experts say were professionals. No bullets. After that, a group of thirty or forty Nicaraguan and Colombian mafiamen entered the Bluefields police station, demanding the release of two jailed Colombian *narco-traficantes*. I heard they put up a sign saying they wanted all of the cocaine that was seized as well. It is a war.

Since then, Babylon activity has been hot here on the island. Last night, seventeen of them came in a big skiff from Corn Island, armed with machine guns and dressed in blue.

I heard the night before they caught a Colombian skiff and some *Peruanos* traveling north. If I don't get fix my papers, I'll have to start traveling with them, *escondido* with the drug and slave smugglers.

A *pueblo* without an artist is like a body without a soul.

Time is light

Time is light. Hold onto a moment. Squeeze it into ice. Take a deep breath and let it out. Send your weary writing to bed.

Jose started smoking rock when he was fourteen. Someone told him that it was marijuana, and it was, but mixed with crack. Jose pulled the same trick on me. The rude-boy. The man encouraged him to keep on smoking the ganja, that it was good for the mind and the martial arts training they were practicing. It was in Managua with an American guy from California. It was months before Jose found out it was crack he was charging up on all the time. By that time it was too late. He was hooked long time.

He always talking about how he needs to quit and this and that, and always goes right up into the ghetto with the first twenty cordovas he's got. If he's got it, a rock man will give all that he has for that piece. It's worth more than diamonds. "If a man has a thousand diamonds, he'll give it all for a thousand *piedras*. Rock man will do anything if he needs to. That makes cocaine more valuable than anything," Jose says.

Jose denies that he's a rock man. "I's not like them other rock man you know. I no smoke no rock during the day all the time," he lies to himself while it sucks the flesh from his bones and life from his eyes.

You can't help it. If you smoke rock, you must smoke more. It grows on people exponentially. At first, it may be cool, but it always catches up on you. You say you're strong, strong enough to control anything, but you are just a man, an animal in search of pleasure. Cocaine is more pleasurable than food, so it wires the brain automatically to make a new priority. Pleasure. Is there such thing as strength? Is will power a myth? There is only nature and science and chemical dependencies that dictate the way we think, wait, feel and need. Lost souls.

May. The rain has come just how Miss Cherry promised it would. It seems to be coming harder and harder and longer and louder and louder by the minute; increasing intensity and pressure by octaves on the tin roof; deafening and piercing the inner regions of the brain. It is so loud that I cannot hear myself think the words and then BAM! Before you know it, it is quiet again without ever missing a beat or a sound. No skipping, no cutting, only fading and rolling into the next wave of sound. All is continuous. Nature is continuity.

My father was a lawyer. I was raised to become one as well. I was grown to become my father, just as you were. I worked into his office and his red Acura Legend. His house in the suburbs and the old Suburban than he bought for his family trips. I naturally seemed to fit right into the legal profession when it came time to pick a career, until something went wrong. I quit believing in the law. I stopped buying into the American sense of justice and right and wrong and respect and civilization. I became lazy. I lost the will to participate. Could I really spend my life *asi*? Bouncing from town to town, staying in some and leaving others. Working my body. Fighting infections and denying the life I was born into and finding the life I was born for. We are not born for anything, only born. No destiny, only products of experience, Birds of Paradise. Mirrors of pasts. Learned creatures of our own light and relative darkness dictated by our distance from the sun.

How long can I keep this up? This life of bumming around and hauling lumber on my back, hammering nails in dirty pants and free housing. Why am I here? Why are you there? Bleeding fingers, mashed up thumbs, broken knuckles that won't close and broken ears that won't listen to the words he's supposed to write.

This pen could be a tool, just like my hammer, shovel and saw. Just like my hammer I fear it. My fingers are *tremblando* in wait of the smash. I fear myself, and only that.

This island is full of animals and vampires waiting to suck your blood if they get the chance. Keep your garlic in your pocket instead of your money if you're wise. They take what they can. There's a group of *Peruanos* here from Ecuador that have been stuck on the island for more than two weeks. The leader of the pack, the pale one with the woman, got even his shoes robbed.

There are some people who only know the smiling side of life. They know nothing of the tears or the shadows.

Hidden in the shadows of the moonless trail, waiting for anyone with anything, lies the dark. The darkness. Stay in the light. Rockman coming a get you.

Nine gunshots ring out from the beach. Babylon. Ten.

I've been spending my days building fish pots with Smoothie. Lobster traps. I know when I sell my stuff I'm gone for the coast. The Mainland. Pearl Lagoon and Orinoco, the land of the Caribs. Black men. Ugly men who no fraid of nothing; who drink rum and bang drums and dance for three days when the spirit comes and takes them. The spirit flies from the drummer's hands to the dancing girls feet. They no put no comb to their hair nor pants on their boonkie when they bath in the rivers or go to the bush. Deh no study dem tings.

The holiness of loneliness.

I want to be alone, alone enough to cry out at the top of my soul, letting it out with all my heart. Releasing it to the heavens that hear it and feel it and add it to their collection of melodies and raindrops. Alone enough to sing in the loudest and purest words that could flow without fear from the inner regions of the gut and eardrum. The current of poetry running connected to God like a bottle of wine or an extension chord, uninterrupted from artificial radio waves or the cries of a rock-woman baby.

God is an umbrella.

Waiting is masturbating.

Inhale the sunshine and drink the rain.

I know that all good writers are good drinkers, so tonight I buy a bottle of Wine Condor. It is not really wine at all, just alcohol with sugar water and *colorantes*. Someone told me it was made with herbs, but people are fools. The wise know this much.

Dear Dan,

I just got a laugh about thinking about how much I was crying the day we were all leaving sunny Lewisburg and our sunny little lives. What a strange memory. That red back door with the number twenty-three on it. We really were a fine bunch of assholes. It's scary that it was no time at all ago.

I am on the Atlantic Coast of Nicaragua right now, on a little island that failed to make the maps. It is called Little Corn Island. What I'm doing here, I don't really know, but the time is passing right on by, just like you. I have been building Lobster Traps and lying in my hammock, eating plenty of mangos, coconut bread and fish. It is a good life here. There is a big problem with crack on the Little Island. The Island smells of cocaine. It seems that this drug makes people "bad" (as much as I disbelieve in morals). Some rock man name Bocario just got arrested for raping his nine-year-old step-daughter. Then yesterday, two Indians got arrested for raping a white woman around on the beach. There is a lot going on here and no state police (Babylon). There is no law. There are a few islanders that act as the sheriff and deputies when somebody is causing problems. It is more like custom as law as that old Jewish Law and Society professor would say. I would like to go back to Bucknell and get laid again. There was plenty of pussy running around there, if you excuse my vulgarity. Things here are as dry as dirt, except for the rain, which has rarely stopped in this month of May.

Well Dan, my candles are burning low and my body is tired, so I will say goodbye. I would love to come pass a Thanksgiving there with you sometime so we could thank God for the gifts he has given us and maybe run a road race or something. Maybe we could just get drunk of some good Connecticut beer.

Tomorrow is Saturday. That means the freight boat will come. That means a little bit of money for helping unload cargo. I'll buy some food and be popular with the mama for a few days. Get me a nice plate of fish and rice and beans. Thank God for the coconut food. *Salud.* Goodnight.

This morning when the light came, it was raining. I took it as an excuse to go back to bed. When it stopped and the time came, I went to the outhouse, the first thing I do everyday. Today I shit all over the hole I was squatting over and wiped my knuckles in it unknowingly. I smelled it a few times as if I didn't know what it was. I tried to wipe it clean and somehow got it smudged all over my toilet paper roll. The me that no one else sees. The me that masturbated once in the back of the family suburban on a road trip to Colorado. Who pees on his feet in the shower.

Smoothie and me finally finished our two hundred lobster traps. My fingers are all mashed up from the hammer. They give us a little bit less than a dollar for one. It has taken much longer than either one of us expected. Smoothie got paid already and he doesn't want to give me my share. He is drinking rum, gladding with the young women and trying to ignore me.

My guitar is a table and I am a lamp. Spaces make words and spaces make rhythms. Spaces make numbers like between one and two, or zero and one, or .9999 and one. Between left and what is right; what is light and what is shade; between the green leaf and the blue sky; between the brown leaf and the dirt; spaces create us where spaces don't exist. A skip in the time that just flows and flows from one being to the next, with no punctuation or meaning, I will just call it life which is running though us all like the breeze, the only thing I can appreciate. The only thing that makes me say it is worth it. All is free.

No more rum, no more rum. You're burning me up from inside. No more smoke, no more smoke. Fire is burning up your life.

Do you know what I think about life, about death and religion, the trinity of philosophy from my limited scope of vision?

This is an unrepeating number. This is pi. This is e. There is no end to it. It just keeps on going without ever repeating itself and only the prophets know which digit will come up next. This number is alive. It has a soul that was born at the beginning and will not seem to die. It is energy; never dying, only changing.

There is a country without lines or names or boundaries and the people there are free. They walk amongst you but they call themselves nothing. They pledge no allegiance and wave no flag but for their mother the Earth. They pass like ghosts through frontiers and down sidewalks like angels of air and water that clean up the mess that evil Babylon has thrown on top of their nature.

Bang Bang goes the poetry, bang goes the song. Bang goes the guns of revolution, but silent are the turning of the wheels that began with the seeds of salvation and rolled right out of Babylon. And that would be a savior. Who could deliver his readers like Moses, with a word from Babylon and into the wilderness?

Open an eye, open a heart, open a mind to make a new start. For life, wake up! Life is all that we have and all that we know. Heaven is for fools and procrastinators who believe it better to be dead. A justification for suffering to appease the paupers and slaves. With a word, all is forgiven. Release with confession. Hell that is waiting for all who keep quiet and refuse to pay their tithes and offerings, feeding the preachers and affording them a life that we must work for. But even the preachers believe it. They've studied it and learned it as fact. The bible is more than words that someone wrote down in a psalm. Divinely inspired prayers and schizophrenic outbursts. People talking to themselves, to their God. God fearing people. Scared people. God protect us from our enemies and strikes down upon them like a ray of light or a nuclear bomb. Send them to hell and send me to heaven. It is my enemy who is wrong. He who is different should die and burn.

The wages of sin are death, a fiery death. This is true. The devil exists, and his name is fire, burning whatever it touches to death. Fire is death, creeping upon the sleeping like a thief in the night. Wake up! Death is filling you up. The flame burns higher with each sip of firewater, each smoke, each bite of burnt flesh. The fire is filling us up. Extinguish the fire with water. Babylon is filling us with chemicals with each bite of packaged garbage they sell us.

Mucus in your lungs, gut, brains and veins. Wash yourself out. Only water will put out the fire. Clean yourself, inside and out. Cleanliness is Godliness. Your body is the temple, your life is your soul, either growing or dying.

The one thing to do while building lobster pots is think. Think about life and about water and think that they're one in the same, washing death out of you, out of my kidneys.

Notes floating out of my pen like bubbles, colorful bubbles numbered one to twenty four. Put them together and you can have a symphony. A pyramid. It's all zeros and ones and the way you put them together. It makes art. It makes letters that makes words that makes feelings. Good notes and bad notes.

I must stop writing about nothing and write about something.

We worked through the rain and the sun, the pain of the cold, the rum and the blood in his eyes when I came back after he sent me home for lunch and found him still at work, sweating like a machine to finish the thirty pots I back up for him. I knew he was punishing himself for showing up drunk the day before. I also knew that I have the awful work ethic of a middle class white boy. I have no hurry. I'm not yet hungry. I sleep in the night dry from the rain. I don't worry about my retirement yet. Smoothie must work for his food until the day he prefers to die.

The devil dances with flame-like hips, seducing you down her pretty road, and happily the young follow along skipping, then walking then crawling crumbling to a stop. The road just keeps moving prettily along, but the young are no longer.

The mosquitoes are biting. Smoothie would have a coconut husk burning.

Sometimes I'm just happy to reach home to the protection of my little zinc walls and a burning candle. The obeah is strong here.

I heard about some girl that is starving to death because she can't eat. She sees worms in all of her food. Somebody done her up bad. The last girl she done that to only lasted six days or so after she started seeing the worms. Don't know how you curse someone like that. Obeah. Voodoo. It's an *intellegencia.* You gotta be careful what you eat.

Jose is dying.

"I soon be dead," he mutters to me walking by groaning and holding his stomach.

He beat the shit out of Myrta a few nights ago. Her whole face is swoll up. Left cheek and right temple. Next time he's gonna kill her. She can't walk because her ankle is broken.

Miss Sherry just told me that the law is after me. She said she don't know if it's the truth, but one woman came by last night and told her that a law man told her that they was looking for the white man. Said something about some problem at home. "Dat's why we ask you if you got any problem with anyone back home." She say something bout me runnin' from jail. People have good imaginations.

I'm taking the whole thing as bullshit, but they still could take me to jail for my papers, not to mention the pound and a half of ganja I got hidden under the concrete blocks in my old house, Jisena's place, that she's now renting to some policeman. I don't feel like the Babylon will look there though.

So now I'm in the hammock, waitin' on the rain. Later, I'm going up to Smoothie's to look the money he owes me for finishing the fish pots before he drinks and whores it all up. After that, I'm gonna go hide out in the bush till I find a way to Pearl Lagoon.

Evening time: Waiting on the police to show up lookin' the white man. I hear a knock on the door outside. It's Jose. He tells me Myrta is calling me to come eat. Myrta is the only person I can talk to around here honestly and intelligently. She tells me tonight that people are always talking about how I'm crazy. How I express myself. Walking around dirty and ragged. "But your not crazy," she says. "You educated. You got good ways".

People around here love to talk. "Small seed sprout big flowers," she tells me.

I tell her about meteors and how they spin around in circles. Just like us. The moon spinning around us. We spinning around the sun. The sun spinning around something. God.

Circles spinning around circles around circles around circles. Spirals. We forget that our lives are three-dimensional. Life is a shell.

We aren't spinning around flat. Our spinning is elevated. We are spiraling up towards heaven. A conch.

The apex. A gravitational magnetic field where the Mayas say some can disappear on certain days, on portal days. Einstein theorized it. The Egyptians tried to build it. The Nicaraguans use their volcanoes. The hermit crabs make it their house.

Around six o'clock, everything comes out just for a bit. Some come to talk with Myrta. Some come look food. Some jump out the water. Some just come to fly around and sing a song before going to sleep.

Myrta tries to explain to me about how it's her own fault that her face is all swollen up still after six days. Her jaw is popped out but it's not Jose's fault. "He was just protecting himself," she explains. She doesn't understand why her family doesn't like him.

I tell her it's because he smokes rock and mashes up all their money quick one time every time. But she says, "No, it's me. I like go mash up the money. Let's say he goes out and makes seven hundred bucks. He gives me six hundred and keeps one hundred that he goes mash up. I go and hit a Plata and want my licky bag o cokes. Then I drink that and want another bag o cokes, then another and another until I finish all dat money. You see, it's not his fault. It's my fault. They like say its Jose, but its me. Him just protectin' he self. My face, him no do me this. I do me this. Let's say you go out to drink rum and you's my man. I gonna think you lookin next woman see. So I pull a knife to keep you from leave, and I swing at you. You bettah protect yourself breddah, and you push me away and you push stronger than you feel, so I fall against the wall like so you see and mash up me face".

So your man shouldn't go out and drink rum and look next woman. He should save the money to buy some food for the children.

"You want to know why your mother don't like him?" I say.

"But they not right. It's me who's wrong," she insists.

"OK Myrta, but I gonna tell you why they don't like him, not right or wrong or morals or nothing". I realize that she probably doesn't understand the word morals, but I continue and I point to little Esperanza who Myrta is holding in her arms.

"Lets say you got your licky baby and every time she goes down to the sea, she come home mashed up in the face. The sea ain't right or wrong, it's just the sea, but every time your daughter goes near, it mashes her up. You tell her no go, but she still sneaks away and comes home all tattered and crying. Pretty soon you start to hate the sea, just because you's a mother and you want you licky gal safe. It's natural".

She smiles and nods in agreement. "I see. I see what you sayin'," she acknowledges. Thinking I'm not crazy makes me feel good.

Rain coming again. I can hear it fade into the full sound in stereo on the tin roof. It rained off an on all day today and yesterday. Yesterday the weather caught me out to sea, diving for conchs and fish. It got me cold and wet up. Today its catching me nowhere but inside.

The police don't come in the rain. They're lazier than I am.

Dookie told me he heard two men talking on the beach yesterday that they gonna come look me again. "The white man that stay by Jisena's place," he heard them say. It may be the truth or it may be a lie, but I don't feel the need to run. I can't hide in the bush until a boat leaves for Lagoon. It could be a month. I'm not going through Big Island to Bluefields. If the police are looking for me, they'll surely stop me for my papers there. I feel like the best thing to do is to take it easy and see what takes place.

I tried forging my papers with this blue pen I'm writing with. I changed the ninety days to one hundred and eighty days. If the police are as stupid as I think they are, they'll let it slide. Benito says not to worry about it. They can't do nothing, he tells me confidently. "Just do what you feel. Things always go alright when you follow what you feel. They go bad otherwise". Benito is pretty cool.

Intellect is waxing and waning, according to what I have read. The living are out in the morning, sleeping in their beds are the deads in their heads on their papers. The police haven't showed up because on Big Island there's a psychopath on the loose after raping and killing a seventy five year old woman up on Queen Hill. Police are investigating. These are the people I would get to share a cell with.

The world outside the window is working. I am pretending to be a writer, resting the wound on my foot and the boil on my shoulder.

Enough of this tale, resist the temptation of the egoist who just sits around and smokes and writes slowly the words that come to mind. "Discipline," he says. "You need discipline. Structure, you need structure, and most of all point. What is your point?" What is your mission, what is you project, and what is your plan? There's a boat here bound for Puerto Cabeza tonight. Puerto Cabeza is a long way up north, nearly to Honduras. From there you can hop on a truck loaded with rice and head to the frontier. I could continue with my life. Forget Marlon and Laguna de Perlas. Forget finding my wife, who's only sixteen, but looks like the Queen of Sheba.

It feels like it would be a hurry.

Black lizard, I don't think I've ever seen you before. I'm too slow. Perhaps I need to hurry. It's never too late to end up in jail. Stop looking for the moment to seize and just play your guitar; or just stare out the window and wait for a moment to seize you.

Passing the evening smoking ganja in the hammock, listening to the gentle hum of the generator and the reggae, country music over at Stella's Place.

Marlon rolled into Little Island last night and like always, we met cool on the sidewalk, letting me know that I listened to the right voices telling me to walk at the right time. Change of plans. We no longer need to head to Pearl Lagoon. Marlon is headed back to San Andres. I didn't see him today, so he must have left last night.

He said there's nothing to do in Lagoon. No work. He's going back to work in San Andres. Start working with arms. One trip with one hundred AK's and you make ten thousand dollars. It's easy he says. You get a skiff and you got work. You can go straight from Lagoon. The world of Colombia and the world of Nicaragua are so different, but separated only by the two-sided mirror of imaginary frontiers in international waters.

He brought his wife and son with him this time. He nearly lost them last time he was in San Andres. He lost his bar. His partner took the music and split. His woman didn't have anyone to take care of her and that is dangerous in these parts. It doesn't take long for them to look another man. Marlon killed the last woman that cheated on him. Shot her in the back in Bluefields, and then split for Lagoon with the next *panga*.

It was good to see him. We smiled and laughed about things. I brought his wife and son some mangos and they were happy. It all made me feel good. So now what? Where to go? When? How to get there? I wonder about everything this morning and meet some Miskito Indian fellow who tells me about Puerto Cabeza and Honduras. Everything I've heard about Puerto Cabeza makes it sound like a hard place. That girl from down the street in San Andres was killed there. The rain is coming damn hard. The sky is dark dark out my window. When the sky is dry, it's just as good a roof as any, and when it's raining, it's just too wet to fix it.

Well, the police finally showed up on the island. I slipped out the back when I saw them prowlin' around, went down to Fireman's down by Bamboo. It is all cool except for some Babylon man is renting out Jisena's little house now. I've got to get the ganja out of there. Right now the door is open, but I don't know if the guy is in there or not. The situation has gotten tricky. A boat left today for Lagoon. I wanted to go but decided to wait until this ganja sells, my mission. My project is to get rid of the grass and go. I am doing nothing. I am going broke slowly. I will soon start getting fat from lying in this hammock. I have no friends. I have not called my family in over three months now. I hope that they have come to accept the death of their son. I have. My name sounds funny when I hear it.

I have every vice a man could want. Ganja, rum, honey and light, and I won't be satisfied until I'm dead.

The police came and took Terry away today. One more rock-man gone too far. He is a big black man that is not from the island and hopefully will not come back, says everyone that knows him. He thieved everyone and everything he touched, and as soon as he touched anything, it was gone. Burnt up.

Back in December for the white Christmas, he found a sack of cocaine worth close to one hundred thousand dollars. It is now June, and he has been broke for several months. They say he just went crazy with the money, drinking rum and smoking it up, just being stupid, shoving dollars into plastic shampoo bottles and throwing them into the sea. He came walking by the house the other day with a Ron Plata in hand, strutting like he needed a cane. He yells at me and Jose, "Hey! How come I done built three houses and I ain't got no home".

"It's true," Jose said. "He don't live no-where".

That is the only way Terry could be here and get away with all of the shit that he pulls. No one knows where he sleeps. He has no upholder. It's surprising because he always looks remarkably clean. His skin is so black that it's blue. His hair is always slicked back. Anytime I see him coming I look down and away to avoid any contact. I know if we met eyes his attention would be drawn to me and any connection with a rock-man like him is going to be trouble.

Jose told me yesterday that Terry came up to him in the morning and gave him twenty cordovas to go buy him a piece. Terry told him everything that he did the night before. He hijacked some guy that lives down in the bottom somewhere, and the guy came after him with a gun shooting. I guess that that pissed Terry off, so he went and smoked a stone, grabbed a glass of gasoline and threw it through the man's window on a burning candle, burning the house right down. The only thing remaining now is the zinc.

Jose tells me how Terry's got feelings too. "I think he's alright. He give me a cigarette and twenty *cordovas* so I can go drink in the morning," he says.

So they come and gone with Terry, and it seems that Terry told them everything that's been going down on the Little Island. Everything. "Even bout Winnie?" Myrta asks. "Even bout Winnie," Jose says. About the Colombians and the cocaine boat deals with Saroh and what not.

Somebody's going to kill him, people agree. Winnie is the *alcalde* of Little Island. He runs the Lobster Company. He runs the town. What he says goes and he doesn't say much. He runs his business and for the most part lets the island run itself.

Around here, the Lobster industry is the cocaine industry. White lobster, found by the ton floating around the seas between Nicaragua and San Andres by the lucky lobstermen braving the seas.

The Downs family has connections with the Morgan family of the Western Caribbean Islands. The Captain Morgan family. The same Morgan that is one of the richest men in Nicaragua. He is still a pirate. The Morgan name is just as big in San Andres. There is a famous cave there where Morgan's ancestors were said to have hidden a big treasure back in the day. Both Downs and Morgan are family with Miss Sherry, so practically something to me.

So here I sit with my Rum Plata, feeling it in my kidneys, begging myself not to take another drink while I unscrew the sweet little silver plastic top.

A few months ago a girl had a copy of the New York Times here, and there was small box about Corn Island. It seems that the Nicaraguan military turned the island over to the US War Machine, saying that they could not control the trafficking of drugs from Colombia. Maybe the US will send them some money. A pay off. Maybe they'll come out here and shoot our asses. Meanwhile on Little Corn Island, we're going to kill the pig tomorrow. I'd like to be able to buy a case of beer and let everyone drink beer and eat coconut fed *chancho* and be happy for a little while. Times are tight around here. Too many mouths to feed and too small a pots. I should be getting gone. It is often hard to believe that this is the same trip that took me through Chile and Bolivia and Colombia and back to Colombia and here, and I'm still as alive as I was living there. Time to soak the beans.

It is a shame I never remember the words I dream of writing. You would all be saved.

Today we killed the pig. Brother Louis whacked it across the skull with the axe head and stopped its heart. It was in real pain for a minute before it lost consciousness. The pig was an asshole anyway. We shaved it with scalding water and cut off the feet at the ankles. Took off the skin and started frying the fat. We then proceeded with the butchering and the frying of meat. Fermin the butcher shared his cuts of the finest meat with me. The liver, the heart and the kidneys were all roasted. I tasted a piece of just about every part of the filthy animal this morning. Then the rain came and I cleaned up. Bumming again in the hammock, I've turned to rum and honey. I feel heaty and sweaty. It is strange to think that I too could be butchered like that, cut up from my asshole to my throat. Split me through the pelvis and smash through my ribs to pull all the innards out. My sweet bread and green shit spilling from the split sphincter.

I'm getting run from my house. I imagined this a long time ago. I will get kicked out of every house I live in until I make my own. Then I will have peace. Just like my house, my book will have no end. It will continue to grow as I dream. I will plant a lemon tree and a fence

There's a rich man who don't understand why the poor man steals. Like a poor man that don't give damn bout how he feels. Like a hunger he's left with after a meal, or an apple that gives him temptation. Take what you're given. Get what you take. Make what you love, and love what you make.

Well, finally I stopped paying rent with Miss Sherry and was accordingly kicked out when I started cooking for myself. For one hundred and fifty cordovas, she'd give me rice a few times a week. I hate rice. I need beans!

I moved in at Heiko's.

Heiko is a crazy fuck. He went away to Managua last week on his "mission" and needed somebody to watch his place. He's got a few nice little cottages on the point where you can see the sunrise and the sunset. He calls the place the Casa Sunrise Project. Rooms that he rents to tourists in the name of compassion.

The moon has changed. The wind has died. I planted a big bed of corn which they say won't grow due to the salt air, but I planted it anyway, and it has sprouted and is coming up nicely. It's a good place to watch things; the birds in the wind; the eyes of the skinny dog; the age of the coconut trees; of course the waves and the cloud's faces; the sea and hoping that something will float up.

Heiko is completely unstable. The last thing he said to me before he left for Managua was about all the LSD he used to take. How much he liked it then and how he wonders about the long-term effects that might be hitting him now. He often just completely flips out. He has no control over it, and says that it seems to be getting worse. He often has the irrepressible urge to just kill someone. Like me for instance.

I don't know what the hell I'm doing here. If I could just get rid of all this grass, I would leave this damned island and start traveling again. I should just give it away and leave. Heiko had a book of I-Ching last night that he took out after a little Black Ticket rum and a few coco leaf joints. The book of changes. I don't even have to ask what it would tell me to do. It would say ditch your possessions and continue with life. Become a beggar and lose the source of all discontent. Follow the spirit and rely on nothing. Sleep where I sleep and go where I go. Avoid being killed by crazy old German screws. Or continue with patience and greed.

Patience makes inner silence and light.

Courage makes strength.

Stubbornness makes fun.

I'm now out of places to go on the Island. Everyone's got marijuana. I shall finish this joint.

Heiko's main problem here on Little Island is the vampires, he says, coming over and robbing his ass. Cutting his plantains and bananas. Breaking in and stealing his shit, gas tanks and mattresses. Sucking his blood. Turning him into one of them. They come over sometimes and make Ron Don. I came with them one time. That's when he asked me to come watch his place. He needs them to come bring him fish. Flesh. Blood. I knew Heiko was bad news. I don't know what the hell I'm doing here now. Heiko's so crazy with this place that he can't take it. He needs to sell it, but he can't. No one wants to take care of it, and he doesn't have the money to pay anyone. He can't take care of anything himself anymore. His house is falling down. His wife left him. The vampires are after him and he has no patience. He may just end up giving the place away. He doesn't know what he's going to do. No one does. All he wants is to leave for his Buddhist retreat in the South of France with the exiled Dali Lama.

There is plenty of food here.

Life is back here on the farm. Drugs are never in short supply. Kidneys are in danger. Water is in the coffee. Air is in the grass. Pelaje just came by with the old San Andres machete I left at Myrta's. Rock man, head of the vampires. Come look Heiko. Two stones. Said he's looking pears to send Bluefields with the freight boat. He gave me some grass and twenty cordovas so his avocados would be legal. Tell them the white man said it was irie.

Meanwhile, I'm back in the hammock for another day of watching the sea and waiting for holes to fill and leave. I've been out and down for a week now with this infection in my leg that *por lo menos* seems to be healing. I went to see the doctor, but he was in Bluefields. I fasted for three days and saw him on Tuesday, skinny and pussing and bleeding all over myself from the gaping bullet hole in my shin. It was a swollen mess, inflamed black and blue. In and out of limping fevers and chills until I let the doctor tend to it and got some antibiotics. My heroin. I need it to get well.

The first thing the doctor did after he took off the pussy bush rag I had the hole wrapped up with was wipe everything off with some gauze and put on some gloves. He put a piece of gauze on the tip of his index finger and shoved it right through the scab that covered the hole in my shin. His finger passed to the first knuckle, and he began to twist it around, wiping out the infection. I nearly fainted with pain, but just had to laugh. After that, he squeezed and squeezed while more puss oozed out of the hole. It was hard to believe that was my leg.

Coconuts are dropping like bombs and I'm still just here watching. *Incommunicado.* I've been reluctant to inform anyone in the old world of my whereabouts for a good while now for no other reason than I have no explanation at all about what the hell I'm doing here. I look up, and it is July. I will blink and it will be November again, and here I'll sit, doing the same thing I've been doing for the last four months now. Surviving. Living. Passing my youth away as if it were already gone. Watching it drift off with the tides and the feathered clouds of the Caribbean Sea.

People are easily *encantado* with the enchanting life of this little island. Trapped. Tricked. Teased into somehow halfway believing that there is an opportunity here; drugged to sleep with a full belly; telling themselves that opportunity is nothing but a poor American dream of vanity. The opportunistic die the same death as the content, but they die struggling in the sandy hill that gives way to only more sand beneath their feet. "Solitude" the dreamer tells himself will fill his hole, and it does, but the dreamer never sees tomorrow. He is not ready to face the reality that comes when he falls sick to the inevitability of accident. He has nothing saved for a rainy day and no one to help him when he is in need. He is weak but he is alive. I was lucky. If not for Fireman, I don't know what I would have done. I laid in his hammock for a week. He and Pamela made soup for me when I began to eat. They say friends are only those who like and hate the same things.

At Fireman's, I practice the *artesania*, making jewelry. It is aesthetic. The polishing of fine shells and stringing them together on braided lines of hemp for necklaces and bracelets. Shiny things for the eye to play with. Prettiness that one man finds and another man buys. Craft. Fireman loves it. He finds beauty in it.

I find boredom. Polishing is a chore. Sandpaper wears on my patience. I prefer to polish a poem. To create beauty and feeling with words. This is what I tell myself. I am here because I have no place better to go. I am here because it can be home. I am safe here. I can make a living. I am not hungry.

The only place better lies in the imagination. The imagination lies on the road but today I am back on the farm. Seek the shade before you burn.

With what little water you've turned me into mud.

If I just want to sit on the porch and play guitar and sing songs to the sea and the *palomas*, who's to say I'm wrong? If I want to smoke a roach and write in my licky book for a little while, who can put me down? I'm not hurting nobody. I'm not doing no one no harm. Ain't nothin' wrong with letting go and expressing what comes to my inside.

Call me lazy, but I can't hear you. Songs don't smog up the air like your cars.

Inhale the present. Exhale the past. Life is waiting for you to take her into your lungs.

Turn off your light. I can't see the darkness.

Heiko's dying. Can't eat. Can't move. Can only lay there on the floor. Pain in his bones, fever, chills, diarrhea. That's what a few days of rum and cocaine can do to someone his age and weakness. He's really an asshole. I can't help but feel a little glad. I enjoy seeing him suffer. He lives in the fire. He entices you down his pretty road of sweet smelling smokes and pleasure filled paths, but the paths are a lie. These paths are false. They are the wrong path. There are many paths, infinitely many, but only one with heart. Don Juan said that.

It is difficult at times to get off a path, especially one that has been walked on it for many years. You have to turn around and go all the way back to the beginning where it started to find the correct one. It is even more difficult if the path was downhill. Retracing your steps until you get back to the right one. The devil's path is one of fire, and the fire burns quickly, growing with all that it touches. The soul is flammable. It must be put out with water and air. The fire burns clean. Drugs are a path of death. Money is a path of death. Excess is a path of death. The wages of sin are death. Morality is health. Energy is wealth. It lies in the breeze and the water.

"Many find it difficult to accept that one mans present could be another mans past, and still yet another's future". Albert Einstein said that.

It is Saturday. The freight boat will soon reach. I got a hundred and eighty cordovas in town and a full sack of coconuts that I need to back up front if I want to sell them. Saturday is money day. *Chamba* day. Game day. I would love to stay here and write all day, but this world I have lived myself into requires money. I have not given up entirely, surrendered myself fully. I need to pay rent. I hate paying rent.

One match left. I still need to catch fire to fry fish.

Last night I dreamt I died from the cold. Today I'm moving too fast.

A glass of rum in the morning because it keeps the dream alive.

Someone came up to me today when I was stewing fish over the fire.

"Too high to write?" he said. Give it up and brush your teeth. Look at yourself in the mirror. Don't be afraid. You are a man of what you believe.

Three days later and Heiko's still sick and sleeping. For a little while, I thought he might die, but today he took a turn for the better. Just wishful thinking. I need to get away from this place. It is bringing out the worst in me, trite and deceitful feelings. It makes me afraid of who I am. At least I washed my clothes today.

Keep a pen nearby in case of something to say.

My dreams of greed and grandeur are always rebuked as a failure. I've got to get off this tropical paradise garden island, but the food is just so good.

Need water.

Thunder crackles. The poet is dead. He died from all this loneliness. From this silence springs his words. Married to this wilderness, he's just been born with the coming of the morn and the again with crack of the sun.

Seen Miss Sherry yesterday and she wants me to come back home to the house. Her nephew that showed up to rent my room turned out not to be worth a rass. "Don't do nothing. Just sit in that room and smoke, smoke smoke. Him say he gonna work. Him say he gonna fish. Nothin' pa pa," she say. "Nothin. Since you left here, things get worse. Things get worse".

I tell her it must have something to do with that room I built. Contagious like a lamb.

I guess she'll soon run to him and I can go back there if I want. I don't want to do that but Heiko's turning into a bad a feeling that arises every time he is near. I never know if he's just going to flip out or something. I spent the last few days at Fireman's drinking rum and cooking food. Smoking joints in the hammock. Yesterday, we filled the floor with sand, a job we've been meaning to do for some time now. After that we made a pizza.

It seemed like I hadn't eaten in a few days. Working and drinking rum, it's easy to forget. I walked home barefoot in the rain before day and crawled into bed beneath the mosquito net that protects me from evil spirits and sand flies. I read a little Albert Einstein and have been trying to get hungry enough to eat a little bit of bread with avocado or banana, but have had no success so far. I try to write about something important and wind up talking about my morning, moaning about the thunder and gods.

Blackbirds drop from coconut trees and try to fly into the wind, but it is of no use. They hover there for an instant and then just float back up into the tree. It is a river this wind. It is a sea, an invisible sea of Ether flowing around us everywhere. It can be seen through the smoke.

The pure mind is a pure reflection. A pool of water mirroring the heavens, with ripples of thought that shatter the purity and break up reality into a thousand spinning circles radiating through the silence. A voice in the night. The crash of a window.

Today I killed for food. A mother lobster and her unborn eggs. I ate them raw, right out of her womb.

Tomorrow I will kill for money. An assassin for the man upstairs. Taking population into my own hands. Morality versus hunger. Compassion versus greed. I have one match and a fresh joint in my hand. It's time to go down. I should drink more water. It is the time of the dengue. Perhaps I should not drink more water. Maybe it's the contaminated well dishing out the back pains.

I am overwhelmed with guilt for the heartless taking of the

mother lobster. I knew she was too small, but I was hungry. I hadn't eaten flesh all week. I felt as though I needed some strength.

I ate the strength of a conch. I ate a belly full of fish. I went diving with Kim in a little dory with his gun. He does not miss a shot. He seems completely connected with the sea when he dives down. He pauses, aims and shoots. He' takes his time. He takes what he wants. Tomorrow he wants to go back out to the reef to look lobster. I'd like to go with him. I was planning to go to town to haul pots in the morning, but maybe I'll stay here tonight. I'll take my ripe avocados to town in the morning with the lobster I kill.

There is nothing worse than robbing a hungry man's food. Nothin.

I'm going to kill that mother-fucking cat when I see it. Kill him and roast his flesh with salt and oil. Now I'll go to bed hungry instead eating the fish sandwich I'd been saving and working for all day.

One of these days I'll finally get off this beautiful island, but first I want more fish. More flesh. *Ceviche* of conchs and wilts. Diving for lobster. Planting for pay. The life is too good here. I tell myself to leave, but it is difficult when you are full. When you are hungry, you become too consumed with the search for food.

They caught Bluefoot the other day with some *Peruanos* and about a half a million dollars.

It was big. The radio said that cocaine was floating in the waters of Little Corn Island. I wonder who found it. Everyone's been walking the beach these days. Treasure Island. Hell, I was out on the dock early this morning, checking on anything that might have washed up on the beach last night, but didn't see anything. That is the nature of this enchanting island, to fill you with hope of riches or success and leave you with nothing for long enough to keep you hanging on. Then she'll treat you with a taste of her promise and take even that away from you.

Got to go talk to Heiko, the worst part of everyday. See what his plans are and subject myself to lazy feelings of worthlessness. Weather. The day is flirting with angst and rainy breezes.

I'm gonna keep moving till I fall in love.

Alchemy. Words from silence. Gold for nothing. Chicks for free.

This morning came and I nearly chopped off my pinky finger hauling cassava for Miss Sherry and the family I've come back to. "Uh oh," I said when I saw the bone and white little specks of tendon beneath the muscle. It is the latest of cosmic accidents and flesh wounds reminding me to leave this island. This will set me back a little while. The *vida* is dynamic. I've moved back to town and the day I reach back, I eliminate myself from work for at least two weeks. The lazy white man is back.

Better go and do something before something does you. The poet has died with his romance and simplicity for the price of the paycheck.

Chopped my finger so bad that it hurts to write.

His father has become a brief voice of the telephone. A two-dimensional faceless tongue; a tone, repeating itself over and over again, "Boy am I glad to hear from you. It's been so long; you had us worried."

The time between calls has been doubling since the day he left home, but the conversation remains the same. No one down here ever goes home.

A wave from the footsteps of his *aeroplane* is played across the news. He tells me everything is gonna be alright until the last river runs dry.

Excuses, excuses excuses. Everyone's got their excuses. People just can't take who they are. Just is an occupation. It's just the car you drive. It is just; it is true; it is you. It is you God, Babylon, in whom we trust. What you buy, where you lie, in the city of tongues.

I went to conquer the city, take it in the name of thought and freedom that will scatter its inhabitants like a hurricane, dispersing them in the fields that grew abandoned without the city walls that had all been destroyed. Inside becomes out and the outside in. People become one. Defenses are down, the strongest defense of all. There is nothing to fight for. You are welcome. You are Jesus' church door.

If I had a thousand dollars, I'd build myself a house with a few rooms where anyone could sleep. Out the back, I'd have a kitchen where you could make a fire and cook whatever food you eat. I wouldn't make you work unless you wanted to and what you'd want to do would be just fine, and we'd play music in the morning and smoke a joint at night and sing to the moon, everything's gonna be alright.

Last night an old *bruja* from down the road died. She'd been stuck on stone and in it bad. She once made me a purge that she boiled from a bunch of herbs; a blackdraft that she said was good for cleaning the blood. Queen of the vampires. Big obeah mama. Today everyone say "her spirit deh walkin' bout".

No one wants to go outside. Better wait until Monday to go in the bush. Sometimes it's better just to wait. We still got a few licky cassava and a pair of big plantains.

Now I got nothing to do today but take it easy. Maybe later on I'll go for a walk; try keep my idleness from drive me crazy, thinking about my *leyenda personal*. All there is to do is wait, six more days out of eight. Spend a little money on things that I need instead of things that I don't. Rent the family.

The present has been written in the stars, but the future is up for the taking.

Light emitted from any point in the universe will eventually return to that point.

Another *panga* loaded with cocaine is said to have sunk somewhere on the reef two nights ago. A few people I know found sacks of cocaine. A guy right next to Heiko found a drum of Colombian gasoline. It is the latest of a long line of treasures and opportunities that have floated onto the beach and kept me hanging on to this dream that I will one day hit it big here on Little Island.

Two weeks ago I awoke in the hammock in Fireman's house to

two gunshots followed by the roaring of engines much louder than any of the fishing pangas around here. "That's a big panga," I said to Fireman who was drunk and passed out in the hammock beside me. He didn't respond. I stepped outside to catch a little breeze, half thinking to go check it out, but in my delirious state of half rum *plata* drunk and half asleep, decided it better to retire back to the hammock for a few more hours. When the sun finally rose, I made my way outside again and walked out to the front to see what was taking place in town. It was clear that something was going down. Two people ran past me headed for the beach by Bamboo.

Fermin was all sweaty and covered with sand. At six o'clock in the morning, for Fermin not to be in bed sleeping off the rum and stone meant something. He was charged up and talking to Randy and some other guy. "Le go!" they said and took off in the direction of Bamboo, Fireman's neighbor.

That was enough for me and I took off walking, regretting that I didn't check things out when it was still dark. By the time I reached the beach I saw more people running so I took off in the bush and started moving fast, passing up gas tank after empty gas tank that people had hidden to come back for later. I should have stopped there and carried a few tanks back to Danny's to sell later, but my curiosity for the panga overcame me. I kept running.

I passed Gun Point and then another point and then saw the panga on the beach. It was a looter's party.

People were all over the boat and engines, smashing the radios and steering control columns, trying to break loose anything that would break free. The compass, the throttle, the radio are all worth dollars.

Teams of four and five were on each of the three two hundred horsepower engines, trying to dismantle them and get them off of the boat. I kicked off my sandals and jumped in the boat, trying to get a closer look. The boat was already filling up with water and would probably soon sink.

I jumped in.

The panga was huge, at least eight feet high and thirty-five feet long. With three two hundreds, it could fly and out run most any police boat, but still no police had showed up. So why did it run ashore?

The people were frantic, stripping anything they could before Babylon came. "Babylon coming, Babylon coming!" people kept shouting.

I looked down in the hull and the other little storage space beneath the floor, but they were full of oily water and nothing else. Anything else, money or cocaine, was already long gone. Better I go look in the bush, I think to myself, remembering the stories of sack top of sacks that people hid in the swamps when the white Christmas panga came in.

I jumped back out and looked for my sandals one the beach, but the were gone. Screw it. I found a little trail that headed through the wild cane fields above the beach. The trail led past a piece of tubing and foam pad from the boat. I thought I might be on to something when I saw two guys that I recognized from the *Barrio Plastico*. One held a large revolver that he swung my way. They were digging through an overgrown patch of cane. "*Que esta haciendo*?" the one with the gun asked. I laughed cause I thought it was obvious that I was looking for treasures. They didn't say anything and I turned and walked back for the beach. When I got back Fireman arrived. We both realized that there was little hope here so we headed back to the house to drink the rest of the rum and pass the Friday eating *tortuga*.

Once my mother told me that I was wasting my life away, as if she had some better way of spending her time. So I left the city and killed my self and sought out ways to prolong my life instead of wasting it. I went in search of energy, of life, of nature of God and of truth. I stuck my hands in the dirt and weighted my back with cargo and greeted the sun when she crossed the morning horizon. I never looked back nor called home because life there is wasted rapidly in high office buildings and automobiles. Death creeps in through air conditioning.

I learned of fire and blood and the tearing of pride and now all I want is to be where I am instead of trying to leave. I have been planning to leave this island for five months now and am tired of plans. Life comes to us unplanned, unpredictably and beautiful, perfect, naked, simple and true.

But on this island there are no roads, no escape without the permission of the captain and the army that he serves. So today I'll sit here letting my insides run out, trying to make sense pass. It is a fool who fills his bucket too full and a fool who's chained himself to his treasure. "This island is full of opportunity. You can't leave here with empty hands. It is full of money. *Asi*! I'm just watching with my eyes open, waiting to jump in," say the drunks in the *billar*. They've been keeping me high on rum for days now in exchange for songs. Juan found cocaine and has been drunk since New Years without falling. He always welcomes anyone who will to take a drink with him.

There's been some Nica songster here who sings ranchero like an opera and smokes crack. Abel is his name. We make a good band. Juan is our biggest fan. Both of us have lost our voices. I have diarrhea. He was supposed to leave here on Monday, but he's still here on Wednesday, just *vagos*in. Too much *vagos* takes its toll on your body. This island of accidents and infections is taking me over and over again until I can reconnect with my *leyenda personal*. When someone is not on their path, they pay. I have paid with my body here, chained to my ganja dream of making a little money. The island is constantly telling me to leave, but never showing me the *salida* or letting me get well enough to go. I must let the traveling wind cleanse me of this salt. I don't feel to step outside today. I don't feel to eat or drink coffee with milk or speak with anyone. I need to be alone in the bush with whoever wants to be with me. Free to work and die as I please. Live how I chose. Adapt to no one else or their habits. Eat what I eat and don't. Build and plant how I want and be there to reap the benefits of all I sow without plans to leave. The space in your yard is infinite.

I want to teach the children here to read. Then I believe I can leave.

Hurricane comin'. Don't go too far from home. Sit back in the hammock and relax. Roll yourself a joint and just take it easy. Hope you don't blow away.

It's your birthday and I just bought you a blank book full of pages to fill, so let loose the caboose and let it slide into the background. The *olvido* is full of *recuerdos* and the morning full of disguise. The wind is coming from all directions and meets in the halo above your head.

This book will be different. The manuscript in my head will come alive in full color as the daily events of my life blossom into a story of love and hate; of drugs and deceit; family and revolution and poetry in time. It will be unhesitatingly fresh and true and it no longer will be, for it is. It is untamed and untangled, unforced and above all else, simple and true. It is the anti-fiction, for I am no writer. I am a listener and a translator of the words in my head that arrive in a flood. It is the rays and veins and kaleidoscope of colors I see in the sky in a breath that only I have taken. Trust yourself. Have confidence. If you have something to say, it is worthy. Your silence is . . .

Myrta just finished crying to me about how Brother John tried to rape her when she returned here from Costa Rica. She was an angel then, the most beautiful girl on the island. Her body was big like Jisena's. Now she's so *flaca*, she's all but sucked away. Now she's nothing, she cries. That's why she smokes rock. That's why she's wasting away. Killing herself. Why she snorts and drinks rum. She wants to kill herself for her family who treat her like she's the last. Sherry told her once that when she dies, she will throw her two daughters, Yenni and Yendi, out on the beach (or on the streets of an island with no roads). Out of the protection of the yard. She ran me once but says she will never do that again. The children are eight years old.

Myrta needs help she cries to me. Someone to be strong, to keep her up but not put her down. To remind her to hold on.

If I could only be back in the cave. In the mountains, up behind the falls, one can be sober all through the day. Alone to work, walk or bathe quietly in the stream's rock pools, watching her ways.

And so it is that the artist must continue to travel. The people complain that you have already played that song. They do not know that the songs change slowly. They evolve and revolve. I must step outside.

Myrta is not doing so well on her quest for life. Neither am I. It just seems so boring. The world of sobriety. Why be sober? It sounds so serious. I never understood that sobriety means a quest for life. To live instead of die. It is serious.

Little kids are dancing outside, chanting "Josana". Some Colombians have been coming by looking for Jisena. It is always a little scary around here to hear someone talking Spanish. Panas. Miss Sherry no like 'em.

"*Buenas Noches*". No one answers.

"*Buenas noches?*" They repeat looking for some signs of life in the yard.

"Jisena? *Buenas noches esta la Jisena alla*?" Miss Sherry tells them to go away.

Since the family got a little money out of the Colombians who got busted here a few months ago, Jisena's been able to stop whoring herself out to the drug runners passing through. They still come around though, hoping to get a little piece. I imagine that she was the best.

The house of drugs, booze and prostitution. Whatever you can pay, for we'll sell it until eight at night. Mama likes to sleep soon.

Coralito's toys are shells and balls and drums, flowers, sticks and cocos. Coral is full of parasites. He shits out little black *lombrisas*. Worms. Millions of them have his little belly swell right up. They are sucking the nutrients from him and just getting fatter in his stomach. He is the happiest baby one has ever seen during the day, but at night he screams and howls like a madman. *Gritando* and crying. It's the worms. He's possessed by evil spirits. *Poseido*. Fireman doesn't how to exorcize the demons. They finally started to try coconut, and it seems to be working. He likes coco.

The days are raining, keeping me inside and unemployed. I feel sleepy.

The further we get from nature, the closer we get to death. More poison, less water.

Spending time massaging my finger, trying to regenerate lost feeling, it is difficult to cope with the possibility that I may remain crippled with this for life.

Last night I dreamt of a pale skinned brunette with red lips. She stuck her tongue into my mouth when we met to lead me away. It was her call to me. She made fun of my appearance and I had to explain to her my fear of mirrors and other games of illusion. I do not like to see the monster that hides deep inside the mirror. He sometimes grabs into my soul and is hard to unhook. She laughed and stuck her forked tongue into my mouth again. I followed her. It was clear that she knew something I didn't, like the eyes behind her disguise or the direction she led me.

I awoke surprised not find myself all wet up. It has been too long alone in the rain. Today I think I'll just stay high. I don't know what it is about smoke bringing words to my pen. There is a connecting of spirits.

The *borachos* are still at it, drinking rum, begging songs from the guitar and talking their war stories. Saturday came and no *chamba.* Could be a tough week.

Smoothie Joe came by drunker than usual, telling me about how he's gonna have my money by Monday. How he never got paid, yet somehow ended up drunk with new sandals on his feet. When he's drunk, he loves to talk about himself and his past. He's a boxer. He tells me about how he can take Mike Tyson. We'll soon see something on the TV about him. Alright Smoothie, just give me my three hundred cordovas. He talks and talks and talks when he's drunk. When he's sober, he doesn't say a word. He just stares off the porch at nothing with a pissed off growl on his black face.

As for me, I had to buy the parasite pills today for the little white worms I found crawling through the shit I took in the bush. I am past ripe, starting to rot. Full of worms and shit.

Myrta's face is all beat up again. Jose threw a sofa at her. Mashed her up. Jose was telling me how it wasn't like he beat her or anything, trying to make himself feel better about his vileness. "I didn't punch her this time". What the hell's the difference. I'm sure that Myrta was asking for it. She's got big balls when she's drinking rum.

Swatting cockroaches on my backpack that needs to be used. Pearl Lagoon, Haulover, Orinoco, up to Puerto Cabeza and on to Honduras. Miskito and Garifuna country. A living museum. A live culture, an indigenous empire, independent, free and autonomous. You can't tell them nothing because they don't need nothing. They won't accept your bribes or your sales, your payoffs or your rules. Your blockades won't work because they don't need a thing. The people are warriors. They can live in the swamps and the bush.

I remember arriving in Costa Rica a few years ago, fresh off the plane from Houston with absolutely nothing to do and no where to go. No plans or knowledge of my destination, occupation or situation, except for the fact that I wanted to find an easy, *tranquilo* beach to just get my bearings and equilibrium straight. I asked around the Coca Cola bus station and after a few nights of shitty towns with nothing but exits, I found Montezuma and a little camp on the beach. I remember meeting a few pretty Gringas from I don't know where. They'd been traveling around for a few months, doing this part of the world. They were pretty boy. Canadians maybe. One looked a little Indian in a black, light summer dress. They asked me how long I would be down here for and laughed when I told them I didn't know, two or three years maybe. I as well thought I might be crazy. How the hell could I last two or three years in this game, with no money and no job? I just hoped that everything would flow together. Then I met the Spaniards.

One was a sushi chef and the other a gardener. They told me about the cave. That is where it began. I had to go they told me. I had to go.

Six months later I found the Caribbean, and here I sit with the months flying overhead like the cool breezes, and two years seems remarkably short. The thought of a year upsets me. I only want to take time as it comes and free myself from this Babylon prison of calendars. I only want some fish. I want to get laid. I want to travel.

A big rains coming. Work may come again on some other day.

Love and Felony.

"I need to get off this island," are the words I see when I lose my mind in the morning. A connection with the day. Seeing the sight that is hidden. The thundering sounds of the unheard. The crashing of silence unbounded. The rays and colors of shuddering light that lie beneath the razors in blurs.

Last night a friend of mine who lives around on the beach was walking home *tranquilo* when he encountered the Chino, the head of the narcotics police around here. The police officers stopped him, handcuffed him at gunpoint and beat the shit out of him. I saw him this morning and he was bad off. His gut was hurting him and his black face swollen and blue. The police had no reason to stop him. They look for anything they can to get their hands on some of the drugs and money passing through here; beating, robbing, shooting innocent people, without warrants or justification.

A few months ago, Chino shot a Chontales man who was here on the island making *chamba*. The man was unarmed and not a threat to anyone's safety. They say he was helping beach a Colombian skiff, just working for a little money. At least the mafia doesn't hurt the innocent.

Smoothie is betraying me. Old dog.

He doesn't want to pay me the money he owes me for building the fish traps. Instead he wants to take me off the island.

He says he's gonna call the police on me and get them to take me for my papers. He says I've been here too long. I say the same.

I get sick to my stomach when I think that I'll probably be crippled for life. My pinky finger is dead from the knuckle up. I haven't really wanted to come to terms with this, but it has been over a month and I haven't recovered any feeling yet. I drink all kinds of things and have pretty much learned to get along with it, except for on the guitar. It is impossible to play anything the same with only three fingers.

The numbness is nauseating and shuddering. I try to massage it and stretch it in a type of finger yoga. I try to make the blood flow to it to avoid any kind of calcium build up. I guess that it helps. I have been hiding in my shed all day, trying to take it easy. I am scared to death of the outside world around me that just keeps rolling with or without us, but it is getting too hot in here.

I need air and the breeze that is blowing from the West for the first time. Hurricane breeze. The days are beautiful and the nights full of hell.

Can't talk now, I'm in the middle of drinking rum.

It is time to dedicate myself to traveling. That's what leaving takes, full concentration of a mind that wants nothing else.

I am now wasting my time, my life, so says my mother. Mama Sherry stole the hammock out of my room. I guess she had enough of watching me occupy myself with lesser things.

The fleabites all over my ass are drying up. My hand is still crippled. My hair is still growing but my feet are still firmly planted. Tomorrow I will look to leave.

There is a ride going to the Caye tomorrow morning I learned after proclaiming today to be a day of traveling. I saw Indio this morning and he said that he wanted to travel. The breeze is blowing as if it were Autumn. I said that I wanted to travel too. I asked where he was going. No one responded, and he walked off.

Indio is a big ass rum-guzzling, lobster-pot-hauling, crack-smoking Miskito Indian. He and Jose got into trouble with Myrta and a machete last night. Sherry came out and wanted to kill him. She always talks about how she is going to poison him. Maybe plant something that makes him go crazy. "You can plant something that makes someone go crazy? Huh," I said to myself.

She is a bad bitch that old Miss Cherry. I wonder if she done plant something around the garden to make me go crazy.

I think I may change my lifestyle and become a vegetarian. Stop hunting and needing to kill. I could kill a coconut and eat the flesh straight from the bone. Alive and digestible.

But the fish, the heart that is beating. Does the coconut have a heart too? It certainly has veins. If it has veins, it must have blood, and if it has blood, then it must have a heart. Its heart must be beating a subtle rhythm of solitude that is inherent in us all. It is too dark to write. My pen is out of ink. I'm gonna take this last five cordovas I saved on *pihibayes* and buy myself a pen. Not a drink. The rum is spirit. It is why some of the blessed have sold their souls to the devil and the sweet stirring music.

Tonight I watched a man die. It was a pana (Spaniard) who was at the *Billar* with us drinking rum and begging music from the guitar. "*No importa*," he said. "*Da le lo que quiera*". It doesn't matter what I played and long as it came from the heart.

His mother was the nice woman who brought pregnant woman's clothes for Pamela. She bought us a beer and wanted to hear the *Ranchero* music that Abel played. He was singing songs about a man that loved a woman so much that he picked all of the flowers from his *campo* when the fight broke out with Fermin.

Fermin was high too. He begged the guitar to sing some Calypso song about old Mister Willy coming down to see what the boy has done. "Well, he pull out de knife and he cut up he wife and we see how de blood does run. And de blood does run and the blood de run." Things were getting hot.

I guess there was some dispute over the game of pool and the two off them rolled on the ground, fighting beneath the pool tables until the Pana boy's mother tried to break it up. The Pana bit a hold of Fermin's ear and didn't want to let go. Fermin cried for mercy "*Sueltame! Suelta me!*" The Spaniard let go.

Finally they got up, and Fermin went after him with a pool stick. All of the black men were hollering to hit him with a pool ball, but he never did. They started to box and Fermin all of a sudden disappeared into the darkness of the night outside. He passed by me a moment later rushing back into the *Billar* with a broken rum bottle in his hand.

I grabbed him by his sweaty arm when he passed by me, but like a lion he swung me loose and headed for the Pana.

They went to the ground again and this time Fermin was on top. I saw Fermin's hand raise and punch down with the bottle. I knew he was stabbing him.

The Pana jumped up with a shocked look of death in his eye. Everything stopped. He stared up at the ceiling for a second then turned and ran into the darkness behind the bar. He had a bleeding hole in his left abdomen that he held as he fled. It made me cringe as he disappeared into the night.

Fermin split, no one knew where the hell to. I sat down with the Pana boy's Mom who was cussing the Negro whose blood ran dirty. How they cannot fight fair like men. I sat with my beer, my body stinging with occasional flashes of shock rushing down my spine, twitching with the sight of Fermin's thrusting hand and the gash in the proud Pana boy's side. How he stood handsomely alone like a boxer with a slight smile the moment before he was stabbed, thinking he had already won the fight.

I walked outside to move on the sidewalk and saw a crowd of people. The boy was on the ground dying. There is nothing that can draw a crowd like a death. *Maldito ese guaro de cana.*

People were circled around his body like vultures. His mother was crying, uselessly trying to tend to his wound. The boy was going. His wet bloody guts, hanging out of the hole in his side, were covered in sand from the beach where he fell. He was barely moaning, able to make no other expressions.

I told her we needed to put pressure on the wound but she said we couldn't, and lifted up the bloody shirt to show his grimy guts. "What is that?" I asked before I realized it was his innards. It was clear that the boy was dying.

We arranged a panga with gas to come pick him up and carry him to Corn Island, but he was already going past the point where one could not return. We still lifted him carefully and carried him to the seaside where Lewis and a next man were in the skiff ready to carry him into the dark sea. He was dead before they reached the big island.

I am leaving in the morning. It is late. I am drunk and tired and need to pack my bag to get off of this little island. I am going Caye.

It is noonish back here at the shack after a premature attempt to leave. It's Wednesdayish. I awoke with the generator and started picking coconuts, taking shits and putting my pants on. I left early for the *Billar* where I was told to sleep if I wanted to leave. Escaping the island seemed like a good thing to do after last night's murder. I need to just keep my mouth shut about everything.

There was a meeting this morning at the *Billar* with everyone that was around last night. Nobody planned it, but it was just natural for everyone to show there and see what people had to say. If the police come, it was agreed that there would be problems for everyone. Fermin showed up and said that he was sorry, but he had no choice in the matter. His blood was hot up and he's a man that can do anything when he gets that way. He no give a rass when he got the rum ina him. I bought a bread. Abel heated some soup. Line offered rum to anyone that wanted and pretty much everyone accepted. We all drank two beers and agreed to keep ourselves quiet. I just wanted out.

The words are evil spirits that have to get out. To exorcize.

Maybe I'll go around to the other side for a day, get cleaned out and eat some avocados. Take it easy and sleep some. Maybe I'll dive some wilts. Take a walk.

There ain't nothin' here but trouble. I've been drinking for five days or so now. A long fiesta. Every morning I proclaim that it is over. Every afternoon or midmorning I take a drink. Today was the last. I've already got an open bottle in my bag from last night. Sounds nice to drink it over at Heiko's. Come back here with some pears.

So here he is. Stuck on an island, roaming around Nicaragua, not doing anything but falling out of hammocks, drinking rum and writing, telling himself that he is clean and free. Secretly trying to get rid of a pound of ganja by keeping it tucked away in his backpack. Minding his own business, not doing nobody no harm and BAM! He gets mixed up in a murder case. Trying to hold a drunk man back with a broken bottle in his hand from killing some poor *pana* boy, he got blood on his hands. Police are coming in. No boats are leaving the land. So here I am sitting over at Heiko's, guarding the house and stealing avocados, trying to stay away from the *Billar* a little while and clean out until the boat is supposed to leave tomorrow morning. It was to leave today, but Matagalpa told me the tomorrow we're going. With all the shit that's been going on, I wouldn't be surprised if they hit the road early. Matagalpa, Abel the Mariachi and Line, the owner of the *Billar*. It's a rough crew I'm taking in with.

I knew that things were bad when I saw Abel and Cain (Matagapla) on the trail coming from Bambu's, picking up my things from Danny's and saying goodbye. They were in the shadows where the sidewalk ends outside of town, where the light mixes with the dark. Death was written in their eyes.

Maybe they were just talking about me, but most likely it was just the stone they were about to smoke. It was as if time was running out on them to burn it up; like they were holding their breath and this would give them oxygen. Maybe they just knew that they were dying. Maybe it was just becoming undeniable.

"How you doing?" I tried to joke.

"What you want me to say?" he struck me and the air of my ignorance of how shitty this world really is. "It is not a joke," he tried to say, but it is just.

"That I'm addicted to this little yellow stone and I don't understand why," he feels.

Whatever, it was bad. I knew it was bad. The moon was changing. The breeze was dying. It was brand new. Neither dead nor alive yet. Still not born from it's non-existing, but things are definitely changing.

Benito just stopped by on his way over to Kim's. We exchanged joints and laughed a little bit about life; discussed briefly an opportunity for us to make some business with this pound. Then he kept on on his bike. We'll see what happens before tomorrow.

Perhaps it is that this island itself once rose from the ocean and that the plants upon it burst into flowers under the first rays of the sun.

Yesterday a rainbow sprang up from the sea above Pearl Lagoon promising this is where you want to go. A huge ray highlighting my destination. This was the end of the hurricane, God's word that it will not rain too hard. Everything is going to be alright. It is now safe to travel. You can leave. You may even find your pot of gold. Maybe even a woman to love you. God speaks with rainbows as words. Communication. Sunsets, sunrises, *sonrisas chiquitas*, eclipses and echoes, new moons and no shadows from the stars. Only breezes can make it all worth it; your pay for a life well lived if you can feel them.

Back at the house, I had to break the bank. Dive into my traveling savings cash and slip Miss Sherry a twenty for all the problems.

"I told you," she scolds me. "I told you 'stop drink rum,' but you no listen. I tell you 'stop running round with those people, Fermin, Fermin, Fermin, Fireman, Fermin, Fireman, Fireman Fireman. Drink rum, drink rum. Look what Fermin done now! Always down at that *Billar*. Now they gonna come look you. People here got bad heart you know'".

Just what I need, a little time alone to write, the idler's favorite pastime. Better than sitting at the *Billar* drinking rum. Things are still pretty hot over there. My guitar is up on the wall in the corner there pretending to be Abel's. She's gonna get lost like that. Clementina in the arms of another man who knows how to touch her better. I know that he wants her. He wants to take her away from me. The marijuana smoke is hazing my eyes and my penmanship. It is making me sick. Clide and hot. "The breeze that was once has died," say the mosquitoes.

This desk I am writing at seems to be the best thing I have ever made. The rest seems to turn to shit after a short while. I'm so tired but if I fall asleep now I fear that I may lose my guitar and ride to the caye.

There is a strong sense of racism here, especially since the fight. Perhaps this racism was the root of the fight. Just now some pana boys came by looking beer. Miss Sherry sent them away because she said she didn't want to sell them.

I fear that the key to a good musician is the rum. The drug use and abuse, Cain and Abel. Sold their soul to the devil of death for the poison they chose to imbibe; the spirit that makes them alive.

I have been writing this book now for years. It seems to be writing me. It is all just imagination.

That sack of coconuts in the corner is for me.

How many times will I tell myself to get it together? Beer for breakfast to get ready for the island. Getting high because I tell myself I'm traveling.

The captain, Armando, is high on *Ron Plata* and cocaine. He doesn't want to leave the fiesta. Says the boats leaving at one o'clock tonight, but I know the rum is and the sea don't mix. Just have to wait and see; be pendient.

Standing on the bed and staring out the window, I count the pangas coming in and out of the harbor, wondering about where they're headed. Armando has a big yellow skiff. It is not in the harbor now.

Abel just brought back the guitar after spending the night with her. Taking her out to the bars and glory for a change. They stayed out all night. From the *Billar*, he took her to the Happy Hut and back up to the *Billar* till now. Running on cocaine and *plata*, just riding it till the crash. No way to live. Try to stay out of trouble and get out the way, but you never see it coming. It hits you where it hurts. It is already on the way. It is punishment.

Stuck in the pauses between words and Jisena brings me a piece of bread and cheese and some milk with cocoa that I spike with rum. She gives it to me and smiles and damn it makes me feel good. As if someone cared about me, as if they don't hate me. Maybe I'll carry a bag of weed and go sit on the beach round the other side of the island if my boat doesn't come in again. Maybe I'll just hide in this tin shack. First I'll go fill some water for Miss Sherry.

Slowly all of the rock men are falling off of the island. They done carry off Fermin. San Fermin. Hot-blooded murderer. "Man of the righteousness, of goodness," he said. "But when I get the rum in me, I is ignorant boy. I ain't had no study. I fight boy. I no give a rass when I get a little heat in my blood. I's ignorant boy. I no study nothing". He didn't give a rass when he got the rum in him. This was his excuse as he explained to all of the men in the *billar* the next morning, as if we were a jury.

Just when he'd about given up on the boat heading for the Caye, Abel came outside of Robert's house and started hollering for him. "Roberto, Roberto!" he cried. "Vamanos hombre, el barco ya esta. Vamanos Roberto!" It was the middle of the night, and Robert was already sleeping, but it didn't take long for him to stammer outside and see what was taking place. The boat had reached and was getting ready to go.

His bags were still about packed, so Robert checked around the room for any loose things and shouldered his backpack. Abel wasn't carrying much of anything, so he helped him out with the guitar and little handbag and started heading for the front where the boat was loading up. On the way out he knocked on Miss Sherry's door and told her he was leaving for the Caye.

"Many thanks," he said and hurried towards the sidewalk to catch up with Abel. He didn't know if she heard him or not. They would certainly figure out that he was gone in the morning.

When they reached out front, Armando, the captain, was loading his yellow skiff on the beach with materials and things to carry out to the Caye. He was sober now. He wasn't so sure that he wanted to carry a gringo out there to the caye. He was the captain. He was responsible for everything that was going to happen. He didn't know Robert. He didn't know if he would be a liability out there. He didn't know if he would be able to work. He didn't know anything about this, so he said no. No way was he going to carry this white boy out there to the caye.

Abel pleaded with him. Robert didn't know why Abel was sticking up for him. Robert's mouth was stuck. Only Abel spoke for him. He guaranteed that Robert could work. He guaranteed that everything would be cool and that he would look after Robert. Armando still refused. Finally Abel took a stand and said he was not going if Robert didn't go. Robert just watched. "No hay fia," Armando replied. That is no problem either. Armando's other two sailors had already stopped loading the boat and stood by watching. Abel couldn't say much either. A moment later Armando gave in and said alright. "Throw your bag in the panga gringo. Le go," Armando said.

They finished loading the skiff and drove it out to a big boat in the harbor that was loading all kinds of things, lobster pots, boxes of nails, wooden strips, sacks of rotten cowhide bait and rations. On the deck, the boat was loaded to its canvas top with lobster pots stacked eight high. Abel and Robert climbed up to the top and found a spot to lie down, their noses nearly touching the canvas top.

The sea was calm. The moon was big and tide high when the boat made its departure. Abel and Robert tried to accommodate themselves the best they could on the deck. Armando's two sailors stayed in the panga, which was being towed by the big boat to save gas. Armando and his wife found a spot in the cabin. The boat stunk of cowhide.

As the boat left out onto the ocean, heading Northwest across the sea, Abel told Robert of the anxiety he felt in his blood. He had been drinking rum and using drugs hard for the last week, waiting for this boat to come and carry him home. He was going home. He was from Rio Grande, a community called Walpa. The caye was fourteen miles out to sea from Rio Grande and the mainland. Klar Caye. It was an Indian caye. A Miskito

Caye. The people there were all Abel's people. He told them that they didn't have to worry there. Everything would be good.

Abel was listless and couldn't sleep. He kept talking and talking about all kind of things. Talking about the work they would do there, about diving and building more lobster traps, about building a camp for Armando. Talking about Puerto Cabeza and about from the Caye they could reach the mainland easily and from there it would not be a problem finding something going up to Puerto. Perhaps something would pass direct from Klar Caye. Robert didn't know what to expect but the boat was moving now. They were moving and there was no turning back. The high boat swayed heavily from side to side in the light sea. It was relaxing. Robert just wanted to drop back asleep. He could hardly keep his eyes open as Abel talked. He asked Abel if he wanted to smoke. Abel agreed so Robert wrapped a little joint from his bag and took out some matches for Abel to light it. The breeze was blowing hard enough through the boat so that no one would smell anything over the cowhide. Robert took one haul and let Abel smoke the rest; perhaps it would help him cool down. Robert had one pound left of the San Andres ganja in his bag. Maybe he could get rid of it on the Caye or the mainland. He didn't tell Abel about that yet. Maybe later on he could find confidence in him, but until then, he would just see what happened.

The boat cruised in perfect time. Rolling over the moonlit sea, its big diesel engine roared over the night air. By morning they were supposed to reach the Caye. Until then they just had to make sure not to fall off. It was goodnight.

The Caye

If I was the captain of this ship, I would sail us right into the moonlight. The shimmering silver burning "V".

La Mar, la Maria, la Madre. The sea. The mother Mary.

In the sea it began. In the sea lies the shell, the mother of all, at the heart of the spiral, the beginning of what never ends and the ending of what never begins. This little caye seems to have begun just so, sprung from nothing. A big pile of coral rocks that for some God given reason have gathered together here in the middle of the sea. It is a floating heap of stones. Like a big ship run aground in a vast ocean. All alone, out of sight of land except for when the tides are low, the weather is calm and the skies are clear. Then you can see a next caye over yonder. It is a strange existence out here on these cayes, strange that life is sustained out here on these salty stones.

The only fresh water is what we collect from the rain. Right now our buckets and drums are full, but it was not so when I arrived here two weeks ago. You couldn't buy a bucket of water. That was when my foot started to get bad.

I knew that my foot was going to be a problem when I saw Abel the night he told me the boat was leaving; the night he told me it was time to travel. The wheels were set in motion long before and the boat was going regardless of the condition of my foot. It was time to go, and I was not going to get left behind.

I saw Bamboo that afternoon. We didn't even *saludar* each other. That cheap old bastard wouldn't even pay for the work I did for him. Easier for his no good old wrinkled ass to try to have me taken off the island. I knew he was thinking that when I saw him that afternoon. He was playing policeman when some face I recognized pointed at me.

"That's the guy," Bamboo asked.

"Yeah, that's him," the face said referring to me.

I don't know what the hell I had done now, but by their tones, they must have been claiming that I did something bad. They wanted me off the island. Some drunk causing problems for the law and orderly. That's how they saw it. I saw it as another case of the rich causing problems for the poor drunk who tries just to mind his own business. The rich are threatened by poverty. I could see it in Bamboo when I asked him for the money he owed me. He's another one of those "*vivos*". Anyway, it was a good time to leave. "The secret to a long life is knowing when it's time to go". Michelle Shocked said that.

The boat left at ten o'clock for the Caye, loaded with lobster pots, ice and cowhide. Abel had to put his ass on the line to get me on the boat. He told Armando that if he didn't take me, he wasn't going. "Shit," I thought.

Eventually we got on and found a spot on the back of the boat where the air was fresh with the smell of rotten cowhides under the stars. We smoked a joint and Abel smoked his last stone, and I fell asleep to Abel talking about something.

The sleep didn't last long before the rain started. It did not stop. There was not a dry spot in the boat that we could find, and by the time my prayers for daylight were answered, things were pretty damn uncomfortable, a condition that did not pass for quite sometime.

The pots have to wait and fill, and likewise the fishermen sit and wait. This is difficult for some because there are absolutely no distractions. There is nowhere to walk to, and even if there was, the stones are too much a pain in the ass to want to get there. There is no booze to fill the days or other work to look. No one puts any effort into the houses because they're really just camps to temporarily pass the sun hot or foul weather. There is no grass to chop down or bush to clean up. It's just fishing and then waiting. Hammocks, hammocks and hammocks. The sea provides abundant fish for this tiny caye, so there seems no worry for food. Cooking and eating are the things to do.

Fish, turtle, lobster, lobster head, turtle fin, are all plenty. And rice! Rice like hammocks. Fish like rice, and sleep and nothing else. Marijuana is a good distraction, so I give myself one joint per day, now that the grass is finally running low. That is fine. Hopefully soon I will be getting off my ass and getting some work. Diving is the best money right now that the grass is done. The last pound sold itself smoothly in less than a week once we reached here. It was perfect timing. The people were appreciative and Abel and I sold it generously. I could not have sold it without him, and just as easily as the grass went, so did the money. Smoothly and nicely. Abel drank most of it when we went to Karawala. That was fine. He took care of me when I was down. I mean he really took care of me.

I was down in the hammock for about two weeks with an ugly boil turned infection on my left foot. It was ugly ugly. *Feo*. Swollen through the ankle, oozing river of puss from the feverish volcano on my foot. I squeezed it before it was ripe, trying to hurry up the process and get off my ass, but that only worsened the situation. The infection spread down to my toes and upwards through my ankles. It got out of control as the veins under my skin filled with yellow puss.

They finally shipped me to Karawala where there was a doctor. Armando told me to go. He is the captain of this camp. The other fishermen on the caye, all Miskito, all agreed that I needed to go, so they took up a collection and everyone put in a few gallons of gas for the cause of sending the sick gringo to the mainland hospital. The mainland is about fourteen miles from the caye. Karawala is another eight to ten miles up the river. It is a good trip. The fishermen carried me out of the hammock and put me into a *panga* with a forty-eight Yamaha engine, and the little caye waved me off with Abel and the captain.

I was in a good bit of pain at the time and probably a little bit delirious from the fever I was getting, but the kindness of the people here made my heart beat. I am going to eat some fish and rice that someone just brought me. "You need to eat," the guy told me.

Does my work have any worth at all? Is there any *valor* in this art? All this imagination and nothing at all but words on a page.

One step at a time, you've gone too far to ever return. You say you're old, just like your father, "well how does it feel" in the complete unknown, where you've finally drifted?

Ah, a pen that writes!

And a blank page.

De quien es este guitara? Pense que era suyo. Nadie estaba usandola. I thought it was for you.

For who is this guitar? It is full of rhythm and sound. It is full of marks and scratches. Asleep and waiting for Zion.

There is nothing better than having confidence in your captain at sea. Here the captain is I.

There is nothing worse than doubt. Choose your captain wisely or do not choose at all.

This morning I reached back to the caye from seas that even the lobstermen in the big boats wouldn't go out in. The only boat going to sea from Sandy Bay was the *Jorgito* and its crew of drunken sailors in the morning after the elections. I went to Sandy Bay to take a walk on the *Tierra Firme* after being on this caye for the last two months. They wouldn't sell alcohol until the evening because they didn't want the Indians causing any trouble until the voting was finished. Just like anything prohibited, the Indians couldn't hide the *chicha* for too long before I found a gallon for sale under the table around the back, and the words started rolling. Some Miskitos started putting it in my head to start writing and telling their story here. To start writing every day about what is happening. About what I see and what I experience.

Captain Kenneth from Slider just walked by the opened non-existent door. Tomorrow we may be hauling one thousand pounds of lobster to the company in Big Island. The seas are too rough for the big boat to come and pick it up like usual, but this lobster has been here for a week now and needs to be moved. The North wind shows no signs of easing up and we can't afford to sit on that amount of production and let it spoil. The weather is high. The lobster is running.

Armando brought in one hundred and seventy one pounds the other day. Cane brought in a hundred and fifty. None of the Miskito guys have brought in anything yet, and as they say, the natives are getting restless. Strike, the boss man here, says that they are carrying their lobster to the other cayes to get out of paying their debts here.

The *Sandinistas* won out the elections yesterday. "In Sandy Bay, Karawala, Puerto Cabeza, Bluefields, Managua, everywhere!" some drunken Indian told me this morning.

The *Sandinistas* are the communists some people say.

"Mistah Strikah hates the *Sandinistas*," Alvaro said.

Strikah says that he does not hate them. He just thinks that they are a "worthless bunch of teifin', cocksuckin' mutha fuckahs".

"They take from all the hard workers who got a house and a little milk for his baby, and give their car away to the lazy mutha fucka who livin out in de bush and ain't got nothin', that ain't nevah worked for nothin. You think I gonna stand for that shit? Noho! Not me".

Strikah is a right wing supporter of Bush and the wars and one of the "many people from across the globe who feel that Ronald Reagan was an angel of light delivered down from heaven as a just and honest republican leader".

Strikah is a Christian man who is, contrary to the belief of the majority of the Indians, is only trying to help the Miskito people. He is self-proclaimingly faultless. "I never make a mistake," he says as I correct him on his addition. Just like we all are, he is trying as hard as he can to produce lobster, produce *dinero*, to produce food for the table the best way that he can. No one can blame him for that. But the thing he does not understand is just that. Every man is just doing what is best for himself and sometimes, what is best for one man is not best for the other, and the Indians have been screwed so many times, that they don't give a damn about you. They don't care if Mistah Strikah's percentage falls. They don't care if Mistah Strikah's lobster gets fucked. The rich don't like to be robbed. They don't care if it's Robin Hood or Sandino's ghost. No one likes losing what they have, but they don't mind if someone gives to them, even if it is taken away from some rich asshole that they never really liked to begin with. There are no rich communists, except for the politicians, who are always rich. Show me a poor politician and he gets my vote. There are none though and I don't vote and or care. The Indians however do. They want Strikah out of here.

Strikah is the boss man here on the Caye. He is my boss. He is a skinny little man that smokes cigarettes from morning to night. They call him Striker because he looks like those big mosquitoes with the sharp needle jawbone. He never wears a shirt and likes to sport a nine-millimeter pistol in his cut off blue jean shorts anytime a boat comes in or he might feel threatened. I work for him now, taking care of the paperwork, dispatching gasoline, weighing lobster and carrying it to Corn Island, making sure he doesn't get robbed by any of his own workmen. He doesn't trust anyone here. He's got a right. No one trusts him either. Everyone wants what they can get.

Strikah works for Bunny. Bunny is the man around here. I've never seen his face, but heard his name everywhere around Little Island and these cayes. It is his money that bought everything you see here. The boats, the motors, the office, the ice-chests, the gasoline; the whole operation is for Bunny. And where did Bunny's money come from? The source of all the money here in the Western Caribbean is *drogas*.

"He gave the Indians the opportunity of a lifetime," say many of the people around here.

He brought them brand new *pangas* and engines, gave them fish-pots, rope, buoys and everything they need to catch lobster. He set them up. He gives them credit for food and gasoline until they can pay it back with lobster. In no time, the Indians can pay off the boats and their traps, their bills, and the pangas will be theirs. They can tell King Crab to go to hell and go about their business, but until then, your ass in here on the Caye, busting it to bring in production. You stay on the Caye all week and if you're lucky, Strikah will give you his almighty blessing to go in for the weekend.

It all seems too beautiful and good to be true. The Indians get a hundred and fifty cordovas a pound before the company's deductions and Strikah sells it for twice that. The conflict arises when the lobster don't walk into the Indian's traps like their supposed to.

"If God does not want the lobster to walk into my traps, the lobster will not walk into my traps. I cannot help that," a Miskito man reasons with me. Strikah does not share the same reason as the Miskito man.

When the lobsters do not fill their traps, Strikah and the Indians begin to have a conflict of interest and reason.

It no longer behooves the King Crab fishermen to sell their lobster to Strikah. They have become so indebted to Strikah's company store and gas station that they can work all week without taking home a dime. They go to sea, find a few little lobsters and what's the use selling it back here to Strikah and the King Crab Lobster Acopio when they won't take home a cordoba of cash money. Better they thief the lobster and take it to one of the nearby cayes and bring home a little milk for the baby. Makes plenty of sense for the Indian, but Strikah does not hold the same reasoning. He gets screwed. "But it's against the law," Strikah argues. The Indians are not quite as civilized as Strikah is. They have not read their bibles plenty as he. It is easy for the commandments to naturally slip their minds when they no longer serve their purpose. "Thou shall not steal. Thou shall not kill," or have they forgotten.

The *Sandinista* flag is red and black. Blood and death they say. Blood and death.

The only thing to take from the world is a deep breath.

Strikah is insane. He is a liar or a psychotic. Perhaps the two are the same, inventing their own distinct and independent reality, separated from the circumstances and real world events around them. Delusional. He creates problems. Everything in his life is a problem. He finds problems. This makes him a problem. The problem.

Some sailor told me other day that Strikah called me a liar. "He said you lie him," the sailor told me.

Apparently when I arrived back from Sandy Bay, he saw me drying out my passport from the salt water, and invented a story about me telling him that I had no passport. This is not the truth. Why the hell would I say this?

This is not the first time his imagination has played tricks on him. The day that my first month of work was completed here, I called him aside to talk about my pay, which we never had discussed.

"What!?" he exclaimed. "Wait, let me get this straight. We never discussed your pay? We never talked about how much money you get?"

"No," I confirmed.

"But I remember going over this with you. Was there never a time when you were inside the store, sitting down on the cooler, and I was standing up at the window and we talked about this?" he questioned me again.

"Nope," I repeated looking in his eyes.

"But I could have sworn we did".

"No," I insisted.

"OK," he said. "Well the number I had in my head was one thousand three hundred cordovas".

That is about eighty dollars a month plus my meals. This is the worst paying job I have ever had. It is also the easiest and the strangest I guess. All I have to do is live here. Which means having to deal with Striker's shit and the problems he invents for the people and things surrounding him, and he invents them for everyone, everyone except for his own faultless self. If I can only survive here for one more month, I can then leave and go meet my family in Bluefields when they come to visit for their Christmas vacation. It seems like a prison, a slave camp out in the middle of the sea.

But the sun is beginning to set behind the coastline on the horizon. It seems to me that another day is done.

Strikah has stopped giving me food. He is completely ridiculous. He wants me to spend back the dribble of money he gives me at his ridiculously overpriced store. When I started working for him the deal was for pay and food. With no discussion or explanation at all, the rations in the pot have grown too small to share around, so naturally I am cut out. So what is there to do but put him out of my day? So here I am in my hammock, passing the rainy morning and watching the activities at the *acopio* on the other side of the horseshoe caye, where I am supposed to be involved. Screw it.

Monday on the caye. There is absolutely nothing to do. Perhaps when the sun rises higher in the sky, I will go diving and risk my life for the flesh that our bodies here crave. Last week I was attacked by a shark that I always thought was docile. A nurse shark. A reef shark. It proved not to be so when it smelled the dead and bleeding fish that I carried in my hand. It came at me hard from the darkness, neither hesitating nor slowing down to check me out or think twice about who he was attacking. It was much bigger than me and didn't give a rass. It appeared out of the distant blue darkness like a dream, like a manifestation. When I saw him coming towards me, I threw the fish I had in my hand, hoping that it was the fish he was after, but the shark did not even flinch for the bait. He was nearly at my fins when I fired one shot with the spear gun at his head. The spear struck him an inch above the center of his eyes. I had no time to think, aim or consider what to do. Everything is silent under the sea. There was no fear or hesitation, only reaction.

The spear stuck into his head and he began to swing violently back and forth to throw the spear. While he swung he pulled the line attached the spear for down, putting a strong tension on the gun and pulling me deeper under the water. I considered letting go of the rifle in hope of getting the shark further away from me, but decided to hold on. If I let go, the gun would be lost. In a moment, he freed himself of the spear and disappeared into the deep blue again.

I retrieved the bent steel *flecha*, and tried to straighten it back and reload the gun as quickly as possible in case he decided to turn back for me, but he was gone; faded out just as he faded into reality a moment before. I dove down and picked up the parrotfish that I dashed away before shooting the shark. Dozens of little fish were crowded around it, picking at the flesh inside the hole where I had shot it. There was still enough left of him to roast and make a nice lunch for Abel and me. I picked it up and headed back for the stones without pressing my luck looking for more fish.

My second work month on the caye here is half over and I only hope to wait out the last two weeks of work until my payday and leave; take a little time in Karawala with a Miskito girl, maybe make a baby as the Indians here all tell me I need to do. If I can only obtain sufficient amount of marijuana I know that I will pass the time fine. The days go by better with her. I think better thoughts and I do better things.

I have joined with the Indians in their plots to get rid of Strikah. "*Waitnum Soura*," they call him. Bad man. They talk about getting drunk and coming out here to mash him up. The Miskito people are warriors. They are big men, strong and athletic. They do not favor the slow peaceful Indians of Talamanca, like Leonardo and Ronaldo. These Indians don't give a rass around here. They'll chop you up or shoot you if you give them a reason to. Plenty of guns have washed up on the beaches of the Nicaraguan Atlantic. Plenty of guns and plenty cocaine. No feel no way. They'll take care of it.

The Indians, led by Lino and Lindolfo, the pastor, were talking about pulling some voodoo obeah on Strikah. Some witch can make up some medicine that will run Strikah from here. "All they have to do is drop a little of this stuff around the house over there where Strikah is, and he'll just pack up and leave. Won't feel for stay here no more," Sonya told me. "Sure, there were some people in Bluefields that no one liked. Always fighting and rowing with the people and that's what happened. Someone got some obeah medicine, and the people just packed up and left. Gone Corn Island. Now they stay Little Island. Just like that".

The only thing about the medicine is that it costs about five hundred *cordovas*, so all the lobster men have to chip in and pay. It is not easy to get the Indians to all agree on something and put their funds together. We'll see what takes place.

The people have been talking about hijacking for some time now. One of the other cayes just got held up last week by a group of Indians from the North armed with AK's and oozies, looking for all the lobster and cash that the *acopio* had on ice. Right now, we've got over one thousand pounds of lobster in the big blue cooler. That's over ten thousand dollars. Good money for a few Indians. I'd like to see them try that here. I sure as hell wouldn't put up a fight. "I'd dive right in that sea and hide out until the shooting stopped," I told Striker with confidence the other day when he asked me what I'd do if something goes down.

"Coward," he called me. He was surprised to hear that I wouldn't stand up and fight like a man.

Damn right I'm a coward. I got no gun here and I'm no dead hero trying to save something that doesn't belong to me.

Striker likes to brag about how he'd do this or he'd do that. "I'd shoot this one here in the head," he claims. "And then wound the others. You know, shoot them in the knees or something and tie them all up. Then I'd go cut some long posts and stick them right up their asses through their mouth and load them all up in a boat and take them over to the mainland and plant them up on the beach there. Show all the Goddamn Indians over there what happens. Bunch of fucking sinners".

He's a real cowboy, Striker. He gets a hard on thinking about that kind of violence shit. I just want to avoid problems when I can. So I sit here on the other side of the caye, passing the time in the shade until I have to head over the other side and check down the weight of the lobster coming in and the gas going out. Today is Monday and there's not shit to do on the caye. No one's out fishing. The fowl don't even lay on Monday. No one works in the Caribbean on Mondays. Not even Mashapa.

Mashapa is the resident ghost on the caye. I am yet to meet him, but they say he was an old black pirate who died here on the caye with his buried treasure. At night he now goes around from camp to camp with the help of the black cat, choking fishermen, enough to hurt and scare the shit out of them, but not enough to kill or do any real damage.

Armando had an encounter with him one night, and every one of Slider's sailors has met him in their dreams. One Sunday when only me and Abel and one other Miskito boy named Condorito stayed on the caye, Mashapa showed up. The Miskito boy just arrived up on the Caye looking for work a few days before, and we were giving him food and cigarettes and letting him sleep in Cien's camp, which we were supposed to be taking care of. Condorito went off to sleep while me and Abel laid in the hammocks listening to the *Chino* on the radio, when we heard Condorito screaming from the camp next door. We just laughed and joked that he was jerking off or something. In the morning he came over wide-eyed and shaking with the story. We told him about Mashapa. I haven't met him yet, but last night got a little scared of his presence for some reason when I was half asleep.

The second most interesting supernatural inhabitant of the Caye is the Toadfish. The Toadfish is a huge fish-like monster that is said to live buried far beneath these stones in the sea. Many swear to have heard him cry, a cry so strong that it shakes and rattles the volcanic stones underneath. I told them I feel like it's some kind of seismic activity from the Earth crust below, but they say no. It is the Toadfish.

A few Indian boys started an enterprising endeavor to find this Toadfish and kill it. They began digging the rocks away behind a camp where the Toadfish was frequently heard. They removed stone after stone and piled them up beside them and reached well into the water, but they soon tired and had to go sea. Their project was never finished and the fish never found. I thought of continuing their work, but in the end decided to lay down back in the hammock and write for a little while. Maybe later.

Road, road, road. Come again please and take me away from here.

I would bore a hole in the moon, string it around your neck and let it shine as the pearl *puerta* of the *diamante marino*.

When you're sick of all your pleasures and all of your creations; bought out and sold out of life and expectation; run out of roads of experiences and explorations; take it out on me. Take it out on me.

Nothing more for do today. Done cook all the turtle blood and fish meat I can handle. Better just sit back and hope too much don't come. Let the joints hit too hard or too small. Let the sun come between you and him. Let'm tell you the ones you loved have changed.

Time to call home you say. Time to say I'm fine and then please call me back if you please.

The man is still screwing me. He doesn't want to pay me and I don't want to work anyhow. I find better things to do and that is fine.

This caye is more like a prison camp than ever-before. My wounds are drying, my feet have been crying from all this walking barefoot on stones. All that I make here is nonsense and imaginary words on an imaginary page. Saltwater cleaned with a freshwater rinse.

It is unlucky to wear pants with holes in their pockets and to dash away cats in the sea. They say bad weather's comin'. Bad weather they says gonna come and follow me.

The moon is full for two days now and life is slowing down back to normal. Slider came back the day she was full with a load of red point Superdragon ganja that sent the Caye sailing. The same day Striker sent his woman back to Bluefields; fired her because she wasn't doing her job. This same day, Patoose, the captain of the Big Boat that comes each week with gasoline, money, ice and rations, and takes away the lobster on ice, well his mother died so he couldn't come with the boat. They gotta find another captain in Big Island.

Meanwhile back on the Caye, life is getting crazy. Everybody is stoned; Misty the baby is running around dirty with her hair uncombed, molesting all the people, most of all her father Striker. Gas is out. Ice is out. The lobster is threatening to go *malo*. We're having a fish fry back at Antonio's, *provecharin'* the good kaya and pretty moonlight, when word comes that the big boat's broke down at sea. Slider's got to go out and pick up some gas and ice. A fight breaks out between two sailors in the *acopio*, and no one stops to break it up. "Let'm kill themselves," Striker says. They fall into the water tank and threaten the Caye's drinking water, and I jump in. No more of this bullshit! They stop for a minute, but soon go back after it.

Tattoo, one of the fighters from the skiff Miss Aura, starts to scream because the other guy, Kato, is biting his ear off. He's a bad dude, the Tattoo. He has eyes like a hyena on crack, like their looking for something to take. He is black black and his eyes are yellow. He's the one who was thiefin' Armando's traps. Well anyway, he's screaming about his ear until they let him loose, and off he goes again with that meager look in his eye and grabs a knife from Luther's bucket. It has a long triangle blade and a fishing line tied handle. It looks sharp.

Woa wo wo everybody says now that it gone too far. Enough fun watching the friendly fistfight, watching the two men try to kill each other with their bare hands, now it has evolved into someone using a tool, and that is crossing the line. Striker's still watching, telling people to let them kill themselves. This is television for him.

"We get fucked if he kills that boy in the *acopio* here. What's everybody gonna say about that. Chuh," Alvaro says.

Alvaro is Alvarito's papa. Alvarito for Jisena from Little Island. He looks just like him, but I doubt that they have ever seen one another.

Somehow the boy, Kato, slips away and swims over to the next side of the caye and seeks refuge by Armando. Tattoo is still waving the knife around saying he's gonna kill him, but he is all alone.

"Get these boys off the Caye," Striker says with authority. "You can't be doin' that kinda shit here. No-o-ah".

Everyone says that he should have stopped the fight sooner, but nobody wanted to jump in the middle of that and get hit up or stabbed for nothing, for two guys who nobody gives a damn about in the first place. Think anybody would risk it for you? They'd stand there and watch me die. The grass is good boy.

By the weekend, Tattoo, was arrested in Sandy Bay for stealing some gringo's camera. The police there shipped him back here to the Caye because they didn't have any food there.

Marijuana is good for the spirit.

Where to begin about what's been happening here since the moon's been full. The ship that was to come, who's captain's mother died, the found a new captain. He's not really a captain though, just somebody's cokehead nephew who mashed up the engine running her too hard through high seas and set her adrift. In this ship out to sea, was the cargo, the gas, the ice, bait and above all else, Striker's new woman, his baby's new Mama. She didn't last too long out here on the Caye before Striker fired her anyway. She looked too good to eyes stranded on a Caye full of men.

You never know when the rainy weather will dry or what a hungry man may try.

The nights are filled will needle joints and Abel's ancient ranchero songs from the hammock next to mine. He is an archive of Mexican opera with a ghostlike voice over nimble guitar bass-line fingers. The mornings are full of tortillas fried in fish oil.

I open my black plastic window this morning, took the flour sack off of the nail and the sea showed the black sail of a Miskito *velero* headed North, back home to Puerto Cabeza. It is the first of December and the sea is choppy and breezy. I just quit my job. I fired myself after finishing my second month of working for Mista Strikah. This morning when I showed up an hour or so after the first, second and third pangas left again, the bossman finally said something about my increasing absence from work and breach of contract. I told him yeah, your right. I don't want to work here. You also said that I was to get food over here, which you stopped giving me a long time ago. So he paid me for most of my time and I let that be that. There are better things do here on this Caye than wasting my days around him in the *acopio*. Even though there is nothing else on this Caye at all, I would rather sit by myself than fill my ears with his bullshit negativity.

I eat a piece of fried fish and baking powder tortilla and head back across the rocks to find myself wondering what the hell to do now after the initial high of the day's second joint has worn off.

"*Cachete*," Abel just asked me if I knew the meaning of. He has turned into the devil. He reminds me so much of my friend Raúl in Chile, it is eerie. A *cachete* is the friend who is always around to beg a drink of *guaro*. *Cachete* is like a little cute pinch on the cheek.

I sit back and watch that sailboat passing by my window and wonder about things like music and how numbers and rhythms and intervals can make feelings. Minor keys; dead, drying, salted fish; stolen mirrors; ropes and buoys, *puertas negras, vagos*. Right now there is nothing to do but *vagos*, an unpaid vacation with nothing to do and no-where to go.

Back to the Island

The hero finished up his last month on the Caye somekind of way. He dove and smoked every day. The time passed. The north wind blew and blew. Everyone was catching lobster, so for the most part, everyone was happy. He had saved a few hundred dollars over the last three months, and rather than going to the mainland and spending it all, he just decided to wait on the Caye for Christmas to come. Life could have been worse. When December twentieth finally came, a hot storm was blowing in. It was time to go.

In a few days his family was coming to Bluefields to pass the Christmas with him. It had been a few years since they had seen each other, and Robert was feeling half and half. It was time. Abel wanted to meet his parents even more than Robert did. They made plans to meet up in Bluefields in a few days, after Abel made a trip to sea and saved a little money. Robert had little faith that Abel would be able to hold onto his money long enough to make it to Bluefields. Whenever Abel had money it was like it was poison. It was like holding fire. He had to get rid of it as fast as he could before it burned him. Robert was still pleased with the idea of it, so they made plans to meet up in a few days and Robert packed his bag, left whatever could not fit and grabbed his weathered guitar. An Indian named Jorge was headed for the mainland and this was the best opportunity he would have to go in. There was a panga traveling South the following day so he could spend the night in the communities of Rio Grande, and in the morning leave for Bluefields. He would still have a few days to kill before his parents arrived, but that too would pass.

Jorge didn't have a skiff like most of the lobstermen. He had a dory. It was a big red dory, cut from a large Saba tree that he worked with a fifteen horsepower engine. It was not really a sea faring boat. It was a fresh water boat or a dry weather boat that was best used to fish the lagoons or carry out divers in the calm ocean. This was December month. This was the North wind. The sea was too high for Jorge to work in, so he was headed home to his community of Walpa. He was carrying in one of his sailors, an old leathery man, his diver and a fat old woman that he had cooking for him out on the Caye. With Robert, the dory was loaded.

The dory loaded up on the rocks of the Caye. They threw the backpack and the guitar in the bow. It was clear that nothing would stay dry. Robert stepped into the dory. It rocked over on its side. Robert had never been to sea in a vessel like this before. It was cranky. He felt a little nervous, but took his seat the best he could and dug himself in. The dory ran out of the harbor and met with the high sea. The salty ocean crashed over the boat. Everyone was soaked instantly. The sea was cold. Robert held on tightly to the edge of the dory and tried to keep everything balanced. The boat cut through the seas as Robert kept wiping the saltwater from his burning eyes. The engine was small and weak but they steadily made their way towards the land. It was only fourteen miles but it seemed to take hours. When the boat rolled over the high waves, he could see the land at times but it quickly disappeared in the canyon valleys. He shivered in the cold sea.

The Rio Grande has a tricky bar mouth. The current coming out of the huge river floods out and meets with the waves of the ocean creating a treacherous system of hard current and short breaking waves that will easily take down a skiff if the captain isn't accustomed. Timing is everything. Jorge was a funny little Indian man, but he handled the dory well, and they made it through bar and into the calm lagoon. It was a relief.

In a twenty minutes time, they reached the community of Walpa. People were waiting for them when they arrived. Jorge's wife, a few young women, a pile of children and couple of Indian men spoke Miskito when they landed. A young man carried the engine up to the house for them, and everyone pushed the dory up on some slim logs and rolled it up onto the land.

Walpa was a small, quiet community of about fifteen houses, all spread out enough to keep a few mango and other fruit trees in between each one. It was a clean village. The people kept it tidy. Walpa was Abel's hometown. Robert wondered which house Abel stayed in with his Tio Juan. Robert looked around for a minute and Jorge called him to come hurry up. He came with Jorge. He was Jorge's guest for the night.

Jorge's house was in the back of the village, amongst some shady mango and orange trees. The house consisted of a big open hall where there was a table in one corner with some chairs, and a dresser against a wall, and several small foam mattresses leaned up against the walls. Jorge showed him where he could put his bag down. He told him to go bathe and put on some fresh clothes. The bathhouse was around the back. It was made of some sticks and a black plastic wrapped around it. Someone had already filled a bucket of water for him to use. The fresh water felt wonderful on his salty skin. It was cool and seemed to take the coldness out of him. He wrapped a towel around himself and went inside to try to find a set of dry clothes. Nothing was dry. He put on some half dry things and decided it would have to do. Jorge told him to give him his wet and dirty clothes. A pretty young Indian girl eagerly took them and carried them to the washstand where she quickly rubbed them clean and hung them up to dry.

The women knew that the men were hungry and cooked up a big pot of rondon with a type of freshwater fish that Robert had never tasted before. It was warm and delicious. He felt like his body absorbed the power of the fish and the coconut stew. He had never eaten a rondon like that before and he liked it. He liked the mainland and the way the people, especially the women, made him feel comfortable. The women treated the men well. They knew what men needed and the men knew what the women needed.

After the heavy breakfast, they sat on the verandah of the house and talked while the food digested. All kinds of people crowded around the verandah, curious to see the white man that worked on the ocean with Jorge. Several young men came around that already knew Robert from the Caye. They were all happy to see him in their community.

The old man that came in the dory with them was Jorge's father in law. It was his house they were in. The old man worked for Jorge as a bubble man when they carried out divers. The weather was not for diving now. It was for working the traps, but Jorge couldn't get to his traps in this weather, so all there was to do was wait it out.

Jorge met his wife in jail it turned out. Jorge killed a man after the war. It was a fight and the other man died. That was the time when Jorge used to drink rum plenty. He hardly drank now he said. Robert never asked what his wife did to end up in jail. It was probably for drugs.

After the food went down and everyone felt good, Jorge brought Robert a pair of blue jeans to put on. They looked new. Robert was a little ashamed that he didn't have any nice clothes to put on, but that was alright. He was moved by the big baggy jeans that Jorge gave him. He put them on and they looked good. They were Nicaraguan style. He belted them down with a piece of rope and put on a sport shirt that Abel had given him some time ago. He looked set up now. He didn't look like a bum again. He was "dudesed up".

Abel cut his hair a few days before. His hair was long, blonde and dreadlocked from the seawater. Until now he had a chance to see the cut in a looking glass. It had been about two years or so since he had had it cut, but he had to say, it looked damn good. It was the best haircut he ever had. Abel was an artist. He could make anything. He had vision and could create that vision. He told Robert he needed to have his hair cut before he left the caye to meet his parents and he was right. He said the rasta look wasn't working. It was the last time Robert ever cut his hair.

When everyone was ready, Jorge carried them to the big town of Sandy Bay. They went with another little dory with a small engine. They carried the girl who washed Robert's clothes and another young woman who was not Jorge's wife. It didn't matter. They were just going to take a little pasear.

When they hit Sandy Bay, they took a little walk around, saying hello to the people until they found a little bar that belonged to one of the fishermen from the Caye. The man was thrilled to have them at the bar. He gave them a gallon of chicha to drink and relax. The girls didn't drink chicha so Robert bought them each a soft drink to sip on while they laughed and talked about each other's history.

When the gallon finished they bought another. Robert was happy to have a little money from his time working. It was the first time he had held this much money at one time in a while. It was only about three hundred dollars, but if felt like plenty.

They drank a pair of beers and when the gallon finished, they decided to go home. Robert paid for the beers and they stepped heavily out of the bar and back to the dory and the river that led back to Walpa.

The sun was dropping low and Jorge's wife had their food waiting for them when they reached back. It was turtle meat, fried brown with rice and boiled cassava. It was oily, but it went down effortlessly after the drinks. In the morning, there was skiff heading to Bluefields at six o'clock. He would have to wake up soon to be ready. There was no electricity in the community, so everyone went to sleep early. They sat around a potash candle, burning diesel from a rum bottle for a short while, but soon retired to the big room were at least fifteen souls slept quietly on the floor.

In the morning, they rose with the sun and rooster. Robert picked a green young coconut and drank the sweet water, thanking God for life. He gave Jorge's wife a hug and a kiss and Jorge a handshake and was gone.

The panga left on time and Robert was in it. It was powered by a two hundred horsepower engine and glided over the oily river like the morning mist. The weather was cool. It took a good two hours to reach Pearl Lagoon, the first stop. Robert decided to get out there instead of going all the way down to Bluefields. He already knew Bluefields and didn't really feel like waiting there for two days until his family reached. Better he pass the time in Pearl Lagoon, the town he had always heard about. It would probably be a little easier than Bluefields.

So he got out, made a little trip around the community and found a hotel that cost less than ten dollars a night. It was right on the main dirt street. It was called Sweet Pearly and had a little ice cream shop and restaurant in the downstairs. It had a nice verandah where he could sit and watch the beautiful girls walk by. He could not believe the amount of pretty young girls walking the streets. He had been on the Caye for too long.

While he was walking around the town's little lanes in search of a hospedaje, an old man sitting in a small wooden shack took note of him and his guitar. He called to Robert and told him to come back later on with his guitar. The old man, who was probably eighty years old, had a magic eye, and a special air to him. Robert checked into the room at the hospedaje, relaxed himself for a little while, and decided to go back and check the old man.

The man's name was Chico. Chico was an artist. He was a woodworker. He could make anything. Little parrots, sailboats, washboards, hammer and axe handles, iguanas, you name it out of rosewood. He was an original and could sing some great old songs that Robert had never heard before. He was an artist, and like most of the artists Robert was coming into contact with, he was a dying alcoholic. The first things they did was break out a pint of rum plata.

"Here," Chico said as he passed Robert the rum and his own guitar after inspecting it once over. "This will help. Play something now".

Robert took a small delicate sip of the hot clear rum and tasted the sweetness of it as he held it in his mouth before swallowing. He started to touch a ranchero Mexican folk song that he learned from Abel. It was a story of betrayal and murder. It was a corrido.

From there the day began. It continued growing hotter and passing through the whole scale of human emotions and songs. As one bottle finished another was brought by somebody who was listening to the strange pair trade off songs. Chico would play one and Robert would play one, and then back to Chico again. Sometimes Chico would play two or beg Robert to play another one, but just so it went until the sun grew low in the sky behind Pearl Lagoon. In between songs the two would laugh and tell stories about their families or places they had come from. Chico had traveled around alot, but Pearl Lagoon was his home. It was his birthplace and he would die there.

Robert could see that Chico's health was failing. His right foot was so swollen he could barely walk. That is why Chico did this work now. It was hard to move around much, so he took his knife and chisel and made anything that people would pay him to make. He made everything perfect. His hands were tough and he worked his sculptures down to the smallest of details. Down to the little removable jibs on the sailboats he carved. Down to the legs of the little rosewood lobsters. Chico was a workingman. He would only abandon his work when he had a chance to sing. He had about three guitars inside of the little shack where they sat on the verandah, but they were all stringless and beat right up, with frets and keys missing. They all looked abandoned.

As the sun was going down all of their energies were too. It was past time to eat and rest, so they called it a night and decided to meet tomorrow. Robert went back to the hotel room, smoked a joint and walked around on the street, looking at the women and listening to the music pouring out of the houses and ranchos.

The next day Robert woke up, took a smoke and walk around the communities. He walked down to Haulover, looking to see Marlon's old bar, and then around to Ritepura and Awas, two Indian communities. The sun was hot, but the breeze was fresh and cool in the shade of the coconut and cashew trees. In the afternoon, he made it back to Pearl Lagoon and found a woman selling fried fish with rice and cassava. He bought a plate and drank a glass of lime fresco. He knew that he had to go to Bluefields tomorrow to meet his family. He did not want to carry his guitar and backpack around with him anymore. It was heavy and burdensome, and he knew he wouldn't need those things in Bluefields or wherever he went with his parents. He thought it would be a good thing to leave his belongings at Chico's place and come back for them later. He felt certain that he would pass back through

Pearl Lagoon on his way back North. He still felt certain about traveling North. That was about it at this point. It was his only direction. He felt like he could trust Chico with his things. There were not many people he felt this way about in Nicaragua, but the old man who he had just met the day before seemed to be one of them. He felt like a special person that Robert needed to commit himself to seeing again. It seemed like a good idea to leave his belongings with Chico.

He asked Chico if that would be cool with him, and Chico said of course. He assured Robert that he wouldn't have to worry about the safety of his things. Robert wasn't too worried. There wasn't much in his possession that anyone would want or have any use for anyway. The guitar was beaten to the point that it could barely play, and the backpack was full of ragged clothes and notebooks of strange scrawled writings that no one would be able to understand even if they could read. His things were worthless, but the thought of losing them still seemed unbearable to him. You think that he would have learned his lesson about leaving things behind, but he didn't. He wanted to travel light. This was no time for heaviness and possessions.

His packed a few suits of clothes in his small military handbag and carried the backpack and guitar down to Chico's one room board shack in the evening. The panga was leaving soon in the morning for Bluefields and he didn't want anything to hold him up. He told Chico that anything he could do to fix the guitar would be greatly appreciated and that upon his return he would pay for any repairs that he made. Chico said he would try his best and that he would keep his things as if they were his own. Chico didn't really have anything except a bunch of blocks of scrap rosewood and unfinished pieces he was working on for people, but Robert knew he would take care of the things. Chico was his friend now. There were only a few friends but Chico was one now. Robert was Chico's friend too. He knew it. They were special in some kind of way. There is a magic that few people understand. Abel understood it. Raul did too. Norberto did. Chico did. The secret is love. The secret is music.

Robert hit Bluefields in the morning time. He got a room in the hotel that Striker recommended. Striker said it was the nicest hotel in Bluefields. It was called Caribbean Dreams. It was alright. After settling into the room and watching the television for a little while, a novelty that Robert had been away from for a long time, he headed out on the road, looking for a bite to eat. He wound up in the market paying two dollars for a plate of fried fish with rice, beans, boiled green banana and cabbage salad. There were women standing around coal burning furnaces slapping and baking corn tortillas on clay skillets. The market was hot and had some flies, but the food was comforting. The meal came with a glass of cold lime fresco that Robert washed everything down with.

After lunch, he found a little second hand shop where he bought a new pair of used pants. He it felt nice to buy something so he went into a real store and bought a new shirt. The shirt was a thin light blue cotton button down with short sleeves. He could wear it with the blue jeans Jorge gave him and with the new second hand brown cotton trousers he just bought. He was set up now. His sandals were a little rough, but sandals came and went, and he wasn't too worried about it. He felt like his parents were bringing him some new sandals from the states anyway. Nicaraguan footwear is junk. Descartable.

The family arrived on the evening flight from Managua. It'd been a long time since Robert smiled so much. He was outside of himself. It was the first time that he felt truly happy to see his family again. He was proud and ashamed. When they got there, he had to sit them all down in the hotel room and explain to them the seriousness of life on the Atlantic coast of Nicaragua. He had to explain to them that the people were the victims of a not so far away revolution. Many were desperate, so they had to be discreet with the flaunting of money and cameras. Bluefields is a rough town, and they had to be aware. Other than that everything was irie.

The family wanted to get out to Corn Island, but they couldn't just go get on a flight. Robert was illegal here in Nicaragua. His tourist visa had been expired for more than a year now, and he couldn't just step up in front of the immigration people at the airport. It was tricky even picking the family up at the airport. To get out to the islands, they would have to take a boat. The Captain D would be leaving in two days, and Robert felt like his family would like the boat ride on the ocean. That was a mistake.

After passing a few days around Bluefields and back in Pearl Lagoon, they boarded the Captain D and headed out on the sea. It was a warm sunny day. The boat headed out past the Bluff and onto the sea as usual. The boat was pretty full. Robert ended up sitting on a bench next to a thin, pretty brown skinned girl named Magdalene who going to Corn Island with her four children. The girl liked to laugh and talk. She was easy to smile and talk with. He remarked to himself how many beautiful girls there were on the coast.

Meanwhile, his sister Annie and mother Nancy were vomiting up their corn tortillas into little white paper bags that the boat owner provided when the sea got rough. Robert didn't even feel the sea. His sister was miserable. Magdalene was eating Zepol to fight the seasickness, and rubbing the menthol cream all over her children's noses and lips, who were also now vomiting. The ship and the travel on the ocean intrigued his father. When he was not staring off into the horizon, he was reading his Travis McGee novel or asking Robert questions that were impossible to answer. Magdalene was cold, so Robert gave her the long sleeve shirt he was carrying. She wrapped up in it. While she lay there on the wooden bench, Robert delicately let his hand contact the skin of her foot, but just barely. It was nothing, but something big. She did not move her foot away. She was probably too seasick and weak to even notice it, but Robert could feel the electrical current emanating from her warm skin. She had a tremendous energy.

The boat reached the Corn Island wharf in the night and the passengers herded towards the narrow exit plank. There was an immigration officer asking for people's documents, but Robert didn't pay him any mind when he tried to stop him. He just grabbed his family and kept moving. The officer was left behind in the rush. Magdalene disappeared somewhere into the crowded night and that was that.

They wouldn't be able to reach Little Corn Island until the morning, so they looked a little hotel room for the night at the place owned by George Morgan. By this point in the vacation, Robert's father realized that he didn't have enough cash. Robert warned him to make sure to bring enough, but the father felt confident that he would find somewhere to change a traveler's check. He was mistaken. They spent the morning racing around the island trying to find somewhere, but it was useless. By the time they reached back to wharf, the morning skiff for Little Island had already left. They stood around in the sun hot for a few minutes complaining about things, and then Robert saw a fisherman he knew from Little Island and the Caye. Luther, the fisherman, was in his skiff, and was traveling back to the island. He was happy to meet Robert's family, especially his sister, and agreed to carry them over to the island in a few minutes. Robert gave him twenty dollars, just to help out the situation.

Luther's skiff was not a passenger skiff. It was a fishing skiff with a sev-

enty-five horsepower engine. The sea was too high for his family who were unaccustomed to this type of travel. The women, Luther sat in the stern of the boat to try to give them a smoother ride, but Robert and his father were stuck up in the bow. The unsuspecting slamming of the seas caught his father off guard and he slammed his ass when the sea fell out from under the skiff. The sea has a rhythm that one must learn to accept, expect and catch with your legs and not your butt. His father ass was bruised up for the rest of the trip.

They were all happy to reach Little Island safely. By the time they arrived, everyone was ready for a beer, so Robert suggested that they try out the Hotel Delfines, the most posh place on the island and the only one place that might accept credit cards or a traveler's check. They didn't. The family was out of luck. Robert still bought everyone a beer, and told to them the reality of the situation. The cash money that they had between the four of them was not enough to pay for the hotel, food and the transportation off of the island. Robert had been in this situation before, but for the rest of his family, the thought of not having enough money was desperate. Robert empathetic. He still had some money in his wallet, so he carried the family around to the other side of the island, on the beach, where there were some little cabanas for rent for about ten dollars a night. Robert could afford two rooms over there, and besides that he knew the people. After the beer, Robert carried his mother and his sister's bags around and checked into the little rooms. It wasn't luxury, but it was a secure place right on the beach where they could sleep safely inside. The situation was a horror for his mother and sister. They had never bathed with a dipper from a drum of fresh water. They had never slept in a leaf top room. The room had a cement floor but outside the room was the sandy beach. The whole thing was too rustic for them but there was nothing they could do. They just had to sleep there for a night and in the morning they would be back on their way to the States.

That night Robert carried them all to a great restaurant where they ate seafood and shrimps and drank beer and dark rum. Robert saw Fireman and a few of his friends from the Caye. They all came around the table delighted to see Robert's family. They drank with them and laughed about Robert's returning to the island. Everyone said that Robert looked big and fat. It was a compliment. Fireman gave Robert's mother a polished shell he had been working on called the Diamante Marino. It shined like a fine jewel and hung from a chain of silver that he made from a roll of wire. His mother cried.

The night was unforgettable and in the morning it was over. His family got on the passenger skiff and made it back to Big Corn Island in time to catch the morning flight to the security of Managua and the Best Western Hotel where their Visa and American Express cards were welcome. They let out a sigh of relief when they arrived at the Corn Island Airport and booked their plane ticket on their credit cards.

Robert kissed them all goodbye and watched as the passenger skiff set out for the southern horizon and Big Corn Island. He turned back around for the little sidewalk on Little Island and began the walk back to Elsa's place on the beach where he still had the key to the room until middle day. He locked himself in the room and wrapped a joint in a dry coco leaf. The world was in front of him again. He was alone again with no direction, like the night in San Isidro de General, Costa Rica. It was an unbearable lightness and freedom that could blow one right off of the beach and into the deep blue sea. He opened the door for some fresh air, and was glad that he didn't have a pile of bags or heavy things to lug around with him. He put on his little handbag with his little two suits of clothes and grabbed his new sandals. On the beach it is better to be barefoot. He decided that he would stick around the island for a few days and then head back to Pearl Lagoon for his guitar and his writings when he was ready. Then it was to the North again. That was direction enough for right now.

It was New Years Eve. He was going to head back to Fireman's to spend the night in the hammock. Tomorrow he would figure things out again. When he gave Elsa the key to the room on his way out, she called him aside. She asked him if he would want to work with her. It seemed like a good idea. He didn't like to refuse work and the little money he had saved on the Caye was about done now. The job would be easy. Raking the beach in the morning and going to Lobster Company for ice. Taking in the chairs and tables at night. It sounded fine. He told her that he would come back tomorrow and start working after New Years. Why not? He liked being back on Little Island. He took a breath of the fresh salty air from the beneath one of the coconut trees on the beach. The sea breeze was cool in the shade. He said thank God.

He passed the New Years getting high with the Fireman and Pamela, eating and laughing about all that had happened in the past several months. The work at Elsa's place didn't last long. She fired him after a few weeks for some craziness involving her rude little grandson. The little boy was going on bad, pointing knives and things at Robert, so Robert picked up the little boy and dunked him into the ocean. He needed to cool down. That was all Elsa needed to get crazy. Robert felt ashamed but didn't care about losing the work. The money was low anyway. He decided to go live by Fireman. Danny and Pamela welcomed him and were excited to have someone else around the house. They played drums and sang, drank white rum in the nights and cooked food over the fire in the day. Robert always brought fish or some kind of flesh, and Fireman took care of the cooking. Pamela was pregnant and finally gave birth her baby girl in Mid January, after weeks of expecting. The baby was named Perla Violeta. They called her Perla. Coralito was two years old now and happy to have Robert around. Robert liked to play with Coral and Coral liked to have the attention now that his mother was occupied with the baby. The night of the birth Fireman built a huge bonfire and kept it burning all through the night. Pamela's labor pains began in the evening. Danny called the midwife, who gave her teas with different bushes to aid the childbirth, but the baby just didn't want to come. By the time morning came, all of the women from the neighborhood were crowding around filling them with all kinds of fear stories. Finally, in a fear Danny called for a panga to carry them to Corn Island. Her water broke on the sea crossing. She nearly had the baby in the taxi on the way to the hospital, but she managed to hold it in.

Before day, Robert cooked a big pot coconut porridge with nutmeg on the fire, but no one stuck around to eat it. Danny begged Robert to take care of Coralito until they came back from the island and gave him a hug. Robert gave him twenty dollars for cual quier cosa. It was greatly appreciated. Robert and Coral ate porridge all day and played in the bush. Robert taught Coral about mangos and coconuts. Coral taught Robert how to fly. Fireman came back two days later and carried Coral back to Corn Island until Pamela and the baby Perla would be well enough to cross back across the ocean to Little Island. They were back home together in less than two weeks.

Their house was made of native sticks and wild cane. It had a grass roof, but a poor one, so they had to buy a sheet of black plastic to hang over it. The house was small but comfortable. Pamela loved it. For her, it was as sweet as the biggest of mansions. It was her nest, and she kept it clean and tidy.

The house was tucked back in the bush amongst a group of shady mango trees. If you did not know the house, you would not find it. You could hardly see it from the trail in front. Every day Pamela raked leaves and dirt from round and round the patio. She kept the yard immaculate.

The house couldn't really lock, and even if it could, the wild cane was easy to just break out. It didn't matter. No one had anything worth stealing. The floor was sand and there was a little upstairs loft where the family slept. Robert slept downstairs in a hammock. Pamela gave him a little cardboard box that he kept his belongings in. It was a little touch of privacy and better than just his bag. It was a sweet gesture.

In the morning time, Danny went to the tourist places and set out a display of his jewelry. He sold necklaces, bracelets and earrings made with pendants from the ocean, pieces of coral, brilliant shells and stones that Robert dove up and carried home. In the mornings, Robert rose early and walked out to the front to see what was taking place. Usually the men sat around in a beached skiff waiting to see what was happening, what kind of work might appear; someone looking a sailor to go fishing, people looking to move some things around or go haul sand. Anything. Every day was different. Most mornings, someone lit up a joint and passed it around. That was how the days began. If no kind of work popped up, Robert would head back to the house for some breakfast with Pamela and Coralito, and then go diving or something. The life was simple and easy.

Some days, when there was nothing else to do, Robert would walk off into the bush and sit up on the top of a high hill overlooking the Eastward Caribbean Sea and take a seat at the base of a coconut tree. He would take a few deep breaths and take out his little notebook that he carried around with him and start to sing the words that rolled through his mind. He would climb one of the coconut trees and haul down three young coconuts and break them open on a stone to drink. He would eat the soft meat until his belly was full and sit down back again with the notebook and write all the things he could hear himself thinking. From the high bank where he sat, you could see far out to sea. Often he felt like he could nearly see San Andres. He knew it was right out there and many days he sat and watched for any kind of skiff that might be running in from there. From high, the sea looks blue and vast. It makes one feel small and insignificant. It seemed like the breeze was always blowing from up atop of that hill. Robert was always happy that he decided to walk into the bush.

Still illegal here in Nicaragua, failing to respect the laws, on a hill on top of the water, thanking God for the breeze and the shade. Spilling out melodies as words. . .

Soon a marnin', I find a new sandal in the jaws of a dog on the sidewalk I was walking down barefoot. Thinking of the pains in my feet and where I'd be walking, I looked around and saw his pair in the sand of the beach. I picked it up and turned back to chase the dog. The sandals are a good fit. Anything can take place when you're walking round soon in the marnin'.

Time to go. No fraid. Fear not. You're just being free, what you have to be.

So what do I do? I get up and go walk around in the bush, looking cassava and coconut, plantains and breadkind. Looking for food. Today, I butchered a small coconut tree. I took its soul to eat its heart. Such is the life. Killing to live. Destroying to progress. Progressing to destroy, and the negation. It is logically equated progression is destruction. They are the same.

Then when I fill my sack with all I can back, I sit and smoke a bit on the beach and sing songs and write in my little book until I finally get hungry and walk back to town. It is what I love here. It is the sunshine and the breeze and the shade from the trees that illuminates the brilliant energy from the rocks and the sea and the crispness of freedom alone.

Cito asks me what the hell I'm writing about all the time. I'm writing about taking him to the doctor for Granny to take worms out of his feet.

I live poor because I do things for free. Just to help people out. To get a meal. To feel good. Eat well. Rest easy. Make friends. Sing songs. Fill water from the well. Fill yourself with God. Transparent clarity. Nothing. Tasteless. Odorless. Colorless. Everything.

Junior's little house panga just pulled in from Pearl Lagoon. Haulover really. I've got to be getting back there. Enough sunshine here in Little Island for now. Time to put the roof on the hut at the Fireman's. Take a nap. Puerto Cabeza. Zabu.

Myrta walks pretty. She swings her arms at her wrists so elegantly. The way her bony hips rock back and forth as she struts. She is beautiful.

God Damn! is all I got to say when I watch you walkin' away. When I see you shakin' what you got in your blue jean behind. The teeth in your smile. The pearl in your ears. Your breasts that hang down over your stomach. Your hands that you cover your breasts with. The necklace that floats. The look that passes through me like, "Plata Tata!" exclaims Jose.

He's drinking rum again. Drinking rum and smoking rock.

High black shoes, smooth chocolate cheekbones, she passed the walk in front of the almond tree I'm hiding in, watching her. Passing time with Jose until the freight boat comes. Look some *chamba*. Some work to buy more ganja and rice. Maybe some vinegar. Maybe I'll pay some girl to wash my clothes. They're all about dirty again. This little island is losing my attention again.

I need music. More music. It is my only savior. My calling that drags me out of the house and into the street when the moon gets full enough for walking bout. It is my energy. My spirit. Without music I am dying and that is fine. It is fine. It is good to sing. People like to listen. It is to dance. A song alleviates the air from evil spirits.

And there she goes again like a hook and line, connecting my eyes and my cock. I need to get laid. All of the women I know are mothers and the men I know, fathers, and they're all miserable. Except Abel. The musicians. They have light. A tormented crying light that wails out in the darkness like a teary siren the instant an airplane leaves the ground.

It is traveling time. Time traveling to Pearl Lagoon and beyond. To Puerto Cabeza and Honduras. Puerto Lempira or Jamaica. In pangas or big boats hauling *heroina* or fish for the North. All I need is my bag and broken guitar, which if I'm lucky, is in the mending hands of Chico, master craftsman and rum slugging singer. He is an artist. Every musician I know is a dying drunk. They have sold their souls to the spirit. It is true. Is there truth? Only fading absolutions that are constantly changing.

I'm tired. I want to go to sleep. I'm hungry. I want to eat. The freight boat is not yet within its dreaded sight. I do not want to work. I still have twenty bucks in my back pocket. I could buy a joint and go to sleep. Buy some rice and go eat; or just go to the sea and bathe.

Bathe in the sea. Clean your dirty soul. Let the salt suck out all the impurities. Piss, shit and mucas. Catch a fish. Drink a young coconut. Make your life a little longer. Make your life the way you please. You can do it. You can't make it. Let it make you. Esperanza.

Mientras, eating coconut and passing the time as well as possible, our hero meets a beautiful girl while playing music with Whykie at the Cubano. He passes a week with her on the beach, waking up late in the mornings and drinking coffee and beer, staying up late in the night, drinking rum and kissing. Dancing with the music. Talking about lovers and pasts and future and ideas. He told her that she made him want to leave. He never told her why he hated backpackers and their plane tickets. By now, she's probably in Peru or around the world in Birmingham, England.

The panga's are flying by, looking for lobster and cocaine. Miss Sherry says not to sleep too much in these days because once it starts washing up it's gonna all wash up. All two hundred and fifty kilos that are supposedly floating around the island right now.

As for me, I went out diving for conchs, lobster and wilts. Maybe enough for a rondon. Off to see the wizard to sell the lobster.

Ballerinas with Punta rhythms; Garifuna girls and a dance that is judged by the style of their stops.

I have been struck by a heaviness that begs for nothing but a hammock.

Diving for shellfish is fulfilling work. Dancing and fighting with the sea and the stones. Angry she can become and throw you where she chooses when she does. Close your eyes, hold out your arms, and pray not to get in the way.

Magdalene has returned. She brought with her excitement and a bright promise of what I can no longer escape. She doesn't care about anything but me. She makes me believe. She makes love incredibly easy. It is decisionless and thoughtless. We met on the sidewalk and it was pure undisconnectable current.

I was hurrying up the sidewalk making a *chamba*, backing a sack of cement, while she was strolling down. Our eyes met and time stopped with our baffled feet. What are you doing here? What are you doing here? We won't let you get away again.

She asked where I stayed and told her, never believing that she would actually take the walk into the bush down by Bamboo to look me. When I finished work, Pamela told me that she had already come by, and would be back later. It was true and then she's back to Corn Island. She says just to call her. Don't be afraid. She wants to come.

Back on the island, living on coconut water and white rum, things get interesting with love. I'm waiting to go to Lagoon. The ride was to leave today to make it to Kukra Hill for the Atlantic Series, but it's waiting for *resina* to reach on the freight boat to fix the *panga*, Sister Chloe. Then she's gone. First to the Caye, and then to the main. Pearl Lagoon where my life lies waiting. Haulover, where the hides my wife. My love, I say, and laugh to myself at my missing her. The imagination of her face calls to me like the track of my footstep. I watch myself and wonder if I am for real. So does she. She came here to see me. Her skin is soft like peppermint and eyes radiate the heavens that rest within her. She is turning me into a poet that sickens even myself.

Death to the poets and all of their wanderings. All of their breezeful ramblings and short-term feelings. Dissolved imitations. Flashbacks faces, wincing pains of the twisted heart in midfootstep, call me to you like water. Death to the poets and all their wasteful ramblings.

"God," I pray in the morning, when the sun is still far from the skies and his silence prevails over the earth like dew. "Give me the power to write, and to create. Something nutritious."

Magdalene where are you? I's a wonderin' if you can hear me callin'. All the letters that I sent to you have fallen like the change that I told you to put away; like the arms I couldn't hold up another day. I feel I should be getting on my way. Up the road, traveling north to Mexico. To Cuba, to Texas, to Honduras and Puerto Cabeza. Pearl Lagoon where I left my guitar, what do I have to be afraid of? Afraid of regret? Afraid of losing you, my sunshine and my breeze. My water, my sea, my energy and motivation, inspiration and imagination. Where have you gone? Managua to your mother? Haulover to your children? Corn Island to your lovers that I'll never see? This is a letter to you Magdalene, because you have not answered your telephone. I'll forget you as long as I can and taunt myself with the confusion of your memory until death do us part. Your essence will now be eternalized in the mixed up collage of scattered faces and shattered memories hanging and spinning circles around my mind like a magnet spinning around my compass. A disturbed navigator. Fuck you! Fuck me! I hope to someday see you again, but until then, I will walk to the rising sun and sleep when the night fills the lightness and walk again when the darkness fades.

Twilight is setting upon the *Islita*. Dawn seems far away. So far that it is not worth fighting for. So far that it makes the eyes weary and the feet heavy. Full of coconut, our hero falls asleep in the shade by the sea. Bare and battered feet feel no more to walk. Alone with the trees, the seas and the breezes. Magdalene has reappeared and redisappeared. This time it is for real. It is too easy to deny. To hard to ignore. To full to choose. Choices are imposters and impossible.

Staring off into infinity . . . thinking off about eternity . . . someday someone will stay with me, but until then I shall be free. So walk along my friend you're free. There is a great big world to see. Do what you feel and feel the breeze. Be what you will and will what you be.

I am disappointed at what I have become. A singer who's lost his guitar. A poet who's forgotten his pen. A fisherman on the land. Wasting away, rotting one day at a time instead of growing stronger. Man does not know his own strength or what he can be with practice and daily exercise. The alternative is withering away to feeble weakness one day at a time. Respect. Backing bricks, you can see the strength of a man's character by the strength of his back. Patience. Everything cannot be done in one day, but something can, if it is even one page. If it is even one stone or a bucket of water carried for someone else.

In the morning I left and went fishing for fish with Alfonso. We gave fish to all the people, fried two for ourselves, and said thank God. Then we did rest.

In Mayan, the word for God is illusion

The Atlantic Series. Two weeks of heated rivalry in the name of baseball amongst Nicaragua's premier baseball Caribbean communities.

Pearl Lagoon, Kukra Hill, Bluff, Corn Island, Bluefields, Karawala, Mulukuku, Rosita, Bonanza, Siuna, Puerto Cabeza and many more meet in Kukra Hill to fight for the crown of the champion. People come in from all over the place for the yearly spectacle. It is the best of the best. This morning at five o'clock, drunk, stoned and asleep, I missed my ride with the company skiff to Pearl Lagoon. "You were never ready," they told me. It seems I'll never make it off this land to find the love of my life. My Clementina. My reason, my purpose, my mission, my music, my guitar and voice with something to say. Breathe. Sing. Dance. Let the spirit fill you and run though.

Something is keeping me here. I know not if it has a reason or purpose, but it has a way. Does the way have a why? No use trying. There is always a time to leave. That time has no fighting or considering or doubtful decision. It just comes as a finishing

Coralito, do you feel alone in the world.

Oh all the words I have wasted on laziness; the phrases that have vanished for fear of the pen, other occupations and lesser diversions. Walking the streets, drinking rum, stirring food on a fire, banging drums or watching sunset and clouds blowing along their days.

They say when you eat conch soup, *sopa de caracol,* you need to go look a girl. It is true. If you don't find one, bad things happen.

Dying on the inside is dying on the outside. That's why I left Houston. The life was getting grey. Void of color. Night after night, making plans to go somewhere else. Some next step. But ain't that what living is? To live is to dance across the floor, in the street or in the sea or in the blue plastic chair on this page. Here we are together taking the same rhythms, speaking the same old blues. If we only had another hundred cordovas to give to the *puta*. And what ever happened to that old lost love of yours? The one that you left and broke your heart. Together hand in hand we'll wander and march through the night covered field of splinters and thorned *diablos*.

The Fireman and Pamela are packing their things and moving to Corn Island it seems. I guess if I want, I can stay and mind the house. Danny found a better life *cuidando* a camping, cafe, tourist place in Big Island called Cafe Mar. It will be a good opportunity he feels, a smoother life for Pamela and the baby. Maybe he can save enough money to take the family back to Argentina to see his dying father. The *artesania* and the *spectaculos* haven't really proved as lucrative as one would imagine, although he does make considerably more than me. I've been crashing in his hammock now for three months with little or nothing to show for myself except for a halfway built, roofless hut and a few fish traps that sometimes catch.

Neutral, resting at zero. Infinity. "I am the mountain". I am the Caye.

The sky juts out of the sea. The volcanoes pierce the heavens above Lake Nicaragua. Ometepe. I am a *vago*, not an everyday person. Undependable and irresponsible. *Por* nada. Not even myself. My teeth are falling out and chest withering. Lack of everyday care. That is everything. Everyday care. Practice. Talent. Justice. Truth. Life. Death. Plants. Love. Change. Reggae music. Control. What are you really in control of? This house is infested with cockroaches. This house is a dead tree. It is out of control.

You were always on my mind.

The spirit of music is the same spirit of the orgasm. Sex. Dimensionless nonsense. Drunkening, deafening earthless shattering calmness that perpetrates every orphus of noise with silence. An orange silence. Che-gong go the bells in the churchyard. Last call for anything short of regret. Forgiveness in fifty-bags.

Come to me Judas, for it is I who have betrayed you. Given you away for bloodshot eyes and ruby slippers.

Hurricanes have come and gone and I stand here in want of you. There are too many songs to be sung. It is the sound of the instant you enter the sea. A rupture of the precious space-time perception.

Trying to catch up with Marijuana, our hero fell on his face. "It was nothing," he says, takes a bit of fresh air and plunges into the lake of fire, never to be heard from again.

If it doesn't feel right to do anything, better just do nothing until the path becomes clear. It won't take long. Just give it a chance. Have a glass of water without sugar.

A few days aback, a neighbor friend asked me to hold her baby. The next night began the *vela*. The wake.

Six months old, pale, limp, *floja*. They say her father, a fisherman, holds the *culpa*, the guilt. They say he was crazy. I used to fish with the guy. You could tell he wasn't quite right. He used to call me over to drink rum because he didn't like to drink alone. They say he used to beat the mama when she wanted to feed him. They say he dropped the baby out of the hammock. They say all kind of things, but the baby is dead.

The set-up started in the evening time. The father didn't even know. He went out to sea in the morning and wouldn't be back until the next day. They got some ice from the company and put the baby in a little cooler while Cien built a wooden box for the coffin. Somebody provided the rum, coffee, Johnny Cakes and dominos for everyone to stay up all night with the mother until the burial the next day. I didn't really plan on going, but the mother asked me to go. Fransisca. She didn't want to let go of the baby. She was just walking around the island, holding a dead baby in her arms, trying to find a skiff to go to Corn Island. It was useless.

I carried the little cane flute and the music started playing from it sad and slowly. As the rum kept sipping, the music kept coming up and up, and by the time daylight arrived, the flute was playing African rhythms while the group of drunkards stamped their feet and clapped their hands, banging beats and screaming into the predawn sky.

From the set-up, the men and I carried a next bottle of rum to the graveyard and dug a small, deep hole for the burial. They didn't make me dig. They just wanted me to keep on with the flute. I was starting to get week by the time the sun started getting high. I was having trouble walking and staying awake. Some woman cooked food for all of us and called me over to get mine. I ate and fell asleep on the beach for a few hours. It was a strange morning. I don't even know when the burial was. When I woke up, there were some guys sitting around with a guitar and a next bottle of rum. They called me and begged me to sing a song. I took another drink and went home to Fireman's after the song, feeling lost and miserable. I went to sleep early.

Today Alfonso awoke and found blood in his hammock.

Bamboo passed by when it was still dark. He knocks on wall. "*Panga's* on the beach," he says and keeps moving.

I awake from the hammock, get Danny up, and out the door we went.

"One". "One".

Life is changing.

Digging.

Dogs.

A lot of drugs. A lot of money. The things are on the table.

The father came home and found his baby dead. Eric. The Capitan.

"*Sayayin*," he used to call me. "*Yo tengo algo para ti*". Money makes people do ugly things. Ugly. *Feo.*

Agua. Agua!

Cocaine floating up in the tide. Babylon arrived and they're floating around the island, seeing what they can find.

Morning came, and the sack is still in the *sacate*, buried in the leaves I cut for the roof.

And look at me. I've turned you all into beggars. Midnight on the island. The moon is up. I broke open the sack. Gave Fireman six. Bamboo three. The Indian people some, and Fonso one. My pistol is next to me. This is no time for sleeping.

I have reached Heiko's. In a rush, I called upon Alfonso and had him meet me on the beach. The trails and the bush are too full of bandits and guns. Fireman's little shanty is no longer safe. People are coming to burn it down. I carried the thirty-eight special and the sack of drugs down to the beach. The darkness was full of vultures and wolves. I fired two shots into the air. You know what that means. Come and get it if you want it. No one came.

Fonso's boat pulled up to the beach. The sea was calm. I rolled up my pants and jumped in. "Into the moonlight," I said and we went out to sea and around to the next side of the island. Things were getting too hot out front. Too many people. I need to be away from the town, where you can see things coming.

So here's how the thing went down. Before day, Bamboo knocked on the house, woke up Robert and the Fireman. "Pangas on the beach!" They raced down the little jungle trail to Gun Point and the beach where a huge Colombian skiff with three two hundred horsepower engines had mashed up on the rocks jutting out of the sand. The skiff must have been leaving the island for the North and came too close to the point when they turned the corner, not knowing how far the rocky reef shot out from the shore. The skiff wrecked on the rocks and was getting crashed as the sea slammed it higher and higher onto the reef. In the night, a late North wind blew in. The sea was cold and rough. By the time the Robert and Danny reached the skiff, there was already a good crew of people aboard, working to dismantle the engines and any parts that could be removed. It was clear that any drugs or money on the boat had long since been removed. The boat parts could still bring a good price though, so Robert boarded the skiff that was being thrown this was and that and crashing against the rocks. It was tricky, but he somehow managed to get in the rush. People were already working hard with what little tools they had, so Robert just had to be an assistant. Danny didn't even bother trying to get in the boat. The whole thing was a little too rough for him. He was good just helping from the beach. They had both seen this situation before, and realized that there wasn't a lot they could do.

They banged and wrenched on things for a good hour or so, until there was nothing more to take off. The sun was starting to raise high. Robert got a couple of marine batteries that would be worth a little money and a big tarp that he could use to roof the little hut he had been working on. It was a good enough morning. Danny went home, and Robert struggled dragging the heavy tarp up the little hill from the beach. Bamboo had brought a wheelbarrow over from his house and said that Robert could use it to carry home the tarp. He helped him put the tarp in and went back to his house for some coffee.

Robert fought with the awkward wheelbarrow along the trail for a few minutes and stopped for a second to look around and examine the situation. A few hundred meters to the south, across a little savannah, he saw some commotion. He saw two men running with sacks on their back. They were headed for a tree line on the other side of the savannah. What was this? Something was taking place. It was worth going over and taking a closer look. Robert knew all of this bush from diving the beaches and his aimless mango and coconut wanderings. He knew that there was an old empty well not far from where the men were running from. When he arrived he saw an Indian neighbor of his, Flubia, standing nearby the well. He rushed closer. Her Miskito cousin was down in the well. The well was full of cocaine. Sack top of sack. The Colombians from the skiff must have taken the sacks out of the crashed skiff in the night and hidden them in the well. Flubia's cousin, Edgar, passed up a sack to Robert.

"Go with this," Flubia said.

Robert didn't stick around to hear the rest of what was taking place. If he would have kept his cool, he could have grabbed three sacks and put them all in the wheelbarrow and rushed them home, but he wasn't thinking. He took the sack and ran with it. One sack weighed about sixty pounds. Robert backed it liked nothing. He threw it in the wheelbarrow, and put the tarp on top of it, so no one would see it when he went back into town.

He wheeled the barrow back to Fireman's house. The house was quiet. No one was around. He looked around, and didn't know what to do with the thing. He glanced at the hut he was building in the yard. There was a big pile of leaves that he cut and hauled over from the other side of the island to roof the hut with. He spread apart some of the leaves and threw the sack in it and covered the sack back up. No one would see it there. The leaves had been there for two weeks already so nothing looked out of the way. He looked around again and didn't see anyone. The thing was secure.

He looked out to the trail and saw a group of people running for down. The word was out about the well. Everyone was running for Gun Point. Robert grabbed the wheelbarrow and headed back down the trail. Maybe he could still pick up another sack or two. When he reached back to the well, it was swarming with people. People were fighting like animals for the drugs. Only the strong were getting away with the sacks now. If a weaker person got a hold of one from the well, someone stronger would rip it away from him and run with it. It was chaos. Robert started to feel bad for the poor people. He already had one. There was no need to be greedy. If he really wanted to get rich, he could go back to the states and work. These people had no chance of ever making this kind of money. Robert jumped down in the well and helped with the dispensing of the drugs. He passed sack top of sack out of the well to people who were waiting at the top to get theirs. As the amount of people grew, the sacks were not enough, so they started tearing the sacks to pieces and grabbing for the one-one kilos inside the sack. It was a pinata. Each sack carried twenty-five one-kilogram packages. Some people would grab two, some would grab three or one, right so until the coke was done. People were diving one the ground and wrestling for whatever they could grab. Several appreciated Robert's help and didn't know that he already had a sack put up at the house. They gave him two kilos and told him to go with that. That's how the people the people in Nicaragua are. They are animals, but they don't want to see anyone starve.

And that was it. In a short time, all of the coke was done and everyone walked back for home, laughing nervously and trying to hurry up along the trails just in case someone wanted to take away what they had. No one tried anything like that yet. Robert put the two kilos in the wheelbarrow and walked along with the group of people for home. Everyone knew that the Babylon would soon come. With so much craziness going on, someone would surely talk and they would surely hear, but they had not shown up yet, so everyone had time to get home and secure whatever they had.

By the time Robert reached home, Danny and Pamela were there. He went in the house and didn't know what to say. Everyone was serious. Pamela said that Robert's eyes were this big. Robert showed them the two kilos. They started panicking. Pamela seemed a little angry about bringing that kind of thing around the house and the children. They didn't even know about the sack outside in the pile of leaves. When she stopped an really considered the situation, she wasn't so mad again. They started searching around the house for a spot to hide the kilos. They buried them in the sand floor beneath a little cupboard that held the dishes things. They paced around nervously and finally sat down and tried to relax. They laughed and held each other's hand. Coralito didn't know what was happening. Perlita was asleep in the hammock. Robert told them about the sack outside. They all started to smile and bust the laugh. "Exito Robert," Fireman said. Success.

Things were just starting to get crazy around the island. By this time, everyone knew about the drugs, and all kinds of people were coming around the house. People who were there in the morning started coming around to see if they could get anything from them. They tried to keep the people as far away as possible, but it was difficult. Everyone already knew that Robert got some, so people assumed that it was in the house. They knew they had to do something, but they couldn't sell the stuff yet. The island was flooded with coke and there were not enough buyers yet. The price was dirt low. Some people had already started selling, but they were giving it away. Some people sold for seven or eight hundred dollars a kilo. By the evening, the price had gone up to a thousand, and by the next morning it was at fifteen hundred. You couldn't just sell to any and anyone either though. You had to know the right person that was a serious buyer instead of someone who would give you false dollars or hijack you when you show up with the thing. It was clear that they needed to wait until things cooled down a little bit. But when would that be?

By the afternoon, all kinds of gangster people started showing up from Corn Island, and by the morning they were coming all the way from the mainland. Fireman's house was right in the middle of everything since they lived outside of town near the beach where the panga crashed.

Fireman went and bought a big machete. They couldn't leave the house alone, so for two days Robert just had to sit in the hammock nearby the pile of leaves and guard the sack. Fireman gave Robert the machete and a big bag of dope that Robert rolled liberally to help ease the stress of the situation a little. So all day he rocked there, smoking and listening to the radio, while Danny went around the town, going to the shop and checking out the movement of things. The next day Danny sold one of the kilos just to get a comfortable amount of money so they wouldn't have to worry about the little things like food and ganja.

It was middle night and new moon when Fonso beached the skiff a hundred yards or so from Heiko's place. I felt like I would be safe there. There was a little open hut that I could crash in for the night, and in the morning show up at Heiko's door and tell him I wanted to stay for a little while.

When I was there working last time, I dug a big hole to mix mud and sand to make a clay oven. I never made the oven, but I knew that the hole was still there. I could bury the sack in the hole and no one would find it. It was the only thing to do, and something had to be done quickly.

I jumped out of the skiff onto the beach snuck around in the dark through the plantain beds and bush, trying to be as quiet as possible until I found the hole. There were a few coconut leaves that had dropped over it, so I softly moved the branches away and shoved the sack into the hole, throwing some coconut husks an leaves over the top of it again. There was no sign of movement or noise from Heiko's nearby house, so maybe everything was cool. I went back to the little hut and tried to rest, but hearing every sound of the bush and imagining the worst of people coming to look for me, I held the thirty-eight close.

The insanity on the little island continues. It exploded. The people have turned into a mob of crazed *banditos*, ready to kill whomever they can take their coke from. Drugs and murder. In the last four days, countless numbers of shootings, stabbings and machetasos have kept the island talking.

Some *moreno* boy was bleeding all over town when Javier the carpenter threw a knife into his leg.

Matazon, the brokenhearted *corazon zapatero*, was shot in the abdomen, but not before he managed to stick his *punuelo* into the gunman's gut. The gunman soon died. Matazon is alive, but in the hospital in Corn Island. Matazon.

Jorgecito chopped the night watchman's head at Oran the preacher's Lobster *Acopio.* Jorge and someone else broke in, were stealing gas and chopped the Spaniard watchman to avoid problems. After being chopped, the watchman gave Jorgecito a dagger in his gut.

I keep a thirty-eight special beneath my writing book. Beneath my sword. I keep the book above my headboard in case anything sparks up in the night. It is beneath the candle. I have to give John something for it, but I don't mind. Maybe I'll give his family a kilo. I was planning on giving them something anyway. The gun is a good thing to have. It is warm and comfortable. It is safe.

I've already given plenty to Fireman. Four to Flubia the Indian. Three to Bamboo. One to Alfonso. This leaves me with twelve. That is enough. Several other people are seriously begging me one or two, but I don't plan to give anyone else a kilo. I'll give them some money or something, maybe a thousand dollars. I'm getting stingy now.

I moved in by Heiko again, and it's a pretty relaxed place to be right now. Up front of the island is swarming.

I gave away fourteen kilos of cocaine to my friends and family here on the island and yesterday when I came out front to the *pueblo*, no one would even invite me to a plate of food. It is a sick drug, this money. This cocaine. They are the same. You can never have enough. More, more, more. You always need more. It is better to be at zero. At zero, you are balanced. Equilibrium. Smoke marijuana. Laugh at the sunset. Smile at the sunrise. Keep to yourself.

My friends have disappeared. My family changed names. Here I sit alone and penniless, with twelve kilos of drugs buried back in the bush by Heiko. Life is funny.

The sandflies are biting me everywhere my clothes are not. I must buy myself some new clothes; new shorts; a new shirt; maybe a woman to cut my beard and dress me up. Where is Magdalene?

I must now make the decision to go sell. The moon was so big last night I could hardly sleep. I awoke to go shit before sunrise, which is where we are right now. Pinkness and purple fill the skies and heaven is on the horizon. It is here we are going to. We may never reach. I am still going.

In my room right now, I have the thirty-eight special loaded with four shells and hidden under my book. Two kilos are in my handbag, and a shirt full of AK-47 shells that I dove up one the reef this morning looking for sunken treasures. I have a bag full of hundred dollar bills. I feel like a movie.

Sailing closer and closer into the night sky, a pinhole of a star grows and grows into a sun filling the space with her brilliant lightness. Her presence is eternal; her subjects are eternity; the wind she blows infinity and the arrival she breathes is called hope. Her name is peace and her eyes are mirrors. Her songs are centipedes and lips like candles that glow soft and warm in the night, coating the walls of the room with golden glimmers and shadows. She is a far and distant dream, an unchained melody sunken to the lowest of melancholy minor keys and diminished half steps, simultaneously soaring to the heights of evolutionary orgasms.

All in all, it's just a bacchanal, a risen fall of ten feet tall guys who call lightning bugs flying around the room to smash into the paper that is filling itself with light juice and not so coherent wanderings.

The cocaine is safe for now I believe. The majority of it is buried in an old hole I dug in the bush for a clay oven. I knew I wasn't ever really going to make the thing in the first place. I just wanted to dig. "Why the hell am I digging this damn hole?" I thought to myself while sweating out the four-foot wide hole. It was just like the straw I cut for the roof. "Why the hell am I cutting all this straw?" Here, nearly a year later, the hole is serving its purpose, just as the straw I dragged down to Fireman's served its. Heiko doesn't know anything about the cocaine. I would prefer to keep it like this. He's just another person I'd have to cut in.

I've been renting this old red house on the bank now for the last couple of nights, just taking it easy and hiding out away from the town for a little while until things cool off and the price of the drugs rises a little more. Right now the kilo is selling for two thousand seven hundred dollars. It is steadily rising and is expected to reach three five to four thousand. Some say it could go as high as five thousand. The game is waiting until the time is right. It is holding fire. I've been passing the time *tranquilo*, trying not to let people pressure me into anything.

Up in Honduras, the kilo goes for much higher. Seven or eight thousand for one. The trick is getting it up there. The border there seems to be a rough place. Plenty of guns and plenty of shooting my Miskito friend Freddy tells me. He just reached back from a trip up there. I need to ask him how it went. I need to buy some toothpaste. I need a woman.

Oh beautiful woman, how you can bring joy to my eyes and sadness to my heart. A smile to my lips and weakness to my legs. An ease to my pain and the onset of my suffering. Unsheathed beauty, tambourine shelter.

"The time has come for everything," the wizard waved his wand. The loss of words overcame the blind man when he realized that the time of his suffering ended and a time of joy had begun. Before he could blink his narrow eyes, the moment top-sized.

The roof became the *suelo* and the *suelo* the ceiling. The poor man became rich and the rich man became old. The elders say it is better to be young just as the dead know it is better to be alive.

It has been a race to get rid of this money as fast as I can. Of the original kilo that I sold for two thousand seven hundred dollars, I remain with only about a hundred and fifty. I don't know how it disappeared so fast. I gave fifteen hundred to Miss Sherry to hold onto. I have been handing away twenty-dollar bills as if they were poems. As if they were poison.

The night overcomes the day and I decide to fast. Clean my dirty blood and clogged intestines. Give me a break.

Write. Just write. Do not be afraid. Something will come out if you only have faith and give praise to the Lord, your holy one. Forget about the details of propriety, audience, truth and the right words and find only a silence that permeates through all. Listen to the words shattering through that silence and confide in the echoing. Generate pages and pages of footprints.

"Create," God said to the idler who wastes through his morning opening coconuts upon rocks. The world is your workshop and your voice a saw. Sing your way to heaven. Blow your cane flute in rhythms of three, high melody, triplets calling down the spirit of music. A metaphysical masquerade and masterpiece of sound, hypnotizing the dancers and players of the court. The music will soon turn into lightning.

Money, money money. You sure are a funny thing. You can change a life of simplicity to one of complication.

Dave is a fat, gringo tourist who has been staying here at Heiko's for a few weeks now, and serves as a constant reminders of what I hate about North Americans. He's always coming around bumming grass and trying to sell me stupid shit that I don't want. Plastic containers, tarps, *masa rica* and shitty bracelets that he brought with him from Granada. He smells awful and rotten, and has some type of skin abscess on his lower calf. When he talks to you, his head and eyes wobble around as if he has no control in his neck, like a jack-out-de-box. He works for an oil company as a first aid person on a rig. He works three months a year and makes enough money to support himself for nine months of vacation. He is a real American asshole. He tells me about the *petrolera* and how the U.S. has Central America in her back pocket. How the oil industry has these Nicaraguan seas planned out as their future oil reserves for when the Middle East has been sucked completely dry. Raping the Earth of her richness. Her blood. Her oil. Her energy. Her life. For what?

For our cars and trucks, plastic factories and power plants. For our excess waste and pollution. Contamination of our seas and our air. Angels slain by ignorance, economics. The evil empire pumping its cancer through the veins of our world, and all you can say is war! Well war I say as well! I will scream it with rage in my eyes and blood in my throat. My hands are clenched fists waiting to explode. My feet are tiger claws tense from my flexed calves and Achilles tendon. You do not see me, but I see you. I am yearning to pounce onto your weakened flesh and quench my taste for your blood. You are my enemy and we will unite against your presence. Your secret will be revealed and the truth of your wickedness *illumbrado.*

We will take your money and spit in your face. Buy an army to resist you. Destroy the structures of steel and drills of daggers. You are not needed. Take your greed and let it rot inside you. Go back to your home.

They've been saying it for a long time; that the end is coming soon. That the Earth is out of its orbit and we're swinging around the moon. What you buy with what you make. The last laugh is gonna be on you. Who you workin' for?

"The time has come to destroy those who have destroyed the Earth".

A yesterday in the life of Robert Kuhn as written in the dark.

All of my friends have problems with cocaine. As for me, I can't even say where mine begin or the extent that they run through my life. My girlfriend could be the devil whore for all I know. Magdalena came, picked up her money and left. Gone Haulover to carry her kid to the hospital. What can you say about that? What can you say about love? It is what it is. You fall where you fall and play whatever cards lie in your path. There are neither decisions nor choices. You take the woman you are given at the time you are ready. Thousands of faces cross your eyes, but only one connects. And what is it about her?

She soothes your wanting and collects your energy. She is a magnet. She is mercy. She crawls through the holes in my head. I gave her a kilo of cocaine and then she left me, sick, weak and unable to eat. She says she'll be back soon.

My friend Doong came by yesterday and stole one hundred dollars out of my wallet and the little plastic bag of ganja that was sitting above my bed. He's the one trying to sell the drugs for me. We've been waiting for the price to hit four thousand dollars for the kilo. I wish that he would leave me alone and let me handle things myself, but he just sticks around. I've known him since the Caye, but things are different now. He's sees money now. The only thing to do is wait. It is the waiting that burns, but I am a patient person. I am in no rush and can hold off as long as I need to. I won't let people pressure me. The treasure is buried in a safe place nearby where no one will find it. When the time comes to move it, I can go with it one time.

Buyers are at the Hotel Delfines with their mattresses filled with cash, hoping someone will come out of the cracks and sell. They all know that there's still plenty of cocaine around. People are just waiting for the right price. Doong says they're paying three eight right now. By next week, it should reach four. Most people say that it will reach five in time, but I don't know about that. Things are getting hot. I'm just waiting for four and I'm gone.

My feet are feeling strong, and you know what they say. "A strong foot is a strong body". It is the truth.

Pearl Lagoon, two thousand five. The Vanguard of the Autonomy. May. The Rainy Season. The sun is high and hot. Bob Marley is singing "Get Up, Stand Up," dah dah duh duh. "Stand up for your right". "Get up, stand up. Don't give up the fight," he says.

There is a black man on the radio, calling for all coast people to unite. People of all races and ethnicity, take the future into your hands. It is yours. Miskito, Creole, Sumo, Ramacaye, you are one. White people, Spaniards and Arabs. You are one.

Finally the trip to Pearl Lagoon came. Fleco, a local gangster, made the trip with his skiff. There was some business going on, but I was out of that. I was just along for the ride. It was a fast trip. We left out on Thursday morning and came back Friday night. It was a three-hour ride with the two seventy-five horsepower engines. The one night there was a complete *bacchanal.* All kinds of rum and cusousa, the Garifuna moonshine, gifatee and beer like rice. Women were on us like hungry dogs. Everything was hard.

I saw Chico and picked up my bag and guitar. He was thrilled to see me. He didn't know what to say. He had not forgotten his friend, and neither had I. He said that he was worried about me, and didn't know if I was coming back or not, but he kept everything safe for me. The guitar was not fixed, but I didn't care. I was happy to fulfill my mission and reach back to Pearl Lagoon. I am free again. We had a drink of rum, but I couldn't sit for too long. The notes were different this time. He looked sick. His crippled foot was hurting him, but his spirits were high. I gave him fifty dollars to help out his situation. It was greatly appreciated. I don't know when I'll see him again.

Since returning to the Island, I have not been working, but have been writing and playing music daily, trying to lay low and pass the rain. Sometimes, you just gotta do nothing. Got another breath, got another year, another chance. But for now, ain't gotta go nowhere from here. Sit and wonder if the rain is coming back. I done pay my rent for another two weeks. If I play my cards right, I'll soon be relatively rich.

So Doong just came by with a few friends and we sat on the porch and smoked a joint and listened to Doong talk virtually uninterrupted for about an hour and a half. I have to admit that he does tell some good stories though. Listening to him is like watching a movie. He talks all about his drug running adventures up the coast around here and Puerto Cabeza. About the thousands of dollars and kilos and arms that have been scattered on the table. About hijacking Indians who don't give a fuck about you; Indians that walk the beach with AK-47's and wait for a panga to pass too close to the land.

John said that once some boys were diving right there out front and they found some sacks of AK's. He himself had three of them, three sacks. AK is a good weapon to have around in case the shit ever really goes down. In case of a war. Maybe Babylon tries to take over or something. The Little Island can say no.

Squalls omen over the horizon. Rain stops and starts and I, on the porch, decide that all these feeling of love are just me wanting to feel you cry. All of the pain in the world adds up to nothing more than a cold gust of breeze.

People here have lost their minds. Traded them for cocaine and given up control of their bodies; their actions; their words; their personalities. They have become their own enemies.

Zombies and fictional creatures of their own imagination. Insane and incoherent.

There has apparently been a hatching of a large group of flying insects nearby and they are swarming my porch right now, making it difficult to sustain my sanity.

The moon is new. The rain began falling just like clockwork. Just like everyone said it would. Now are the days to be planting.

I walked around the island today, planting marijuana seeds all over the place. If the seeds grow, we will all be rich with thoughts and love songs. Friends and energies.

Energy is the only thing that is worth it. Saving. Collecting. Hording. The only hope we have for the future lies in the next deep breath.

Sit and watch the rain with marijuana on the telephone.

I have seen the dawn in the east, and it is dry. I've seen the flooding of the mountains and it is sorrow. You are killing the world with the things you buy. Success is your imagination. Your riches are an illusion veiled over your poor living. Simplicity is the only solution. Refusal to consume is the revolution.

Make your mark by erasing.

"Only those who can admit the light into their gizzards can translate what is there in the heart". Henry Miller said that.

Dear Lord, I pray that you grant me wisdom to behave wisely with this woman I believe that I love. Magdalene. Asleep in my bed, beneath my mosquito net, beside the pistol on my table. I am on the porch with the Western land breeze, taking a breath of fresh air, the only thing worth taking.

The end of May. All deals have been made. Negotiations are finished. The money is in hand. I have sold. There are thirty four thousand dollars hidden inside my guitar. I am in a ten dollar a night hotel in Corn Island, preparing to catch the Captain D to Bluefields. It is good to take a little time away from Little Corn Island. Everything is very serious. Love, money, guns and drugs. Questions of faith and betrayal. *Cosas de la vida* and death as well.

Doong tried to kill me. Showed up in the middle of the night with some Tasbaponi boy, Enrique, wearing masks and ordering me out of the house. Magdalene and I were asleep in bed when they knocked on the door. Magda knew right away that something was wrong.

"Robert. Robert," she tried to wake me. "Robert, they're here.

Don't answer the door. Don't. Shh. Its Doong". Magda dreamt all of this a week earlier. It was like she was ready for them. We were out front in the town that night and she didn't even want to come home. She said that she was going to stay with her cousin out front. She said that she just had a bad feeling about going home. I finally convinced her to come home with me, but she wasn't happy about it. We had to fight about it. It was all just like she said.

They knocked on the door again. This time I was awake. I didn't say anything. Banging on the door, they promised to shoot up the little board house if I didn't come outside. "Where is the sack, Robert?" they asked.

"We're going to get it in the good way or the bad way. Where's the sack?"

They fired a warning shot. "Bang!" went the night.

By this time I was up, pacing around the room, looking for something, anything I could use as a weapon, anything I could use for protection. I gave the pistol back to Brother John a few days ago. It would have been good to have it now, but that is irrelevant. I picked up a spear gun I had in the corner and loaded it. I looked out of a little hole in the door, and thought that maybe I could shoot the masked gunman who was standing on the porch not far from the door. I stuck out the point of the spear and took aim. If I missed, the man would surely blast down the door and kill me. The man backed down off of the verandah and stood on the ground about ten or fifteen feet away from the door. Better. I didn't have to make any decisions about pulling the little trigger.

Magdalene was under the bed shaking and trembling, curled up in a ball, crying and telling me to go outside and give them anything they asked for. I felt awful for getting her into this. I had to do something. I held the spear gun and opened the door. I stood facing gunman, half of me inside the door and half out. The man in front of me held an AK-47, and the second who was on the ground at the corner of the house held a pistol. The mask was a primitive, frightening array of white and colored rags with some coconuts leaves and bushes hanging over his face. They looked liked monkey men.

"Give us the coke Robert. We're going to get it in the good way or in the bad way," he repeated.

About seven yards separated us now, I on the porch and him on the ground. Doong was still around the corner off the side of the house. "Doong! Enrique!" I called.

"Who the fuck is Enrique?" Enrique replied. Doong didn't say anything, but I knew it was him. The two of them had been coming around too much in the past couple of days.

Their guns were pointed at me. Energy filled my body. I grabbed a black handkerchief that was on a table near the door and threw it out the door. Before the cloth hit the ground I bolted from the doorway and off of the porch, sprinting for the beach as my feet hit the ground. I heard a gunshot fire and felt a surge of joy knowing that you never hear the shot that kills you.

Another shot fired as I flew by Heiko's little house. "Heiko," I called as I passed by running. I don't know why I called his name.

My feet flew down the beach for a short distance until I made a sharp cut for up and darted into the bush, never once stopping and turning back to see what was behind me until I was a good distance into the dark bush. I crossed beneath a barbwire fence and down into a plantain bed and stopped to listen for any sounds in the bush.

The moon was full. Full, full. My mind raced to Magdalene. I heard nothing but silence in the bush. Some crabs and iguanas rustling through the dry leaves, but no people. I continued creeping through the bush, from tree to tree and shadow-to-shadow, slowly working my way back to the house on the beach to find out about Magdalene. I still hadn't heard her scream, so I comforted myself hoping that she was not being raped or tortured as her dream had forecasted. I was glad that she didn't know where everything was buried but prayed that she was somewhere safe.

I snuck back through the bush until I saw the house. It was dark. I saw no one and heard nothing. I carefully went back to it and climbed up the stairs onto the verandah. The house was empty. Magdalene was gone. I hoped she made it down the beach to a friend's house or went by Heiko, even though I knew she hated Heiko. I just hoped that the gangsters hadn't kidnapped her and carried her off somewhere.

The first thing I did was put on some clothes. The whole time running about in the bush I was barefoot in my boxer shorts. I had to go into town and check out things.

I started walking the trail back to town. The moonlight was bright. My feet couldn't move fast enough. I felt like the hijackers could be hiding in any of the dark patches of bush. I started running. My feet moved faster and faster until I was sprinting over the dirt and rocks that led back into the town. I reached quickly.

The sidewalks and lanes of the town were empty. I saw Bernaldo and a group of Indians who were incoherently drunk. Bernaldo had sold off his drugs a few weeks ago, and had kept drunk since then. It was probably past two o'clock. I walked down the sidewalk towards Alfonso's. Maybe he could lend me a gun. I had to find Magdalene.

Ahead of me on the sidewalk I saw two people. It was Doong and Enrique. I stopped and made them go ahead further. I did not want them to see me, but I felt like they already had. I went back to the drunken Indians, looking for strength in numbers. I found them right where I had left them, falling over and talking to themselves. I told them I wanted their help. They couldn't understand anything. I told them lets go out front and get more to drink, and they started to follow me. They were all happy to see me. One of them kept touching me. He seemed drunk to the point of turning gay. I kept having to throw his hands off me, but I finally got them moving on the sidewalk and towards the front where Alfonso lived.

When we came near Alfonso's house I left the group of Indians. They were lost, mumbling and grunting. They stunk. I went to Fonso's back door. I knocked, but no one answered. I knew he was probably sleeping so I kept knocking on the door and calling out his name. He finally answered the door, rubbing his sleepy eyes. "Wha happm?" he asked.

I apologized about waking him up at this hour of the night, and he me told not to worry about it. I told him I needed a gun. I told him about Magdalene and the hijackers who came by and what was happening. He said he didn't have a gun. I felt like he had one, but maybe he did not want to lend it out. He gave me a little machete. It was a good machete. It was sharp and of just a good length. It wasn't a big long bush chopping machete, but not too short either. He told me not to worry about things, and that he was sure everything would be alright, but to be careful. I thanked him for the machete and went out on the sidewalks to take a look around the village and see if anything was moving around.

Everyone was sleeping except for a few rock-men that were still up walking in circles around the shadows unable to sleep and trying to figure out how to get another piece. I nodded hello to the men and kept on walking. There was no sign of Magda up here. I wanted to go back around to the beach.

I forked off of the trail I came into town on, and took another road back to Heiko's. It was a little longer, but I didn't know what might be waiting on the road.

When I arrived back at the house it was just how I left it, still no Magdalene. By this time it was well past three o'clock and would be daylight shortly. There was nothing to do until morning came. I could not sleep so I laid down in the hammock with the machete by my side. Thoughts raced through my head as I took some deep breaths and tried to calm myself down. I didn't want to smoke. I just rocked in the hammock and waited. The roosters crowed and the Eastern night sky soon began to show some color. I took of my clothes and went down to the beach close to our friend Kim's house. I walked into the ocean and dove in. Under the water I could hear my name being called. It was a voice inside my head. "Magdalene!" I cried out inside of myself. I turned over on my back, spread open my arms and floated in the rippling sea, staring into the heavens. In the purplish sky, the daylight was erasing the stars of the night, but a few still lingered above. The moon was dropping low in the west.

I put down my feet and waded back up to the shore where I could see an angel in white running towards me. I walked onto the beach and grabbed Magdalene as she ran to me crying. "I heard you inside," she told me. "I heard you calling and I came out and there you were".

"I know," I said. I held her tight against me and said thank God. "Come. Lets go from here".

In the night when the two gunmen went chasing after me, Magda got herself together and made a run for it. She headed for Kim, our neighbor friend's, house and they let her in to sleep for the night. She spent the night crying, telling them that she thought that they had killed me. Kim and his girlfriend tried to calm her down and get her to sleep but she could not stop shaking, like there was a tremendous cold inside of her. There was nothing they could do at that hour of the night, Kim told her. In the morning they would go out and look for me. Kim didn't have a gun, and they did. They just had to wait until daylight.

We went back to the house and got our things together and went out to the front. It was time to sell. Things were too hot. It was time to get off of the island. We made the contact with a short Colombian buyer named Eduardo that I had been talking to. He was ready anytime we were. We just had to bring the things out to the front. He was staying in a room at a hotel called the Lobster Inn. It was a small room, jammed with dollars and drugs. I asked him if he would lend me a gun, but he said he couldn't do that. I understood. It was daytime now and things seemed a little bit safer in the light, but I still wanted some protection. If I carried the sack of drugs out of the bush just so, everyone would know just what I was carrying and we would be easy targets for hijackers.

On the sidewalk out front, I saw an old Jamaican fisherman fellow that I worked with on the Caye. George was his name. Jamaican George. George was a tall, lean salty looking old black gangster who came over from Jamaica twenty years ago. He was a rough cat. He'd been in jail all over the place, Nicaragua, Jamaica, Honduras, all bouts for running drugs. He was a seaman, and in the Caribbean, the sea and drugs go hand in hand. He was tough. No one was going to mess with him. He didn't need a gun or anything. He had a long scar down his long face that was partly covered up by the thin scraggly beard he wore. He smoked cigarettes plenty. He drove an old Jamaican skiff called the Trying Man. No one was tougher than him on the ocean, even though he had over sixty years. His eyes were cold, yellow and hollow. He was a nice and easy man though. He lived up in Sandy Bay with his Indian wife and three children. I knew all of them. He carried me in from the Caye one time and invited me to his house to eat and meet his family. They were all pleasant people and the children well behaved. I saw him on the sidewalk and begged him the favor to accompany me on a walk back to the other side of the island and back. Magdalene felt much safer with an escort. Having

George around just made everything a little bit cooler.

We walked home, put the ten kilos in an old backpack I had, and walked the beach back to town. It was about ten o'clock in the morning. No one would be expecting us to walk the beach back and there might be people waiting for us on the faster highland trail. Everything went according to plan and we made the sale without any problem. Thirty seven thousand dollars Eduardo paid me in new, crisp one hundred dollar bills. I checked the money and it seemed real enough to me. Eduardo didn't even bother checking the kilos. I gave George a thousand dollars for the little walk he took with us, and more than pleased, he shook our hands and told us to be careful.

The money folded up into a big roll in my pocket. Now what? We had to leave. This island was not safe. Neither Magdalene nor I felt to go back to the house on the beach again. It was too far away. Too remote. Anything could happen back there. It was better to be in the front, in the town amongst people. We got a room at the same Lobster Inn where we made the sale. The room was safe and nice. We checked in in the late afternoon and walked up to the top of the island to visit Fireman and Pamela, who were renting a big cement house with a big grass yard. They sold off a long time ago, and were waiting to get their papers together to fly home to Argentina. Since the cokes fell and we all split up, we had hardly seen each other. Things got tense. Danny wasn't there when we arrived. He was out somewhere. He was using drugs a lot lately and things were funny. Pamela was there with another one of our friends, Ann, who was renting the house with them. It was good to see everyone. We told them that we were leaving the island and a little bit about what happened. They were shocked. They thought it was a good idea to travel. Pamela told us that they were leaving soon too. We didn't talk about Danny. It looked like only Ann was sticking around, but she was leaving soon too, maybe in a couple of weeks. We wrapped up a joint and smoked again before Magda and I left. Magdalene didn't like that. Magdalene didn't like anything about drugs or alcohol, but she took it easy while we smoked one last and said goodbye to each other. I wished that Danny had been there, but that was how that goes with friends.

The night in the hotel was hot and sticky with plenty of mosquitoes. Magdalene and I got up early and took breakfast by Alfonso. I gave him back his little machete and said thanks. He said not to worry about it. After breakfast, we walked back around to Heiko's place to clean up the little house, pack our bags and get the hell off the island. The panga was leaving out at two o'clock, so we didn't have much time. At the house, we started throwing our things together into bags of stuff we were taking with us, and stuff that we weren't. We wanted to travel light, without all of the cheap rubbage and rags that could be easily replaced. We were just about through packing when we saw two Indian boys running down the beach, headed back towards the village. It looked strange, but we didn't pay it too much mind. We continued packing, when out the window, we saw Jamaican George hustling down the beach after the boys, carrying a sack of something on his back. Something was definitely going down.

"Come on Magda, let's go check this out," I said to her. We went down onto the beach and walked around the bend towards where the men were coming from, and then we saw it. A huge Colombian skiff had run up on the beach. "Here we go again," I said, and took off running up the beach towards the skiff and the people who were already a work at dismantling what could be removed. I jumped up in the skiff again amongst the people who were hammering away at the Yamaha two hundred engines and the steering column. It was all the same. The guys had already gotten one of the engines off and were working on the next one. I helped with what I could, but could tell that I wasn't going to get anything out of this skiff. I got off a big radio antenna that I knew Heiko could use and gave it to him. There were a few sacks of food things, coca-cola, sprite, apples and oranges, tuna fish and bags of chips, thing that the mafia people could eat while traveling. What there was still on the skiff was plenty of gasoline. The hull underneath was full of it. Flooded with it. People from all over the island brought all of the buckets and little gas tanks that they had and were filling them up. Anything that could hold gas, the people brought. There were several hundred gallons in the hull of the skiff. After people had gotten all out of the skiff that they could carry, they poured a little trail of gas and threw a match at it and the skiff blew up in flames. No one wanted any problems with the

Babylon. They would rather burn the skiff than give it over to them.

Magdalene and I didn't stick around to watch the rest of the party. We hurried back to the house and got our things together and left. We told Heiko thanks for everything and split. We still had a little time before the skiff left out. I gave Magda about half of the money to hold onto just in case there were police around searching people. I was already illegal in the country and didn't want any more discrepancies about what I was doing here. Even if we lost half of the money, it would be better than losing all. I told her to wait there at the skiff. There were a few people back in the village that I wanted to give some money to and say goodbye. I gave a few hundred dollars to the guy who ran the little league baseball team and passed a few hundred to Jisena just because, and tried to hurry up back to the skiff. I arrived to find that the passenger skiff already left. I felt my stomach drop. Magdalene was on it, and she left with the money. I suddenly started to panic. What if Magda was not who I thought she was? What if she just wanted the money and now ran? How could I find her? Why didn't she just wait for me and travel with me later? I started to panic. I had to get to Corn Island and find her. I had to get off the island.

I asked around the town if anyone was going to Corn Island, but no one was going. I found a guy, Jimmy, whom I worked with on the Caye that had a skiff. He said he would carry me across for a hundred dollars. No problem I said. Let's go. He got the gas, put his propeller on the engine, and pulled the skiff onto the beach. I threw in my backpack and guitar loaded with money, pushed the skiff off and jumped in. Jimmy dropped me off on the secluded North End section of Corn Island. It was a good drop off, better than the municipal wharf where Babylon would surely be swarming. There were no people around, and the road was right close by. I took off walking, all my belongings on my shoulders. I had to find Magdalene now. I found a telephone and called, but got no answer. I called and called again, but it seemed like her phone was turned off. Where could she be? For all I knew, she had already left the island and was landing in Managua, where I would never find her. I hailed down a taxi and told him to carry me by the airport. The evening flight had not yet left, and she wasn't there. She had to still be on the island. I tried calling again but had the same result. She must have cut off her phone, I thought. I had to get a room and settle myself down. I got a room at a cheap place by the wharf. It was the hotel that I always liked the looks of. The room was nothing special, but it seemed safe; no windows, no bathrooms, one door, a fan and an *escritorio.* I put up the guitar and the bag and went back to calling Magdalene. The situation seemed hopeless. I nearly gave up, when all of a sudden I got an answer.

"Where are you?" I asked. She could tell I sounded desperate. She just started to laugh, and said, "You never trust me did you?"

"Where are you?" I asked again.

"Right here," she said. "Where are you?"

I told her the hotel I was at by the wharf, and she told me just to hold on. She said she would be there in two minutes.

I went out on the verandah and took a deep breath and looked up the road. It really took about two minutes, and there she was, rolling up in a taxi, a big smile on her face.

"Ahh," I sighed to myself and I grabbed her and hugged her tight. She just laughed and told me that the phone was broken, and she had to carry it to someone to fix it. She said that she couldn't wait on that little island any longer. She wanted off and wasn't going to let that panga leave without her. She had the money put up by a friend. She just laughed. I had to laugh too. We went up to the room and I showered and tried to cool off. I had to say thank God again.

Haulover

This money is making me depressed. It has made my life seem like an incandescent joke with no remedy or solution in sight. It has taken away my freedom and given me greed. Taken my strength and given me idle weakness. I cannot eat. I have sores on my feet.

I walk down to the street to have a beer in the bar by the wharf. "Who took my money? Who took my money? Who took my money?" the crazy drunk on the barstool next to me chattered to himself before he called me by my name. How he knew my name and my age, I do not know. He didn't know either, but he did. I tried to ignore it, but could not. Everything he said pierced through my being and into my past. I tried to believe it was a coincidence, what he was saying, but it was not. We had never seen each other before. He knew my university and my worries from knowing how to listen. He was listlessly drunk. He was past the bounds of consciousness and living in an elevated drunken state in which nothing was hidden or unreal. He heard what the universe shows, the vibrations that pulse through everything. The sober cannot hear over the hum. "Twenty two thousand, three hundred ninety two, one hundred and seventy five, five thousand and seventy two. Twenty and twenty. Thirty thousand and . . . " he mumbled to himself. He knew the exact number of dollars I had in my guitar. He was charged.

Two torturous weeks after leaving Little Island, we have finally reached Haulover, the small village where dreams are made into realities. Corn Island was full of sickness and depression. Immigration officers fattening their asses on my pay check, while they do nothing but give me a hard time. Babylon. The time finally came to pay my dues to the government. I had to get legal; get my papers straight if I wanted to stay in Nicaragua. Hot nights full of sand flies and mosquitoes that love the stillness of the air. After ten days of waiting and regretting the decision to follow Magdalene away from the outlaw's haven of Little Corn Island, we escaped on the Captain D to Bluefields.

The only positive things about Big Corn Island were the hours upon hours that Magda and I were able to spend together on the bed with absolutely nothing to do but wait, getting to know ourselves and our respective bodies.

Little Corn Island was the beginning. It was the entrance. Haulover is more advanced in the game.

Smoking Haulover homegrown, our hero sits back in the breeze and the country music over the Lagoon of Pearls and reflects about his life as a book. He cannot quite grasp if it is fiction or non, or whether or not he is really holding the reigns of this backwards bull. "*Tu sabes major que nadie* . . . and I went to the wild side of life". Freddy Fender's voice sounds like Fats Domino.

A group of Creole children are climbing around on the balcony like staring monkeys amazed at the white man.

The truth about God is that he gives us only so many breaths to breathe. That number is set or variable depending on the truth of *uno*.

"That weed make you thinkin' them things," she says.

I say to free your mind is to free my pen.

"Free yourself," she says. "And don't come write no craziness bout me no more".

She is my model. My inspiration. The skin of my red eyes. And she is sleepy. The afternoon breeze makes her so. She yawns and blinks her black eyes. Rolling eight balls. Shining mirrors. Looking glass.

"Stop talk craziness and come lay down. Make we sleep. Come *amor*". The end.

Magdalene.

Eyes of black pearls. Ear of precision and nose of *olores*, you are going blind. Your smile is sincere as your coco like rice.

I love you plenty and your just right sized breasts. You keep me fed. You keep me clean. You are an angel that God of the road has sent to me. You have rhythm and fluidity. Honesty and brutality. Be careful in what you say to me cause you might make it hurt. Clarity and sobriety. All your five senses and more.

I am going to lay down beside you and taste your neck. Is the beat too slow? Have the late hours of the half moon sky made you so sleepy? Have a drink of water. Blow out the wick. Take the night and all that it is.

"Un beso de una puta"

It has been two full lunar months since I have left, and since returned to, Little Corn Island. Two life changing months of planting and nothingness, aimless waiting for something that I am not sure of. The *lunada* was wonderful. Magdalene showed up vexed about a pound of sugar that I told her she could stick up her lovely ass. Better she never showed up at all. I am getting fat. Plenty of food. Plenty of fish. Plenty of coconut and breadkinds. The soup has left me *empachado*. It is time to get moving. Time to get living. Time to get working. Time to fast. Curiosity is what killed the cat, and the road of excess leads to the palace of wisdom. The palace lays at the end of the road. The wise have all abandoned their excesses. The foolish are still on the road. I'm leaving Little Island again for bigger and better things. There is nothing here for me now.

I sing to myself, searching for the *diclofenac* put myself to sleep and this earache to rest. Life is hard in Nicaragua. Death is an infection. Godliness is cleanliness and Christ the resurrection. Amen. Hallelujah say the preachers in the churches. The word of God is in the beaks of the birds, the chirpings of the crickets and the rolling of the midnight waves.

Magdalene, where is the *diclofenac*?

Mosquitoes are biting in Haulover; big mainland, sharp-nosed mosquitoes. It may be time to be moving on and find somewhere else to be. Do what you want. Everything works out for the living. Get some sleepin', stop your drinking and sometimes your smokin' too. Drink plenty of water. Say goodnight.

People who sing have words in their head. That's their soul talking. People who live through this world in disgust are disgusting.

This house is falling down as I watch the river flow freely down the stream to its destination in the sea somewhere outside Bluefields, where it will turn salt.

For sometime now, I've wanted to tell you what is happening or where I am, but I guess I've just been a coward or too busy, or too tired to pick up my pen.

My hands are soft and bleeding, growing calluses with this Nicaraguan lifestyle. My attempts to make life here in Haulover have been slowly weakening my sense of moral. Magdalene has got me crazy and alone; fadingly weary. I guess it is about time I'm going. I've been trying to build a house for us. For her. That has been my life for the past month, and it doesn't want to happen. Hauling sand, mixing cement, making bricks, digging holes, buying lumber, tying rods, I'm sick of her. I'm sick of her shit and the life that she's sending me to live. I'm sick of myself and my money that I have to spend. The time ahead of me seems long as I spend the afternoon drinking beer by Marlon. Marlon is from Haulover. He has a bar here. It is miserable. My life in the United States seems like a distant memory of a long forgotten person.

The little dugout canoes with their black plastic, triangle sails come blowing past in the fair North Eastern breeze. They are good days to be working, but who am I kidding? I am no kind of working man.

I'm out of here on the next freight boat heading North to Rio Grande. I'll leave my money here with Magdalene to build her damn house for her four children. I don't care about nothing no more. I was better just being a lonesome vagabond.

Magdalene's come home way too late for the last time. She's come home way to late for the last, last, last time.

I'm going up on to Rio Grande. I give up. My belly is too hungry.

It's too cold in my bed.

Back to the search for the money in Magda's suitcase. I found the pearls in her pocket. I got the key to unlock it, but the money is missing. We need to have a talk. We haven't said a word for days. Gonna hurry up and run out the door. Find some food to eat with the girl next door.

So you think you got a good woman? Ha! A good woman's got chu.

Laid up on my back with a dog bite that quickly developed into a fever. I am at a loss. Happy Birthday. Hopefully I will stop oozing puss and start walking again soon. It will not be tonight. The strong survive. The weak die off. Nicaraguan hard life.

I went home and came back with a machete, determined to kill the dog, but he was already put up behind the gate. I'll find some way to kill him. Don't feel no kind of way. They say a cigarette butt in a piece of bread is a strong dog poison.

"White shrimps are starting to hit," says Menrod. "That's what we've been waiting for. The big white ones".

It is September first. September has finally arrived and as promised a plentiful bounty here on our bank of the Pearl Lagoon.

Callwah, snook, drummer, tarpon and the abundant and delicious, tough ass stone bass.

The stone bass is a smallish, sharp pointy fish with razors on the cheekbone and bony spines shooting out of its ass and back. It looks like a Chinese star. Black and silver are its shiny scales that blaze in the moonlit night like reflectors in a gill net. Like flowers.

Menrod say that it's all about the tides. "There's a guy that just started killing them at the bar mouth out at our bank, and he no know a thing about tides. You see we understand when the tides are running. We know about the moon".

Menrod and Negro are dorymen. They work the fish and the shrimps here in Haulover. They worship the God of the moon, as do the rest of the fishermen and farmers, the natural men. They work in the night and always know what is happening with the moon. Where she is. When she's rising, when she's falling. When she's full, when she's new and the changes that are affected by her. The tides, low and high, flooding and ebbing, are controlled by her. They are what dictate the coming and going of the shrimp. The shrimps then call the fish and the fish call us. Everyone is going out for a meeting with God. Some will lose their lives. Some will gain it. This is the nature of living as I see it in Haulover. On the banks of the river, on the Pearl Lagoon, in the waters flowing in and out of her mighty mouth, leading to infinity and the Atlantic ocean. That would put Haulover right in the lungs, the capillaries diffusing the waters in a swampy flesh of mainland. It is the lowlands. The heat and humid pressure is deadening at times. The mosquitoes are a plague. The breeze is hallelujah. The women are beautiful. It is the Pearl Lagoon. The water is fresh. It is nice to drink. It is good to bottle it up and carry with you in the dry weather. Very fine. Plenty shrimps. Plenty fish. You just have to have the gears and go out there and get them. The life is free.

Coast people have a free lifestyle. You don't need to buy everything, or anything really. You can survive with little or nothing, but you must be a hard-working man. You've got to fish. You've got to plant. You've got to chop and you've got to dig. You have to build and you have to destroy. Kill and give life. Balance yourself as the natural man and you will thank God for the results, the faith and energy you will receive. Life is rewarded you. Life eternal, if you can live with the laws of goodness that Jesus Christ brought to us and the teachings he was crucified for; his revolutionary ideas that showed the people they were free. They didn't need the Romans or their calendars. They were not slaves. They were free with the water that God gave them to carry themselves to heaven. Cleaning their souls with nothingness and air, they were free. God has given us all that we need to live. Our medicine, our food, our life-blood is free for the working and the faithful. Take it. Accept heaven with a deep breath and then another. Expel the devil from your fiery gut and lungs. Exhale. Piss.

The night is coming to a close and again I must ask myself how things have gotten this far out of hand. My shirt is ripped open and I am standing in the kitchen, looking for a sense of clarity in this big foggy mess I've fallen into. Love, sex, money, whores, thieves and the nature of women.

Tonight Magdalene tried to kill me with everything she had in her. Now she is asleep, exhausted beneath the mosquito net. I told her she wasn't leaving until she gave me some explanation for the thousands of dollars she's been spending and lying and deceiving me about.

She wouldn't talk. She wouldn't say a word and when she tried to walk out the door again, things got rough. She's a tough bitch to let go of. First she tried to smash me with a glass. Then she tried to stab me with a knife. After that, she tried to stone me with a rock that little Esther brought her. Finally, begging for life and water, I let her up and turned my back to her when she threw a stone into my back with all her force. After wrestling and holding her down again for a half an hour, I released her. Better she killed me. End this life of misery that she drags me through. I could leave her, but I want nothing else but her in this life. Her and the top of the house made of wood. She wanted ply-cem, so after I told her no, she bought it without my consent. She took the money from the little bag I had it hidden in, and used it as if it were hers. Now that I tell her I don't want her spending any more of my money, she refuses to return the thousand dollars she took out of my wallet. She is a whore and a thief who wants nothing less than exactly what she wants. She knows no compromise or respect. After thoroughly defeating her in battle tonight, she mysteriously returns to sleep in my bed. I try my hardest to understand what she is thinking, but I cannot. I am afraid to enter the bed, so I am standing in the kitchen writing.

"Mama Magda, you gonna die?" little Esther cries the whole time I am pinning Magdalene down.

"No baby, bring mama a knife from the kitchen".

Why do I build her this house? Why do I love her? I feel the wires around my heart are twisted and cross, wrenching it from the bones of my chest. I cannot catch. I cannot believe I allowed life to lead me here again. I will never love another. The end.

I only wish there was some way to make her feel this hurt I am feeling inside. The only thing is to leave. "My feet know how to love someone as my heart knows how to pound". Townes Van Zandt said that. She would only smile for now she has what she wants. She has used me efficiently, the way a mason uses a stone; to build her house of bricks. I'm happy to have helped her.

My life has suddenly whirl-winded into a nightmare here. I cannot escape it. My love is my life, and I have ceased believing in it, as is the expiratory nature of belief. I've lost confidence. Her vision is blinding. Her touch more precious than air. Belief is a troubled belief and disbelief holds the tiny heart of belief. She wants me to build this house. She wants to build this house. She wants us to build this house. She thinks it will be for her, but she is sorely mistaken. This house will be for me. The greed is sickening me. Mine, mine mine. My money, my money my money. My house. Let go of everything and live. Prove yourself fool!

And so I just don't know how I'll make it through the night. You still haven't left, and I'm not about to leave. If morning somehow reaches, I will welcome it and thank the lord for helping me find it. Perhaps she will touch my leg and make it all alright.

All of the slow, painful love songs on the radio have come true. I have ceased sleeping and eating. Magdalene just asked me where I'm going to sleep. I tell her the bed. The only instant of comfort or sleep is when the warmth of her flesh touches mine before she realizes it and pulls away. It is hope. For a second, I feel alright.

I am hallucinating. A crazed maniac, out of control, shuddering and shaking and wearing thin; about to explode all over Magdalene and then retracting back into the smallest molecules of the corner; inside myself.

Screaming until I'm hoarse and tired; kicking until the muscles in my legs won't snap; crying until I am no longer hungry, afraid or willing to love again. I nearly snapped off her neck, but I hauled back the reins of my advancing forearms. It is pitching a fit. A fit over money. A fit over betrayal, lies and thieving money because I wouldn't give it to her. Selfish, foolish or ignorant, there is no saving or wisdom with money it seems, only the loss and withering away like broken-hearted dreams.

The soul is white like an apple. Pure and unforgetful. Blood will not show on walls of red, but they still need to be washed. Dirt shows clear on a shirt of white, as sins show on the soul. Clean yourself with fasting and praying, drinking water and singing the well of the world is in my heart. Take off your shoes and throw them in the sea.

I awoke yesterday, wrapped in wet blankets, pouring feverish sweat from my weakened body, and recalled where I was again. Staring at the tin roof, I wondered how I had gotten this far away. Who am I? What am I doing here in Nicaragua for this long? The heat was so that I could not catch. The tin rood made the little room like a big oven. The fever had me for six days. It has been a long bad dream, until yesterday when I felt I could fight no longer. I felt death taking over the daylight. They brought me a young coconut and got some pills down my throat with it and out I went. Hours later in a sweat drenched bed too short for my legs, Magdalene held my hand. "You coolin' down moy. Any hotta would have given flame".

"I'm afraid," I told her.

"No fraid moy. You no go die".

I haven't taken a bite of food in five days, but today she stewed some vegetables for me in coconut milk and I was able to force them down. They tasted damn nice. It is heaven to breathe again. Hell has been inside me for six days and I pray that it never returns. *El dengue es mortal.*

Two days later, it turns out to be malaria. The fever returns harder and hotter and pill resistant. Life with Magdalene is a constant battle as she rattles my sanity daily. I have been imprisoned in her village of Haulover. Locked in the house and life that I've now spent too much money on to back out now. So I jump on the floors and pull out my hair and scream at the top of my lungs at Magdalene, cussing her for tricking me and leading me into a life so miserable and then threatening to make us live like animals. If I stay here, she promises to make this life hell. If I leave she says she will follow and torture me. I cannot wait to sell this house and leave her and her family homeless and penniless, heartbroken and growing old with her immaculate pussy no longer able to trap anyone. Alone to die like her mother, begging money from her prostitute daughters. I am hurt because she does not love me. I am hurt because she used me. I am hurt because she is still using me and I don't want to walk away from the five thousand dollars she is hiding from me. It is a disgusting situation that makes me a helpless pathetic schizophrenic. Life is cruel and funny to those watching from *a fuera.* They are the ones on the outside.

The fever has broken with my will. I want to hurt her. What kind of love is that?

Negro just came by. He is the reason for our present conflict. Magdalene hates Negro. She says that if I go fishing with him one more time, we're going to live like animals. I know she is telling the truth now and that is it. I hate it when she tries to boss me. She won't leave me because she can't leave, but she can make my life a living hell until I have to. Neither of us wants to leave the house. It is set in stone. Anyway, Negro is my current fishing partner. We made plans to go fishing last night when the conflict arose. After an earthquaking explosion, I had to step outside and cool down my temper on the porch, when a messenger of Negro's came by answering my prayers for rain or an excuse not to go out fishing. Negro's woman caught him fooling around with another woman and threw his ass out of the house. She went out of line. He had to beat her then, and I didn't care what else so long as we didn't have to go out fishing. Buy me some time around the ultimatum. Cool things down with Magda the she-devil a bit. So now, Negro himself comes by. "Hey paddy, I need a place to stay and, how many rooms does this house have? I figured since it was so big that maybe I could. . . ". Sorry Negro. My woman doesn't even want me in the same dory as you. She would rather blow up this house than let you stay in it. I don't know why she hates Negro so much.

Magdalene comes home. "Your *amor* Negro was looking for you," she sneers. I haven't responded to her. She doesn't know what he wanted.

The community of Haulover is drying shrimps right now. Everyone. They harvest the little sea-bob shrimps like beans. They set them out on sheets of black plastic, drying them in the sun, covering every open space of cleared land throughout the community. The fishermen come in every afternoon with their *pangas* or moto-dories full to the point of sinking with small sea-bob shrimps. All you need is a trawling net and a motor, and then you rake the coastline for the thick and seemingly endless sea-bob. It is disgusting if you aren't accustomed to it. The whole place is rank with shrimps from top to bottom. Our house has been full of shrimps for the past week. As for me, I don't know what the hell I'm doing here in Haulover.

I don't know what I'm going to do. Since the fever, I've spent most of my time reading or staring out at the big muddy river, bay flowing down to the sea, spending my money and telling myself that I'm going to make life somehow. There seems to be no opportunity here. I wish that my friend Chico was still living. We could sing and drink rum. He could show me how to work with wood. I could make guitars from rosewood. Chico is dead. He died a week after I picked up my guitar and backpack from his little shanty. I heard the news on the radio in Little Corn Island. I felt to cry. I picked up my things in the knick of time. After the burial, his family took all of his possessions from the house and carried them over to the beach and set them a fire. It was a good thing I picked up my things when I did. These writings would not exist. It is a pity.

Instead, I will dedicate myself to the only art that I pretend to know. I will write. I will write unrelentlessly and unhesitatingly. Unapologetically and unrefined, I will create something of strength and glory. What I will have in Haulover is a beautiful house that will not fall down right now. I will have a space of my own in which no one can tell me shit so long I can put a little food on the table. Plenty of food on the table.

The marijuana is tickling me, and I cannot help but smiling. The sun is so hot above my head it is drunkening. My handwriting is getting slurry. I am within the moment. Right now!

Sitting on the porch, watching the river to see if the boat is gonna pass by. Maybe Miss Orel is coming back with Aisha, Magdalene's eldest daughter. Rayon, Magda's youngest son, asked me to watch for him. Miss Orel is the children's great grandmother who recently left

Haulover because it was killing her. She left Mr. Wonki alone, and she went to stay with her daughter in Kukra Hill. Wonki sent Aisha there because he can't visit her since he hates Orel's daughter so much. She thieved him five hundred and fifty dollars in a bad business deal some years ago. Everyone does bad deals down here. Everybody is thiefin' and lyin'. Wonki gave us the land to build the house on. He assured us that there weren't any problems, but now some other guy, Cecil, says that his grandfather chopped the land clean some years ago, and now he wants us to buy it. I fly through money here.

Gene is the father of Magda's children. Three out of four at least. He is Orel and Wonki's grandson whom they raised as a son. Gene is a rock man now. He makes life hard on everyone, thiefin' all of the shit from their house and selling it out. Getting crazy and beating up people, cussing up Orel and Wonki. He is a problem. He even stole a little radio and fifty dollars from me when we first came to Haulover and were staying in Wonki's house. He cannot mind himself, much less any of the four children he brought into this world. I now hold that responsibility. I am a stepfather. I always hated the thought of stepfathers.

Magdalene doesn't like me talking to drugs men. She hates it. She gets very upset when I mix up with them. I cannot say no to people with food or ganja. The vast majority of men my age here are hopelessly addicted to crack and rum. It makes it difficult to have friends.

The heat is sweltering. Plenty sun hot today. Going to sit in the back with the breeze. Maybe I'll catch myself.

Slowly pissing away my life and my money here in Haulover. A good woman is hard to find. I've bet on love over and over again, and over and over again after losing, I tell myself to live and learn. I pass most of my time here at the *edificio* that I'm slowly constructing. I have no other escape from Magdalene's wrath. She drives me from the house we're currently renting with wicked looks and an evil tone of voice. That means go work.

The construction zone is more peaceful. We are putting up the second story. Renaldcito is sticking the bricks while I mix the cement and pass bricks. The house is getting higher and higher. I fear that Magdalene will try to boss me from this house when it is finished.

She cannot. I've spent too much time, effort and money to let her run me from here. The house is mine. She can live with her family down below, but the upstairs will be for me. From up here, you can catch a sweet breeze and elevated perspective. I need to finish this house so I can travel and leave Magda to mind herself if she wants to continue treating me with complete disrespect. She is a hard teacher who makes me sad for ever coming to this Haulover. I tell myself that life will continue, but I don't really believe me.

It has become more and more apparent that all Magda cares about is getting her house. I was happier penniless, worriless, womanless and homeless. Someday soon I will return there, although I fear that I will not be quite so happy and free as I once was, only lonely, dirty and hungry. I feel that I have no fight left in me. I feel, I feel, I feel, who cares how I feel? Do you? You care how you feel. Perhaps my thoughts and words can relate to your feelings and that would touch you, but probably this has turned into nothing more than incoherent ramblings again.

What was the story? That happened to the plot? Our hero got stuck in Nicaragua. The gringo trail has led in and out of alleyways and cheap hotels from Buenos Aires to Bluefields, trying to save a buck and make a few more miles, but has it finished? In Coroico, Bolivia I played the *charrango* with the saddest Frenchman I'd ever met. The road between Coroico and La Paz was littered with crosses and stars of David where busses of Christians and Jews slid off the mountain pass and into the clouds. That was the decent into the jungle. The *bajada* into the tropics and out of the Andes mountains, the *Altiplano* region where enraged underpaid miners stones buses at roadblocks because they've lost their voices and no one is listening to them. The trail is full of hard-times. Nicaragua is the poorest of all Latin American countries, and it seems I've dedicated myself to here. People are hungry. They'll do anything to eat. They are interested in only survival. Thieving means nothing.

Looking back on my life in the States, I now realize that I spent most of my time driving around in a car with the windows up, sucking down freon and burning gasoline; listening to some overplayed songs over the radio and existing oblivious to the outside.

I awaken suddenly in the middle of the night with the lucky feeling that I've narrowly escaped death again; the nightmare overtaking its victim. Who knows the voodoo that you do. The obeah is strong. Handwork. Bull piss. Panty water. Lord.

"Too much smoke in your lungs," Magdalene tells me. She can see the future. She has feelings. She can light a moment and make me believe in the madness of a sadness that we love to hold.

It was there on the sour, four-night-old *hospedaje* sheet with Magdalene that I realized I did not want to return to Managua. A hot and dry city of hustle and bustle, *pandilleros* trying to kill you or take your money. There is no winning amongst the savages and taxi cab drivers. It is contaminated from head to toe. It smells of *chicharon*, cheese, *carne de vaca* and unregulated car exhaust. Pork meat and immigration officers who only say no and give problems. Ann finally got off the island too and is opening a beautiful hostal on the *Laguna de Apoyo*. Her hotel in the hills is a heavenly refuge from the city's hellishness. The lake is pristine and deep. Small *mojara* fish ripple in the still volcanic waters soon in the morning. We are making plans to leave, but haven't realized them yet.

I've been out of words for weeks. It is raining. It has not let up for days. Everything is wet here on Buttonwood Caye. My underwear and t-shirt are hanging over the fireside trying to dry, but the fight is futile. Everyone else here is building lobster pots for big Winnie the captain. They don't really need my help at all. Where they need help is in the kitchen, and I've got the pot on the fire. I don't know what I'm doing here. Washing dishes and black pots and chopping up wood for the fire. I left Haulover four days ago, trying to hustle a little money on the ocean, hauling fish pots for my neighbor Mr. Winnie. When we reached here, I found that Winnie already had enough sailors so I just sit here watching. They gave me one day on the sea, but that was a few days ago and we didn't catch much.

All day I have been trying to gather the courage to go bathe. The North wind is blowing hard and cold. I have no towel or dry clothes to put on. Another lobster and fish rondon is on the fire. I tell myself to go bathe before we eat, but I'm still sitting in my bunk, trying not to look awkward. Who knows when we will go back in? It will be a few more days. Better I stayed on the land and built windows and doors for the house. That's all that's left before we can move in. Windows, doors, the toilet and septic tank. The rest is all vanity.

The zinc leaks above my bed. Water does not pour through, but a cold spray periodically wakes me up throughout the night.

Weather comes in hard on the cayes. This caye is called Buttonwood Caye. It is a small little button with a few dozen coconut trees and two small fishing camps. There is nothing else. You could throw a rock from one side to the next. The wind comes in hard off the open sea and runs through you.

The people here smoke cigarettes all day. I just watch with silent eyes. I rarely speak. Silence is an ocean, infinite says Rumi.

All day I think about Magdalene and getting home. All of the things I could be doing there rather than sitting here on my bunk. "Experience," I tell myself.

The camp here leaks like a xylophone and I have no dry pants to put on. I prance around like a prince in my underwear, day dreaming of places far away from here, where the people would be dreaming about being on a little coconut island in the middle of the Caribbean. Nowhere for go. Nothing for do.

Days later, still here on the bunk, waiting for a ride off of this little caye, the rain has finally stopped. Our bed sheets and clothes are hung outside in the sunshine, evaporating. Winnie, the boss-man, has gone to sea, leaving me alone here at the camp. There is nothing to cook and nothing to do but praise God for its infinacy and listen to the gentle roar of the waves breaking over the coral reef. Why I am here, I don't know. I am learning to be a fisherman. Patience is a prison.

The torrential downpour has left the near-by mainland village of Set Net Point flooded beneath a few feet of water, the radio told us yesterday. All of the well water, toilet holes and trash pits have become one big contaminated lagoon. It is a disaster area with no clean water to drink or wash with. All houses built on too low a' stilts are under water. There is nowhere to walk except in shitty water. It is infection waiting to happen.

A *panga* from Pearl Lagoon was to arrive this morning with Clorox, medicine and some rations to try and help out the situation, but with the passing of the hurricane a few weeks ago, relief funds are low. Set Net Point was the last land we saw before heading to sea. We picked up rations and ate middle-day there. I hope we don't go back there right now.

In all these years of living, have we learned anything? Have we figured anything out or are we just deteriorating from our original fall from the womb. Was that the garden they speak of?

Magdalene's upset that I nearly ate all the row in the pot. I walked all night through the sea. The north wind and the pouring rain. Caught fish and ripped the eggs out of their womb; sailed home and brought the balance to you. You gave it to your children. The fish row is a symbol of fertility. According to some, it can give you babies if you otherwise cannot make them. Men and women love it.

I remember that in my childhood, I was a collectionist. I collected all types of things that valued: coins, hats, pins, baseball cards, knives, rocks. Now all I want to collect is words.

Yesterday, Ralston, Mr. Renald's son, chopped a man's arm in Manhattan. Manhattan is a farming community in the highlands behind Haulover where many Haulover men work. The man was Mr. Lester who was giving Ralston lodging at his camp in the bush where they farm. He is his uncle. They were planting beans. They say that Ralston nearly chopped his arm clean off. No one understands why. You know back in the bush they keep their machetes sharp and shiny.

Ralston likes to chop. I don't know how many people he's chopped up, but several. He doesn't say anything, just walks up and ching-chang, done. He hasn't killed anyone yet, but plenty people have come close.

Magdalene says that she thinks he has some kind of brains problem. You can see it in his crazy rolly eyes. It is worse when he is drinking rum or smoking rock. He might chop you just for looking on him. When he's in town, keep one eye on him. The community of

Haulover is happy when he stays on the farm because as rock-men go, he's one of the worst. They say when he not drinking rum he's one of the best people. He works hard in the bush and will help anyone with anything. When he's drinking, you'd better keep your door locked.

They backed one-armed Mr. Lester the three-hour walk out of the bush yesterday in a chair. He arrived low on blood, so his son gave him some of his own. It doesn't look like he's going to die, but he will be crippled for life.

They say that Ralston now has the gun that Mr. Lester used to keep at the farm there. It is a gun that Roy, Ralston's half brother and owner of the camp, gave to Mr. Lester to mind the farm, but Ralston took it from him after chopping him up.

Now the question is, who will go back there and take the gun away from the waiting Ralston. The police are ignoring the situation as they say that Mr. Lester has no proof. The truth is that they are tired of Ralston and keeping him in jail. They say that no jail can hold him anyway. He has already escaped from jail more times than Billy the Kidd. He even escaped from Bluefields jail once, walking through the swamps for a week before finally busting up behind Kukra Hill and making it back here to Haulover. There is no law around here anyway. The police are only concerned with drug business. The rest is every man for himself.

Mr. Renalds himself is tired of dealing with Ralston. They've pretty much exiled him to the bush of Manhattan, but even there he is making problems. They say this time Mr. Renalds ordered his eldest son Roy, to go back there and kill his brother. It might not be so easy now that Ralston has his gun. In Kukra Hill a few years ago one man killed his own son because he went on so bad. The boy was a rock-man and a bad thief and the father finally got tired of him. What can a father do when his creation becomes a threat to the community?

We eat fish for breakfast. We eat fish for lunch. Fried in the morning and steamed in the after before noon. Fish rondon, fish for fun, fish for food and fish for you.

I fish for my love in the night. When the moon is above for the light. Making life as it takes and taking it home when she wakes.

But here I stand alone. Full belly, full pot and home. Nothing to do but wonder if this fish got away.

And then there are days like today, when all the pretty girls are gone, and all I feel to do is give up. I never made it to Bluefields this morning. The boat left early. I reached late. Magdalene went. She ran off and left me here alone, turned me into stone, without the heart to do a thing. Locked up and unable to work. I should have gone to Bluefields, but something told me to stop when I was waiting for the *panga* to speed down there. Should I stay or should I go? The question of my life. Can I withstand the temptation calling me to go drink rum? Can I distract my spirit for long enough to avoid the confrontation, or will I give in? I've got food to cook. Cassava, fried fish, carrots and cucumbers, but Magdalene won't be back until tomorrow afternoon.

It is the following afternoon. Magdalene did not come back with the boat. It looks like she decided to spend a few days more in Bluefields, doing what, I can only imagine. Bredah, her first-born son, came and told me that she sent a few sheets of zinc for me to back up to the house. I guess she wants to roof over her washstand. Her pilah. That is good. She'll be using it plenty since I'm not planning on buying a sink. Better I hit the road before I go too far in the hole; see what else there is to see in this world; return to the pretty things I've seen before, or maybe just keep on moving. *Adelante siempre.* The past is always a failure to return to. It has always disappeared.

I am considering going into the gasoline business. It is the ugliest drug in the world. I will do my part in the killing of millions of innocent and ignorant helpless human beings everywhere. The planet is doomed. Every living thing has its death ahead of it somewhere.

The marijuana has given me a scared feeling of the outside world. It is a claustrophobically secure feeling of insidedness. It is like holding on tight to the arm of your chair so you cannot be blown away in the spinning hurricane outside. The arm feels sweet. Sucking you out of the hole in the wall, feet flying parallel to the ground, the earth is coming to an end, and I am buying a part of it. I will then sell it back to you. You will thank me for the service. Cheap gas.

Like all good drugs, the more you buy, the further and faster you can travel. Why walk when you can drive. Why sail when you can hit it. Don't wait around for a bus when you can fly.

Behind every fire is a fool and this gasoline burning fool is filling the earth up with smoke like the smoker filling his lungs. Cancer to the planet. Death to the cynic.

Wars, plastics, pollution and accidents are all caused through a spirit filled liquid more poisonous than *guaro*. We all do it. We can't get away from it.

I traveled all the way around the world, from North to South and East to West, trying to escape from it, the modernization of everything, and come to settle in a little Creole Indian community on the Western Caribbean coast, yet it follows me still. I travel, but travel by gasoline. How far might I have come on foot.

Gasoline and cocaine. They've brought me where I am today. I'm not proud, but well, you do what you gotta do, and sometimes there's no getting around the steps God has set for you. Am I ashamed?

"The result of drugs is death," a sign painted on a wall in Pearl Lagoon said this morning. The result of life is death.

When rhyming becomes the problem, give it up and go fetch a pale of water. Down the old dirt road, through a shallow running creek, in the right hand fence, there is a gate that leads to the well beneath the palm roots. The water there is fresh to drink. It tastes like rain.

It is on the way to Big Creek, back in the bush where all the young gals go to wash and bathe. The water is clean and the sand is white and oily. It is a fine place to pass an afternoon if your woman is making you feel like not being around.

"Bread and jelly is the nicest thing in the world. I would eat it night and day," say the children.

Awe to the creator is the gateway.

"They killed me harse this marnin," Gilley said this morning as we dragged the dead horse out of the stagnant bloody ditch it staggered into with its last breath and dropped. It was right in front of our house. It was a bitch to haul her out of that. It took about fifteen of us to drag the horse down the sidewalk into the savannah about two hundred yards in the bush behind the last houses and leave her at her final resting place.

It didn't take long for the vultures to arrive. By middle day, there were flocks of them circling the dead meat buffet.

That is the type of thing they do to you here if they don't like you. It's better than killing you I guess, but what did the poor horse do? Magda says that it's through Gilley's wife Millie. "She got a tongue of fire. It puts her in problem. Likes to talk! Huh".

They killed the horse with a peg. That is a sharpened piece of iron rod with a little catch on the end of it so it will rip out the meat when you haul it back out. There is some speculation about who the murderer was, but it is pretty much agreed that it was another one of the neighbors. They must have stabbed the innocent horse before day.

Millie and Gilley are our neighbors, right across the sidewalk. I don't know how many children they have. Plenty. They keep an immaculately clean yard. You will rarely find a fallen leaf in it, much less a plastic or piece of *basura*. As a leaf falls from the cashew trees, Millie is there with the rake. Magdalene is envious of their yard. She tells me that if I keep chipping ours down, every time the weeds start to grow up, ours will come clean and pretty like theirs. My hands are blistered from chopping down the bush that was our yard. Now from the balcony above, you see the dark mud through the patches of grass. It is a beautiful thing. I would like to see the whole of everything chopped right down to the bare roots. Clean and new.

We have a few trees that we've planted around the yard, but I fear that the horses and cows that are constantly grazing and shitting around the community will eat them down.

We are getting into dry weather time after several months of rain. The people are harvesting young corn, which little girls carry around the town peddling for one *cordova* an ear. Every season and time has its fruit to enjoy. Before the corn came in style, it was apples and oranges, which you could find in abundance. Now the apples are done and the oranges will soon be too, but mangos, avocados or something else will reach. Star apples are another nicety that is ripe now. The perfumy rose apples are green and flowering on the trees.

It is Saturday, and for most of Haulover, Saturday is the day of rest. Many of the families here are Adventist people and remember to keep the Sabbath. I am not, so I'll try to do a little work since I do not feel so tired to rest. I have some lumber to pick up in Pearl Lagoon at the planer mill. I'm going to borrow a canoe and paddle up to Pearl Lagoon. Since the breeze is coming from the North, I can sail back down with my load. Maybe Magda will accompany me and help paddle. She is a good helper with anything she wants to do. If she doesn't want to do it, forget about it because she will be worthless.

I've been induced into smoking marijuana until I am dim enough to take this despair without shivering from hypersensitivity. This Magdalene issue has become a problem. If I knew where to go, I would leave. A walk to Pearl Lagoon is not far enough. I must walk to Kukra Hill, continue to La Fonseca and keep going on to Rama, the gateway to the world; the world's gateway to the Atlantic Autonomous Region of Nicaragua; the land of the highway. I live beyond the end of the road. If there was a boat headed for up, I would head for Sandy Bay and Karawala, the Indian communities of the North. The people there treat you good.

I could head East out to Little Island, but no boat until Wednesday. If I leave here before day, I could reach Kukra Hill before the sun gets hot. Who knows what to do? Get more marijuana. Get started killing myself before the pain intensifies. If I only wasn't so damn tight.

If I'd only give to Magdalene all that she wants in a timely fashion, perhaps she'd treat me better. Perhaps not. Maybe she'd treat me worse. What she wants is perfection and I am in no means a perfect man. I am not pure. Perhaps Magda is. I am stained and wanting. I am tired of all this.

No matter what you think about communism or leftist revolutionary parties or Daniel Ortega and the Sandinistas, what the revolution accomplished in Nicaragua was a good thing. Many innocent people died and were misled as a result of the direction it took, but at its heart it was a pure and positive. It rid the country and the world of a fascist tyrannical dictator named Somoza. Somoza murdered and plundered the country's people and resources for generations, making himself, his family, friends and a few other gringo supporters rich at the cost of the poor peasants. Anyway you look at it, he was a bad man. The Sandinista revolution ended that. They set up free elections and tried very hard to do some good things. This is true.

What has happened since the revolution, the contra scandal and the decade following is a bit sketchy.

It was the night before Christmas and all through the house, people were having sex. In the bathroom with the lights cut off, a couple lived together on the floor while Miss Beverly, Magdalene's mother, peeped on them, got vexed and threw them out of her house and bar. Miss Beverly is a Christian woman. She does not believe in love. She says it has never existed. She is fallen.

She sells beer and rum on Saturdays and Sundays. Holidays don't matter either. We're open for Christmas.

I'm going up to Ann's in the volcano. Beverly should be back tomorrow.

Around Managua, people are leaving and talking about war. Nobody wants war again except for Daniel. Everyone wants peace, but the thugs want to make us fight for it.

Reporters are getting shot. Radio stations are being shot up. The truth is being hidden at all costs.

Busses are burning. Fireballs are stoning. Little jacks welded from nails are flattening tires at busy intersections. The media is silent.

All Daniel has said is that they'll recount the election votes. Ha! He didn't say anything about all of the liberal ballot boxes dumped in the gullies in Leon and Managua.

He didn't say anything about the *pandilleros* that he bussed in from Chinandega, Matagalpa and El Salvador, the hoods and gangsters terrorizing everyone.

The whole thing didn't calm down until some Salvadoranian gangsters started killing up the Nicaraguan ones.

Daniel didn't say anything for about two weeks. Then it was only Gringo's get out and down with capitalism. *Ranchero ranchero. Ratero ratero.* Take it as it comes.

Corruption has reached to heights that the people all know about it, but feel they have neither the energy nor power to do anything about it.

This life full of sin and boredom is killing me one-way or the other. Get it together or get on the road, but don't just sit there and write. There's nothing to say that hasn't been said, but maybe it was in something you never read, so I'll give it my best to say what I know before I'm laid to rest.

Drink your water before you eat, not after. Eat your fruits alone. Eat your fish alone. Eat your breadkind alone. Eat everything with vegetables because they make everything better. Sing music. The road of excess leads to the palace of wisdom. The palace is at the end of that road. If you are sick, fast. If your head hurts, drink water. Take deep breaths all the time. There are angels in the air and in the water. Don't use cocaine. Don't eat pork meat. Behind every fire there is a fool. Behind every night there is a day.

"This whole life is a preparation for death". Plenty people said that.

When someone asks what you did, what are you going to say?

Did you create? Did you plant fruitful seeds or did they cut you from your roots when they realized that you were no good; when they saw that your house was falling in around you; that your world is caving in.

Today a *panga* left for Corn Island, carrying family and friends to see Oriseli before she dies. It is agreed upon that she's soon dead. She has AIDS.

Oriseli was a friend of Magdalene's and mine when we were there on Little Island. She was Fonso's woman. She started getting sick when we were all there and she said she was going to Bluefields to take some bush medicine. Later she told us that none of the bush medicine was helping.

Everything was a little funny. She called Ann begging some money, even though she'd just gotten off of Little Island with two kilos in the rush. We'd heard that she had SIDA, but people say all kinds of things.

Oriseli had a Honduran fisherman few years ago in Corn Island. It was he who gave her death.

He was a black, rusty man; a fisherman who came to port in Corn Island every forty five days or so after fishing Nicaraguan waters for lobster. Like all of the Honduranian big boat lobstermen, he'd come to port with loads of money in his pockets and like so many of the girls who swarmed the docks of Corn Island whenever a Honduranian boat came in, Oriseli needed help. She needed a man.

She had two kids with no fatherly support to keep food on the table, and whenever the *Hondureno* came, he brought good help. He took care of her she said. He sent money and always came with plenty of fish and small lobster. He treated her good and even though he had his woman back home, Oriseli was a good woman to him for a few good years.

One time he went out to sea and did not come back in again. This was the last time Oriseli heard from him. She once again had to start looking for herself.

About the same time, Alfonso finished the house he was building with some cokes money that fell a few years back. He needed a woman to cook, clean and who knows what else. Fonso and his wife Erlinda had finally left after several brutal arguments and fights over other women, next men and me no know what else. The relationship seemed irreconcilable. He had some Pana woman back in Rama, but Rama's a long way from Little Island, so he took Oriseli into his house.

This is when I met Oriseli, Fonso's new woman. We used to all hang out around Fonso's or down at the beach by Bamboo or by Fireman's, smoking joints that she always sold overpriced. I'd play music sometimes and everyone would laugh and feel good. It was before Fonso's woman came from Rama and I suppose before Oriseli had any idea about the SIDA, but maybe not. Maybe she knew all along, but didn't tell anyone. There's a belief here that when you have SIDA, the more you spread it, the more strength you gain and longer you last. Some people love to spread it, seasoning up as many people as they can with it before they take bed. This is what Oriseli did after she left the island and came to the mainland.

Around this time, Oriseli's mother received a phone call from a woman in Honduras inquiring about Oriseli's health. "How is your daughter feeling?" the woman asked. The woman was the fisherman's mother who found the phone number amongst her son's personal things. "She's doing fine," Oriseli's mother responded, "Why?"

"Because my son is already dead," the woman said. She told Oriseli's mother to go get her daughter tested for AIDS, so together they went to the health center to make the check. They took the test two times, and two times it came out positive.

Oriseli cried and cried, pleading with her mother not to tell anyone, but her mother could only hold the secret so long before telling her other daughter, Oriseli's sister. This is how the word got out here in Haulover, where the sister lives.

She told a bunch of people in Haulover that she had me when we were in Little Island, but this is a lie. She tried to seduce me into taking her home one night at a party behind the dive shop, but I refused out of the strange awkwardness of the situation. I thank God that by this time I had stopped drinking rum. Many other nights have ended with me taking less beautiful girls to bed or the beach. The morning I first met Oriseli, I knew that Fonso had not been so fortunate. From the half ashamed look that hung over the two of them as they stepped out into the ten o'clock sun in last night's disco-ranch clothes, I could tell that things had gotten hot with rum and cocaine, sojka music and you know what else.

They were stepping out, looking for a panga to send Oriseli back to Corn Island to bring some clothes and things to stay there by Fonso. This was the beginning.

I had just reached back to Little Island after being on the Caye for about three months. When I left, Fonso had just started building the house, and now it was finished, with a big kitchen and hall set up to run a little business or food shop or something. It was deh.

Fonso is probably one of the most sought after men in the area. He has two houses, one right in the center of Little Island and one in the back. He has a skiff and an engine. He is young and set up. He is my friend and I pray that he is alright.

Two days a-back, Oso came by to trust a gallon of gasoline to go down the lagoon and cut some paptaw sticks. He said that he done had the contact to buy the lobster pot strips and he just had to deliver them and come pay me. "Alright," I said and dispatched him the gasoline. Yesterday he went into the bush to cut the sticks.

He never went far before he came across the bodies of three dead *Peruanos* who were traveling their way up to the states. It looks like someone carried them across from the beach and shot them in the swamp, hoping to take their traveling money.

Peru is a country in turmoil. *Peruanos* pass through here like cocaine, trying to escape revolution and hard-times facing them in the South American highlands. First they go through Colombia. From Cartagena, they fly to San Andres where everything is still legal. Then they take the back door into Nicaragua. From there on out they are contraband. This is people smuggling.

In San Andres, they wait until they collect a large enough group of like-minded travelers and charter a boat to Little Island. Maybe someone will send a few kilos of coke to deliver to a contact on the Island, but for the most part, the *Peruanos* travel clean. They are not drug runners or rich. They are running themselves, trying to find something better. When they reach Little Island, the struggle begins. They are refugees. They are illegal, *sin documentos*, and the people like to do them up because they can. They are frequently robbed and harassed because they are ignorant of the run of things here.

For reasons that I do not understand, Nicaragua, and apparently the rest of Central America, does not accept Peruvian refugees. As with all contraband business, their movement gets dangerous. Since there is no law to protect them, the *Peruanos* can trust no one.

In Little Island, I remember many times people hijacking the poor travelers, taking their money, clothes and belongings and leaving them to hide out in the bush, without food or shelter and afraid of the police who are sent out to capture them and send them to jail on top of it all. They need to get off the island and onto the highway headed for Managua. They need to reach Rama.

To get to Rama, they need to get to the mainland and this means passing through the lawless Haulover. There are all kinds of contacts between the Islands and Haulover. Everyone knows one another. Someone in Little Island calls someone in Haulover and tells them to meet the skiff coming with the *Peruanos* at such and such time. They pick up the *Peruanos* on the wilderness beach and then cross them across the lagoon and put them on the road. The people who are involved in the movement get paid well, but sometimes, this is not enough. Sometimes they want everything. This is when people die and things go bad.

Oso's not talking to the police. They have him in custody, but he's denying everything. The police are everywhere, walking the bush and swamps, but they don't know here. They'll never find anything.

I am not telling a story. I am a story. The words of this book are the unignorable resonations of the chimes inside my head. They disappear when listened to. They go outside and let me stand in the middle of them all. This is meditation.

Outside, there is a world going on, around and around with all kinds of movements and vibrations, hustlers for food and less valuable commodities, such as *dinero*, the symbolic representation of wealth. These trifles have come to concern me in the very least. My health concerns me.

I have visions of distant lands where my feet have carried my years. Old friends and lovers; old wines and songs played on old guitars seem to call me out of the open doors of this unfinishable house that I have endeavored to create. I am not a builder but I am trying. I need help.

I used to be a *viajero. Vagando* over the high and low left behind lands of the Americas. Has my adventure finished? Life has become quiet in Haulover. This is the frontier of Nicaragua, where the world will soon meet the untamed *Caribe*. We are warriors. We are Indians and Garifunas. Here there are no roads and even less law. They say the *caretera* will soon reach, connecting us with the *Pan-americana*. It is inevitable. It will be passing right in front of my back door. The highway. The road that I ran off of so long ago. It has caught up with me again.

My lungs have grown clean of her carbon monoxide moanings as my brain has cleared from her eighteen wheeled roarings, but I feel that I will soon take her back. The highway has been the death of every love of my life. Could my only true love be this incessant rambling road?

No. I will soon escape through the front. I will take to the sea and bring my Magda with me. We will follow each other as far as we can run or until we reach Texas again. If they will not let us in, we will break through her iron curtains and claim the land of the free for ourselves. The Autonomous Atlantic Coast is the land of the free. Free to do as you please. Free for the farmers and fishermen to live. Free to sit on your ass all day long if you want, or free to walk down the bush road to bathe in the creek in the free savannah.

Who ever dreamed of free money? Here it floats in the sea and washes up on the beach. It is quicker and fairer than the lottery. It is cocaine and it's all thanks to the thousands upon thousands of drug users in the helpless cities of North America. "Bring more," I say. Let them die out a little quicker. "Down with the *Estados Unidos*," say the *guerilleros*. Have some more poison. Each grave is one less problem for humanity. The damned are damned and the dead are dead. Let it be free, all of life. Give us your water, for it was given to you. Plant trees instead of weapon factories. Plant trees of life along the roads and fields you've been using for waste and cattle production. Give fruit to the people instead of guns. Use tax money to plant and fill up the country with fruits for all seasons. Sustain life.

The past several days have been filled with sick weakness. Fevers and cold trembling beneath thick covers followed by sweat sessions beneath the same wet sheets. Energy is low. I pass the days in the hammock catching breezes and reading Ernest Hemingway, Ruben Dario and Antoine de Expury's *El Principito*; trying to recover from the fevers that we blame again on malaria. The fever has not returned for a few days now, but I still feel uneasy. I consider making a fast after I finish these malaria pills. The sleepless nights are filled with recollections of better times in past lives, university friends, beer drinking taverns and winter days inside eating fraternity house greasy food and watching movies with the blinds closed tight. Nicaragua is far from there.

I'm still confused about this situation with Magdalene. My love grows stronger and more rooted each day. If not for her, I would be dead by now. If not for her, I wouldn't be in this sickly situation either, but that is irrelevant. I don't want to leave her alone. She doesn't want to stay here alone, but it seems impossible to get any kind of paperwork straightened out. Bush has closed down the walls so tight that nothing comes in or out. I hope he suffocates to death underneath his homeland security blanket.

The music is playing too loud to write. The music is simple here. Reggae, ranchero, gospel or country is constantly coming at you from one side or the other.

And again that wavy feeling rolls through my soul and the true morning is unfolded. The incandescent silver streak, shining purple and *rosadito* comes stripping through the black page of consciousness, like a crack between a double door. What lies behind the *puerta negra* is pure energy waiting to be unbound. The black room is full of light begging to be released into the darkness outside where the pressure is less dense. This is the law. I'm going to sharpen my machete; make myself useful.

The fasting has been long and tiresome. Today was the sixth day of life with lone water. Tomorrow is the *ultimo*. The *septimo*. God is creating light. One day at a time is the only way to get through this. I know now that I will make it.

The hours of meditation has been filled with abrupt roaring silences reminding one of the absurdities of the ego. The I. I am a warrior. I am this, I am that. I am nothing! I am only a heart beating along with the rest of this eternal motion. I am two eyes observing this thing we call life.

Breath is important. Breezes are holy and purification is forgiveness.

I am a flute, empty as can be. Letting the wind of life make its melody, holding on to nothing is being truly free. I am a river. There is no me.

"Beyond the mountains, there is peace. . . . We will all soon be at rest". Goethe said that.

Fasting is a restructuring of the framework of the soul. It bursts the frames and splinters like an old wineskin filled with new wine, or something like that.

Marlon has just convinced me to open a gas station with him. He will be the one running it. I will be the one putting up the budget. I don't know if it will prosper, but in life one has to take chances. Marlon helped me get to where I am. He helped me reach San Andres. Maybe I would have reached without him, but not that night and not on that boat. So what is money? It is a game. It is not life. Food is life. God is life. Money is for play with when you've got it. It is to fight for when you don't. Fight for it or fast. Think, wait and fast. With those three, you can accomplish anything. You can cure sickness; move any mountain or manifest your dreams or destiny just by learning to listen and go with the currents that God passes through us. Try telling that to a starving African child dying of the AIDS that his mothers gave to him; or an Iraqi man who was bombed and had his leg blown off walking down the street trying to buy a loaf of bread. Life is not fair. Life is not just. God is good and grace for the lucky few. For the rest, he is unapparent. No worry, God will take care . . . of some of us. The rest will perish. It is all the same and all for the better. There is a world of suffering. Perhaps it will be better next time around, or perhaps the screen goes blank. The dead cannot write.

Write, write, and write. The words will come. Just begin, and something will finish. In Haulover, the time of the gill-net fish has stopped. Now they are picking with line. It is dry weather and the time for working in the bush. It is the time when beans are free and corn is plentiful. Life is full of seasons. Seasons for everything. Ebo, star apple, rose apple, and oranges are done but mangos soon begin. Fish are out, but beans are there. Take life as it comes to you and your belly will always be full, even if it is only with air.

How else can you know a man but by the color of his smile, the cracking of his wicked teeth, the smell of his foul breath? Words are nothing. Eyes are full of betrayal. They are the weakest of all your senses. Rely on your nose to know true beauty. Feel your way through the labyrinth that time places ahead of you. It's not what you touch, it is what you feel. The echoes of the mind are full of wisdom. Take today and understand the incomprehension of the moment. Feel which way the wind is blowing. See where the moon is and know how she is shaped. Think about how she will be tomorrow. The tides are omniscient. Why are we so far detached? Turn off the lights and disconnect yourself from man's confusing imitation. Your hours are all wrong. Your timing is off. Who ever heard of an alarm clock anyway? Wake when it is time to wake. Sleep when it is time to sleep. Eat when it is time to eat. Fast when it is time to fast. Slow down and wait on yourself, there is no use in being ahead. Let your footsteps catch up, and you will find what you were looking for. Nothing or love? Love or nothing. If that doesn't work out, keep on moving.

The floor has been sandy for so long, that you don't even notice it under your feet until you sweep it out. "How nice and clean," your feet say on the new smoothness of old floor.

Now take the mop and soapy water to see where the true beauty and freshness of the tile is. So are we.

Maintain yourself in the face of daylight and you will find shelter beneath the rays of the soul. "Dignity," say the beats of the street. Unconscious dignity. The kind that comes playing it straight and noting else. How do you get out of this? How do you get into your dreams?

When the moon is bright enough for writing, the words just come. Get out of your bed and accept them. Capture them. Be a cane flute for God. Be a guitar. Be a song. Music is everywhere and rhythm is everything. The pulsating tidings of the night are trembling with tremolos of the toads and crickets, the breath that rattles inside of my brain; floating clouds of hieroglyphic metaphor meteorites, buzzing with electricity and whispering the secrets of the universe. Shock waves of neon and incandescent purple illuminating the half eyes, hovering over the dim and variable reality rest in front and down below. Heaven is first a state of being before *llegando a la despues*. It is a pleasant place of the present life where all becomes nothing and nothing shatters through the midnight and the dawns of the morning. Who is writing?

So in comes crazy Borhey, Ralston's brother, drunk as a monkey and snorting like a hog, begging me to let him clean my fish. I passed him the knife and gave him five cordovas for half scraping them. He said he would chop off his finger for a pint of rum. I said that he'd have to beg Magdalene the machete. Magda said no, and he started making a scene in the house, kept on molesting and frightening the visitors and everything, begging until everyone was sick of it. Finally I told him that if he killed himself, I'd buy him two pints. He jumped right off the verandah one time, and it was done.

But I like to smoke. It puts words in the brain to write down so you can find them again later. A photo, a frozen mirror, pealed like a plum you're left alone to let the world see the flesh inside of you.

The way to do it is first to make the door. Then make the frame, and then straight edge the house.

I want more light. The darkness is *demasiado*. This book is getting boring. It needs more action. More excitement. Tomorrow morning, soon before the day, I'm going to the beach with Marlon. We're going to paddle over before anyone else has a chance to reach and walk the beach. They say cocaine is drifting. Maybe we'll find the sack. Maybe we'll just find some coconuts.

The most beautiful gift that anyone has ever given me was a blank book. I gave it away when it was full to someone who just threw it away. I cannot forget it.

Don't be a shell.

"Every challenge is a gift and every gift an opportunity," Clint wrote down.

Magdalene likes to fight. She says she will never stop until death. She says she will never stop loving me until then either. They tell me I need to beat her as she plunges a conch shell into back. She likes to rip off my shirts. I have to go back to Bluefields and buy another. She fights me with hatred and loves me with hunger. She is beautifully hideous.

My only goal now is to finish this book one way or another, with words whatever they may be. It must be complete.

The wind and rain were her skin and hurricane her soul. It was dry weather. Nothing anyone could do about it. It was the time to be digging wells. The time to be on the shrimps day and night, paddling about in a dory, fighting the East breeze. Catching mullet in the hand net, and billapow on line. It was the fish. The lobster and the white stuff were drifting on the sea. Magdalene went to Orinoco for the night for a burial, and Robert was at home alone. Spending several nights a week fishing and away from home was making life funny with her. A large row erupts from the house next door and noise interrupts the writer's string of concentration, but he keeps right on through knockin' it out and uttering words that describe his present situation. A little girl from down the road was raped yesterday. She was an eight year old. The boy had 17 or 18 years. A big young man. He was from Haulover and staying in their house. They say the girl walked out to use the bathroom. How they don't have a toilet, they go back in the bush. The young man followed her and told her something he was going to do to her. She said "no not with me your not!" She came back to the house bleeding and crying.

The little girl's father was out fishing and hasn't come back yet. The young man packed his bags and hit the road, not to be heard from again. The trail southwest out of Haulover goes first to Kukra Hill, and then to Rama, and then to the rest of the world. This type of thing happens frequently in Haulover. There is sickness.

The man from the beach came in to his pickniney with fever. Mr. Wenstein got his teeth in. Robert got stoned and stared at the computer for hours, drank coco. The neighbors yelled and the ranchero music blared from the bar down the sidewalk. Robert grabbed a guitar and started singing. The Moon was full.

It is nights like these that make me want to give up everything again and take back to the road. Start all over. Find a new life. Take a new woman. Live alone. Build another house. Live in the bush. Sing songs. Drink wine. Howl. Forget whatever I've made here; time is already spent. At the end of it all we are all naked, stripped of illusions and confusions, possessions and obsessions. They are chains. They are prisons. The bigger they are, the heavier. Lighten your load and give it all away. None of it matters anyway. You can always do it over again if you want. Throw into the sea and it is returned to you ten fold. Be brave. Throw it hard and blindly. Let the poor catch it. Your eyes are too high to even see these things. It will be fun. The making is the fun part. Once you have it, throw it away. The creation is beautiful. Let someone else squander its purpose. There is plenty more out there. Plenty more and plenty better. Here you have a dory. Give it away, and you find a sailboat. Give away the lagoon and you find the sea. Give away stale love, and find fresh truth. Jump and you will fly.

You know where you can go. Where is the first stop? You can walk there. From there you can catch a bus.

I've returned to Haulover after a tiring week in Little Island. I have been inspired to leave, a momentous occasion for the traveler. Everything else has lost all importance in this world. Magdalene, work, house, children, and progress are all indifferent. The only thing holding any promise in my mind is the Northland, the *Pan Americana*.

The Indians pass through the unknown Northern Autonomous Region with pangas, dories and who knows what else. This is too risky with the pocket load of one hundred dollar bills of crisp drug money I'll be carrying through the zone. Indians don't give a rass and I've heard of many a man less conspicuous than myself hijacked in the zone. This time I'll stick to the highway, maybe pass a couple of days by Ann, playing guitar with the tourists and gathering strength for a long awaited journey of epic proportion.

I can take the freight boat to Kukra Hill and avoid Bluefields. From there I can make the hike up to the cross roads where trucks pass to La Fonseca, the Flor de Pino and the Heart of the *Palmera*. From there, the river may be flooded due to the rainy weather, but we can paddle across in a dory. The Pana people there are friendly and helpful. They live mostly on milk and cheese, cow and pork meat. They are an oily and acne covered set like most of the Rama and Inland people. This is where the Caribbean ends and Latin America begins. Try to remember your way home. Your parents are supposed to be worried about you.

There's one more bag of cement to mix, a few small jobs I could finish up tomorrow, and on Monday, I can leave. I don't know what will become of Magdalene. I don't know how she will react. Her violent nature has begun to push the limits of my rationality. I no longer know who is more crazy, her with the hateful outbursts or my tranquility and seeming indifference the whole situation. Carlito over in Little Island told me that he would "assen" her if he was me, after witnessing one of her episodes. It is only at night when her fits occur. A look passes over her eyes and through her soul, warning of the darkness and hatred that has just entered. It is the worst sight in the world to see. I would wish that you will never have to see such a thing. By the time you see it, it is too late. You can try to run, but she will follow and track you down at all costs. She will neither rest nor let you. It happens especially if I drink alcohol or smoke marijuana. It sickens her. I cannot stop smoking now. I'm smoking for Magda.

I am considering restarting my email, revitalizing my childhood character. Resurrect him.

I don't know why everything has to be so dramatic with life. Life is a drama. It is a round up, shoot em' out, love story of a girl warmed with fire of phosphorus and lit up for the world to see. It was always there, the words and the story. It only needed illumination and translation. A little bit of energy thrown into it, and the invisible ink highlights itself. The words become understanding and thought.

Magdalene says she wants to wait until December to leave, after Aisha's promotion. It is the beginning of July, and I told her that I'd be leaving this month. It is the fourth. The Fourth of July. Happy Independence Day, whatever that means.

My belly is full; full of bait, lies and deception; murderation. I do not know what America thinks of my disappearance from their country. I have dropped off the radar. The paper trail has finished and junk mail exploded. The boxes have broken and hearts all forgotten that I never intended to stay here forever. I was just passing through, connecting the North and South and understanding the relationship between the two of them. It started a long time ago when a bomb of an airplane crashed into the twin towers of New York City. My other half was shattered and I caught a one-way flight to Buenos Aires. It cost four hundred dollars, and brought me all the way here to Nicaragua though love, heartache, theft, betrayal and a million other sincerities that I never counted on. Magda will never understand this, nor will she care to. Her care is for her children, survival, house and food.

She knows nothing of a gringo on a hike. She uses the bed as a tool and her love as a means to her ends. She is selfless in her selfishness, just as we all are in the cosmos.

Clint has developed into a cosmic person, one of the *gente cosmica*; one of the people driven by the stars and the God in themselves, surrendered to his direction. They come into your life with a reason and purpose. Whether they know it or not, they are on a mission, and you are their project, just as they are yours. It is important to know these people when they spring into your life, although you may not recognize it until they are gone. They come with gifts of some kind or another and you will be wise to recognize them for what they are worth. He was down here for a month. We caught up with ourselves. My old friend.

Poor Clint. Clint was afraid he was going to be exploded along with the house and the twelve drums of gasoline we had selling in the living room. Magdalene got bad and tried to light it all afire. There was a sealed five-gallon bucket she was trying to throw the match in. I had to go leave the bucket over my the neighbor Miss Cora, where Magdalene couldn't go ignite it and even if she did, it would blow the other five hundred gallons to kingdom come.

I must write this book. I must complete it. I must publish it for someone to read. This is the matter of the most pressing importance. To accomplish this I must return to the United States of America. I must fill the circle and the sooner the better, before Magdalene kills off the whole left side of my brain. Clint brought to me advice and support of my dreams. He told me to leave here immediately and put some distance between Magda and myself so I can see things clearly. He feels that my vision has become distorted from too many blows in the head from Magda's clubs, sticks and stones.

I try to rationalize the situation with masochistic themes and morbid psychological theories of happiness through misery, but he is right in some of his aspects. He hates Magdalene and will feel sad for me if I remain here with her. It is because Magdalene hates Clint. He drinks and smokes too much for her company and she doesn't want me ending up like my friends. They are both right. I need to be alone for a little while.

I need to take a walk.

The rain is pouring like it wants to keep on. Work continues as normal for most people, but I stick myself up inside like a bear in the winter. It has been raining for weeks. Everything is wet. Clothes are hanging all over the house, hopelessly trying to dry. They'll wait there for a few days mildewing until they're folded up half dry and put in the *ropero*.

On the brighter side of things, the sound of the rain is mesmerizing on the zinc roof with its crescendos and *bajandos* of intensity. It makes me want to smoke a bowl. There is nothing else to do.

My dreams of taking Magdalene to the states with me seem dim. Bush has made the immigration process extremely difficult for people in the third world. It seems that we are the root of all the grand nation's problems and must be eliminated. Clint tells me there's even talk of building a wall along the Mexican border to keep everything out and everything in. I say fill the whole thing with rain. It sounds too much like East Germany for me to have any respect for Bush and his laws. Fuck you Bush! I hope that you burn along with the rest of your Nazi right wing comrades. I don't know who is running the whole circus up there or where it began, but it is spinning out of control. The lines have been drawn and . . .

"On its wobbly axle, the wheels roll steadily downhill; there are no brakes, no ball bearings, no balloon tires. The wheel is falling apart, but the revolution is still intact . . ." Henry Miller reminds that all of my attempts at writing are futile, for he has already expressed his possession of the complete vision of the full picture so precisely.

Use your writing for good instead of evil. Use it for whatever you can, but write. Let the words there are to say be said. If you can control them, control them. If you cannot, let them control you. Let them be purposeful or playful, but let them ring true as a song in the night.

I want Magdalene to accompany me on my travels.

Al Norte

Enough talking. I'm on the road. I left Haulover a few lifetime filled days ago, and have reached a small cabbage and lettuce farm in the community called Tisay, in the mountains outside of Estelli. We left Managua this morning determined to travel north after hard-times in overpriced private and under-attended public hospitals. We have supposedly solved the mystery of Magdalene's belly bottom pain in her womb. The womb is swollen and twisted causing pain and complications in both of our lives. The doctor was ready to fix the problem with a surgical operation for three thousand dollars.

In a state of shock and panic, we agreed to make the surgery the next day. After reviewing our financial situation and the cost a Bluefields surgeon would charge, we decided to hit the road and travel. Here we are in the mountains.

My greed is eating me alive. I have fifteen thousand dollars in my pocket right now because I was afraid Magdalene would steal it after her vows to kill me tonight in my sleep. We got in a fight about our presence at our present rural location. She is cold. She says its better she goes home before this *viaje* goes any further. Perhaps she is right. I told her good bye then.

After our quarrel, I went for a walk through the mountains overlooking Estelli. I breathed the fresh cold wind and meditated over life and song and troubles. It was so beautiful that I wanted to kill myself. I took out my new Navajo knife, stuck it to my chest and pondered over the slow death that would follow as the blood leaked out of my self. I looked to the steep cliffs and setting cloud hidden sun, and wondered about releasing my soul at the moment of impact;

shooting it out through the top of my head towards heaven. I wondered if it would work or I am foolishly mistaken about this whole killing myself business. I wondered if I was being selfish or a selfless martyr, bringing eventual true joy and feeling to contrast the initial pain that my family would experience. I imagine the sweet tears Magdalene would cry and how long she would remain alone.

I always believed that if the horror of life became unbearable, that a symbolic suicide was superior to murdering myself for real. I thought it was better to abandon everything, killing my old and tired self to start anew with a fresh new life, changed for the better and free of my old worries and stresses, but today I realize that I have run out of directions to run to. I'd already killed myself once before and my new life already exhausted after only a few short years. Where would I go to abandon this abandoned life? Back to the states? Resurrect the dead? I'm already going there. I've already been there and killed that person. All this thinking is shit.

Magdalene says she's down to one hundred pounds now. Some boil on her neck and itch on her skin has got her down. I have the same itch. She doesn't want to drink water.

Is it true? Is she dying? Is this fresh cold getting better or worse? She says it's because of bad treatment. She says this fresh cold is the end.

She wants to eat more meat and take in plenty of chemicals before she is dead so that not even the worms are going to want her.

She says her eyes are pale, her hypnotic black eyes that are the same color as her pupils.

"Why are you checking me and writing?" she laughs and puts her head under the blanket.

She is cold as usual. We are on the top floor of San Pedro's highest hotel, the Hotel San Francisco. San Pedro de Atitlan, the highland of Guatemala. We are far from the coast.

She says that she's going to tear these pages up. "Only one man write bout me, and that man is God".

The church bells ring with timely purpose, a precise moment in between each one. First a high tone ding, and then a low dung dong, or is it the other way around, dung dong. There's always just a moments silence between each one. It creates the instant to think about the melancholy of the situation.

On a brighter side of things, I gave my five *quetzal* coconut banana bread to a little girl hanging out the window over a rock wall above a backstreet cobbled road in San Pedro.

Is this love? It there a God involved? Is marriage a sin?

Magdalene is about to get her period. If she doesn't, there is something wrong. A fast would be good for her, but who am I kidding? She is taking her sickness out on Robert, and why shouldn't she. He is the one loving her to death. She was demanding more money today to go home and get the operation. She already has more than enough money to go.

In our fights, Magdalene attempts to break all the windows of this glass room. She tries to throw the furniture off the balcony. She wants to destroy and put me in problems. Since we have left sea level, she has been cold and sick.

The best part of life is to leave something beautiful behind, something you created for others to share. Love.

"*La infermedad es el resultado de un comportameinto que no va de acuerdo con las reglas establecidas por la comunidad. El alma de desprende del cuerpo, se va muy lejos y con frecuencia se pierde in los lugares sagradaos en el mundo invisible habitados por seres distintos al hombre; en aquellos lugares . . . es hecho prisionero*".

Sickness is the result of a behavior that is not in line with the established rules of the community. The soul releases from the body and goes very far. With frequency it loses itself in the sacred places of the invisible world inhabited by beings distinct from that of man; in these places . . . it is made prisoner.

We made it to Mexico. We are illegal here. To enter Mexico, you need a visa. To get a visa you must apply for one in your country of residence. For them to even consider giving us a visa to enter, we would first have to go back to Nicaragua. We have come much to far for that. El Salvador, Honduras, Guatemala, there was no way we were about to go back.

We reached the border at La Mesilla and saw the bridge crossing into Mexico. The border looked like a big market with little shops selling clothes on either side. Hundreds of Mayan Indians walked back and forth across the border busily doing their business without paying anything any mind. We looked at the border. There was a big sign saying "*Bienvenidos a Mexico*". Magda took a picture of it.

We looked down a little road to the left saw the immigration building. We looked again at the bridge and said to hell with it. If they catch us they catch us and send us back, but let's go.

No one said a thing as we crossed amidst the crowd. On the other side things were much the same. We were hungry after the day of traveling on the buses from Quetzaltenango and Huehuetengo. Chela and Huehue. Chichicastanango. Mayan places. High mountains and cool fresh air. We got some tacos and roasted corn. Real Mexican tacos. Meat and onions grilling up on a big iron skillet with little corn tortillas. *Culantro* and peppers. Hot pepper! Pepah pepah!

We soon figured out the *rumba* of things and made a contact with a chartered bus heading up North to Tabasco, carrying cheap clothes from Guatemala. The woman who was in charge told us that there would be check points and that we would be on our own if they took us down. We knew we were taking the risk, but we were going forward as long as we could.

We wanted to reach San Cristobal de las Casas. The woman said that the bus could drop us on the highway at the entrance to the town. We left out at dark.

The bus passed a few checkpoints in the border zone, but the police didn't check anything too closely. The bus had been traveling for about an hour or so when the police stopped the bus again. This time they boarded with a little flashlight to check everyone's papers. Magdalene was asleep on my shoulder. I knew he would question me. I had my passport ready when he shone the little light in my eyes.

"*Gringo*," he said.

Yeah. I pretended to not speak Spanish.

"*Y la muchacha? Anda contigo?*" he asked.

Magda rolled her head sleepily. How she's black, I hoped that she could pass for a Gringo too.

Yes, I told the man.

He turned off his light and turned back towards the front of the bus. A knot loosened in my stomach as the bus started rolling again for the North. I love traveling.

One of the biggest problems with modern society lies in the difference between doctors and priests. They should be one in the same. The *sacerdotes* and the physicians are equal and should hold the same position.

San Cristobal is a revolution town, a Zapatista town. They march in the street and have the support of the majority of the people. They wear ski masks and wave a red and black flag. It is the capital of Chiapas, the center of the Mayan world in Southern Mexico. They are the same Indians as in Guatemala, only separated by mountains and politics. The altitude is high and energy crisp. The sun is hot and the shade is cold. The line separating them is sharp; a wall of nothing. It is a beautiful town that one can imagine living in.

The last couple of weeks of traveling seem to be wearing on Magdalene, and I feel that we should rest here. She is still sick with a cold and pain in her belly bottom. I feel like it has worsened. She had a fever the other night and this is a good place to catch ourselves. There are all kinds of doctors here, traditional Western ones and indigenous bush medicine healers. The market is full of fresh local fruits and vegetables, sweet baked things and stewed fruits. There is a kitchen that the owners of the clean cheap hotel let us use, so everything is *tranquilo*. Next week we can head up to Oaxaca and Mexico City. Continue for the North.

Sitting on the curb outside of the cheapest hotel in Oaxaca, Magdalene and I are breaking up. Do I care for her? Do I love her unconditionally or is she too much to bear? I want to change her, but she does not want to change. I want to make her care, but she would rather not give a kick. She spits on the floor constantly. She would rather throw her trash on the road than wait for a trashcan. I cannot take it. Why don't I pick it up for her and wait patiently? Why didn't I pay the three thousand for the operation in Managua? I hate her constant spitting. It is a constant reminder of the sickness inside of her. Every morning, there is a pile of spit on the floor next to the bed. She cannot stop. She cannot change. Why don't I change and stop caring? If I only stopped caring I could live freely. I feel a duty for the world. She will throw garbage anywhere she pleases until death. She does it because it hurts me. She don't think nothing of my writing. She don't give a shit about nothing or nobody. She doesn't even drink her medicine we bought in San Cristobal. She says, "I no have to".

Leaving Oaxaca, the busses departure is delayed due to the teachers strike against the unfair wages and last week's assassination of one of their fellow professors. There is tension in the streets. Everyone is broke and pissed off, so they're blocking the roads out of town, pissing off everyone else too. They're involving everyone in *La Lucha.*

People have already taken over the plazas and broke out the windows and shut down the finest hotels downtown. Graffiti is on the walls and to me it looks like the situation is just getting hot.

Magdalene just farted and it stinks up the bus. She told me to put that down too.

Yesterday I watched you waving away. Watched your bus shrink into the horizon. Watched it all so clear. Watched it all disappear. Yesterday I cried.

The breeze was blowing hot across the plains. The sun was droppin' down into the shade. The moon was shrinkin' down into a quarter and I left thinkin' where to go from here. I hitched a ride with a truck for the border, haulin' limes from the South. I took one or two deep breaths and stretched my arms to the sky. I don't know if I tried or tried not to, but yesterday I cried.

Your teeth I seen through the window, your smile through the pane. Your whereabouts I am wonderin', your everlasting memory. Yesterday was just a day away, but lord it seems so far away. A hundred million miles they had to put between us. Miles and two police cars.

Yesterday they picked Magdalene up at the border. We were twenty-six kilometers south of Matamoras when they stopped the bus. This time they wouldn't take the story about her passport being under the bus or the whole "she's with me" line. This time they demanded her papers. When they saw there was neither a visa nor Mexican stamps, they put her in the police car. There was no talking that could get us out of it.

It happened fast. They ordered me back in the bus and they put Magda in the back of the car. It was just daylight.

We left Mexico City in the evening. The bus rode all night and would have reached Texas in the morning. The immigration stopped the bus at dawn.

When they put Magdalene in the back of the car, I could tell it was going to be a problem. They told me that they were carrying her to Reynosa and that I could go meet her there, but I had to get back on the bus. Before the bus pulled back onto the dusty flat highway, Magdalene started fighting them. I could see the look in her as we headed for Matamoras. I knew the look all too well.

I told the bus driver to put me down at the first place I could catch a bus going to Reynosa. He had to pull off of the highway and pass through a dead little town where the Reynosa bus passed. He asked me why I never told him that the girl didn't have papers. He said that he could have paid the police a little something and he would have overlooked us. It was too late for that now. I had to find Magdalene.

I waited in an empty café dusty parking lot for an hour or so before the Reynosa bus passed. I sat on the bumper of an old junk car. It stunk of piss. There was no one around. The border zone was poor. It was barely seven o'clock and you could already feel the heat of the day coming on.

The bus finally came and within an hour or so we were at the Reynosa bus terminal. I found a locker to check my bag into and went outside into the torpid sun. The day was heavy. I was already sweating and had to find somewhere to take a shit. Across the street from the bus station was a place that *alquilar*ed *banos*. They rented bathrooms. It cost about a dollar and they gave you a towel, soap, toilet paper and nice cool shower. It was the best thing I had seen in days. After the fresh, I was ready to go.

I quickly found the immigration office but there was no Magdalene there. It was just a big building with all kinds of office people and bureaucrats. The holding cell was twenty miles or so South of town. After tearing through all kinds of red tape, I got in with the boss-man there that knew about Magdalene, the *negra.* I tried to explain the situation to him, about true love and fear of marriage and religion and all that jazz. The man was sympathetic but it was way too late. They were sending her out of Mexico this afternoon, and that was all. If we had tried something like that before she was caught, maybe something could have been done, but she was illegal now and in custody. We crossed the line and now she had to get out of the country. He told me where to find her, and that I had to hurry. He said that she was "*maltratando*" the people there. Mistreating. My mind raced through the wars that Magda and I had and the look I saw on her when I was leaving. I imagined the things that they told her and the way she reacts when she is unpleased. Imagined a caged wildcat clawing and tearing at anything coming close.

Your people are *maltratar*in' her I told the man and left in a hurry to find Magda. I ran back to the bus terminal and tried to explain where I needed to go. None of the busses went there. After asking around to all of the ticket vendors, I found one who said they would talk to the driver and find out if he would drop me there. The driver agreed, but wasn't leaving out for another forty-five minutes. I just had to cross my legs and wait.

The bus finally left out and dropped me off at the little immigration holding cell outside of town. It was a small building and the officers there wouldn't let me come in. They told me they would send for Magdalene. I walked around to the side of the building where there was a little barred window. Magda stood and smiled peacefully at me from behind the bars. Thank God I said.

She looked calm and easy and just tilted her head and laughed when I asked what happened. She warred the people. She kicked and bit and pulled off their ties when they tried to put her in the cell. She turned over their desks and scratched the officer's face that told her I never loved her and already abandoned her and went back to Texas. She spat on them and fought them with a reckless abandon that comes when you no longer are afraid to die. She went crazy she told me. She said she never would have done that if I would have been there, but she thought I was gone so she didn't care. She didn't care about life.

I wanted to hold her with all of my strength, but could only touch her hand through the jail windows from which I had to stand outside. I touched her face and wanted to kiss her but could not.

She was the only woman in the cell full of men. The men were from all over Central America, Honduras, El Salvador and Guatemala. They were all trying to get into the states. Magda already made friends with all of them. There were about twenty of them in the cell with her. I was worried about all the men, but they all treated her with respect. They laughed and joked with her about all kinds of things. Everyone told their stories about how they got caught and about how as soon as they reached back to their home country they were turning around and coming right back to try again. Next time they swore not to make the same mistakes. They thought that her Gringo carrying to Texas was a myth and were happy to meet me.

The treatment there wasn't bad. They gave her cookies and coca cola, anything she wanted to eat. There was an old man caretaker of the place that just wanted to see her happy and not fighting. The bus was coming in the afternoon to carry them back to Guatemala. There would be a physician on the bus and two armed police officers to secure the safety of the detainees until their release in a free country. They carried Magdalene to a doctor for a check-up and promised to feed her until she was released. The *federale* bus ride was the safest way for her to get out of Mexico alone. At least the police would protect her. The immigration officers assured me that I didn't have to worry for her safety while she was in their custody. I thanked them and apologized for her beating them up. They said that in all their years of doing this job, they had never had someone go on the way Magdalene did. I knew that.

The bus came around four o'clock, and they loaded the prisoners out of the cell and onto the bus in a single file line, each one having to sign their name before entering the bus. When Magdalene came out of the cell they gave me a chance to hug and kiss her goodbye, and that was that. She promised to call me as soon as she could and walked up the steps onto the bus. I watched her through the window as she took her seat and laughed at me when she saw me gazing sadly up at her. I could see her blushing.

In a few minutes, the bus pulled out and headed down the long, flat, straight highway for the South, crossing the Mexico's northern desert. I stood on the side of the road and watched it until it turned into a small dot on the vast horizon. I am so small in this big old lonesome world.

I had to get back to Reynosa now. That was all. It was time to go back to Texas and finish this thing.

I stuck out my thumb as a big truck passed slowly by the immigration station and jumped in when it stopped. "*A la frontera*".

I took a night bus across the border and back to Houston. It was a traumatic experience. The whole Texas border region was a war zone with Homeland Security issues taken over the minds of the crazed people. The United States immigration officials were the rudest and worst people I've met in all my travels. They did not want me to come back into my own country, and I was legal. I was going home, but they did everything in their power to keep me out. By the time they finished with me, all I wanted to do was go back to Mexico where the people treat you like people. The gringos handcuffed me, frisked me, searched me, interrogated me, threw me around, roughed me up a little bit, apologized when they finished and saw that there was nothing they could do to hold me, and let me go on my way. Its none of their damn business what I do in Nicaragua. No, I don't have any ties with Al-qaeda. See my passport here. It's good. Now get out of my way. It's none of your business why I don't have a driver's license. I'm riding the bus. They asked if I'd ever been arrested. I lied and said no. Can you be arrested for lying? They looked me up on their computer but didn't find anything. I just took everything cool and crossed into Texas trembling and afraid as everyone else.

Gringolandia

The bus passed through several military checkpoints in South Texas during the night. Each time they boarded the bus with their guns pointing, checking around and carried off a couple of Mexicans. I just hoped that they weren't going to haul me down. I felt more like a Mexican than a Gringo. We rolled into Houston at dawn. I didn't even recognize the crowded city, but knew that it had to be Houston. I could tell that a lot had changed over the last four years. I called my parents from the downtown bus station and begged them to come pick me up. They were more than happy to. It has been long day. It's hard to believe where I was two days ago and where I am now.

Life is a long running experiment to improve my rhythm.

I awoke this morning with a deep tiredness inside of me, the kind you get from staying out until three thirty in the morning, drinking wine and telling stories with old high school friends that you haven't communicated with in years. The kind you get when you haven't drank wine in years.

It is a crazy and sick world here, full of beautiful girls and greed called ambition. It is full of cars and air conditioning and sitting on your ass for days at a time even though you think you're moving around. This is the illusion that cars create. The only thing moving is your brain. You see things pass you by and reach a new location, so you feel like you're moving, but it has all just been sitting on your ass.

The pain of living without Magdalene grows worse every day. It's like a hole in your gut that was filled with wine the night before.

She says you make your own happiness wherever you are, but I don't know. False light fills the orange night sky while the true moon seems to have disappeared along with the stars. For the first time in years, I know not where the moon is; what time she will be coming out of hiding; whether she is waxing or waning, full or empty. I know that I too will soon grow empty if I stay here in this city of Houston. I've been here now for a week and must start learning how to leave again. I love my mother. I love my father. I love my sister too. I love her man and I love our friends, but where is my Magdalene now?

I want to play music every night. I want to sing every night. What is this self-empowerment?

Writing is improvisation.

The end was supposed to be the return to the States. You thought that was the closure of the circle. The journey should begin and end here at the home of Mom and Dad. The story began in Argentina with a cold fever in a hot bed's thick woolen blankets in a windy beach town called the Sea of Silver. It begins in Buenos Aires and Bariloche. It begins with Peace and her radiant Chile. There it should end. It should end in Nicaragua in the bed of my loving heart. I do not control these words as much as they control me.

Now the test is if he can turn around. Can he take the road again and if yes, how soon? Will it be soon enough to save the life of his future wife? Hold your life. It is the only death we will have as we know ourselves.

Tomorrow night in Texas, they are going to murder a black mother for the sake of our justice system. Some say she killed someone. Some say she killed no one. Some only cry.

They try to consolidate her. Say that after eighteen years in a rotting cell, she will now be free. No more pain. No more suffering. No more loneliness. No more. It doesn't appear to help as she wails and sobs for her life, balling and trembling, howling for help.

Redneck accents are anxiously awaiting the murder. "So be it," they say in support of the U.S.

This is America. "Ain't nothin'changed. Ain't nothin'changed".

She will now join her dead daughter as the dogma of death continues and grows stronger. Thirty-five executions this year already.

I remember the night in the Andes where the glaciers meet the hill; away from the cheap classrooms of Santiago, the moon explodes over the rim of the mountain and through the curtain of night, its red veins pierce the darkness.

Where a half a joint of *Paraguayo* is enough to hear the explosion.

Where firewood is insufficient and the morning too far away, and sleeping bags cold on the rocky floor that sucks the heat out of your body. Where no roof interfered between myself and the God I'd been so desperately trying to perceive. Who else is there? There's no one for miles. What else is? Only the dried up shrubbery near the foot of the ice. There are no nets below to catch you crossing the gorge. There are no fires in the night. There is no peace in the peace. It is raw as the Andean Condor. It is as free as the holy moon with her red veins spider webbing through the sky. It is as cold as the fire rocks I throw into my sleeping bag and dry as the wind in my ear. Hallelujah, praise the lord. Breath can warm you.

Adelante

He took the bus to Austin and caught a flight up to New York City. He had some business to see about with some Conch Pearls that he bought when he had plenty of money in Corn Island. He had heard that the pearls were valuable and saw that they were beautiful so he thought he would get into the jewel smuggling trade. If the pearls were worth half of what he thought they were, he could stand to make a quick twenty thousand dollars.

The pearls were fake. They turned out to be pieces of conch shell polished finely until they resembled the true conch pearl. Their luster and flame of colors could only be discredited with a microscope. Robert didn't know a thing about the pearl business. He learned quickly however on the streets of Manhattan amongst the Jews in the diamond district.

Traversing the majestic blue empire, dancing off stone rooftop corners and cutting the lines where shadows meet their maker of light, the man realizes that all of his pearls were false; pearls in the downcast eyes of strangers irreverently stomping by, pearls that they guard so closely. They are all masters, these strangers of Fifth Avenue. How else could they have survived so long amongst these lions and tigers of New York City. They are masters of the arts and masters of money. They take it all so nonchalantly. The man is destined to lose every dollar that has so loosely fallen into his possessions. It falls like sand between his fingers. Perhaps one day, he too will become a master. A master of zero.

Can he capture the smile the taxi rider's eyes? Can he create beauty as do the leaves of Central Park, casting their outlines upon the concrete sun ridden floor? A trumpet drives by slowly in the traffic, playing along with some ragtime band on the radio. Time freezes for a moment and emotion takes over. There is no harm in writing. It passes the time better than drinking and cheaper than moving. The thoughts behind the eyes watching behind the driver's side window suggest a world where nothing has changed. Brakes squeak from all directions like obnoxious birds singing to heaven. They are not birds. They are corrosion. The longhaired beautiful people know. They've forgotten about the dead and their haircuts, coats and ties. They've made something that works and they aren't selling it. They give it to someone else who can take care of it. There is no describing it the man realizes and jumps down off from the stonewall to find his way back to the subway and on to a door in Brooklyn. The sun has now fallen behind the buildings and creates no more lines and edges. The world is covering with the shadow. It is cold and silence and breath will be the only comfort left tonight.

The Gemological Institute of America takes care of the rest.

The sun falls. Businessmen with destinations, black skinny pants and paten leather shoes take the sidewalks. A skinny dog that looks more like a rat leads its master on a walk. There are true birds tucked behind the green of the leaves soon ready to redden themselves and fall to the ground, brown and dry. It is a crystal day.

There are pearls in the windows and in the hearts of the children rolling down the hill. You will soon learn it. You'll learn it when the will has escaped the light grips of your fist and when the desire has all floated away from your burning ears. All that remains will be the pearls. Looking for compassion or humanity in the eyes of strangers, he finds nothing. No smile nor acknowledgment; nothing. Only cold countenance toward their personal destination, reminding him he is no one to request an unpaid for emotion or connection? They are all proud of themselves and for good reason. They have mastered these sidewalks and there is no one, no stranger who will pull a nod from their necks. But to him they are not strangers. It is as if they are each beautiful old friends of his whom life has kept apart for all these years since birth. He listens to the conversations that two sisters share in front of him and makes it his own. He understands and steals a precious look from their eyes even though they think they cannot spare one. He knows his glances are not dimes and gives them freely. The street bench is temporarily his, but if anyone wants to share, they are welcome. He thinks that recognizes everyone and loves their stories and passing cellular phone conversations. He fears only the undeniable darkness awaiting in the hours of night ahead. When it arrives he fears only the morning.

He wonders how many women Donald Trump has in his International Hotel and Tower and consoles himself with the fact that he wants only one. She is, however, two thousand miles from his location.

There is a bicycle hanging in a doorway by a ladder in a renovated brownstone building in Brooklyn's Jamaican district. Ackaye and Salt Fish, sunflowers and sunglasses, Rasta Chinamen and police officers mix up on Norstrand Avenue where even the street preachers are surreal.

Dust devil in an old black guitar bag on the street. The park closes at dusk. Brower Park. Back angle parking. In search of more words. Only park-benches and green young girls in long skirts; squirrels with grey outlined tails; orange hats on black people; big green crunchy apples in hard white teeth; golden earrings hanging down low; pigeons are landing in the worn out field.

Two chords and a chorus. A girl picks up the guitar case, empties out its trash and carries it away on her bicycle. Shaggy dog walkers appear now, use your imagination. Hairnet ants and Jack Hammers and children hollering, "Drop your gun! Drop the gun". Drum symbols and the pigeons flap their wings. "Guinness for strength; Fuck Bush!; No Direction Home; One Hundred Percent Pure Lambskin," say the walls. "Be a servant," the man reflects.

"The spectacle is capital accumulated to the point where it becomes images," from The Society of the Spectacle.

The Bible prohibits usury because it creates a spectacle, an illusionary symbol of wealth and security and happiness. A number that becomes alive and feeding, growing upon itself, it dies and diminishes the more its size shrinks. It is exponential and horrifying, imaginary yet enforceable by the gloated ones with the money to pay the officers of this enforcement who, like everyone else, have become dependent upon her overflowing interest.

A glass of water, a glass of wine, life, death and comfort in-between like a white table. A tortoise shell guitar pick, the accessible "Unity and Division Within Appearances" and the accessibility of life through freedom and will manifested through desire for truth and a desire to understand why the soul is calling you somewhere. What does life have waiting for you there if you follow your self to what you hear and imagine? There are certain things that one must do for one reason or another. One voice may be calling you to New York City or a spirit calling you to leave. Do things right. Follow yourself, wherever you lead. Ignore signs and you will soon grow numb to their subtle warmth or word that intuition graces you with. You will become a block, hard, grey and crumbling. The sunshine won't touch you nor breezes blow through your hair. It is the end of the spirit and the beginning of homogeneity, the antithesis of life itself; cold and boring without ever even thinking differently. Thank God for spontaneity and follow her every nudging.

Today he's headed North to Connecticut and then on to Boston.

Rene Marguitte pushes forward the evolution of the mind with paintings that can't help but evoke some sort of thoughts or dizzy feeling.

The poem is a pitcher of water, orange with words mixed into her essence. She pours it all through a clay filter because she questions its purity.

You don't have to tell me. I know it's a war. I know it's a war of Babylon against the good and the just, the poor, the weak and the simple. It's a war against the world. A war against the soul and a war against the dead.

There are no more wounded heroes rising to tie up all the scattered ends of human unity. There is only the poet, the artist and the storyteller. It is the genius that is the thread running through the broken confusion, forging a unity. It is a global union the whole world must see, understand, and join that will bring an unconquerable power to the human race. It is a world of workers, paupers and unorganized forces waiting for a common vision that each individual part of the shattered mirror can see and reach their hand to and grab. When each tiny fraction has got a hold of that vision, an eruption of energy will blast through the dark clouds with radiant red veins shooting through the sky. The vision is the sun and the moon revolving in the heavens that spins inside each particle ever created. Songs of joy will fill the air with vibrant colors of orange and indigo. Individuals will explode and their emptinesses gathered and fused. "Through tragedy, the myth attains its most vital content. Its most expressive form; it rises once more like a wounded hero and its whole excess of strength together with the philosophic calm of the dying burns in its ashes with a last powerful gleam". Nietzsche said that.

After days of being here on the couch, with blunts in the ashtray and the nights full of shows and beer, I have decided to move on up to Ipswich, to the house of my dying grandmother and dead aunt. The only thing undying is the cherished world of the immortal song. Immortality. God is love, and what happens when love has vanished? There are more important things to worry about some people say. Your retirement for instance; your bank account. "Nothing," the blind man argues from the corner of his barstool crying for moments and smiling at their adjacent counter-moments. There is nothing more important than finding you. Not money, nor fear, nor art, nor music, nor literature, nor excuses, nor pearls or girls or words that express what is hiding. "I miss you," the sadist whines. "I'm coming," he hollers into the night wind.

I finally talked to Magdalene on the telephone. Two weeks since I left Houston and still haven't made it to Niagara Falls. As far as Boston I am. My days have been slowly escaping. Seeing Aaron has been unwordable.

Missed the one fifteen to Ipswich. Have to wait on the three fifteen at North Station.

Bob Dylan is the first surrealist in song. Max Ernstein, A. Beren and Salvador Dali, throwing out their instincts and impulses in divine expression. "Anxiety is divinity," one of them said.

"The suns not yellow, its chicken," Dylan said with all seriousness. The song is not the revolution. Life is an effortless rebellion.

It is the most natural progression the human body can go through. It is the search for happiness and the realization that no such thing has ever existed. It is the search for healthiness.

Life is a vacation from death, and a short one. Don't spend it enslaved to the Gods of your checkbook. Live enslaved to your freedom. Let it drag you down the righteous path of rebellion. There is nothing more. If it is a vision, run to it. Abandon yourself on the brink of a brilliant discovery and stay there until the flood currents carry you away with the Gulf Stream. There you will find it. A death worthy of true nobility. Life.

The trees are blushing with the surprises of autumn. The loose leaves are flying past the windows of the train as the passengers await their destinations of Syracuse, Rochester and beyond. Only the Amtrak is running out of Albany. All the roads are all closed. It is the snow belt of the Canadian border. The man just likes watching the leaves fly by, listening to the lovely Hong Kong Italian girl gently conversing with the stranger sitting next to her. He loved the motion, the movement, and the thrill of traveling. He felt as if he were released from prison as the train wheels gather momentum. The smooth rhythmic rocking of the train, the stretching frontiers of his experience, he only hated the stopping; the intervals like Schendenacky, New York and the slowing heavy start up legs. The sky was blue and hard to show a hint of the blizzards blowing over the rails three hundred miles ahead.

The autumn changes to winter without law or permission. "God is funny," the Chinese Italian girl rationalizes with a subtle British accent.

"Excuse me, do you have the time," she intimates to the hero, who's mind fills with visions of his brown skinned love that he thinks is awaiting his rapid return to Nicaragua. How contrasting was the apple dimple flesh of the girl sitting behind him. He was pleased to listen to her soothing subtle voice, speaking to the stranger of the places that she longed to travel to. He prayed that he would not fall in love with her.

She worked in India, teaching English, Math and Art to children of the untouchable class. Her father is moving to Cambodia to teach prostitutes to sew so they can work in factories as an alternative.

She hates the news because they marinate the stories for entertainment. Her emotions cannot handle the strain of the newspapers. She cannot take watching Bush speak.

The hero cannot believe that this Bush is a real person. He seems more a cartoon or clay-mation character. The whole show was a joke impossible of being taken seriously. The only thing that could be funnier would be a bomb. The hero imagined how it would feel to be an assassin or a spy for the resistance, but knows it would be better to go back home and grab a machete and walk into the bush to plant a field of corn and pumpkins and sleep with his wife.

Politics was on the tip of everyone's tongue. "How do you feel about this? How do you feel about that blah blah American bullshit public and talk Republican and Democrat liberal fascist voting approval rates?" Serve your country in the senate and fatten your ass with pale skin cancer golf clubs and shopping bags taking Mom out to dinner with the family dog.

Mackinaw apples shine red upon the trees in New England orchards. I smile as the American death count goes up in the Middle East.

Live for love. Die for it if is calls. Serve it valiantly, for nothing can be more truthful, pure and unregrettable. Failures are not a failure. They are a triumph.

Speed trains hiss by in the opposite direction. The movement is fascinating, bringing the long held visions closer to reality with every revolution of the wheel. God is glorious when no pain is involved.

Give me wine. I wanna feel it. Let the last drop drain into the plastic cup as I shake the empty bottle for more. It is not enough. It is never enough until sleep reaches and even then it is nice to leave a half glass on the table for the ten thirty A.M. The swirl is surreal. The heart is objective. The blood clings to the walls of the glass and it reflects light. It is a dark shine, deeper than the sea of Atlantis and truer than the crimson of autumn. It is blood waiting to meet the soul and violet waiting to meet the tongue. The senses burning with the passion of a hundred daggers, stabbing through life's silver curtain.

The train will be waiting in Syracuse for a short while. If you want to walk around, there is an exit behind the dining car. Niagara Falls is in a state of emergency. Wine is warm like winter. Reason is false.

He envisions his love and the distance between them and her far away reality. He shivers. The smile she brought him was painful and piercing.

He wished to fall asleep and when he awoke, the train was pulling up to the Bolivian high plain Chilean border in the midst of the Atacama desert and surreal salt plains of Uyuni with a pair of *payaso* puppeteers from Colombia and a red headed freckle faced immigration officer trying to turn him back to Antafogasta. He ducked down beneath the train window and hid way to Bolivia with a prayer and a song from his guitar in place of papers and exit stamps. The Bolivians aren't too strict on formalities.

The cold air from the night still lingered inside the drafty train cars, the morning sun outside like a fresh bolt of oxygen. How long can this luck keep up? How long will this train roll? Where will the morning sun greet their waiting lungs?

Through snow and sun, the empty train rides on to its destiny. I and I alone will ride it till its end.

Three thirty A.M.. The train reaches Niagara Falls. There is a payphone outside in the freezing rain. The wind is blowing sharply. Jerry wraps a big spliff and the two friends discuss all kinds of old shit and new shit down in the basement while burning it. Jerry's house is warm and has a nice smell inside. His wife seems happy even though she's just been woken up in the pre-dawn hours by one of Jerry's old university wino friends. She smiles and greets him welcomingly. She says that she remembers him and he tells her the same. She has gone back to sleep now. The writer cannot sleep.

My grandmother sleeps for sixteen hours a day. Her sleep is gradually overtaking her waking life until finally the consciousness will fade into the eternal dream. Sleep twenty-four hours a day. No one will even know when she dies, much less herself. It will just start to stink.

It was uplifting to see her again with my aunt. They are both still alive. They reminded me that I too am still alive.

It was on the trip I made getting back to San Andres. This is the same trip. That was when I got involved in the drug trade. This is not a confession. It is a story if you want to hear.

The trip started a long time ago. So much has changed since then, since the trip began. It began with a plane flight back to Costa Rica; Quepos; songs being made up in hotels overlooking soccer fields where young girls shoot off firecrackers from the *cancha* down below the verandah. Bang goes the sound of the bass drum.

From the mountain jungles of Talamanca and the Indians who ride down to the Western Caribbean from their farms with plastic bags of pounds and ounces shoved underneath their saddles making the ganja stink of sweaty horses. It is better to have ganja and no money than money and no ganja.

After Talamanca and the nasty sores of popylomoyo on my ankle and the ounce buried in my backpack, I stopped for a few days of rest in San Isidro de General. I kissed Marylee goodbye, saw some friends on a farm up in the mountains and took the afternoon bus to Rivas after camping out a few nights in John the Saint's abandoned cabin in the hills, where Michael and Barbara used to live. They are long gone now.

The border crossing was easy. There were no worries until a cop woke me up in the pre-dawn hours outside of Managua. He checked my papers and the backpack, but never found the *bulto*. You gotta stay cool.

I made it out to the islands without any other problems. A drug boat carried me back to San Andres and back again. The ganja saved my ass and got me to where I am today, rolling around the world with a blanket and a guitar. Still.

Can you put yourself into a character that is not yourself? Is that what art is?

Can you put another character into yourself? That is the question. Who are you kidding? Life is hard. You have to stay hard or you get soft. That is the thing. Live hard and you will be hard. "Perhaps I'm getting soft," the writer says to himself. Tomorrow is a hard day, laying down a hardwood floor.

Words mean nothing; letters to a poem. All we've got are our hands, and they are meant to be touching you.

I must be strong against my dreams. Girls and temptations of other colors and numbers from the past and future. I must live against it and survive. I must return home to Magdalena safe and unharmed.

I got a vision of you, dancing round in my head, striking me in the gut and knocking out my wind.

"Kindness in words creates confidence. Kindness in thinking creates profoundness. Kindness in giving creates love," says Lao Tse.

The glass of water and the glass of wine each occupy their space on the desk. It is life's most powerful contradiction and most enduring question, life or death?

Standin' in the kitchen in her morning gown, Magdalene stirred the beans that were beginning to boil. It was a long road getting here. The beans were soft already, just needing to be heated enough to kill any bacteria beginning to ferment in the pot. Just long enough to sterilize the spoon. Magda knew well how to care for beans.

Robert was alone again. He was two thousand miles or more to the North of her. He really didn't know where. All he knew was that it was cold enough. Cold enough to snow in October, and cold enough to make him jump around like a madman, dancing to the music in his head just to stay warm. Life on the shores of Lake Ontario and the Great Lake Erie is windblown and grey. The people are beer drinkers, pizza and hot wing eaters and hunters of deer. The women are singers and the men are factory men. Robert was an assistant carpenter to an old friend of his, Jerry Mahl.

Mahl was married man. He was experienced with the blue collar. He'd been around the factories and unions and they all wanted him.

He was a working class hero. His shoulders were strong and eyes keen. Robert learned alot from him about things. Music, love, work, life. To him, Jerry was a pretty good example at the time. His wife, Lisa did not feel the same about Robert. She thought he was a bad influence on her newly wed husband. She thought that he dragged Jerry down into the lonesome world of drinking and ganja smoke.

Magdalene was at this point surely wondering what the hell Robert was doing away from home for so long. Robert was wondering the same thing, but sometimes we are swept away by currents flowing stronger and harder than anyone is capable of swimming against. All the time really. The only thing to do is ride them out to sea. Swim out the rip with force when you can and swim back in. The swim was far for Robert it seemed.

He just got a computer from his friend Jerry who had since purchased and updated one and was no longer using the Window's Ninety Five Microsoft Laptop. The year was two thousand and six. It was a fine computer for Robert to carry back to Nicaragua. That was a part of his mission in the states. To get a computer.

The kitchen was cement. The countertops were made of white ceramic tiles, *azuleros*, with a pretty little flowerish trim around the ones stuck to the wall. It was a strong kitchen that the beans were hotting in. There was a sink but no running water, only a hole that ran into a rough septic tank built into the ground outside the kitchen window. The kitchen window was a little rough too. Robert hadn't gotten around to putting up the trim around the windows and doorways yet, so there was a little space in the upper right hand of the window between the wooden frame and the cement, through which a beam of sunshine could pass. A beam of sunshine or a skinny mosquito. The house had plenty of things to do yet before it could be considered finished. Magdalene didn't mind though. She loved Robert just the same. She didn't love him because he was a carpenter. She didn't love him because he was a musician or a poet. She just loved him. This was the hardest thing for Robert to understand.

So there she stood in the kitchen, boiling the beans and waiting for his return, waiting for a phone call or some sign of life. She was busy though, so nothing was torturing here.

Two months had passed since the Mexican police separated the two lovers. Visions of her deportation bus sinking and shrinking into the fine line until it finally disappeared across the barren horizon down a long straight highway outside of Reynosa haunted him. From that second the string between them only stretched. It stretched as he hitched a ride back to the border with a truck loaded with limes from the interior. It stretched as he crossed the border in a midnight greyhound bus bound for Houston.

The bus passed through the war zones of South Texas and up into the smoggy city of Houston just as the sun was coloring the sky.

The string stretched as his patience ran out of Houston and took him to New York City, West Hartford, Connecticut, Boston and finally on a long snow drifted train ride into Niagara Falls, the honeymoon capital of the world. The string could stretch no more. It felt like it was ready to snap. He was ready to go home to his woman so he bought a plane ticket back to Houston where he would pass through on his way down. The tension of the string felt like it would ease as the distance between him and his love grew closer rather than augmenting.

The room his friends in New York had given him was already a mess after three weeks of habitation. His dirty cement caked clothes had taken over the floor. Pieces of paper with strange writing covered the dresser. Books were scattered about all over the carpet. He prayed that Lisa didn't enter. He was ashamed, but still couldn't think of another place to throw all his mess. It was time to sleep. He had another long day of work soon in the morning. It was October Twenty Seventh, the Friday night before Jerry and Lisa's Fourth of July Halloween Monster Mash Birthday Bash. It was the War on Terror Show. It was the night of his Sister's Third Annual Halloween Party. We were getting drunk and ready to go. Robert stepped down the stairs to the cold basement and smoked a bowl of some pretty decent Canadian homegrown. He came upstairs and got on the computer with some words to say. He hadn't yet decided what to wear, but the glass of wine on the dresser was still half full. After a long week of work it was time to cut loose. He bought a big bottle of wine. It was payday. He bought a five dollar phone card to call his baby at home in Nicaragua. He told her he was coming home. He was standing up but swaying a little like a hot breeze was blowing across the room. He decided to take a drink of water. Everything else seemed a mystery. Life, love, the rhythm of words on a computer screen, they seemed as beautiful as a telephone call, or a birthday, or a picture that you painted of a flower singing notes of lovestruck fragrant melodies across the canvas in light purples and burgundies. Chiantis.

He pulls up the beaded shades on his window and decides to put on a mask. Forget about things for a while. No thanks. "I've had enough to drink," as he reaches for the glass at his side. Tomorrow is the opening day of goose season. Even though Robert didn't have a hunting license, he . . . "I am Jack the Ripper. I am looking at you through different eyes". "I've killed Robert and taken over his new computer!" he laughs. "What is happening Robert?" Robert cries. "Scream as loud as you want," the Ripper says. "You'll never take my mask off Robert". "You working on your computer with your Scream mask on?" Jerry asks as he passes by. "I can be the funky Grandma," Lisa says.

Robert hauls off the make to talk a sip of fresh air and a breath of water, thanking God that he's alive. The glasses are half full. The blood and the water. He puts the mask back on and takes another sip of the wine. When he starts drinking, he really just wishes someone would come and knock him out. He kicks the piñata. He screams at the top of his throat. He throws the whip around some poor drunkard of an old friend's feet. He sprints across the tight rope and grabs another glass of warm red wine with a dab of honey and a little bit of cinnamon. It is Saturday night. We goin' church in tha monin. Shot me a goose. Feathered and stuffed her in the oven for three hours and served her up for thirty meat-eating-trick-or-treaters. They said it was like roast beef. His teeth are rotting. His mangy legs itch at night. His head goes round and round through the equations of the universe as lighting strikes his cerebral vortex. Life is short and life is funny, sweet honey brown fountain and down with the water. Amen. Hale to the *lucha*.

Tonight he was disguised as Jesus Christ, the messiah in a white tunic gown from Egypt. Last night he was Jack the Ripper. Jerry was a Lion. Lisa was the tamer. Swanny was a dead man crocodile hunter. Ma and Pa were dead rock stars. Vince was the prom queen and Pappy the angel headed hipster with the devilish wife. Janel was half black and half white. Franky was just swankin'. Everyone is dressed as their characters.

Two days after the party Robert bought a plane ticket back to Texas. He did a few odd jobs in the week ahead and saved a few hundred dollars more, and packed his bags and said goodbye again to everyone. His father carried him back to the Greyhound station one night after having a few beers at a bar. The bus left out at eleven o'clock. It hit the border before day, and as the sun rose, he was walking the streets of Nuevo Laredo, looking for a bus headed south past Monterrey to Real de Catorce.

Clint still hadn't got back to the States. Robert left Clint in Nicaragua after their visit in Haulover and Little Island. He was supposed to start chiropractor school in the fall after his trip to Nicaragua, but apparently put it off. He was in Mexico now. He bought a motorcycle and was touring Central America like Che Guevara. He spent a month or so in Guatemala, and had taken his time coming North. He hadn't cut his hair or his beard since they separated in Nicaragua. They met in the desert mountain gold mining town of Real de Catorce. Only the ghosts of gold remained now, but some artists, Wichole Indians and occasional tourists resurrected the place.

The old friends passed two days in the mountain town and then walked down into the desert; passed through Estacion de Catorce and continued on to a small desert Indian community called Tecolote. Don Louis was the *jefe* there. They carried a bottle of Mescal to the leader and begged him for a place to camp. They told him they wanted to find *medicina*. Don Louis showed them where plenty grew and gave them a place to spend the night under the protection of a big old cactus tree.

"One thing I know is that handwriting don't mean shit. It's better doing this in the dark, when the light don't shine so bright. That's what I like about Big Bend, desert places, no concrete, no obstructions. The simple pleasures in life are great," Clint says while taking a bite of his beans.

Life is what you make of it. It is a blank page. It is a stretch of night waiting to be burst open by the fingers that claw at it from underneath. It is the tone your voice makes when it rings in your head. It is whatever you create it to be. It is a game. It is a song. It is a dance.

"Rhythm is life. Life is rhythm on toilet paper. That's good. We got ourselves a scorcher here. We got something to put out," Clint says to himself as he circles the fire. You don't have to hold back. You can let it go. That's all a part of the medicine taking you. It's the pain in your gut that tells you to let go. Let it rip. Take a breath. Have a sip.

"These are beautiful little cacti". These are beautiful.

Howl at the moon. Let it all go. Haul it over. Get back home. Don't forget, even if the candle burns out, words do not.

"I wonder how Chaves y Chaves made that tea?" Clint asks.

The one thing we have is burn.

The one thing pure thing we have is water.

Do not burn the water.

She is mother. She heals people with hugs. She is the Cactus Tree. She is an amazing woman. People go to her. She is Ama.

Carl Johan Calliman. It is called the Mayan calendar and the transformation of consciousness.

How specific can your colors get? That is the question of poetry.

"I think I'm a deer or a rabbit".

"Full moon," Maya and Clint.

To know what you're looking for, and to sit down when you've found it. Get up, run around and jump up!

Nuestro amores no se acaban. Nothing is finished. Smile for passion. Smile for love. *Siempre*. Smile for love. Chase after it. Hold onto it while you have it. Let her up and let her get a breath of air. You do not want to kill it. You want to love it. Don't you see! It is all so simple. It is just what you make of it, so make it beautiful. Make it warming and make it magic.

Make the charrango play! Let it live. Throw more wood on the fire and let it blaze. Let it burn all night and if it don't like it, we'll turn it off. Shut the book. Take a breath.

"It's a really cool sound. It's what they put in movies at the scary part," says Clint.

He burns the songs that the night brings out and plays through him.

“It’s like water dropping”. Twingy twangy twang say the sounds of the anything.

What you pull from the void, from the darkness, a ha! It is light. What else could it be?

“On its own,” Clint says.

“Have you had enough medicine?”

When you have, turn off the light. Clint has to take lots of medicine to make him feel good. You don’t need any. Drink water. Turn off the light.

“Yeah!” Clint laughs as he blows into the fire. “Everything wants to live!”

“Mo Fiah!”

Life is medicine. Food is medicine. That is the one thing I know. When you’ve had enough, you’ve had enough, I say with a serious look in my eye.

Food is medicine and I’ve had enough of it. I can feel it like a punch in my hollow gut. It is clear that the light is not turning off right now.

Clint says something, but I don’t make out the words.

That tree is going back to the atmosphere. We’re all.

That is the beauty of language. We can tie it together, or we can break it apart. How are you night? My hands can’t keep up. They are sweating.

That’s like the one in India.

Magdalene, I have not let you go! I love you! It is you woman.

“Women are powerful. They know. They don’t need to tell you. It is just what it is, like this tree. The Cactus Tree. You are behind me. You are the root when we sleep”.

“Think of all the women. They’ve overcome more than I can even imagine. It is time of the woman. How could we think of burning this tree? We should give it a hug. How long have you stood here, waiting for us to find you?” Clint stammers.

I laugh a devilish laugh.

Don’t let the candle burn out.

“Are you the one with a question?” Well, there is no answer. It is never ending. It is right now.

Everything compacts and it expands, the grand energy. Be a Jedi.

We should stay here for a few days. Eat some more medicine. Tea! Tea!

What do we have that we could make tea with? We ain't got nothing. We burned it all.

Don't they make sage tea?

Don Louis is the real thing. He is the master of the desert. He understands.

Clint wants to be a professor. The lesson is a campfire. He would never be late for class. Clint is trying to name the tree Ama.

He is wondering if we can stay here for weeks eating peyote. You can stay here for your whole life, but there are important things to do. There are engagements to meet. There are cows going off in the night. Clint is doing the cow-face pose.

Here's the answer. Relationship is touch. Clint says that he's found a way to touch the soul. He talks about kissing.

Fire always burns up.

Hay animales! Owwuh! Yo soy un coyote. Yo soy un lobo. There are definitely animals out there, animals of the night. I am a coyote. I am a wolf.

If you start going crazy, don't panic. Just eat another button. Just don't go over the edge. "There's always another edge". The night is what the light makes of it and you can't take it back.

"Oohhhmmmm," Clint says. The night welcomes that sound.

Consume and you too will be consumed until life as you know it turns into an undecipherable system of numbers and dots and symbols and triangle and . . .

The blues, the muse, or the news which is which. Whatever you use to fill the page, but write you must write, for as long as there is someone to read.

Clint is getting out into no man's land. He is a character.

Clint asks if I want to write a poem. I tell him I am.

"David told me about this book where these people go do all these drugs or something like that or these crazy psychological problems about how candles burn." It's very simple but very complex when grasshoppers start flying into the flames and killing themselves. So, as the wax is burning the night, the one thing to escape for is love. If I have nothing else to say, let it be that.

I've saved the fire. The muse will getcha. I will not put my hand into yours Mister Fire. I will control you and hold you between my fingers until they sweat and burn because the wick has burned down too low. There is no return from the cold night. Ash. It is the newest cleanser. It is whatever you want to make of it.

I am a wolf. Jack Nicholson. It is cold. It is sad when light goes out. When light goes out, the squash is alive.

Desierto. Cierto. Ser. To be.

Amanacer. Manana. Give me some light.

Permanacer in the darkness, when the heat has disappeared.

The night seems infinite in her darkness, and then bam! Hello moon.

You will not sleep tonight. You will shake and breeze, but sleep you will not. But breath is life and to shiver is warm, and tea is good if you're going to be awake, and if you're not, you'll go beneath the deep eyes of Don Louis, what you forgot when you slipped beneath the blue eyed angel of the *sierras.*

Crickets play the charrango.

I want to be the inventor of words, the creator of languages. I am not the mother. Ama. Amachi. Oh my God.

The sun was high in the sky when Clint and Robert realized that they needed to get back to the town. Their minds were not made up until the heat of the day became unbearable and they knew that they did not have enough water or strength to make it through another night.

They slept what little sleep they could beneath the shade of the Cactus Tree, but that soon was not enough. They decided it was best to move.

They packed up their little things and cut a dozen or so peyote buttons for the walk home and started walking under the heat of the desert sun, their heads wrapped in white shirts like Arabs. As they walked their feet moved unknowingly attached to their bodies. There was no hunger and no pain and no heat, but their feet kept moving like a treadmill. There was only the dreamy fear that they were dying. They laughed desperate laughs and kept on rolling as they chewed the alkaline little buttons, swallowing the juice while they stepped. Even though they moved with strength and speed, they still had the feeling that if they didn't soon reach the little dirty room they had rented behind the bar in Estacion de Catorce, they would drop. They arrived to the desert spring train station just as dusk was hitting.

When they hit the room, they loaded a joint and got a gallon of water and drank until their bellies could hold no more. Robert lit a fire in the shower to warm the water and went to bathe, but felt such incredible cold underneath the water, he could only wet himself briefly and wrap up in the towel. He retreated for the room and climbed into bed shivering beneath the thin covers. Clint took a shower. He came in and put on some clothes to go into town and get some food and a beer. He begged Robert to come, but Robert was afraid of the town. He was still shaking beneath the sheets and wanted to stay inside behind locked doors and closed. It was irrational, but he was afraid of the people outside. He felt like he might die. He was freezing. Clint looked meager has he got dressed with his bushy hair and long beard, that he hadn't cut in nearly six months. Traveling in Latin America will do special things to a man.

Clint left the room and Robert lit a candle, hoping it would warm him up some. He breathed deeply for a good while and eventually went to sleep about the time that Clint came home. He met some girls and ate some tacos. Robert didn't feel to eat. He just wanted to sleep. He stopped shaking and felt comfortable in the bed. In the morning, they would leave on their own separate roads, one for the north and one for the south. They imagined that they would meet again someday, but knew neither when nor where.

Daylight came and Robert took another shower. This one was better. He felt strong and new. The two friends went and ate some beans and eggs with tortillas and packed the bags onto Clint's motorcycle. Tomorrow Clint would reach Texas. Robert didn't plan on going back there right now. He was excited about getting on the road for South. He'd done enough playing around and was now ready to reach Nicaragua as fast as possible. Clint was talking about school and family and things like that. He was ready too. The two of them smoked one last joint and Robert watched Clint as he rode his motorcycle into the desert road heading north. After Clint left, Robert got on the morning bus to San Louis de Potosi. From there he could hit Mexico City by night, and from Mexico City on to Oaxaca by morning.

There once was a cactus tree that lived in the desert. Her name was Ama and she had many heads and arms. She is a protector and a guardian and has been standing there for many years. She was there before the old wise men walked the deserts as boys. She was there before the days of Christ and the nights of Lucifer. She is strong and steady, watching us as we sleep because she understands everything and don't need to say nothin'.

The streets of Matehuala smell of roasting meat. The doorways look a hundred years old. The buildings are made of rock, clay, hay and cement with iron poles that stick out a foot and a half from the upper wall.

Today in the streets, on the plazas, beneath the biggest tree in the world, it is cold. Days after the young American journalist's murder, times were strange and hard in Oaxaca.

The rain blew a little in the wind. People in the crowded cities bothered him. Their looks; their prayers; their begging and selling; his obligations to buy; his desire to go inside; his desire to sin; his desire to touch and be warmed; his curious visions and ancient feelings of his dearest Magdalene, his salvation and downfall, *retrograsada* and waiting at the end of this straight line he is running on.

It wasn't until he walked out of the town towards the mountains and took a haul on the windy pipe and a breath of fresh air afterwards that he realized why he felt bad. The turn onto a dirt road instead of the *cantina* was a good idea. The *tamalitos* are *calientitas*.

The farmers are reaping their corn, picking it from the piles of stalks that they already cut and throwing the corn into woven baskets.

Sleep has slowly disappeared as beds have changed into bus stations, food into marijuana, marijuana into food, thoughts into visions and visions into words that will never be heard through beats in the night as footsteps in the slippery rain and amazingly winding up where you started for, the bus station. Terminal.

Man of the plazas, with his hands on his knees and closed eyes raised to the heavens. His destination is the future and his beard as long as his hair. His possessions in a sack by his side, no one could ever guess. He wears his peace like a coat, protecting him from the cold breezes of freedom.

The day has come for the hero to finally return to Nicaragua. It is a sunny day in Managua. The bus from Guatemala City ran all night through mountains, valleys, bridges and checkpoints. It keeps on running. It doesn't stop.

Night reaches and after a long nap the, the hero awakes to sound of a woman's voice and guitar singing soft Spanish folk songs behind his room at the market bus terminal. He wakes up and tunes his charrango.

He scrapes the last of his Mexican bowl and tells himself it is the end. He goes down to the bus terminal to watch how the people are, but doesn't feel comfortable around all the hustling commerce and neon sounds of the blaring television, so he walks across the parking lot, sits down on a yellow cement tire stopper and starts to write.

It is the night he's supposed to meet Magdalene, but she hasn't shown up yet. He feels like something's wrong. It's eight o'clock at night and the next bus from Rama isn't supposed to come until eleven thirty. Nothing makes sense about why she's so late.

Maybe its just Managua, but the closer his time comes to seeing her again, the more beautiful every female figure appears. On the street, in the buses, in the shops and hotels, the young girls pop out everywhere. He grows erections in his sleep on the buses that are difficult to put down. The boy who shared the seat on the bus ride felt like a woman brushing up against his shoulder. He wondered if the boy was gay.

The hero does not know if his woman has lied to him. He did not even know if she was his woman. Three months is a long time to disappear. He keeps wondering what her face looks like, if he will still love her the way he says he does. He wonders if it will be awkward.

Buses come in and roll out, full and empty. They are rolling pages of religious poetry. "*Yo honro los que me honran y me hayan los que temprano me buscan*". Today he wondered if his love was the kind that glorified or the kind that killed. God is alive in Central America.

The hero can handle Managua in small doses. It makes him want to go drink beer. Life makes him want to go drink beer. Beer makes him want to go drink beer. If wine existed here, it would certainly be the wine sunshine.

In Managua, everywhere is a dump. Where you feel to piss, you piss. When you have trash in your hand, you throw it. Pieces of plastic float down the canals like boats stuck in a traffic jam. It is a mess in every way.

Bus stations are a much nicer place to hang out than cafes. There are always people there and always movement. You are not obligated to do anything. In bus stations you can blend in with the transitoriness of everything.

And the Magdalene, well she never arrived. The hero waited and waited through the day and through the night with his hopes high in the cloud. Bus after bus passed with no sign of love. The last bus passed through from Rama again at eleven thirty. It was cold and dark. The hero went and drank a beer and started planning and thinking about his next move, looking with calm reflection at the blank page in front of him. He knew that you always have to keep doing what you want. Everyone must. Beauty arrives when people's paths intersect while both are doing just what they want, and their wanting occupies the same space-time. All else is mere emotion. If truth lies in the action, then emotional imaginary worlds hover above us like stars in the night of egoist thought. The world disappears with breath and meditation and oneness can happen. He knew he was finished in Managua.

In the great web of hell fire, there is nothing left for the protagonist of a story to feel but brimstone. Family, wealth, fame and accomplishments all burn away to ashes. Women and heartaches, the things that seem so pertinent and important at the time, are nothing more than bridges to help us get through this dream a little smoother. The rest is all up to you. What makes you feel good? What makes you feel on top of everything? What fills you with spirit? If you deny that, then you are a coward, and you will feel it when you come face to face with your maker. When that day comes, a New Years Eve of immense proportions, will you have the strength to look the moon and the heavens in the eye and tell them, "I did the very best I could"? Can you look at your life with the confidence of a child and admit to it, testify it. Purify your guts. Liquefy your dreams. Solidify your reality. This hollowed out shell of the universe demands nothing but respect. This meandering path of salvation demands nothing more than truth. It is the sadness behind the face of clown. It is the smile of the moon at dawn. It is all we ever cared to see in the waves of the sea. Where else have we to go? "The heavens have all been explored and they are empty." The conch shell world is spiraling into your soul and moving the trimmings of your bowels. Respect it. Listen to it when it screams to you. It is all that is left of the childish dream of heaven and it begs to be released. Search for the right road and you will find it. You will find it if you are one of the elect, one of the chosen. If you have not been chosen yet, do not worry. You won't anyway. Keep on at the grind, toiling away your precious energy in the gears of the machine you keep spinning. Pay it no mind. The machine will not let you go. Its treadmill clockworks keep ticking away at your lifeline like a chisel of time. You have to let yourself go. It is grey and it is cold, like a fog at four thirty in the morning. It is the smog over the oily streets. Only the heat of the sun can burn it off, but where has the sun disappeared to again? It is lost in the wheels of chaos and the parallel tracks of daylight. The thing about learning to fly is you've got to jump.

He arose soon in the morning to take a fresh cool shower and check out the buses; feel which *salida* would lean on him or strike his fancy, even though his course, he felt, was already fixed. He smiled.

"In the wonderful peace that fell over him, it seemed as if he had climbed to the top of a high mountain; for a little while he would be able to look around him, to take in the meaning of the landscape".

"Human beings make a strange fauna and flora. From a distance, they appear negligible; close up, they are apt to appear ugly and malicious. More than anything, they need to be surrounded with sufficient space- space even more than time". Henry Miller said something like that.

About the Author

Multicultural poet and musician Robert Kuhn was born in Houston, Texas and moved back in 2010 after bouncing around the world for twelve years. Texas, New York, Pennsylvania, Australia, Chile, Colombia, Costa Rica and Nicaragua all played home for him as different doors, jobs, occupations and art forms opened and led him on from an Academic All-American Line Backer to a vagabond fisherman farmer writing the critically acclaimed songs he has carried throughout the Americas. Broken hearts, broken backs, failed marriages, violence, riches, drugs, labor, poverty, music, poetry, dirt and salt; so it goes and continues.

Back in Houston, Robert joined forces with like-minded musicians (including extraterrestrial ancient bluesman Little Joe Washington), surf rock n' rollers and reggae ragamuffins to form a band and recorded the album "Everybody Knows". It was Little Joe's last studio work and recognized by the press as one of Houston's Top Releases of 2014. Kuhn's latest album, PERSEVERE, a transcendent collection of psychedelic folk rock n'roll was produced at home in Galveston, Texas after his last tour was cut short by a nearly fatal van wreck in Colorado. It is scheduled for release in 2021.

This world is changing so fast. Robert hopes it will again take him back on the road to share this rich new music with the friends and family he's made along the way.

CPSIA information can be obtained
at www.ICGtesting.com
Printed in the USA
LVHW032311130723
752117LV00011B/1536

9 781948 712514